DISAPPOINTED RAVEN AT PERTH MINT

To Find the Girl
from Perth

By David Chadwick

With illustrations by Simon

cuke (press

cuke (press

Cuke Press
PO Box 151471, San Rafael, CA 94915
www.cuke.com/cuke-press
cuke-press@cuke.com

To Find the Girl from Perth
by David Chadwick

ISBN-13: 978-1-7322877-6-1
Copyright © 2008 by David Chadwick
Library of Congress Control Number: 2019945775

FIC027260 - FICTION / Romance / Action & Adventure
HUM026000 - HUMOR / Topic / Travel
MUS052000 - MUSIC / Lyrics
Region - Western Australia
Thema - adventure fiction, humorous fiction, romance wholesome,
travel and holiday, Buddhism

Cover Design: Paul Michael Speir
Cover & Illustrations: David Chadwick
Book Design & Production: Paul Michael Speir
Author Photo by Raymond Rimmer

www.girlfromperth.com

10 9 8 7 6 5 4 3 2 1

This book was originally Published by Speir Publishing in 2008
2020 & 2022 (with larger font) Cuke Press releases prepared by
Paul Speir

For my beloved sons
Kelly Bernard and Clayton Randolph

If the only prayer you ever say in your life is thank you,
that would suffice.

Meister Eckhart

TABLE OF CONTENTS

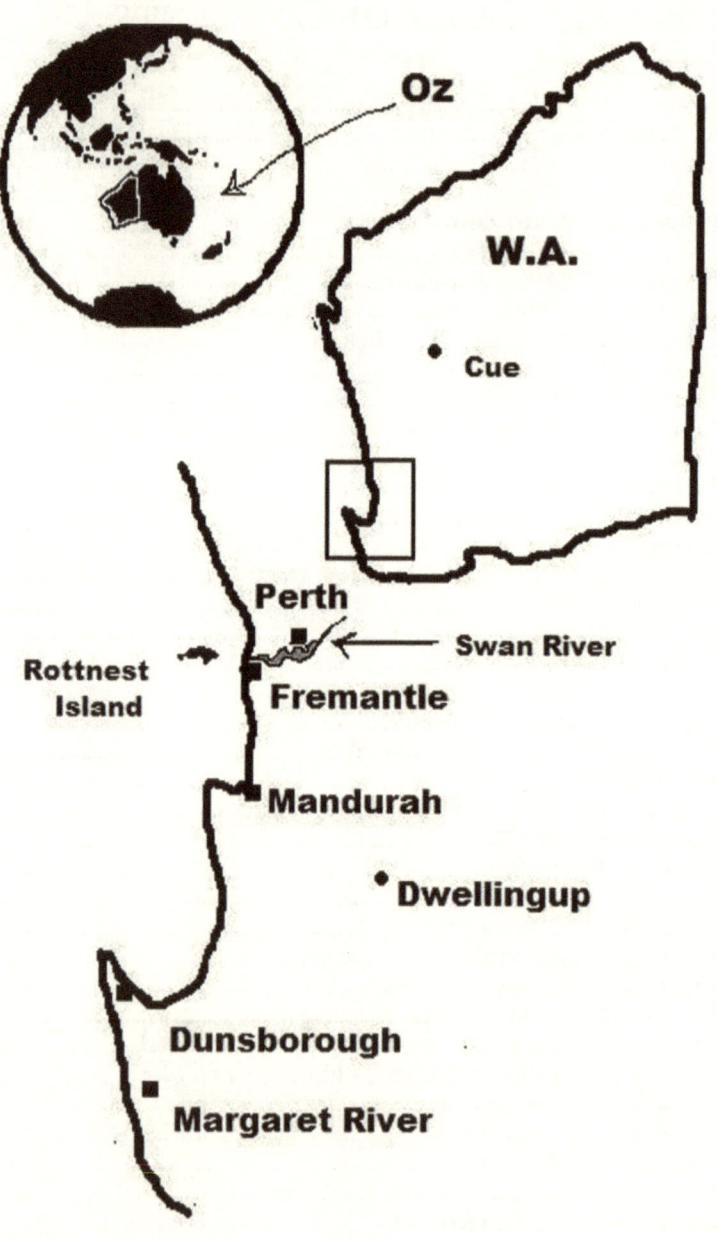

MINDY'S AXE

SONGS

ACKNOWLEDGMENTS

Bowing with grateful thanks to:

The NaNoWriMo (National Novel Writing Month) folks for hosting that great annual event. I used it to best advantage and wrote the first draft of this book in 2005 becoming one of more than nine thousand proud winners that year. To be a winner, one had to write a novel of at least 50,000 words in November, download it onto the NaNoWriMo site which counted the words, erased the file, and awarded the prize—a downloaded certificate which hangs on my wall.

Paul Michael Speir for agreeing to publish the book and for personally helping with the final stages of the text and layout and art and cover and the offshoots such as the color illustrations book, the audiobook, website, and so forth and for tirelessly keeping up with it and me for months, far beyond what any other POD (Print on Demand) publisher I know of would have done or permitted.

Those kind and skillful people who read the manuscript at various stages and who made valuable suggestions. First was my dear partner and mate Katrinka McKay who vetted it throughout the process and who always cheerfully answered my never-ending queries.

Heather Bussing for spending a good deal of time on the manuscript early on, a most helpful contribution to its development.

Kelly Chadwick, elder son, who, though extremely busy, carefully read through the book in its final stage, scrupulously observing details, and who made insightful, competent suggestions.

Others who read all or part and sagely advised: Andrew Atkeison, Berndt Bender, Cheryl Foltos, Ryan Madden, Avi Peterson, John

Tarrant.

Andrew Atkeison for his creative ideas and for creating a set of superior color illustrations for the story that are available from Cuke Press as *Color Dreams for To Find the Girl from Perth*.

Ahdel Chadwick, my keen-eyed mother, for finding numerous errors in the first printing (see the Changes/Errata section of girl-fromperth.com).

Lisa Clark, Jonathon Green, Alex Murawski, and Raymond Rimmer for further advice and assistance with illustrations.

Carol Homiak and Rick Levine for medical counsel related to the story.

Dotty Woodson and Kelly Chadwick for botanical council.

David Cohen for tech support, also the competent staff at the Computer Recycling Center in Santa Rosa, CA.

Richard Baker, Sarah Bercholz, Clay Chadwick, Elin Chadwick, Susan Chadwick, Lyn Dillin, Colleen Gildea, Daya Goldschlag, Theresa Green, Gregory Johnson, Arnie Kotler, Michael Katz, Howie Klein, Bill Porter, Jim Richardson, Renée Roehl, Ward Ruscoe, Dennis Samson, Alan Senauke, Peter Spowart, David Stanford, Ellen Steube, Bridget Sumser, John Sumser, Ian Sweetman, Steve Tipton, Carole Tonkinson, Elizabeth Tuomi, Dan Welch—for miscellaneous support and advice along the way intentional and non.

The wonderful people of WA with my apologies for any misrepresentations of them or the venues herein—memory moves, imagination grows, artistic license, and so forth.

A few Ozzies in particular for teaching me all that Oz slang, much of which they'd argue with each other over what is still used and which is more associated with the Outback or Tasmania or wherever and whenever.

Indispensable WA mega-pal Francine who gave me tons of inspiration, material, and tidbits to sprinkle throughout— also a name.

WA-ite, Ross Bolleter for various suggestions and especially for his wonderful tango and ruined piano music which the reader is advised to acquire and listen to as part of this whole trip.

Kurt Vonnegut for saying, "American male writers have done their best work by the time they're fifty-five and then it's pretty junky after that."

Again, heartfelt gratitude to all of you and to any whom I forgot to mention. Let me know and you'll be included soon. Which reminds me—all errors are my sole responsibility. I would be most grateful if you would inform me of any errors you encounter. You, dear reader, can contact me at davo@girlfromperth.com.

David Chadwick
Sonoma County, CA
October 27, 2008, at 63 years old

PS: And thanks to Paul Speir for making the changes necessary to republish this novel as a Cuke Press book.

INTRODUCTION

GEORGE WHAT?

It was August in winter and I, upside down in the land of the numbat and black swan, yanked about in the third year of this millennium. May the rest of it be this engaging.

I went on a whim to visit a dear chum, meet her family, friends, and homeland, curious to explore, anticipating only the warmth of new acquaintance, the excitement of unknown flora and fauna, the joy of walking about. There was that, but then there was the unexpected as events propelled me with brazen mates into a bizarre treasure hunt for another lass, one in danger of the grave.

My mother created treasure hunts for my sister and me on Valentine's and birthdays. At the time they seemed enormously challenging. They faded from memory until I was reminded by an eccentric Australian named Bobby. His game was plotted in no maternal spirit.

Life can be seen as a treasure hunt—the path, the way, the Tao, the road up the mountain—all imply we seek some fortune, which is of course ours to begin with—true nature, enlightenment, god, emptiness, the all-in-all, whatnot. Or we could be seeking something external—mythic goals, mammon, idols, pleasure, fame, winning ticket. I just went to Australia to visit a pal and poke around.

I wouldn't have gone if it hadn't been for almost suffering a heart

1

attack near the end of 2002. I'd had angina, chest pains, for four years. This condition seemed to be pretty much under control. I was used to it. I remember when it first came on—before I knew what it was—I'd be working up a sweat at the gym and get this unique feeling in my chest like there was a piece of rusty iron embedded there. Later, I was walking my son Clay up the driveway to his elementary school and felt a slight pain where my heart should be. It kept happening.

I made an appointment and walked over to see my family doctor. I lived in a nice little town where I could get anywhere on foot. He said it was either my heart or my esophagus and forwarded me post haste to a cardiologist next door, Dr. Garfield. Garfield thought the problem was my heart not getting enough oxygen because of a partially blocked artery. He hooked me to an EKG reader and later shot me up with thallium and had me trot on a treadmill. He looked at the x-rays and couldn't see anything suspicious. But still he thought it was dammed blood and not the esophageal path. He put me on a beta blocker, an aspirin a day, and a tablet to keep the cholesterol down even though it wasn't all that high. My blood pressure wasn't off the meter either. I started wearing a round nitroglycerin patch twelve hours a day. That gave me slight headaches for a couple of weeks.

One day not long after the first visit, I took my seven year old son Clay to our family doctor's office for a checkup. Hadn't seen him since he'd sent me to the cardiologist. He looked at me and said pleasantly, "Oh, you're still alive."

Because occasional attacks of angina continued, the family doc gave me a prescription for nitroglycerin pills to augment the patch. It's the most effective medicine I've ever used. Nitro! Boom! When you see people in the movies go, "My pills! My pills!" while desperately searching their pockets, fumbling with a bottle, downing some pellets that take effect immediately—that's nitroglycerin. I would go long periods without needing it at all but when I got angina, nitro took it away like a stiff breeze grabbing a discarded candy wrapper.

I discovered I could also make angina subside and disappear by being active, something that would make friends terribly concerned. I would walk slowly, accelerating the pace until I could feel increasing pressure in my chest, would back off and again slowly push ahead and soon could go even faster. In this way I could keep pushing the angina threshold higher. I'm not a runner but I knew I could run if I wanted to. All I'd have to do is work up to it. A doctor neighbor called it "walking angina."

2

George What?

After that first visit to the cardiologist, I'd dropped by a bar and had a beer and bummed a cigarette. Then I didn't do any more of that—or caffeine—for some time. I walked a lot and I was careful what I ate. But I didn't sleep enough and was obsessively working on a book. I remember once when I saw Garfield I told him I'd been up all night and he opened his eyes wide and said with sincere alarm, "Don't do that!" And then he relaxed and said, "You're the healthiest patient I've got—but the youngest."

If I'd taken all this more seriously and been disciplined and pure, it might never have gotten worse. But after awhile I started drinking a glass of wine now and then, caffeinated tea, a latte, and then bumming a cigarette here and there. Then I'd do more than a little—especially if I was working late I might drink strong coffee and get crazed and go buy some rolling tobacco and smoke a few and throw it away and sometimes more than a few and then maybe drink a bottle of wine or maybe two. And I'd smoke pot some too. A Swiss neurologist buddy cautioned that studies in Europe, which he said American medicine never pays any attention to, indicate that when you smoke pot you're ten times more likely to have a heart attack—like tobacco—just at the time you inhale it and it stimulates you. But then I looked into that further and found the same was true of making love, taking walks, and doing a lot of things.

I took ecstasy with a lovely lover. I hadn't planned on it, it's a little speedy, but a libertarian doctor friend said he didn't see ecstasy coronaries coming into the emergency room and told me not to worry. At a time that I had to minimize caffeine intake to avoid chest pains, I had none on this much maligned psychoactive. I ran around on it. Made love on it too. But I'm going astray here. The point is that my indulgences and rationalizations increased. There was more and more inhaling and imbibing, especially alcohol and tobacco—the truly dangerous drugs. Not incessant drunken chain-smoking, but too much for my heart condition at the age of fifty-four when Y2K arrived and didn't destroy civilization.

I don't think it was those bad habits though as much as the stress that made my condition worse or got me the angina to begin with. I was stressed out by writing about Zen, which people assume is supposed to reduce stress. Then I got a divorce, amicable but still a divorce, and had all these debts and a house I loved and my young son loved and our dog and cat loved and friends loved. But there were so many expenses.

I'd done three books and it was time to do a fourth, but nobody in publishing I knew was interested in what I was writing at the time.

I kept spending and the payments didn't go away. I was juggling a bunch of credit cards, paying one off with another, taking out new loans. I really like to ride the edge—I'd get off on having to come up with a lot of money and not know where it was going to come from—but I'd taken it to such an extreme that keeping up was too tense.

I started noticing my angina patterns were changing. It was coming on more often, getting unpredictable. I hadn't been to my cardiologist in over a year. I think I was embarrassed my habits weren't so smart. I made a list of important phone numbers and kept it on me. Elder son Kelly called. He'd had a bad premonition—he gets these. The last time it had happened, he'd called his boss two days before he died. I started to get things in order.

It was a stormy dark night. The angina was acting like a dangerous stranger. I decided to go to the local emergency room after getting a few more things in order. Then the phone rang.

On the other end was one of son Clay's chums, the darling daughter of a quite attractive woman, a dear friend and stimulating conversationalist whose curvaceous body comes to memory as well. We'd played around but were just good friends by then. We'd drink, and I noticed at times she didn't do well on booze. Indeed, that was the subject of the phone call on that evening of my advancing angina.

"Hi David. This is Denise. Mommy's drunk. I've taken the keys from her. Could you come get us?"

Denise was eleven and didn't know exactly how to tell me where she was but through a series of questions and answers we eventually came up with the coordinates. It was about ten miles away. When I arrived there the rain was coming down like the whole sky falling at once. Denise ran over, gave me the keys, and hopped in the back. I started to walk to her mom who was sitting in the driver's seat of her car ten feet away. My chest hurt so bad I could hardly move—and moving wasn't making the pain go away.

As rainfall clobbered me, her mom insisted she was fine and could drive, but she said it singsongy like a crazed drunk. I asked her to please get out and she said no need. We went back and forth on this until I informed her that my chest was hurting, I was surely close to having a heart attack, and that if she didn't get out of her car and into mine right away, I might die. That did it. I drove Denise and her mom (who later got into AA) home, and, as I handed over the keys, said I was on my way to the hospital and might not be able to help them get back to their car the next day.

Thunder pealed. I walked into the emergency room and told the two fine people there what was happening to me thorax-wise but said I was only coming by to see if there was anything I needed to bring with me later when I came for real—that I wasn't quite ready to check in yet as I needed to go home first and finish up a few things—and then I'd be back in a while.

These two hospital workers looked intently at me, smiled, and spoke to me slowly in the same tone of voice I think one might use to try to get a psycho to drop a gun.

"Now, why don't you just come in here and let us take a look at you?"

"Sure, I'll do that in a while. I just need to go home for a little bit."

"Well, maybe a nurse should check you out first and then you can go home for a little bit."

"No—I don't really feel any angina at all right now. Of course that's probably because I'm just standing here. If I don't move I don't feel it."

They kept coaxing me in until I entered their territory and then a nurse came and finally she got me to drop the gun—no, I mean finally she persuaded me to stay, listened to my heart, and asked a few questions. But they didn't rush me off to an operating room. I just lay there for a while on a gurney and then I sat up. As I'd said, as long as I wasn't moving, I felt fine. I ended up squatting there all night talking with them—it was a small hospital—not much happening. A doctor came to see me at one point and said later they were going to send me in an ambulance to a bigger hospital in the bigger town down the road. He said what I'd had for four years was stable angina but now it had become atypical angina. It was important I have it taken care of before it changed to unstable angina because that signals a higher likelihood of heart attack. He said I don't want that because even if it doesn't kill me, it still kills part of my heart and makes life harder. Still they let me sit there till sunrise.

Garfield wasn't around so another cardiologist came to see me in my room at the big hospital. He was from India and exuded confidence. He said the problem might be my esophagus—heartburn instead of heart attack. I said no no no. I know heart and esophageal troubles can have similar symptoms and hospitals make lots of money because of this similarity, doing all these tests, but I knew it was my heart. I could barely make it to and from the toilet a few feet away.

I called family and friends from the phone list I'd made. Talked to mother, sister, and son Kelly in Spokane who didn't say "told you so," but couldn't get through to my ex-wife Elin and younger son Clay. Their phone was continually busy. Good friend Dennis drove over to tell them what was happening. Elin had the phone off the hook for some reason. She never does that. Weird.

The doctor had me wheeled to a room with a treadmill on which he wanted me to run. Is that a joke? That would surely kill me. He wasn't worried and I tried but I couldn't even begin to do it. So he gave me a drug that forced my heart to speed up and I really thought that was going to be the end. It was unbelievably extreme—like taking amyl nitrate if you've ever done that—it made my heart beat faster and faster and stronger and stronger till it seemed it would explode and there was this highly unpleasant, enormous pressure and then little by little it slowed down and went back to normal—no, to the abnormal of the moment I could lie down with and not feel like an over-ripe bomb.

The doc smiled. He wasn't worried. Not, that is, until he started to look at the readouts from the brutal test he'd just put me through. While I was rolled away in the gurney, I saw in the corner of my eye an alarmed look on his face and jerking head movements as he scanned the results of the near murder they'd just committed.

Back to my room. Friends and family had arrived. Elin, Clay, Dennis, plus Andy, author of the excellent *Zen's Chinese Heritage*. A nurse told me I was going to have an angioplasty later in the day, maybe that night, maybe tomorrow. She came back in thirty seconds smiling as if everything was just fine and said I'd be next.

The doctor came in again and told me some things about the operation. Something about the LAD in the front of the heart being blocked. I remember saying to him, "People die in this operation, don't they?" and he answering forcefully, "None of *my* patients do." I liked that answer at the time and felt confident as well. In fact, I wasn't worried at all. The bliss of total denial I guess.

I was only mildly sedated. They punctured my thigh and ran a tube of some sort up the big artery there. It had a tiny video camera in it. I could see the play by play on a monitor.

The doctor was talking to me and being his confident self when all of a sudden he went, "Shit!"

"Shit what?" I asked with apprehensive interest.

"You've got a hundred percent blockage."

"Hmm. I guess that's bad?"

"Bad yeah....um." All of sudden he wasn't so confident. "You see—usually there's something to work with," he said. "But there's no light in the tunnel. If we miss and knock a hole in the artery wall—well, it's right next to that big old pump there." Now get this. He says to me, "What do you think?"

"Well gee, I'm not really experienced in this area."

"Ah, maybe we ought to just sew you up and put you on drugs."

"That doesn't sound good."

"Or we could go for it."

"Sure, go for it."

"Okay."

I closed my eyes because I couldn't make out much of what was happening on the screen. I didn't really feel like watching TV at the time anyway. I went deep inside and relaxed, trying to do my part to help the doctor. I still wasn't worried. I just lay there as if I were waiting for the score in a game on the radio, forgetting the game was being played inside me. After a couple of minutes I asked him, "Well, what's happening?"

"Oh," he said with a tone indicating he'd forgotten I was there. "It went great."

"What happened?"

"Just punched a hole in it with a little pin and then knocked it all out and put a stent in there and blew it up with a balloon and then pulled the balloon out and we're out now too."

I couldn't believe they brought along all those tools with the camera and could manipulate them at the end of a tube that went from my thigh up into my chest in an artery that, no matter how big it is, is still rather narrow. I could only see it in terms of there being tiny people in there operating a camera and mini-jackhammer, little tools on their little tool belts, their service vehicle parked nearby.

But wait. "What happened to the stuff you punched out?"

"Oh, it just became little chunks."

"And where did they go?"

"Your heart gobbled 'em up."

"What? I thought that would give you a heart attack!"

"No—your heart's really strong."

"Okay, but why didn't I have a heart attack because of the total blockage?"

"Because you're old enough to have grown collaterals around it. That's why younger men die more often when they have heart attacks. Haven't had time to build up the little helper tributaries."

Back to bed. My buddies were there waiting and happy that all went well—especially Clay who gave me a big relieved hug. After a while I said I was fine and tired and they could go. Elin and Clay were expected out of town and I told them don't worry, go on.

I had to be completely still for six hours because the thing to fear at that point is the incision into the thigh artery opening up and all the blood in me running out onto the floor. My nurse was a friendly yet strict, somewhat effeminate man who told me I absolutely couldn't move at all. After a couple of hours my back and legs were aching really badly and he said I'd just have to tough it out. Then he went off duty and a compassionate female nurse came on who added morphine to the drip. I never liked taking opiates for fun, but I sure liked 'em then.

The next morning a spirited, zaftig, red-headed friend in her mid-twenties picked me up and took me out to eat at a real down home place. I hardly ever eat hamburgers but I did then, a jumbo. That night, alone at home, I made myself a BLT with a dozen pieces of bacon—and I fried the bread in the bacon fat and added lots of mayonnaise. After that I went back to a fairly low fat diet, nothing obsessive. And I felt normal. I felt great.

I did have a scare a week later when I started to get chest pains again while eating evil potato chips and watching a 49ers play-off game. A cardiac nurse I know had commented that a high percentage of angioplasties have to be redone. I insisted on seeing the doc immediately. He calmly asked me some questions and said that this time for sure it was my esophagus. He gave me a scrip for some pills to take for acid reflux but I didn't fill it—just ate more carefully so it wouldn't happen. I'd always told Garfield I had two types of angina.

I wrote a song about this experience called *It Was a Stormy Dark Night*. It had a chorus with a stolen line I'd always wanted to use in a song.

It was a stormy dark night
My chest was painin' a might
Turned left at the blown and blurry light
To give my drunken friend a necessary ride

—chorus

George What?

It was a dark and stormy night
It was a dark and stormy night
It was a dark and stormy night
It was a dark and stormy night

The nurses put me in a dress
The doctor drilled away the stress
Friends and family prayed and touched and blessed
Edward George and Snoopy sent their best

(repeat chorus)

I told my family doctor I was going to sell my house, pay debts, travel for a while, come back, and live a simple low stress life. He bowed and shook his head, looked up, sighed, extended his hand, and said he should do the same thing. I didn't tell him I never filled the scrips for the heart medicine prescribed after the angioplasty. And I didn't go back to either cardiologist.

My realtor was a buddy and said he'd make a lot of money on my house, but he begged me not to sell it with its spa, gazebo, voodoo rhythm fence, cushioned attic where people could smoke contraband while kids ran around downstairs uncorrupted, office above the shop garage, artistic mosaic patio which Dennis helped to make, antique stove, speakers in various rooms, fecund apple tree out back from which had come so much apple juice, sauce, and gallons of "Bad Apples Hard Cider" to enhance our wicked parties. But I was dead set on a dramatic change. Wenger at the Zen Center said I was shedding my skin again, something, he added, he'd seen me do periodically. The house sold for a goodly amount in one of the best markets in the country after an exciting few months of real estate drama and a host of improvements. Paid debts and went off traveling. Clay joined me for a month that stretched from ten days at our favorite Zen monastery through the blistering Southwest to Fort Worth, but then, after a touching parting, he flew back to the Bay Area and I was off to another side of the world.

On the first part of the journey I went to George What, better known as Western Australia. Everyone there calls it W.A. Dubya A. I like to write it without the periods—WA. WA was the first abbreviation I learned in WA. Abbreviate and recreate—that's what they do with names, with language. They don't say George What—I did.

It was my first attempt to play with words as they do. Here's how it went:

Aussie: Where you been in Australia, mate?

Me: I been only in George What.

Aussie: Come again?

Me again: George What. George as in George Dubya, my prezi, and what as in eh? George What—Dubya Eh? WA!

He thought I was off my crumpet, but I swear that's the sort of thing they do when they talk. A fun lot—at least my sampling of them. Party hard—with booze, with each other, with words. Good on ya!

And they were there on both sides of the fence to give the game what they got, to throw their bloody all into the WA treasure hunt to find the girl from Perth.

It happened something like this...

FRANNIE'S FIREDANCE

PART ONE

WANDERING AROUND

CHAPTER 1
LION CITY

I was dying to see Francine. She and I had been great friends for a time in America. We were just pals, as she'd say, but we both got a little teary in the remembering after she'd gone back. When we first met she said she felt like we had been in a past life together. We just stared at each other. But not gooey. She had come over to take care of Mark, the severely brain damaged son of close friends of mine. I'd seen him grow up. He'd painted my back door and done some research for me in Japan. But he'd had a terrible blow to his brain stem in an auto accident that killed his best friend. They'd given Clay and me a ride to the local Fourth of July fireworks show just a week or so before.

Francine lived in Perth, the capital of Western Australia. While visiting out of town relatives, she'd seen a notice in their church weekly of an American family seeking a caretaker for their severely impaired son. That's what she did—take care of intellectually challenged people, as she called it. She looked at that notice and said, "I'm going to America!"

I met her a couple of days after she arrived in California and she spent almost every minute of her painfully little time off with me. I lived walking distance from where she worked. I also spent a lot of time with her at my friends' home. They were old Zen friends, the father an Englishman who'd been one of the first Westerners to live in a Japanese Zen monastery, the mother from Japan.

Soon after we met, Francine took out her scrapbook to show me photos and mementos. The following quote was on the first page:

Whatever you would do or dream to do, begin it. Boldness has genius, power, and magic in it.

When she first came to my house, I showed her the same quote scribbled on a piece of paper taped on the wall above my computer. I get sent a lot of smarmy, feel-good crap homilies in emails but some ring true to me or, as in this case, are actually inspiring. It's a quote attributed to Goethe but I researched it online and would say it is more of a quote from one of his liberal translators. Anyway, I believe it, so I don't care where it came from. As far as I'm concerned, I said it.

I was touched by Francine's selflessness and kindness, the care with which she looked after my gangly young friend who'd lost so much of the connection between his brain and body and speech. She fed him, changed his diapers, bathed him, talked sweetly to him. He loved her. She made him laugh. I could make him laugh too— just make fun of his father or say something about sex or marijuana. He was good natured and knew everything that was going on—he just had no way to respond except laughing, grunting, kicking. I know it sounds hard to believe, but even though he could understand what we were saying, he could not clearly, consistently answer yes/no questions. He was cut off in so many ways.

Francine was around for six months. The last two weeks of February we traveled in the Southwest—lowly humble Death Valley, always amazing Grand Canyon, magical Bryce Canyon in knee deep snow. Behind the facades of Las Vegas she placed our one bet, after a long distance consultation with her father on his lucky numbers. Lost five dollars. Then she flew off and Mark, his family, Clay, and our boxer Lola missed her. And I missed her and she me. One would call the other now and then to say hello and hear what's up. But she was gone.

Two and a half years passed. It was August, 2003. I was in Singapore, the hub of a half-year trip to Asia. It's one of the cheapest places to buy air tickets. Francine had a month of vacation coming up and we'd planned to meet there and go on to Thailand, but she called before I left and said her mom's melanoma had taken a nasty turn.

She couldn't leave. I would go to Australia for a month instead. She assured me I wouldn't be in the way. Maybe I shouldn't have gone, shouldn't have bothered her at such a difficult time. I've noticed Australians don't like to say no. And Texans don't like to hear it. But I thought she really wanted me to come so the first thing I did in Singapore was to get a ticket to Perth—with the Student Travel Association. I'm always a student—and their prices are among the lowest.

John Tarrant, a Zen teacher and writer from Tasmania whose barn I had moved into upon selling my home, gave me a phone number for Ross Bolleter, a Zen relative of his and musician of note in Perth. So I had two people to look up in that remote spot.

But first, Singapore. I'd been there a decade before for a few days with one year old Clay and his mom—on our way to Bali. Singapore is a good city for walking—day or night—safe and civilized as can be. Easy to ask directions, English being the lingua Franca. It's just one degree north of the equator and full of lush green growth. But the people don't have that laid back tropical vibe—maybe because the ocean winds keep the weather somewhat mild—almost always between 73 to 87 degrees Fahrenheit. There's high humidity—I spent my days wiping the sweat from my face with a cloth handkerchief, making me feel like a desperate character in a Bogart movie.

I stayed in Little India the first night, the funkiest part of town, got up in the early dark to go hang out in a Hindu temple—sitting on the floor and watching the ceremonies and devotees go to this altar or that statue. Lots of flowers, incense, dabs of paint on faces, clanging, chanting. Then to coffee, pastry, and newspaper at a sidewalk table by a busy intersection as the city got going for the day. Walking on past store fronts, to museums, a vast Chinatown with Buddhist temples and shopping streets, Muslim areas with mosques to admire for their restrained aesthetics and lack of idolatry.

At the modern art museum an elderly Chinese man struck up a chat. He inquired as to where I was staying and what I was paying and found me a much better deal in a low end Chinese hotel—a real bed and my own bath. He paid the bus fare for us to go to my fairly grubby hotel in Little India and insisted on carrying the extra bag on the way back. I offered to take him to dinner with me but he declined. He said his retirement allowance, publicly assisted housing, and government medical insurance covered him pretty well. Finally he settled on ten dollars Singapore to dine on later. As he walked off I figured that to be about five American dollars and sixty-eight cents.

I loved the new spot. I'd walk around the city in the day and hang out in the evenings with working class men of Malay, Indian, Bangladeshi, Indonesian, Mid-eastern, and Chinese descent. I'd chat with the Philippine bar girls who had rooms in the hotel, would eat food from stalls representing a variety of cuisines, drink beer, coffee, and bum cigarettes. A popular dancehall for youths was across the narrow street. Almost everyone in Singapore is conservatively dressed—lots of well-to-do folks fashionably attired—so it was a treat one late afternoon to see a dozen punk kids with purple and Mohawk hair, piercings, and torn jeans come running out of the alley and under our awning to sit till the predictable daily downpour passed. A young guy from Ohio who was going on to me about Australian versus Indonesian girlfriends and Singapore prostitutes, ran to get his camera.

So there I was in Lion City where there were never any such felines—a case of mistaken identity or hyperbole. But there was grand foliage everywhere overflowing in this sultry metropolis. In the Botanic Gardens are stately, looming trees, tropical vegetation galore, spacious lawns surrounded by flora I soared through and lost myself within. I entered an interior garden devoted solely to orchids. Walking among varied forms of the sturdy flower was in turns fascinating, dreamy, lovely, humorous, frightening. It was while being mesmerized thus that I met an unanticipated traveling companion. That's what happens when you travel—the unforeseen, and new friends.

"Ah, so many members of this family of perennial herbs. God awful beautiful huh?" A guy next to me, the only other person in this area of the garden, gave me a start. He looked like a local but, having opened his mouth, he was definitely American.

"Oh hi. Yes," I said coming out of my trance. "Yeah, really. Wow." We 'Mericans sure know how to describe subtle feelings.

"Look," he said pointing, "these are brown terrestrials."

"I can't believe they're flowers. But the ones under that tree clearly are. They're so purple."

"Look at these rare leafless orchids." He turned around. "I love these fragrant cymbidiums too. And did you smell those awful white ones over by that gate?"

"Yeah—like rotting meat. Did you see the cool-house for orchids from mountain areas? I want to go there."

"It's not open yet. Where you from?" he said.

"North of San Francisco—Texas originally. Hmm. You sound like the East Coast but then there's a little South in there."

18

"New Orleans."

"Oh, wow. Yeah. Yeah. I used to live there for a while—in '64. City people sounded a little like New York—it's really a distinctly different part of the South. Started going there in '63 cause my sister went to school at Sophie Newcomb. Love it. Great city. Whatcha doin' here?"

"Going to Australia for August."

"Me too. Where to?"

He was on his way to Melbourne where he had a distant uncle related to his mother though she'd never met him, a businessman it seemed. He said he was planning to start his trip there because he didn't have anyone else to look up. He'd just received a message at his hotel that this relative, Uncle Rudy, was flying into Singapore and he should go to the hotel within the airport and meet him there tonight late. He was surprised when he got the message because he hadn't mentioned in correspondence where he was going to be staying in Singapore.

His name was Jackie Gupta—told me to call him Gupta. His father was from Calcutta and his mother was Irish though she'd come to America as a baby. He was thirty and into real estate—writing up mortgages all over the country from a cubicle walking distance from the French Quarter. That's a place I've stayed up all night a number of times. As we ambled out of that heavenly garden toward the street, I dropped all the Louisiana place names and drunken anecdotes I could think of. Once had a great old girlfriend there I still love a bunch. Worked in a pork bar-b-que stand for seventy-five cents an hour. We walked the few miles back to the center of town.

"My father was a realtor," I said. "You enjoy real estate?"

"Pays better than teaching high school biology."

We entered a large modern bookstore to look for something basic on Singapore. Found what we wanted and browsed around some more. I was surprised and pleased to see they had a couple of copies of a biography I'd written on my Zen teacher. I signed them at the desk. Gupta put on a pair of glasses and looked a copy over.

He said he'd been to the New Orleans Zen Center a few times. I've met the teacher there so we knew someone in common, sort of. He went there to try out zazen, Zen meditation. He decided to stick with practicing yoga most mornings. Yoga is about as old as anything in human culture and came from the land of his father, so he felt a strong connection to the tradition. But more than that he just liked the stretching, the limberness, and the healthy overall feeling the movements gave him. But he said he probably should meditate too. I pointed out that yoga is meditation, is the or one of the roots of all Asian meditation.

"Or maybe some ancient form of meditation is the origin of the yoga," he said.

"It's all pre-historic," I said. "We can only guess."

He returned to the book in his hands. "Also by... Ah. It says you've got another book. Zen Failure? An American Zen Failure in Japan? That's bizarre."

"That's the subtitle," I said.

"You failed huh?"

"'Fraid so."

"I didn't know they graded you."

"An attempt at humor," I said.

"So you didn't fail?"

"Humor revealing the sad truth."

We came upon a lively, painted, contoured concrete skate board park nestled within the shade of trees. Admired local skating youth. A teenager was sitting on a bench strumming a guitar. We stood close by and listened. Gupta asked if he could play and the guy handed it to him. He went through a nifty riff.

"Well done," I said. "Where'd you get that?"

"It's just a little improv."

"You're good. I play too. But not that well."

"What d'you play?"

"I've played lots of stuff. But mainly my own songs. Not much in recent years."

"I write songs too. I'd like to hear."

"You first," I said.

He continued with the same chord progression and started singing.

Travelin' alone has a kick all its own
But sometimes round a bend
You happen to find an accomplice, like-minded mate
Co-conspirator, friend

I remember once in Marrakech
Got involved with a rambunctious princess
Had to save her from a gang of bandits and cutthroats
Her daddy gave me a bag of silver
Said I'd live to spend it if I took the river

Lion City

Wavin' bye to her from the stern of the royal rowboat

And I don't know where I'm goin'
Don't remember where I've been
But whatever way its blowin'
My sails are to the wind

Washed up on a Southseas shore
Friendly natives, pungent flora
They crowned me king and festivities began
I was eeny meeny mining for a paramour
Then the hon I wanted hinted I'ze to be the main course
Took a potty break and zipped off in a catamaran
(Thank you darling!)

What the heck am I thinkin'
To get into all these fixes
Maybe shoulda stayed home drinkin'
With my homies down in Dixie

A guru by the Bay of Bengal
Hypnotized me when we mingled
Sent me walkin' up along the Ganges to her source
Must have passed it cause
I was lost and freezing in the snow
When a Yeti found me and led me below
To a yak who got me back on course

So where the heck am I at now
And what's gonna happen next
When things get cruddy will I have a buddy
Who pulls me out of a wreck

Travelin' alone has a kick all its own
But sometimes round a bend
You happen to find an accomplice, like-minded
Mate co-conspirator
Friend you can scramble round with
Friend, you can babble on to
Friend you can climb out of the rubble with
Friend, you can hobble on with
Friend, a travelin' friend

"Good lord," I said rather stunned. "Well done indeed."
"Your turn," he said handing me the guitar.
I looked at the kid who nodded. I strummed a C and sang.

Pocket song, so short, so true

"That's it?" Gupta asked.
  "It's a pocket song," I said.

A friend of a friend, a guy named Mike from Texas, had driven me around the day before and shown me some of the sights. One place we stopped was near the skateboard park. It's not really a sightseeing sight but it's no secret. It's Lee Kuan Yew's home. He's the semi-retired strong man who'd run this place since the Japanese lost out. Humble digs for mister big. There was a guard station with one guard on hand—seemed rather minimal. Lee's popular—goes shopping with his family without bodyguards. My tour guide had read both of Lee's books and recommended them. Lee scoffs at American media interviewers who question him about Singapore's civil liberty shortcomings, executions for drugs or guns, caning of juvenile delinquents. Lee answers that Singapore prefers not to have the chaos and violence of American cities. People seem content, are not living in fear, and support their government. They have a high standard of living and drive more Mercedes per capita than anywhere else. They also pay more for cars than anywhere else—keeps the traffic down. Singapore is clean as heck, sort of square, comfortable, affluent. There's a legal red light district too. Lee says you can't stop it so why try? I wish he applied the same compassionate and realistic thinking to people's universal and insatiable desire to alter their body/mind chemically.

Two days before, I'd met a young hip local on a bus, a photographer who helped me figure out what to pay and where to get off. It was his stop too. He said Lee's okay and Singapore's okay but it's a little stifling for an artist. He preferred New York City and its dangers to the conformity of his home town. I went to dinner with him and a young couple and it cost more than I'd spent on food up to then, about $35 and lots of meat. These well-educated young professionals had plenty of spending money and I figured I'd better stick with my lower class friends out front of the Chinese hotel and the cheap eateries that abounded where I'd spend a few dollars on a good meal.

As I'd use this currency, I'd calculate both US and Singapore dollars spent, not principally out of financial concerns—though I budget much more carefully when traveling than when at home—more so out of a curiosity, an amateurish enjoyment in playing with numbers.

Gupta and I had an early dinner outside at one of the upscale tourist eateries—a restaurant on Clark Quay. It wasn't too expensive either—there being so much competition. It was nestled among the many restaurants and night clubs on the bank of the Singapore River, a wharf once clogged with sampans and commerce, now clean and uncluttered. Sight-seeing boats passed under the bridges, beneath glistening skyscrapers and older well-lit brick and stone government buildings on the opposing bank. A cover band pounded out a Stones song while we savored shrimp, pasta, and salad. It started to drizzle and a motorized awning spread out over our heads.

My new friend and I were soon to be parted. Too bad. We really got along. I was to pick up a ticket to Perth the following day and fly out in two. He was off to Melbourne the next morning. He invited me to come with him to the airport to meet his uncle. Changi Airport is awesome and I didn't want to break up the flow of conversational tangents either—a little Buddhism here, Hinduism there, Islam and Christian asides, real estate, a dash of Bush bashing, American geography, psychoactive agents we've known and loved, and of course, Singapore and Singapore women, which we'd become experts on. They were lovely. I'd read in the paper, the well known Straights Times, that a study of Asian women found Singapore's to be the most sexually aggressive of Asia. Neither Gupta nor I had noticed that, but it was nice to speculate as these fine specimens of human evolution passed by or sat near. We paid attention to other things as well. He, being a biologist was always commenting on the surrounding tropical plants, birds, and insects. I liked all that but I would get distracted by artifacts. Like trains, airports, and coins.

"What are you doing?" Gupta asked me as we waited for the subway train.

"Converting the fee to American dollars. Figuring out which way's easiest—fractions or decimals."

"It's like half. Singapore dollar's like half an American dollar."

"No, it's more like nine-sixteenths," I said.

"Oh my god. You're a fanatic," he said looking at me askance.

In the sleek clean subway car on the way to the airport Gupta fell asleep, travel weary. There were no closed doors between cars so I could see way down through them. It was past rush hour and there were so few riders that everyone was seated. In the back of the caboose I had a clear shot of a long row of stainless steel poles for standing riders to hold to—shiny vertical pipes running down and down the middle through the cars for what seemed a hundred yards, waving with the bends of track back and forth, then the bars closing in accordion-like, severing the depth view as we rounded a bend till the queue of cars whipped and straightened to reveal that lengthy line of bright poles again, a pleasing example of unintentional industrial op art.

The people who run this place sure believe in rules. It's well known there are huge and effective fines in Singapore for spitting, chewing gum, or littering. But one would be unlikely to receive such a penalty because you hardly ever see any police. People are just well-behaved. Japan's like that.

There was a sign running along the wall above the windows, a row of images with circular red borders and red lines running diagonally through the center indicating the activities pictured are commuter no-no's. No bicycles, no roller blades, no gum, no smoking, no kissing, no flammables, no durian. I laughed at that last one. I've seen that rule written down in other Southeast Asian countries—at the entrance to buses. Durian, the "king of the fruits," is a wildly popular vile smelling melon—the Limburger of the fruit world, which is honored at the beginning of the park along the Singapore River by a large performing arts center, the Esplanade, which looks a lot like half a giant thorn-covered durian.

The subway rises to the surface revealing Singapore suburbs, high rises gleaming. I wondered if at that point I should call it a train instead of a subway. "What do you say when it's both above and below ground?" I asked Gupta, but he was too groggy to care.

We pulled into the airport. Gupta yawned and stretched. The passage from the train led to a shiny, cavernous foyer. We gazed up at silver escalators that seemed to have no end.

"It's the escalator to..." I paused.

"To a better place," he said.

We glided up and up past daringly designed reflective metal and glass, then walked through vast sparkling spaces to a waterfall welcoming us to the Ambassador Transit Hotel. While Gupta went to the john, I checked out a brochure. There were spa, gym, and pool. Some rates were reasonable—for rooms with bath or shared bath by the hour or the six hour block. I'd wrongly assumed it was all super-expensive. When Gupta inquired at the desk about Rudy Dugan, heads turned, a phone was quickly lifted, and we were provided with an obsequiously polite escort to the Presidential Suite up top.

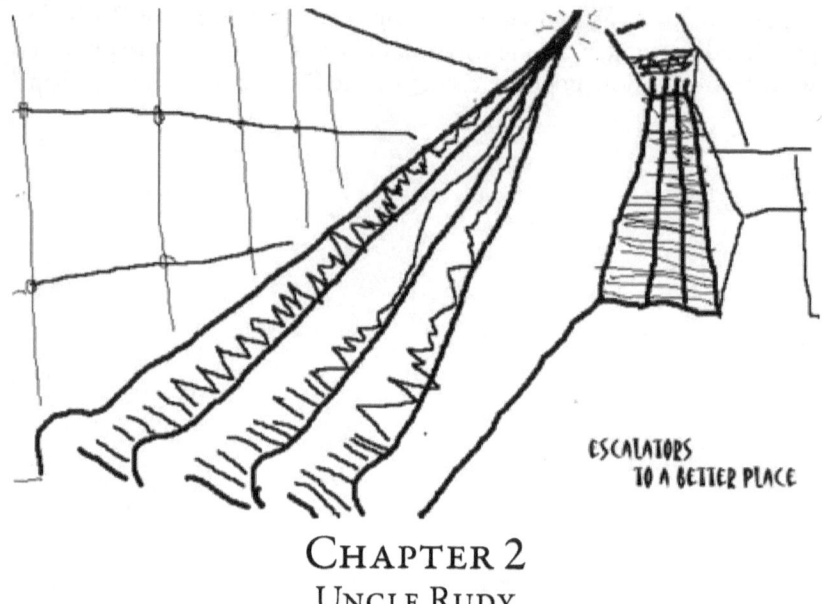

ESCALATORS
TO A BETTER PLACE

CHAPTER 2
UNCLE RUDY

A serious fellow in a white suit answered the door and let us in without introducing himself. He escorted us to a balcony overlooking the darkened causeway with slowly moving bright boat lights and the shadows of the Malay Peninsula beyond sprinkled with twinklings of human activity. From behind us came the sound of an evening jet descending.

Before long a large man came out to join us and introduced himself as Rudy. Gupta and I responded politely and shook hands with him. Rough hands. He was a tough looking guy with a coarse voice who seemed more like a retired boxer than a businessman. He offered us drinks, which we accepted—all agreeing on Jameson Irish Whiskey. We sat and looked out at the night view while he called for the other guy to bring the booze in.

"So we're relatives huh?" he said looking at Gupta.

"That's what my mom says."

"I know who she is. I never met her. My mother knew her—may she rest in peace."

"Oh, I'm sorry," said Gupta.

"Thank you. It's been a long time."

The booze came. Rudy poured a couple of generous shots in each glass. Rudy and Gupta took theirs with ice and soda. I drank mine straight.

"Who's your friend?" Rudy asked.

"David's a writer from near San Francisco."

"Never been there. What do you write about?"

"I've written about Japan and Japanese Buddhism and about it coming to the West. And I like to write songs. Never sold any of them though."

"I don't know anything about Buddhism," Rudy said. "I don't like Japs. I don't like them buying everything up here. I wish they'd stay home. Umm. That's only half true. I like Japanese women. They can come here."

"Yeah," I agreed, "I love Japanese women."

"Where you going?"

"Perth."

"To write?"

"No—just to visit an old friend—and a Buddhist teacher there I've never met who's supposed to be an interesting musician. I just want to walk around and see what there is to see and get to know people. I'm looking forward to it. I like Australians."

"Yeah, not as uptight as Americans, huh?"

He turned to Gupta and asked him what he did and they went on about real estate.

Rudy's the type of guy I take one look at and know to choose my words carefully—like meeting a redneck or a biker in a bar. There won't be a problem if I don't say too much, don't stick the ole neck out, and most importantly don't do anything that might give the impression of assumed intellectual superiority. Even though I'm a blabbermouth I never get in trouble with people from tough sub-cultures—probably something I learned growing up in Texas. Not saying Rudy's insecure or looking for a fight—this is just what came to mind watching him talk with Gupta.

Rudy looked at me for a second, head tilted, like he's not so secretly sizing me up. He got up and went to talk to the young guy in the white suit. The sound of the front door closing. Rudy returned and poured me some more Jameson. Good guy. There are two types of pourers—those who pour what they think you want and those who pour what they think you should want. I think he's the former but I can't prove it because he poured himself a generous amount as well. He offered me a cigar, high quality I bet, though I really wouldn't know. Gupta declined. Rudy held up a gold lighter and clicked on the flame. Jameson, good cigar, the Singapore view, unexpected companions, don't need a credit card—incalculable.

They talked about the Irish side of the family, how they were related, the IRA, and the old country. Rudy said family was important to him and therefore Gupta was important to him.

"Even if your mom did marry outside her race. I don't have a problem with that. I got a lot of respect for Indians. They're tough. They're smart. They survive. They stick together. Everybody feels sorry for them starving to death and suffering. I don't. It's just a matter of time before them and the Chinese are gonna be dividing up the whole world. White people are getting lazy and arrogant. Maybe it's better we inter-marry. Anyway, we're all people, I know—ain't room for racism in this world anymore. Don't mean to offend. Just telling you how I see it."

He said more than I expected. Gupta and I just nodded and sipped.

"Don't come to Melbourne," said Rudy. "It's not so interesting and it's cold now. I'm busy. Can't really show you around or do nothin' for you."

"Well that's where my ticket's for," said Gupta. "I fly out tomorrow. I understand if you're busy... It's nice meeting you here. I don't have to bother you there."

Sound of the door to the hall closing.

"Hey," Rudy called out over his shoulder to... his assistant I guess. "Stevo, bring it in now."

Stevo brought in a large brown hotel envelope and put it on the round glass table in front of us.

"You go to the desk downstairs here and they'll give you refunds for your tickets—both of you. If you don't have them with you it won't matter—they'll take care of it."

"What?" said Gupta with some annoyance in his voice. I just sat there wondering what's going on.

"Now just hang on," said Rudy. "Here's two first class tickets to Perth—round trip—open-ended." He turned to me. "I took the liberty of having Stevo get you one too. I think Gupta here is a little wet behind the ears and could use a mature guy like you along."

"But I've already got a ticket to Perth. It's waiting for me."

"This is a better one," he said.

Gupta started to say something but Rudy turned to him and cut him off.

"I got someone else to look after you there. My niece. She's young and..." he clicked his tongue searching for words, "young and full of piss—she'll wear you out showing you around. She'll be a good guide. She's dropped out of college. I think you two guys will be a good influence on her. She needs to meet some serious people, people with values, people who think. I get a little worried about her sometimes."

"Uh," said Gupta, "uh, well... I guess... okay."

"Good," said Rudy. "Good. Here." He reached into the envelope. "Here's some money so you don't have to worry about bummin'. You should have a good time while you're there."

Whoa—there were a bunch of hundreds in there.

"Oh, I can't..." Gupta started.

"Forget it. You're family." He leaned back. "Listen—these tickets are for the day after tomorrow. She'll meet you there. You stick with them—make sure they don't get in any trouble," he said to me.

"You know," I said, "I've got these friends to visit."

"He's got enough there to bring them along too. Keep an eye on 'em. Anything happens to her we'll all regret it."

That sent a chill down my spine. "Now wait—I didn't sign up to be a bodyguard."

"Well, you just make sure everything's okay," he said pointing. "Both of you make sure and you won't have anything to worry about. It's good you go," he said to me. "She's a looker and they might need a chaperone. And she's a jewel. She's a jewel of the family. I'm asking her to take care of you. You gotta take care of her."

Good lord. What the hell is he talking about, I thought? I tried to talk to him some more but he stood up and said he's tired, gotta get some rest.

"Oh yeah. Let's meet on the 29th of August at Jessica's in Perth," he added. "Melinda knows where it is—that's her name—Melinda Dugan—same last name as mine. Well, Dugan Waters. Waters is her married name. But she's separated. Uses both. Nine P.M. I like a late dinner. The 29th. That's a Friday. Jessica's is a great seafood restaurant. You can sit facing the river. My treat. Look forward to hearing about all the fun you had—all the good clean fun—seeing each of you fit and healthy."

I tried again to beg out of this deal but it was no use. Time to go to bed. Nice to meet you. There's a pre-paid taxi waiting. Have a good time in WA. Neither one of us could get a word in or out as Stevo escorted us to the door without a word himself or a nod and it's closed.

We turned to the elevator door. It was open, a hotel employee standing there.

"This way please," he said smiling.

NAKED CLOUDS OUT THE PLANE WINDOW

CHAPTER 3
FLYING NUDE

Gupta and I luxuriated with hedonistic satisfaction in first class where neither had been before except in passing. What cushy seats with lengthy legroom, shoulder space, extra attention from the cutest stewardess, tasty snacks, first class booze—though we weren't partaking. He said it was too early for him and for some reason I don't like to drink or smoke on planes. Maybe it's the altitude or the dry air.

I told Gupta about a friend from Mill Valley who was bumped up to first class. He mentioned to the gentleman sitting next to him how comfortable it was and the gent said, yeah it was good, but nothing compared to Air Force 2. "Air Force 2?" my friend replied trying to figure out what the man meant. "Yes, I used to be Vice President of the United States. My name's Spiro Agnew." He said he thought the guy looked familiar.

"I'll bet our airlines just give you bigger peanuts with first class," I said. "Singapore Airlines is the best even without first class, but with first class it's in the stratosphere."

"Do planes fly that high?" Gupta asked.

"This one is on its way out of the earth's gravitational field—on the escalator to paradise."

"You speak truth," he said smiling at the stewardess. "Management obviously doesn't have to worry about affirmative action in their hiring."

"Hey Gupta," I said, "Do you think if I write a book about Australia and put in some really good plugs for Singapore Airlines, that they might pay me?"

"Can you do that?"

"I don't know. Never heard of it. They have product placement in movies."

"Do the movies get paid?"

"I don't know. I wonder."

"Isn't that selling out?"

"Heaven forfend! Are you kidding? I'm dying to sell out. Please let me have a chance to sell out—and for a product I really like. Hmm. Maybe I should do a whole book based on product placement. I'll start making a list of what I could stand behind." I pulled out a little notebook from my shirt pocket and wrote "Products to Place" at the top of a fresh page and then "Singapore Airlines."

Gupta watched on. "Is this going to be another neurotic thing?"

"What do you mean, *another?*"

"Like the way you calculate exchange rates and stuff like that."

"If there's fun or money in it," I said, "I'll do it."

"You seem to have more of the former."

"True. Got to put more into the money thing. Starting with— product placement."

"I think you've got to get really famous before anyone's going to pay you to endorse their products," he said.

"You don't have to be famous to sell advertising space. Only to sell a product based on who you are. I'm not talking about that. Maybe they'd pay based on a flat fee plus sale of the books."

"Well, try it, but I doubt if there's going to be much of anything happening on this trip that would be interesting enough to write about."

"Of course. Just speculating. I don't really plan to write anything anyway—pretend I'm going to, pretend that any publisher would be interested to begin with, pretend I have big contracts awaiting while bumping around as clueless as Jacques Tati."

"Poor Jacques. Poor you. Truly tragic figures."

My god, I've only known him a couple of days and already he's ridiculing me like one of my sons. Come to think of it, he's just Kelly's age.

We flew on in first class splendor. Gupta kept flirting with our stewardess. She lives in Singapore and wants to live in America. He could help with that. I could see Gupta trying to get the nerve to ask her out, knowing full well he's much more attractive in these seats than he'd be further back. I didn't blame him. All the stewardesses seem to come out of the same tantalizing mold, but hers, I told Gupta, must be the new mold—she's beyond gorgeous. Gupta wasn't paying attention to me—even though I had some excellent observations to make. She'd absorbed him.

No matter. I love to fly. I like to look out the windows but I also enjoy thinking about being way up shooting forward this fast. I turn it into a meditation, shut my eyes, and cruise along into vastness. I only meditate this way while cruising, not when going up or down. Especially not when waiting to take off—then I think about airplanes. I don't believe they're going to get off the ground.

How do planes do it? I certainly understand people who said we'd never fly. I still think that. I look out at the plane wing while we're taxiing and think, nope, it'll never work. It's impossible. It's too heavy and there's all of us and our luggage. And if it does take off, it will only go up for a few seconds and hover in space like cartoon characters do when they run off the edge of cliffs and then, after the shocking realization thin air is not going to hold us up, we will drop to the hard ground where we explode.

At times such as this I turn to a higher power. I ask myself, "What would syndicated Miami Herald humor columnist Dave Barry do?" I immediately know. He'd go, "Ha ha! Those nutty airline people are just pulling a practical joke on us! They'll drive this hunk of metal that's the size of the Sears Tower around a while and go through the safety procedures with the passengers and rev up the engines while winking at each other and trying to hold back giggles and then at the last moment go, 'Just kidding!'"

But Singapore Airlines took it further than that. As I was thrust back in my seat and saw the ground receding that morning, I told myself they've really gone to extremes with this hoax by creating a long outdoor stage where everything is built gradually smaller and smaller so it looks like it's getting further away but is actually just right down there thirty feet or so with the plane wheels still touching the ground. I remember Clay looking out of the window on a flight years earlier and, in his wee toddler voice, remarking at how small the houses were. He understood.

The stewardess is busy with other passengers so Gupta will talk to me again.

"Is it love?" I said.

"She's so beautiful and friendly. But I just got over a very emotional relationship and am more interested in something superficial."

"It doesn't have to be superficial to not be out-of-control, insane hyper-stupid love."

"Sounds like you've been there."

"Indeed. I don't want to go crazy like that—not now anyway. A little comfortable affection without the mania would be fine."

"And some hot monkey love," he added.

"Or sweet potato love."

"Is that Zen?"

"I think even romantic love is an expression of our ceaseless quest to awaken to our true nature."

"You mean that sex is a substitute for religion? I thought it was the other way around."

"Nope."

The conversation moved on past our mutual desire not to become endorphin slaves. He said one of the things he's looking forward to in Australia is testing the Coriolis Effect, which is the way water swirls in opposite directions in the Northern and Southern Hemispheres. He had a friend who saw a demonstration right at the line of the equator in Ecuador. A woman poured water into a container being held by another. On one side of the line (painted on the floor) it swirled one way and on the other side of the line it turned the other. "Must test it," he said. He went to the airplane restroom and reported the toilet and sink both had so much suction that the water didn't cooperate with his examination. He was sure all drains in the Southern Hemisphere went clockwise.

Moving on from the Coriolis Effect, we agreed we had the absolute best type of movie viewing setup with our own screen with many choices and good sound. Airplane movies are usually hard to see and harder to hear. Not with this setup. I'd spent a little time watching a Discovery Channel show on roller coasters. Gupta said he'd like to have a choice of air disaster films like *The High and The Mighty.*

"That one really got to me as a kid," I said, "wondering if they're going to make it to Hawaii after they got beyond the point of no return—and what will happen to the little boy who's asleep."

"I liked another John Wayne film I saw named *Island in the Sky* where they crash in remote Canadian wilderness," he said.

"Don't know that one. *Airplane!* and of course the sequel. So loony. Almost everyone poisoned so only the nut case can fly it."

"*Twilight Zone*," said Gupta getting animated, "where the guy played by John Lithgow has the extreme fear of flying and the gnarly gremlin is tearing out wires from the plane engine!"

"Yeah that was great. But the best airplane crash scene in a movie that I know of is *Fearless*. They feed it to you little by little. Seemed realistic as heck."

"Totally—I was chilled to the bone."

"Stop! Please! Please stop!" came from behind us.

We turned to look. Oops. We were freaking out the poor woman there. "Sorry," said Gupta.

"Excuse us," I said. "I'm sure everything's alright on this flight."

"I don't know," said Gupta stretching up and craning his neck to look out her window. "Don't you think the smoke coming out of that jet is a little suspicious?"

"Stop it!" she said.

"That was cruel," I said, nobly coming to her defense. "Sorry ma'am. I won't let him get out of hand again."

She returned to her magazine and then looked up at me and shook her head as if to say, "Naughty boys."

"Are you going to forgive us?" I asked.

"Okay. But that was horrible. Don't do it again."

"Sorry. Sorry. Sorry. It was his fault. He made me do it." That made her laugh.

She's cute and by herself so I went around and talked to her. That's another good thing about first class. I can get out without bothering Gupta. Our neighbor is from Kuala Lumpur where we stopped on the way—capital of Malaysia. They speak a lot of English in KL, as it's called, just like in Singapore—former Commonwealth states. She got bumped up to first class. She said she always asks and every now and then it works. She was on her way to Perth to see her sister and brother-in-law and to buy dolls to put in her collection or sell on the Internet. She looked like a doll. Cute little woman. I could feel the juices flowing in me—or whatever it is that happens. But she was way too straight for me. She had four sisters, all married. She was thinking about marriage already. I was just thinking about how nice she'd be to cuddle up to. But it was just thinking. There was nothing there but an interesting conversation.

It's not just she who has to be on guard though. This is how men get trapped too. It's like men and women just say hello and if the chemistry is right, they start spinning webs to catch themselves in. Thank gosh it almost never works but sometimes—we're caught!

34

And it all starts from the first glance. It might even be over after the first glance. I imagine all those deluding chemicals swirling—clockwise in the Southern Hemisphere I suppose.

I asked if she's Muslim but she's not—she's Catholic.

"Ah! I've got a Catholic book," I said and went back to get my shoulder bag. I got out a book on Pseudo Dionysius and asked if she'd ever heard of him. Nope. I told her he's a third century monk named Dionysius, or a fifth century monk who signed that name, not to be confused with the god of wine, Dionysus. Almost the same—it's what the names Denise and Dennis came from. She nodded trying to keep up.

"Okay—so he's phony Dennis right? Pseudo Dionysius. He's possibly the most influential writer on mystical Christianity, a big influence on Meister Eckhart." I can see that doesn't ring a bell. "That's okay," I told her. "Eckhart fell out of favor—the Franciscans had it out for him."

"Some of them can be mean," she said. "I know—I went to a school where they taught."

"I've heard that from others all my life. Meister Eckhart's quoted in the movie *Jacob's Ladder*." She wasn't familiar with it. "Good movie," I said. "Pseudo Dionysius is quoted by Saint Thomas Aquinas—I swear I read—1300 times."

"Oh—he's one of the great Saints."

"There we go. And Pseudo Dionysius taught him everything he knew—or a lot of it. Here, let me read you some." She was amenable.

I read her a paragraph of stuff on the first cause, a term he often used instead of god and he listed everything it wasn't, which was everything people thought god was. It's not truth, it's not power, not this, not that, and on and on.

"Then what is it, what is god to him?" she asked with concern.

"Beyond conceptual thinking," I said. "Beyond any definition or attribute. Here—he says beyond any affirmation or denial."

"Hmmm."

"I love this guy," I said, "He says to his fellow monk Timothy not to bother to try to share this lofty teaching with people who can't imagine anything beyond instances of individual being. What do you think of that?"

"That's very interesting. What does it mean to you?"

"That the supreme being is not a being, that the truth about you and me and god and Jesus is not bound by the constraints of this realm of separate being—of being beings."

"They didn't teach me that."

"Didn't they teach you it's a mystery?"

"Yes."

"Well that covers everything they don't bring up."

Now she wants the book. Nope—I gave her the basic info so she could buy it, suggesting she order it from Many Rivers Books and Tea in Sebastopol, California, where I got mine. I point to the address on the bookmark—130 S. Main Street, Suite 101, Sebastopol, CA 95472.

"Just say you want the book on Pseudo Dionysius and tell 'em I sent you."

Gave her the bookmark and she wrote the name of the book and my name on it. Another convert. Before I went back to my seat I got her name, Mai, and sister's phone number in Perth.

The plane flies on. I hear Sonny and Cher in my memory bank.

Gupta was asleep. I settled back in my seat and ruminated on Australia, which I knew nothing about except what I'd learned from Francine, Tasmanian John, Mr. C. Dundee, and rumor. It's the rumors that had stuck. I'd always had a dread of going down under because such a point had been made of all the lethal critters there. That guy from Ohio in Singapore, the one who took the photo of the punk kids, told me Australia's got something like ten of the twelve most poisonous beings on earth including a lethal spider so aggressive it's been said to bite through shoe leather to plunge its terminator venom into toey flesh.

I was sure Francine would do her best to protect me, but still I trembled with distress as I closed my eyes, and, falling into light slumber, visualized myself in a serene park with kangaroos, koalas, emus, sea gulls flying over a lazy beach. That worked for about one minute and then I find myself floating into a long hall under a sign, a sign that reads, "Welcome to Australia, A Great Place to Die," which features a diorama of everything there that could poison or chew on me. Then a sinister looking large brown snake starts crawling out from the display. Brilliantly colored, variously shaped reptiles, spiders, crocodiles, sadistically grinning kangaroos with fanged teeth and spikes on their swinging fists and barbs on their tails, threatening emus, and fantasy critters that writhe and slither their way toward me as I back nervously into the shark-infested sea, the floor of which is covered with fatal stone fish, the waters crowded with bright ribboned poisonous turkey fish, deadly sea snakes inching up to my pinkies, and the streamers of the super-toxic box jellyfish with their minuscule barbs I am unprotected from by the fact I'd forgotten to don pantyhose on my legs, arms, and head, which I had heard about from Tasmanian John who was once surrounded on three sides by these cold wet insta-killers. Luckily the fourth side was open. I swim that way with him to safety.

I was back in my seat. Barely awake. Gupta was still asleep. The nice tiny woman behind me was reading peacefully. I sat up and followed breathing in and out, in and out. In stages, dream dangers were gone, my companions were gone, the airplane was gone, my clothes were gone, my body was gone. I was gone. Breath alone nakedly hurled ahead 35,000 feet up at 550 miles per hour.

LOG MAZE

CHAPTER 4
THE GIRLS FROM PERTH

"MELBOURNE'S GANGLAND WAR BURNS RED HOT," was the bold headline of the newspaper.

"Did you see that?" I asked Gupta, tapping him on the shoulder. We'd just walked out of the plane into the airport. He turned around.

"What?"

"What the man was reading."

"Who?"

"The man sitting in the waiting area."

Gupta stopped and turned around. "I'd say he's waiting in the sitting area."

"Did you see it?"

"Yes. I wanted to snatch it away from him and scarf it down before he could catch me."

"What? Maybe you saw a different headline."

"I saw his Cadbury bar."

"Not him—reading, not eating. The guy next to him. I meant did you see the headline on the paper the guy sitting next to the guy eating the Cadbury bar was reading?"

"The guy eating the Cadbury bar isn't reading. He's eating."

"That's right. And the guy next to him is reading and not eating.

38

So look at what he's reading."

"Why didn't you say so?" He walked back and took a look. "The *Western Australian*. Hmm. Latest count—twenty dead. Melbourne of all places. Hmm." The man glanced up at him. "Excuse me, sir." Gupta looked at me and grimaced. "Maybe it's for the best I came *here*," he said as we walked on.

We exited the customs area—Gupta with just a big overstuffed backpack and me with my worn shoulder bag and trusty rolling suitcase/backpack combo. We got in line at a money exchange place. A young blond woman in front of us went up to a window.

"You're staring at her. She's making you breathe heavier," I whispered in Gupta's ear.

"Mmmmm," he grunted approvingly.

"Have you already forgotten the one you were in love with five minutes ago?"

"She wouldn't give me her phone number. I've been rejected. But you, you stud, you got that Malaysian woman's number."

"That's because I wasn't drooling over her. I have no second chakra intentions with her. Anyway, don't let me cramp your style."

"She's German," he whispered. "She went through customs in front of me. Ah, there she goes. Lost forever."

He stepped up to the window. Another opened up and I went to it. In a few moments we're done and ready to head out.

"Just a second," I say.

"Oh no," Gupta said watching me scribbling in my notebook.

"Interesting."

"What's interesting?"

"Well, one thing is that the US, Singapore, and Australia all three have dollars."

"Mildly interesting."

"The Singapore dollar was worth 57 cents US, which is about 4/7ths of a US dollar and the Australian dollar 65 plus US cents—just a tad more than a penny short of 2/3rds of a US dollar."

"Could you be more exact? I can't take this sloppiness."

"Good for you. I'll go back and recalculate to finer fractions."

"I take it back."

"Now, to continue. The Singapore dollar is worth point 865 of the Australian dollar, which comes out to 55/64ths, which is... one 64th short of being 7/8ths."

"Wait a minute. I thought you said yesterday the Singapore dollar was 9/16ths of the US dollar, not 4/7ths."

"You remember! That's right, but 4/7ths is only a 64th more and it's easier to relate to..."

"Relate to a fraction?"

"Yeah. The exchange rate fluctuates and can be different in different places so you can play with small percentages to get the numerical relationships you desire."

"Desire? Desire numerical relationships? Seek help."

"I'll try to think about sex more."

"Please."

Out the door to the lobby. A bunch of kids jumped up and down and cheered a guy entering in front of us. A woman kissed another on the cheek and squeezed her hand. An older man near us was drunkenly blubbering all over a younger woman dreading to depart through the door to customs. Gupta rolled his eyes in disgust that expanded as the man started throwing up into a trash can.

"Jeez. Take it outside, fellow," Gupta said softly toward me.

"That could be you in the future," I said to him.

"That could be you in the present," he said smiling cruelly.

We continued walking toward the exit.

"I see someone I know!" I said as Francine ran up, gave me a hug, and then pulled back, looked at me with a smile and said in Australian, "How you goin'?"

"Good yeah," I answered appropriately. "And you mate?"

"Good yeah. I see you haven't forgotten what I taught ya."

"I studied my notes," I said.

"It's good to see you."

"Yeah. You too. And how's your mom?"

She looked down. "She's not doing so well. I been stayin' at home with her and dad for a week. It's hard. You'll meet them soon."

"Oh," I sighed. "I'm sorry."

I introduced Francine to Gupta quickly and explained he's looking for some young woman who's to meet him. We look around. Not there. We walk. Smack dab in front of the exit is a yellow Porsche convertible with "GUPPY!" written in dripping shaving cream on the side.

"That's her," said Francine.

"Why do you think so?" I said.

"Guppy for Gupta."

A young woman behind the wheel was waving. She is good looking—a fiery redhead with a gleam of fun and trouble in her eye you don't have to be close up to catch.

"You're Guppy and you must be Davo," she said.

"You got it," Gupta said. "And this is Melinda, Francine. Francine, Melinda. Francine's here to pick up David."

"How was your flight?" she asked, as Gupta put his backpack in her trunk.

"It was alright," he said.

"You must both be tired," she said.

"It's good to have arrived," I said. "But I like flying."

"I like flying about fifty percent of the time," said Gupta.

"Fifty percent?" I said.

"Yeah. Half the getting there is fun."

I groaned.

"You ready for more fun?" Melinda said.

"Sure," Gupta said.

"Where you going?" she asked Francine.

"Dwellingup."

"In a hurry?"

"Not really."

"Then follow us Frannie."

Francine looked at me. I nodded. "Righto Mindy," she answered. They didn't waste any time getting into the diminutives.

Francine had to open the rider's door of her car from the inside. I was delighted to see my dear ole buddy again, all chipper and bright with that nose turning up a bit, dressed in faded jeans and a black furry coat that minded me of the weather. I'd left the oven summer of the American Southwest and muggy tropical Singapore for winter in the Southern Hemisphere. Perth is near the ocean and it wasn't so cold, similar to a Sonoma County winter day where I live. Good thing because the heater didn't work and it was rather open-air, there being a window stuck down in the door on the driver's side. I put my bags in the trunk and closed it after fetching a sweater. She threw some of the clutter from the front passenger seat and floor in back with the clutter there. That clunky, dented, rusty old Honda looked as if it had been broken down and sitting in the parking lot for years. But magically it started okay and backed up and so I relaxed as she headed to the exit where Melinda and Gupta were waiting.

Francine managed to keep up with the peppy Porsche as we zoomed along a country road.

"Oh, on the wrong side again," I said.

"Oh how clever," she said, "never heard that one before. Scare you?"

"It jolts me at first."

"You've been over here on the left a bit?"

"Sure. This morning in Singapore, Japan for four years, a few other places briefly. Remember? I was in England."

"Sure. You're an old hand at it."

"I've missed it."

"Finally back where you belong."

"At home when I get nostalgic for driving on the left, I just look in the rear view mirror and pretend I'm there."

"You feel superior?" Francine asked.

"I've tried to figure out if there's an advantage one way or the other but I can't see what it would matter."

"I've heard that the left side is better if you have to fight cause it leaves your right mitt on the side of the threat that's comin' at ya."

"So righties," I said, "which are nine out of ten people, can pull their sword and defend better?"

"Yep. But fewer than nine out of ten people carry swords these days," she pointed out.

"I read that archaeological excavations of Roman divided roads revealed they were for right side use—except in Britain. Weird huh? And then Napoleon went right so the Brits *had* to keep left. You drive on the left here because you were part of the British Empire."

"Don't tell anyone here it's because of the wenchin' Poms."

"Oh yeah—Poms. Now why's that again?"

"They're ruddy—from bein' in the sun or getting' pissed all the time—their noses get red and bumpy like pomegranates."

"Pissed is drunk," I remembered. "What a weird thing to say."

"Schindlered."

"What?"

"Schindler's List—rhymes with pissed. Remember?"

"It's all coming back to me."

Francine had to concentrate for a while to follow Mindy's navigations onto a new road. We cruised along.

"So here I am in Australia," I said looking out the window at the green and yellow countryside, excited to be in a place altogether new.

"Yes, here you are in Australia. Take a good look. You've never seen anything like this before."

"I know. Never." It may be just more planet earth. It could look similar to where I live, but it's elsewhere, a place with its own name, and today I'm seeing the birth of a new world. "Look there—Australian sheep. Australian trees. An Australian road sign."

"And there's some Australian flowers poppin' up," Francine adds, "and an Ozzie Ostrich and Emu farm."

"Ostriches and Emus," I repeated tilting my head quizzically. I asked if Ostriches were from Australia. Nope, they're from Africa. Right. Right. I know that. We have them in the US too. But there they were with Emus and it seemed like they should come from Australia as well. She agreed and suggested maybe they were originally intended for Australia and their delivery was misdirected.

"When am I gonna see kangaroos?"

"You may see some but they're not so easy to find around here."

"Well, that's okay," I said. "There are Australian clouds above—following us into the Australian future."

"Coming from the Australian past."

I looked at her. "And there's Aussie Frannie."

She glanced over at me. "And there's Yank Davo."

We follow Mindy into an area called Sequoia Park. Sequoias? In Australia? Yep—there they were—not giant but they were redwoods. Maybe received in return for some of the Eucalyptus trees. Not a fair exchange. We pull up beside Mindy at a place called The Maze.

"Maze? Maze! Great. I love mazes," I said. "You know this place Francine?"

"Always wanted to come," Francine said getting out of her car.

Even though it's a convertible, Mindy's car reeked of pot smoke. She got out barefoot and went running into the trees. She's an energetic puppy. Gupta made a face to me like he's stoned out of his gourd. Francine teased him for his bloodshot eyes. He offered us a hit on Mindy's pipe. Francine politely declined, so me too—with effort. Mindy came running back calling out she couldn't wait. She rested a camera on the hood of her car and got us together in front of it till we heard a click.

There was a giant maze there alright, made of logs, but there were five other smaller ones—three hedge min-mazes, a stone maze, and one that's a paved path. We took the big log one first. Francine bought some water in case we got really lost. Mindy brought her digital camera along.

"My treat," said Gupta going up to the window. "How long do you think this will take me to go through?" he asked the woman there.

"Most people come out in forty-five minutes or so," she said.

Gupta synchronized his watch with her, told us he'd find us in a while. Then he was off into the entrance. We looked at each other somewhat puzzled and went in. We were wandering around inside a while later when he came up to us.

"Made it in 19 minutes," he said. "I've got to keep going. I'm trying another route. You can follow me or I'll find you again in a while." And he was off again. A while later he came up to us. "Yeah— you're almost at the exit," he said. "The second time I did it in 18 minutes. I just came back in through the exit cause I heard you over here. Want me to let you find it?"

"Whoa! He's the maze wizard!" I said. "Yes, let us find it—I think it's over this way."

We made it out about ten minutes later.

Eating wallaby pie at a picnic table outside, we quizzed Gupta. Had he been there before? Of course not. Did he know about it? No. Did he see some map? No. Is it the same as a maze somewhere else? No. Was he an Olympic maze champ? No. He said he had a system that worked for any maze whereby he'd go through the whole thing without repeating his steps. Actually, two systems. Two? He didn't read it anywhere. Figured it out himself. And he wouldn't tell us. Sadist.

We sat there a while and relaxed. Gupta yawned and then put his head on the table. I stretched out on the grass.

"You boys take a nap," said Mindy. "We'll go look around for a sec." The women were off and we boys were out. But not for long.

"Any interesting dreams?" Francine asked.

"I dreamed," I said looking up in a daze, "that we were all in Mindy's Porsche and left it in the middle of the road and flew off like superheroes and then we realized we'd forgotten it but we couldn't fly anymore and so we had to walk back to get it and when we got there, there was an enormous traffic jam because everyone was waiting patiently for us to come move it, and they all waved at us smiling as we drove off into the sky."

"How about you?" Mindy looked at Gupta.

"I dreamed everything was upside down," he said rubbing his eyes.

We went through the smaller mazes. Most enjoyable. Gupta would sprint through them and come up to us from behind.

We visited the Maze zoo, which had kangaroos, wallabies, koalas, wombats, dingoes, and a funny little marsupial called a quokka that was just as cute as the koalas. They had Western Australia's official mammal—the striped numbat, which eats up to 15,000 termites a day. There was a large flightless bird with a blue neck—the Double-wattled Cassowary that looked like a cross between an emu and a wild turkey. There were reptiles. A cobra had its hood opened.

"Naja-naja kaouthia," said Gupta.

"What?" I said.

"Naja-naja kaouthia," he repeated. "That's scientific for Asian Cobra."

"What a name," I said.

"That's why I remembered it."

"Look at the Frilled Lizard," said Francine.

"Oh yeah," said Gupta.

We crowded around. It looked like a little dinosaur, like a raptor—reddish brown, bright yellow inside its mouth and the frill was like a cloak that it wore.

We spent a while with a cute Kookaburra bird that Mindy said sounded like a crazy person laughing.

There were emus of course but, "No ostriches delivered to the right place for a change," I said as if disappointed.

"What?" said Gupta.

"I'm not going to tell you anything till you tell me what your maze secret is," I said.

"Just follow me and you'll see pretty quick," he said. "I thought maybe you'd figure it out by now."

We all followed him back into the big log maze. Somewhere around what must have been the center Francine said she knew and Mindy said she thought she knew too. It was so obvious I should have thought of it. He just honed in on the same direction all the way. That explained the two systems—going right or going left. He said when he confronts a new maze he goes through it turning right every time he can. Then he goes back through it turning left every time. He said if you always go the same way, you keep moving through it without repeating yourself.

Mindy challenged him, saying it seemed one could end up going in circles that way but he said nope, it was an infallible system and he challenged her to draw a maze that didn't conform to his rules. I pulled out my little notebook and a pen and so she tried. I watched and it became clear he was right.

He said most mazes have a middle and usually he gets a sense from the first two passes which way is shorter for each half—right or left. If there's time, he keeps going through it till he figures which side trips can be eliminated so finally he can come to the most direct route through the whole maze.

"That's when I get into trouble though," he said. "When I deviate from always going the same direction because I think I've learned something, I might be mistaking one place for another and then I get lost—sometimes finding myself walking out the entrance. I hardly ever have enough time to figure out a whole maze."

"Doesn't that ruin it for you?" asked Mindy.

"No—it just turns it into exercise, a nice walk—and like I said—when I get into the details of trying to figure out the shortest route I can get lost."

"But not for long because you can always just start going the same way at every juncture and then you'll cruise through," I said.

"Right. But I love going through a maze without thinking—just walking along and enjoying it."

"It turns it into a meditation walk—like a labyrinth," I said. "They're cool too. A lot of churches have them."

"There is a way to bring the lost and confused type fun back into play," Gupta said.

"That being?" Mindy looked up at him.

"Hide and seek."

"Cool," I said. "Who hides?"

"A battle of the sexes," suggested Francine.

"Now you boys give Frannie and me a head start and then try to find us," Mindy said. And then it was maze hide and seek in which Gupta's method was useless and we'd all get lost and would stumble on each other screaming.

"Here's another thing that mazes are good for." We heard Mindy's voice coming from around a turn and then there she was with her skirt up giving us a full moon.

"Nice ying-yang," said Frannie. Mindy had a tattoo just above her right buttocks.

"Nice butt too," I commented. "I'm grateful. Thank you."

Gupta was speechless and Mindy turned a summersault.

STUBBY HOLDERS

CHAPTER 5
FIRKIN' SEXES

Driving home from the maze, Frannie followed Mindy onto a side road that led into a shady woods.

"Here we are," Mindy said as we exited our cars. "Now everybody into the bush for a secret mission."

She and Francine said bush. Gupta said he didn't see so many bushes, that it looked like we were in a forest. It was a Eucalyptus forest, but not the kind of Eucalyptus we have in California that Gupta said are Eucalyptus globulus otherwise known as bluegum. Mindy guided us to her special secluded nook.

"I grow one here and," dancing a short ways off, "one here and," twirling around to an opening beyond two trees, "one here and," and she went on to dramatically show us thus six spots.

"First time I've been on a garden tour—to see what was not growing," said Gupta.

"I'll be planting in a couple of months Guppy. You're welcome to join me—and then of course in the harvest."

"It'd be a long commute."

Finally I realized we were in a dormant clandestine contraband sacrament garden.

Gupta spied a flowering plant. "Ahhh. Look over there! I think that's a modesta, a rare carnivorous plant. I just happened to have

47

studied it."

Francine went over to look at it with him and they took a while to get back to the car as she answered his questions, the ones she could, about all the plant life surrounding us.

We stopped at a liquor store where Mindy got some Australian wine because, she explained, I'm from California, and gin because she's from Melbourne, Irish Whiskey for Gupta who is half Irish, and beer because Frannie is from English stock—and French. She wouldn't let anyone else chip in. That seemed fine to me but Francine got more beer and paid for it. Good manners. I noticed she included a lottery ticket with her purchase and tucked it into her coin purse.

The woman who checked us out opened her eyes wide and said, ah it looks like a party. How she wished she could get off and join us. I'd never seen anyone in a liquor store be so enthusiastic about what they sell.

Mindy's got a handsome little white wood cottage by a creek where we sampled the recent purchases, took a pleasantly revealing dip in her spa, and lay back on deck chairs in soft earth-tone Balinese sarongs. Gupta and I fell asleep. We awakened to find Mindy and Francine weaving multi-colored hemp cords they tied around our ankles. Francine said we shouldn't take them off—just let them be till they fall off.

We walked to dine at an ABC restaurant—Australian born Chinese. Then to a pub with an acoustic Irish band. They three ordered beer but I was full—can't take the volume—and got a shot of single malt scotch. Their beers, Emus, were served in bottles placed in padded sleeves.

"What's that?" I asked.

"What?"

"The uh foam doomaflochies."

"This," Francine said, "is a stubby holder. We drink our beers in stubby holders. Can you say 'stubby holder?'"

"Stubby holder," I said.

"Good boy."

Gupta tried to test the Coriolis Effect by pouring his drink into an empty glass. Then he's off to the loo and back with a report that the toilets indeed flushed clockwise. He'd tested his toilet at home in New Orleans and said it was counter-clockwise. I commended his dedication to pure science.

Francine and Mindy got all excited making a list of sights Gupta and I should see and things we should do while in WA. I got out my notebook and wrote, "The Wonderful WA Women Suggest:"

"Don't say 'women,'" said Mindy. "Makes me feel old. Say girls."

"Yeah, you're never too old to be a girl," said Francine.

"Okay. I'm just... just try to be..."

"Pussy whipped by feminists," said Francine.

"Yes. Yes—thank you. I obeyed them. Now I'll obey you. Obedience to females is the key to a successful life," I said looking to Gupta who remained neutral. "It just gets confusing when you contradict each other."

"Keep trying," said Mindy. "Gotta be on your piggies."

"Piggies?" I asked.

"As in 'this little piggy went to market,'" she said reaching down and pinching my big toe through my shoe.

I tore the page out and started a new one. "There. 'The Glorious Girls from Perth Suggest.'"

"The girls from Perth, the best on earth," said Gupta raising his beer in its stubby.

"Ferdinkum," said Frannie following his lead and we toasted the girls from Perth.

Then it was back to the must see sights and the must do deeds. In Perth the Swan Bells top the list. Then there's Kings Park. Then to other towns, national parks, an island, museums. Mindy wrote them down. I made my own list. She gave her list to Gupta. We ordered more drinks. Soon nature called. Again.

Gupta, still holding his list, and I stood swaying before two doors. Over one was a sign that read *Firkin' Males* and over the other *Firkin' Females*.

While eliminating ethanol rich fluid, we read a poster on the wall between us with a photo of a huge, swarthy, unsavory, bald-headed guy in a jail cell. The poster said, "Use the date rape drug and have a new roommate for five years."

"That's not right," I said.

"It's not? You're pro rape?"

"No silly. I think it should say, 'Use any drug for date rape and have a new roommate for five years.' The so-called date rape drug is just a downer. A drink with something like that in it used to be called a Mickey Finn. Alcohol, which is a downer, is by far the mostly widely used date rape drug. You don't get five years for that."

"Nevertheless, it's a pretty cool sign," he said. "I'd like one in my bathroom at home."

"Yeah, I'm reminded of my all-time favorite public restroom

sign," I said.

"What was that?"

"A sign above a urinal at the Sand Dollar Restaurant in Stinson Beach north of San Francisco that said, 'Please don't throw cigarette butts in urinal as they become soggy and hard to light.' It was so good it was stolen, dug out from the wall."

"Maybe destroyed in disgust," Gupta laughed while zipping his pants up and dropping his list on the floor at a spot that was a little sticky and wet. "Yuck," he said looking down at it. He gingerly picked it up by a dry corner and placed the piece of paper in the waste basket.

Francine came out of the woman's side. Mindy was not at our table. Francine said she wasn't in the firkin' women's room either. Gupta and I looked around and didn't see her. Finally we found her outside talking to a guy who looked like—like an Aborigine.

"Wow," I said and mumbled on semi-drunkenly, "is that my first Aborigine? Have I never seen one before? Hmm. I'm sure I have. Maybe in San Francisco. We've got people from everywhere there but I can't remember. Seen them in movies."

Gupta was not paying attention to me. He was watching Mindy and the Aborigine intently. Mindy was angry. Gupta walked toward them and, as he approached, the Aborigine went away.

"What was that all about?" Gupta asked her.

"Nothing—just a crazy guy."

Gupta sat next to Francine on Mindy's couch under a strangely hypnotic painting created with many tiny colored dots—a snake in a tree wrapped around a dark-skinned child who looked at us with deep black fearless eyes. There was another interesting object on the wall next to it as Gupta pointed out.

"I see you've got two sharp, dangerous weapons," he said, gently touching the blade of a mounted machete.

"Got that in Darwin," she said, "for going into the jungle. What's the other sharp weapon?"

"The axe," he said eyeing a fine looking guitar. "May I?" He took it down and tuned it while Mindy brought in a bottle of port for night caps. Delicious. Gupta added background jazz chords to our roving conversation.

Francine told Mindy I don't believe we exist and Mindy asked then what exactly do I think is happening? I came out of the painting and said I must have been drunk to give Francine that impression but they won't let up on me so I said, "I think religion is about..."

"I don't like religion," said Mindy.

"Spiritual path?" I said.

"I don't like spiritual path," said Gupta causing trouble.

"Philosophy," I tried, "love of wisdom."

"I don't like that," said Frannie.

"How about the universal perennial teaching?"

"What does that mean?" said Francine.

"Let me try it this way. A lot of wise people throughout time all over the earth have said that the key to understanding it all is to realize there is no self, that it's just something we assume exists, an imagining that we think is in the center and believe in. And all phenomena likewise, as Buddha said, is like a bubble, a dream—I can't remember—he said it's all unsubstantial things like that."

"There seems to be *something* here," said Mindy.

"Sure. It's not what we think it is, it's said—everything totally screwed up by the self idea—I don't really know," I said.

"Good," said Gupta. "Then that's the end of that."

"However," I continued, "not knowing is to me the highest teaching. How about this—the Surangama Sutra says, 'Things are not as they appear. Nor are they otherwise.'"

"That's good," said Gupta. "I'll stick with that. You see," he said, "the problem with David is that he's a Zen failure. It says so in the title of one of his books."

"It's true," said Francine. "He really doesn't make any sense, poor boy."

"It's very sad," said Gupta.

"I'm so sorry," said Mindy.

"But that's not stopping him," said Francine. "I never heard anyone go on so much about something they say they don't know anything about."

"I'll stop now," I said, "talking. But I can sing a song that might shed a little light on the subject." Gupta handed me the guitar and I launched into a song that starts with the chorus.

—chorus

Now tell me who did I write to
When I went and wrote that letter
I addressed it dear to you
And it's the best that I could do

Did I write it to your head
Did I write it to your heart

To your memory your bed
To your shadow to your star
Tell me who who who did I write to

(chorus)

Did I write it to your face
Did I write it to your smile
To your hidden private place
To your thought stream, to your wiles
Now tell me who who who did I write to

(chorus)

Did I write it to your fingers
Did I write it to your toes
To your odyssey your goddess she
Your doppelganger soul
Now tell me who who who did I write to

(chorus)

"Thanks for the clarification," said Gupta, "but shouldn't that be 'Whom Did I Write To?'"

I hand Gupta the guitar. He plays a sequence of dreamy jazz chords but his eyes are more on Mindy than the strings.

Mindy asked if I was working on something at the present. I said I was toying with a story about my boxer, Lola.

"Lola is beautiful," said Francine.

"Do you miss her?" Mindy asked.

"Sure I do," and I sighed. "The story is called, *Lola, Come to Me as a Woman*. It's about a guy who has not been all that successful with women and who keeps wishing some woman would show up who related to him like his dog. Lola is an inexhaustible fountain of love and devotion. Sometimes I say to her wistfully, 'Lola, come to me as a woman.' She always wants to lick my face or my toes or walk with me or be with me or prance around me. So this guy has a boxer like that and now and then says to her, 'Lola, come to me as a woman.' Lola dies—of cancer as boxers tend to."

"Oh," sighed Mindy. "Lola died?"

"Just in the story. Then one day the guy meets a beautiful woman named Lola and they fall in love and she is his dream come true, his Lola as a woman. She has an insatiable desire to serve him and please him. And she always wants to be with him—to massage him, make love, follow after him wherever he goes. Naturally he gets tired of it and all sorts of problems develop."

"I'd like that sort of problem to deal with," said Gupta.

"What sort of problem?" asked Mindy.

"Right now I'll leave that up to your imagination."

"Oh—you mean like you can't lock a girl inside the gate and tell 'em you're going off somewhere? Can't get rid of 'em?"

"That could be one problem. Constant devotion can get tiresome," I said.

"I've had that problem," she said. "Maybe when you've finished it you could send it to me. Might give me a few pointers. Yes, I've had that problem."

"Tell us," said Gupta.

Mindy told us about her failed marriage to a guy named Gelar. She's awfully young to have had a failed marriage. She was maybe twenty. She really loved him she said and he loved her like crazy. He had a problem drinking and taking hard drugs though he never got violent. She liked to have a good time too she said but not hard drugs and he was just blotto too much of the time so she sent him packing. He was a talented artist and had been an art teacher at a school in Perth. Gelar did a dumb thing. To show her his devotion, he had tattooed her name, MELINDA, in large letters on his chest. Since they've been apart he's tried desperately to find another woman named Melinda to be his mate. He searched in phone books, club membership rosters, in bars and gyms, on the Internet, and through the newspapers. He has dated a few other Melinda's so far and even showed the tattoo to one as if he did it for her, but she saw through his scheme. Nothing has worked out.

"Never get a name tattooed on you," she said. "Actually, never get a word. They get old. The drongo!" She shook her head. "Gelar's out there now... somewhere—looking for a true love named Melinda. I hope he finds her."

"Drongo?"

"Drongo," she repeated.

"That's sad," I said. "Of course men are more like dogs than women. Your story's true. Mine is fiction. Yours would make a good song too—*Lookin' for Melinda*—*a true story*."

"Hmm—'Lookin' for a Melinda,'" said Gupta. "It rolls out of the throat nicely. Hmm. I've got a fictional love song. It's got a machete in it too."

"Good. Let's hear a fictional love song with a machete," said Francine.

"This was written during the initiation ceremony of a fraternity I was pledging."

"Frat boy!" I said.

"Yeah," he responded without enthusiasm. "I had to write a love song on the spot for the president of the fraternity and sing it to him in front of a bunch of hooting drunk Southern frat boys."

"A gay love song?" I said. "Shocking. And with a machete as well."

"You know who John Belushi is?" he asked.

"Animal House," Said Mindy.

"He OD'd," said Francine. "The dummy."

"Yeah, sad. And to me mainly Saturday Night Live," said Gupta. "Anyway, his name is invoked."

"Delightful," I said.

Gupta sang.

You're lookin' like a dream tonight
Spread out on that bearskin rug
Before the crackling oak log fire
You've got—John Belushi Butt

At first was your Karl Malden nose
And then that Marlon Brando gut
Not even now Depardieu toes—not those
Can vie with—John Belushi butt

Are you ready for my Teddy
I'll go steady if you let me
You are heady—better 'n Betty
Take machete's wild confetti

I'll bring to you your favorite pipe
And latte in a heated cup
Jojoba oil and Handy Wipes
For you've got—John Belushi butt
Yes you do, yes you do
You've got—John Belushi butt

That was almost the end of the story because we nearly died laughing.

Gupta and I spent the night on the living room couches. He went right to sleep but I sat up at Mindy's computer and checked my email on Sonic.net's excellent webmail center. There were Internet cafes in Singapore but I didn't yet have a digital jones so I hadn't connected to my boys. I wrote a lengthy report to Kelly the wise elder in Spokane and Clay the fierce younger in Sebastopol, telling them about what had happened since I left Texas—the flight to Tokyo with a five hour layover. There I met a man who was going to Inner Mongolia, or was that Outer Mongolia? I showed him my little short wave radio and he said he wished he'd brought one and I said he could probably buy one right there in the airport but later I thought I'll probably never use it and I wished I'd given it to him. I wrote them about Singapore, meeting Gupta and Rudy, and lots of what had happened all day including The Maze and list of things to do and see in WA. I saved it. And I told them I loved them and missed them and felt a little melancholy.

The next morning I rose late. Gupta was doing yoga.
    Mindy and Francine were chatting and making breakfast. Gupta wound up his stretching and said good morning to everyone. Soon Mindy handed us two glasses of orange juice. Glug glug. Correction—mimosas. I gasped appreciatively.
    "Didn't want that gin to go to waste," she said.
    We ate and hung out for a while and then I said, "'Bout time for Francine and me to be on the road."
    "Oh no!" cried Gupta. "You can't leave! You've got to stay with Mindy and me. Remember what Rudy said?"
    "Come on. I remember, but Francine has things to do and I want to go with her."
    "We'll come with you."
    "No we won't," said Mindy.
    "Uhg, uh—then I'd better get a hotel room," Gupta said.
    "Don't worry, it's fine for you to stay here," said Mindy.
    "Then uh... well... he was quite um convincing that...oh please stay."
    "Let them go. Rudy is overly protective. Don't worry about him. I'll take care of him. He'll do anything I say. We'll smoke another cone and you'll stop worrying about Uncle Rudy."
    "See Gupta," I said.

"Oh, okay. But I do remember how serious he was about your sticking with us."

"Me too, but tough luck. He's not my boss. So Bye!"

"Goodbye Mindy and Guppy! Good to meet ya!" said Francine.

"Bye Frannie! Bye Davo!" Mindy said, coming up to hug and kiss us goodbye.

"We'll see you both soon Gupta. Mindy will take good care of you," I said.

"Bye-bye," he said with resignation.

He'd accept his fate. I knew the most important thing to Gupta was not that I stay but that he do so. He's clearly smitten with Mindy.

CANOPY TREEWALK

CHAPTER 6
DWELLINGUP

Simon! Throw the ball to Davo! Good! Good! And good catch Davo! Okay Simon, he's throwing it back to you! Get it! Get it!" Simon tried to catch the ball but missed and went awkwardly running after it laughing.

We were on the way to Francine's home and stopped in Mandurah to visit some friends of hers who lived in a large two story house. I hadn't played catch in a while but was holding my own with Simon. It was a good way to interact with him and gave me something constructive to do. After a while we went back inside and drank hot chocolate. Simon showed Francine some drawings he'd done. She responded with genuine interest and once again made my heart melt to see how naturally kind she was—and patient. Not that his art wasn't good. I liked it—simple line drawings. Simon is a big, good natured fellow. He's forty years old and has Down Syndrome. He was one of a dozen patients living in Mandurah House, a home for the intellectually challenged—the brain damaged and retarded. This is one of the places where she works.

"It's a busman's holiday," I told her.

"Bushmen don't have holidays, do they?" she replied.

"And neither do Bodhisattvas."

Her job is not always as easy as throwing a ball. Some of the people she works with at other places can't take care of themselves at all—like Mark whom she tended to in Sonoma County. Some are a lot harder than Mark who didn't give her any major trouble. She says she prefers working with people who can take care of themselves at least a little and who are somewhat socialized and cooperative. Sometimes her wards can be feisty and cantankerous, opposing her every move as she changes their diaper—jerking around or spitting on her face. "Spit is okay, but phlegm's awful. It's the worst. I've had 'em vomit on my head and piss on me and shit on me, but the worst is phlegm," she says. That series of images stuck with me. What an occupation.

But nobody was spitting phlegm on her or anything else unpleasant. She's popular, eliciting big smiles from staff and patients alike. Her dream she said is to help this home out with a substantial gift. The government is pretty good at providing for unfortunate people in Australia, but of course it's never enough. I asked her what specifically she'd want money to go toward and she said if it's a small amount she could buy more games, recreation equipment, furniture, and create a bigger lawn. If there's more money after that, the plumbing could be re-done and a new roof and they could buy the house next door and the lot behind and she continued to innumerate ways to help out till I realized she'd have all the retarded, brain damaged, and otherwise mentally or physically disadvantaged people in Australia well taken care of if she could—and then she'd extend her largess to the rest of the orb and all its suffering beings one degree of latitude at a time. Bodhisattva.

Back in the car, continuing on rural roads, Frannie talked about her mother.

"It's not easy to be there at home with her. She just sits in the dark. She's not the same. I can't help. I want to but I can't. I go out and work in the yard and do little things but..." and she couldn't talk anymore. There was nothing I could do but feel sad with her.

After driving along silently for a while we entered the little town of Dwellingup, population 452, and parked in front of a hotel and pub.

"Dwellingup's a one pub town," she said.

I didn't know it was so small. Considering its prominence on the map I thought it would be much, much bigger. Just shows how sparsely populated Australia is—twenty million in an area larger than the US.

After introducing me to the bartender and the other five people in the pub, she got us a couple of beers—an Emu Draft for her and an Emu Bitter for me.

"No Fosters? I thought it was Australian for beer."

"I never had one. And what do they come in?" she asked, holding her beer up to prominently display the foam sleeve.

"Stubby holders," I said proudly.

"That's right."

The friendly locals called me mate and Davo and her, mate and Frannie. I love the way Aussie's talk, the way she talks. The inflections go up. It's got a cheerful, positive feeling. But it's not always clear to me. It's not like they're slurring their words but they do cut off a lot of consonants. And they tend to talk so fast—like trying to keep up with any foreign language I guess. I remember the first time I took Frannie to a bar in California. After we'd had a couple pints of Guinness she got somewhat garrulous and was going on and I just sat there and stared at her and finally said I loved listening to her but that I couldn't understand anything she was saying. The background noise didn't help. I came to understand her better and better as time went by.

Time to go. Frannie ordered a six pack for Ron. Ah, company I guess. Then it was a short drive to her home on the edge of the national forest. That's not such a big deal in Dwellingup where everything's on or almost on the edge of the national forest.

"Here's the front yard," she gestured dramatically at the brownish green semi-hibernating lawn bordered by a picket fence and dirt clod beds with bulbs and flowers planted and some still in pots. "And here's the front porch with rocking chair for keeping up with the neighborhood. This bed (complete with pillow and covers) is for sloshed friends who need a place to crash, mainly Freddy who comes at times in the middle of the night and is often gone by the time I'm up."

A quick tour through the living room and kitchen, peeking into two small bedrooms. Hers thick with bedding, clothes, a mirror, sculpturettes, paintings, writing on the wall, a dresser, a stand for beads and scarves, a dark wood armoire with doors half opened and coats and blouses spilling out. The next bedroom has less going on but is piled with paintings, some half done.

"Mary's an artist."

So is Frannie. Or maybe she's more of a craftist. A step down from the kitchen into the ante-room off of which are a small stuffed storage room for her art and craft supplies and bathroom with tub. It's a small house but plenty for her and a friend.

There are little touches of her neo-Aussie baroque artistry on the walls, the floors, the ceilings, the doors. She opens the back one.

"And here's the patio and backyard and laundry hut and that building used to be a garage and that's firewood on the right side of it and the left side's just got junk. It's to be my studio."

A nice size back yard. It's a great place. God, I can't believe Francine has her own home. Someone with her type of employment and lifestyle would be unlikely to own a home in my parts. She bought it for $5000 down with payments of $200 a month—where I live it would be more like $50,000 down and $2000 a month.

"And here comes Stubby! Hi Stubby!" she calls out.

Oh my gosh, there's a pit bull coming at me full bore. Nice doggy. Lick, lick, lick—good doggy. Relief, he's friendly.

"Stubby's Mary's dog," she says as he turns his attention to her.

She opens a couple of beers and puts them into stubby holders— oh, I see what they're named for. She designates one stubby holder to be mine, not only for the duration of my stay but to take with me as a souvie. It's got that funny little furry animal on it that was at The Maze museum—a quokka, she reminds me.

"But hey—I thought those beers were for Ron," I said.

"They *were* for Ron—later on. And that's now."

"Ron's coming later on which is now?"

"You're dense."

I thought for a minute, then, "Sorry, sorry. I get it. Later on— late Ron. Here's to Ron."

We built a fire in the iron stove with a glass door as the light outside the living room window went from blue to black. Stubby snuggled up to us in turns. It made me miss Lola. I looked at the fire and at the paisley fabric on the yard-sale couches and walls decorated with home-made paintings, day off dabblings, a string of tiny colored lights, and masks staring down at us. On the end tables and shelves are knick-knacks, rocks of interest, twigs and twine and darn and heck she's made and collected. I looked at her and admired her innocence and purity and mystery. Sometimes she seemed to shapeshift from one appearance to another. She was thirty-seven but could look like a teenager, then like a crone.

I went to my suitcase and retrieved some gifts I gave to her in the warmth of the fire. One was the *Botany of Desire*. Another a bag of lint I'd saved from the dryer. When she taught the kids to make paper back home she'd commented that laundry lint made the best. So I saved it. While she was inspecting it, there came a knock at the door. Some mates dropped by and the intimate spell was broken as more wine and beer flowed and smoke rose. One mate was Banger, a former boyfriend. He came staggering in and gave me a big booze smelling hug, said he was dying to meet me. I excused myself in time and went back to her absent roommate's bed and crashed.

Next morning I was up early, amazed at where I found myself, built a new fire in the living room, using waxy cubes to get it going, and sat zazen floating in the flame, a delicious special effect not found in any meditation hall I know of. Stubby came in from his round soft bed by the back door and sat with me. An hour later Francine got up and made tea that we sipped quietly by the morning's hopping flames.

In the anteroom I watched as she split a short piece of firewood into smaller pieces for—for what? The water heater! My gosh, she has a wood-burner. When it was done heating, we took showers, put on fresh clothes, ate granola, and drank black tea with cream. Doing the dishes in her small sink, I studied the crystal bobbles, purple doo-dads on the window sill, rainbow spiral painting, and impromptu guest poem scrawled on the wall, a patchwork of blues and greens.

"Now that you're here on my turf," Francine said while combing back her long light brown hair, "I reckon it's my turn to show you some of my favorite spots for hangin' out."

From the dirt alley behind her house we took a narrow path that led into the national forest. It smelled superb. She said that's mainly the jarrah—it's a jarrah forest. I asked her if there's an unfriendly plant there like poison oak or poison ivy in the States. Nothing round here like that. Onward into the bush, Stubby running up ahead and returning at her command to be leashed as a guy with a Labrador approached.

"You're dog friendly?" she asked.

"Yeah, yours?"

"Yeah. What sex?"

"Female."

"Good. Mine's male."

We chatted while Stubby and lab romped around. We've got to be careful with Stubby because the fine for having a loose pit bull is $5000 Australian, which I multiply by two-thirds to get the easy

Yank equiv—threes forever. She's required to have "Dangerous Dog" signs posted on the fence.

Continuing down the path Francine taught me plant names and uses. There was a red kangaroo paw and it did look like that and then there was a green one. Some flowers were out—yellow buttercups blooming from a shrub and blue leschenaultia with its white center and blue landing platform for the bees, "the floor of the sky" to the Aborigines. To me it's all just plants and trees and flowers. But to her there is much finer delineation. I've had that relation to other people in my life. I meet them and learn all the names. My vocabulary goes from plant and flower to ficus and narcissus. Then we go our separate ways and I revert to plant and flower.

We came to an area where junk resided between the trees—a totally rusted Austin Healy with no doors or windows or tires—overgrown with vines, a broken and molded easy chair, a mattress mostly reduced to springs, little stuff such as marbles and a shoe horn. She mined for something useful or ornamental—a trophy of our walk to bring home—and selected a tarnished serving spoon.

We came to a cemetery. She pointed out a tombstone inset with a glass case holding a chromed motorcycle engine—enshrined there by the son of the woman biker who loved doing what she died.

Back home we got in Francine's wounded car and visited a few of her favorite further flung outdoor haunts—a high bluff overlooking a vast plain extending flat to the horizon. There was something man-made, running along for miles. Then to a walk along the Murray River with swimming holes and white water flowing over and around large rocks. Here's where she frolics in the summer and where she saw the deadly tiger snake in January.

"Where are the deadly tiger snakes now?" I asked.

"Oh they don't come out till spring," she said.

"Spring? There are flowers blooming and it's feeling a little springish," I said glancing around at the ground.

"They don't always kill you," she said reassuringly.

She took me into the woods a ways and showed me a large sprawling tree with enough room in its lap for us to sit for a spell. She said one day she'd walked way over here and gone swimming by herself and it got dark with not enough moon to see her way back so she curled up and slept in the lap of this tree. Wow. Like Johnny Appleseed.

We visited a friend of hers at his small fruit winery and admired his wood carvings, went to a local art gallery where she talked to the luscious owner about doing a crafts workshop there for kids. I was tempted to inquire about the woman's availability but I knew there probably wouldn't be any opportunity.

The Forest Heritage Centre was jarrah leaf-shaped with three large rooms in the form of rounded sections that narrowed to sharp points, the middle one the largest. There was a treewalk on a railed platform that extends sixty meters into the canopy of the forest that surrounds the center. Most the trees around here seem to be jarrah. One of the blades of the building is an active woodworking shop.

Here I learned the meaning of the name of the town. "Up" is an Aboriginal ending used in a lot of Australian place names because it means "place." So I assumed Dwellingup meant a dwelling place. Wrong. To quote from the Forest Heritage Centre's literature: "This prime location, near the Murray River, was a traditional Aboriginal camping place long before European settlement. In fact, the Aboriginal meaning of Dwellingup is 'place nearby water.'" The most memorable item in the forestry center was the Snotty Gobble, a glob of a plant the Aborigines used for chewing gum.

At the Dwellingup Museum I learned this was a logging town. The logging was coming to an end as the forest now is mostly protected. There was a big fire in 1916 that just about burned everything down but the town got rebuilt and it turned out jarrah has a large swelling under it in the ground that stores carbohydrates so that it can come back strong after a fire. The genus of the jarrah is Eucalyptus and the species marginata. Now I see why there are so many types of Eucs—it's a genus. And Marginata is the name of the street Frannie's house is on—129 Marginata Cresent. I see we can take the "timber route" on the Hotham Valley Railway and hoped we would have time to get to it.

There was a mine nearby. We drove under the sluice, the conveyor belt that runs for miles from the mine to the processing plant. Francine says it's the longest of its kind in the world. Ah, we saw that from the bluff.

When we got back home her roommate Mary had returned. She's talkative and funny and part Maori from New Zealand. Mary brought some more Emu Beer. I told Mary I saw the roller-blader with turban and guitar at Venice Beach she'd mentioned when Francine had put her on the phone some months back to introduce us. I learn she's about to go to Scotland for half a year. Before long they decided to go to the pub. I begged off.

I determined to make myself useful. After some snooping, I found rags under the sink and got to cleaning. Right away I was content in a labor of love, which made my passions smaller and the invisible world large.

Moving along the kitchen surfaces I read the messages chalked on the front of the fridge painted with olive blackboard paint. There was my flight number and time. I drew a square by it and checked it. Then I made two more little squares and wrote "vacuum" and "dust" next to them. Then I wrote "finish off wine" by another square and uncorked a partially full bottle of red and soon checked that one off. "Good to have one completed," I said to myself and wonder about the habit of saying out loud what has just silently gone through one's mind.

I searched around but there was no more booze. Then in cleaning I come across a maroon, waxed, cardboard container with spigot atop the fridge—booze in a box, wino stuff. I gulped the cheap, challenging port and wiped and vacuumed and gulped more till Frannie and Mary came home at two. After expressing disgust I could actually drink the port in a box that's been sitting there since forever, Mary retired. Francine was already in bed. I stoked the fire, crawled under a blanket on the couch, Stubby curled up next to me, I petted him for a moment then got up and went to the fridge and marked checks in the squares by vacuum and dust.

Frannie made Indonesian food for lunch. She marveled at how clean and tidy everything was. She'd been up early helping the man across the street with a sick dog.

"You look tired," I said.

She feigned staggering. "If I can just last long enough to serve out one last meal before I drop."

Mary sat down as Frannie put the food on the table.

"Thank god. I'm starving," I said before gratefully taking my first bite. "Haven't eaten since lunch yesterday."

"Poor dear. I run off and party while you stay home famished and cleaning," said Frannie.

"Hey, I got to finish off your booze and a free place to stay and I ain't here to cramp your style. Anyway, you're usually off being Florence Nightingale to the brain damaged. Actually, their union paid me to come here and tidy up as a small way of saying thanks."

"You've done well."

"That's the secret to life—serve women, listen to women."

"How many exes do you have?" Mary asked.

"Depends on how you count 'em."

"Should we ask them how good a job you've done on this obedience or is it more likely disobedience?"

"That would indeed cast another light on the issue. I may fail to live up to my ideals, but, however feebly, I aim to be up to them. It's not just serving women. Men have female in them—it's the female side of things that I strive to serve. It's like Lao Tsu saying that the mysterious female is the only door to the Tao—or something close to that."

"Sounds good," said Frannie.

"Sounds like the same as when people say Jesus is the only way," said Mary.

"Same thing," I said.

Mary looks up. "Jesus is a mystic female?"

"Sure. Like saying Christ consciousness is the only way to union with God. Or we must get beyond conceptual mind in order to realize the absolute, know our true nature. Just different metaphors and myths to help us wake up out of our little painful worlds."

"Food for thought," said Mary.

"Booze for thought," I said, "As in the opium of the masses."

"Boobs for thought," said Francine.

"As in sexual sublimation," Mary said.

"Back to the food," concluded Francine.

"Amen," said Mary.

"Looks like you need more sleep," I told Francine when we were done. "I'll clean up."

"I thought I was the boss," she said with half closed eyes.

"That's my feminine side talking to your masculine side."

She complied. Sauntered to her room.

Mary went out to do errands and took Stubby. I peeked into Francine's bedroom, saw her sleeping peacefully and sighed, wandered around, and realized I'd better get these idle hands doing something. I went to the woodshed out back, started rolling rounds into the sun, sharpened an axe with a rusted file, found a sledgehammer and splitting wedge, and got to it. By late afternoon there were dark clouds overhead and a mountain of firewood all ready to burn. Francine had been back with the living for a while, expanding a nearby garden bed, transplanting. She and I stacked the fresh firewood in the shed and set aside the shortest stuff under the back steps for the water heater.

"It smells like rain," I said.

"Looks like rain," she said looking up.

"Feels like rain," I said, hand on head.

We taped plastic over the open window in her car just in time. It rained hard. We sat out on the back patio and watched the sky spill into the jarrah trees, on the shed roof, into the yard—in sheets and blankets. Thunder and lighting!

The cement at my feet was charred. She said it's from a fire made by some ruffians who snuck in one night when no one was home. They left a bunch of empty bottles and burned her firewood and two of her wicker chairs to keep warm. They almost burned the house down—as indicated by a blackened area on the wooden siding.

The fiberglass roof was leaking behind the wicker couch down the line where it met the steeper-pitched composition shingle roof. We watched the rain and smelled the pungent air snug under blankets while sipping red wine and eating Brie smeared on French bread. As we sat there I wrote down a poem and read it to her.

I picture you walking into the woods alone at night
High grass and unpicked flowers
Running between your fingers
After circling around an opening
And greeting the spirits of that spot
You curl up in the hollow of an old quiet tree
And fall asleep
You dream of flying over the branches
I dream I'm the tree
Without grasping, cradling your gently breathing body
That has come for a while to be within mine.

That night a woman named Della who lives down the street came over. Francine put on some Afro-European music and they made masks and painted them and glued on sequins and whatever they fished up in their little boxes of ornaments. Francine showed Della the lint I brought and they laughed. Mary returned with Stubby and joined in by painting post cards for later use. I lay back exhausted from a day of swinging axe and sledge and looked on in admiration, happy to be doing nothing on the far side of the world with mellow gals, snoring canine, and gracious fire.

CHAPTER 7

INDIAN OCEAN

Francine and I were arguing when the phone rang.

"That was Mindy," she said to me as I scrubbed the soot on the patio. "She and Gupta want us to join them. I accepted their lunch invitation. At the Indiana Tea House on Cottesloe Beach. Can we leave soon?"

"Where is it?"

"On the coast south of Perth."

"Good lord, you just got back from up there."

"No problem. This is a place I wanted to take you."

"Okay. Let's go," I said.

Frannie had just gotten back from driving Mary to the airport. They left before sunrise. Mary lingered over Stubby at the door and told him she'd miss him. He responded with licking.

As soon as they were gone Stubby and I went back inside, ignoring the guy sleeping in the bed on Frannie's front porch. Stubby went back to sleep but I set about doing things to please my hostess. When she returned I had her enter via the front gate, previously suspended by one hinge. Now it swung and latched smoothly. It's under an arbor covered with twisting vines from which I picked some of the petite white flowers and arranged them in a small emerald green vase in the living room. Impressed by the beauty of that decoration, I'd searched elsewhere in her yard and the bush for more flowers and greenery—like the yellow ones and blue ones that are called... uh... yellow and blue flowers. Before long my hurried and artless arrangements littered the house, many in antique bottles she'd collected.

When I started cleaning the soot off the patio she said I'd done quite enough and could stop now and enjoy myself. I said I was enjoying myself and she couldn't make me stop. This is the argument we were having when the phone rang. That ended it. I cleaned up—myself, not the soot—and we were on the road.

One perk for us from Mary's trip to Scotland was that Frannie got the use of Mary's car and Frannie's heap could hunker down in the drive. She said maybe if it got a long rest it would get well.

The Indiana Tea House. Where have I heard that name? Frannie pulled into the parking lot. Beautiful old building. We went inside. It's not what I'd call a tea house. It's a restaurant. But it's a cool name. Still just us so we walked out back to the esplanade.

"It's the Indian Ocean," I marvel. "I'd been thinking of it as the Pacific. I forget. Looks like the Pacific but it's not. It's the Indian! Here. I wade into the Indian Ocean for the first time."

"You're so easy to please," she said.

"Not at all. It takes an entire ocean."

"If it had been a drop of water you would have gone on about how terrific it is."

"Well, each drop contains the whole ocean—that's the nature of things."

"Is that Buddhism?"

"I guess, sure—and a lot of other isms if you dig into 'em enough—and listen to poets and artists and saints and physicists and lunatics."

"You'd know the latter best I bet."

I pick up a conch and listen closely. "I hear the sea calling!" I said.

"Ah, my mobile." She reaches in her pocket. "G'day." She listened to her phone as I listened to the shell. She hung up and told me, "They're up top."

"That's not what I heard."

"What did yours say?"

I do my best to imitate the sound of ocean waves. It's a Three Stooges answer and I hint at that by doing a Curly "nyuk, nyuk, nyuk, nyuk." She catches on and thrusts two fingers of one hand at my eyes—I deflect with a vertical palm before the forehead and nose—she counters with a double index finger attack. I fall back onto the sand. The advent of global culture is a remarkable event.

Gupta gazed at Mindy while she went on about an expanded itinerary. "We must go to Darwin—sleep with the feral people in the long grass, go into town with them during the day to bum from tourists and hang out. Mangos are all over—in the trees, on the ground. Get ripped at dusk tokin' on a bottle bong."

Gupta smiled happily. It looked much like he would follow her into shark infested water.

"Feral people?" I asked.

"Mainly Aborigines with a mix of bums and hippies," Mindy said. "They live wild. Some even wear animal skins. Darwin's not tamed yet. They say it's a place fit only for misfits, missionaries and mercenaries."

"Followed closely by the merchants, mechanics, and morticians," Gupta adds.

"And then we could hop over to Queensland," Mindy continued. "Crash on the beach. But gotta watch out there—they've got hideous pot laws."

"You can get high on each other," Francine said.

"That we could. Guppy even wrote me a song. Sweet boy."

"Davo wrote a poem for me," said Frannie.

"A platonic poem," I said, somewhat embarrassed at her timing.

"Can you recite it?" Mindy asked.

"No."

Gupta was writing on a napkin. "A poem for Mindy," he announced and proceeded to read.

Darlinger
Wild thinger
Ferdinker
Your Wanker,
Gupta
PS Good yeah.

"You've a knack for pickin' up dialect," commented Frannie.

A waiter came up to the table with menus. He looked East Indian. "Would you like anything to drink?"

"Wine anyone?" inquired Mindy. After a glance at the wine menu, she ordered a bottle of—sounded like Lew's Chardonnay.

"I think I'm also in the mood for an afternoon delight," she said. The waiter looked confused but Frannie told him the wine would be fine. Mindy and Gupta looked at each other and she excused herself to go to the loo.

"I feel the call of nature myself," Gupta said departing as well.

"Hmm. Afternoon delight," I muttered, looking down the menu.

"It's usually off menu," said Francine.

"I've gotta go too," I said. "Back in a flash."

"You might want to wait a moment," said Francine.

"I'll just be a second."

Funny. Gupta wasn't in the men's room. When I came out I heard a racket from inside the women's room. Banging. There was quite a commotion going on in there. Then grunting. A high sigh. I went back to the table.

"Good lord. I just figured out what an afternoon delight is."

"Your Australian is improving in roo leaps."

After lunch we hung out on the beach, white capped ocean waves rolling in beyond. No one but us. Gupta ran out to the car and got the guitar.

"Sharing time," I said. "What you got to share, Gupta?" Happy to be his straight man. I know what it's like to have a new song and want to play it for friends.

He took the guitar and bluesed away.

Let me tell you baby
Plain as it can be
Bird got sky
Fish got water
And baby you got me

— chorus

You got me babe
You got me babe
You got me babe
Babe, you got me

Openin' a door
Who is that I see
Rain got air
Wind got leaf
An' it's come to be

(chorus)

Babe you got me
Babe you got me
Babe you got me
You got me babe

From the first hello
To the last goodbye
Sun got shine
Moon got beam
An' till death do us die
(chorus)

He handed me the guitar without asking.
    "Nah," I said.
    "How about something short."
    "A pocket song. Sure."
    "A pocket song?" asked Mindy.
    "You'll see," said Gupta.
    I composed myself and sang:

Stubbed his toe—oh!—oh!

"Bring the boys with the nets," said Gupta.

As soon as we were alone he grabbed me and proclaimed, "I love her! I love her! I've never been so in love." Five minutes passed and he's still going on about how great Mindy is. "When I'm with her, even a parking lot is a beautiful place. We were in downtown Perth and I was so high, high on her. I forgot who I was and what was happening and then I heard something—it was my voice talking to her and then hers saying something to me and I looked at her and could feel this warmth and I was so blown away my legs almost gave out."
    "The madness has taken hold. You poor guy. Hmm, or you lucky guy. She's young and so yummy. Oh well, this is what people in the

South are famous for."

"What?"

"Incest."

"Incest?"

"Well, you're kissing cousins."

"Kissing very distant cousins. Humph," he grunted as if insulted and then continued with his love-crazed review. "She's smart as a whip too. Says she'll go back to school next year and that she can study as hard as she can play. Wants to be a schoolteacher. She'd be great with kids. She'd be a great mom."

I put my hands on his shoulders and looked deeply into his eyes. "Come back, Gupta. You've been snatched. It's not too late. Keep awake. We'll run hide. Or else you'll become one of *them*."

He didn't seem to notice. It's too late. "What a heavenly play-mate," he sighed. "She's something to keep up with. There's been a lot of drinking and smoking grass in the last week. This is one hedo-nistic culture and she's its goddess. How do they survive it?"

"They don't. Like everyone else."

"Right. Well, we might be poster playmates for co-dependence, but we're always active together. We don't veg. I never feel out-of-it drunk with her—or stoned silly—no matter how much we do. There's something about her presence that makes me feel clear and energizes me. And she's so amazing." He turned away from me and looked out over the ocean. "But I can't help but feel a pain too. I know we're only gonna be with each other for a while. Even if I stayed she'd move on. And being with her fuels an unquenchable thirst I nevertheless feel compelled to try to satisfy. And when I get over the edge I tell her how wonderful she is, and suddenly she's not the wild-child anymore and she looks down modestly and waits for me to stop."

"That's what I'm waiting for. No, just kidding, go on."

"Oh—do I have to go back?"

"Hey—look over there," I said. Above the steps to the beach we could see Mindy talking to a man. "That's the same guy as before."

"No!" Gupta said, "The Aborigine. He's following her, man. Mindy won't let me intervene. I ran after him in the city. She got mad at me and told me to leave him alone. She says she'll take care of him. I ask who the hell is he and she doesn't want to talk about it. Says it's her business."

Back in the restaurant, Frannie and Mindy were scheming.

They suggested we get together again at Margaret River, the

most famous wine producing region in WA. Frannie's got a weekend family reunion in a few days down that way. They glance at us.

Gupta and I bowed to the floor in unison going, "We obey."

Mindy said she and Gupta had to get going to an aerial ping pong game.

"What on earth is that?" I asked.

"Aussie rules footy," she clarified.

On the way out of the restaurant Mindy and Gupta were cutting up in front of us in all their glory—ridiculously happy and silly, caught up with themselves and letting their infatuation take them for a ride—not just him. Lovers can be disgusting and irritating but their fun was infectious. They were playing Mindy being a school girl and him the teacher who caught her smoking pot in the restroom. They looked the parts. An older guy walking in with his wife took it at face value and said jokingly to Gupta, "Kids! What can you do about 'em?"

"Ah, he naughties 'em" Mindy said loudly as she walked on— shocking the heck out of the poor old couple and leaving Gupta, who instantly knew what she meant, red-faced and looking away.

DUNSBOROUGH BEACH

CHAPTER 8
DUNSBOROUGH

"Now we're going to be with my family for a couple of days," Frannie said, "and I want you to please remember to be careful what you say—no talk about sex and no talk about drugs."

"We're not *doing* any sex or drugs—except for grog and caffeine and a few bummed fags on my part."

"That's not what I mean."

"Well, there's the ever present possibility of masturbation going on in private. Won't bring it up—I promise. It would surely make things most uncomfortable."

"Yeah, very funny. But you like to talk about drugs—the good drugs, the bad drugs, how everyone takes drugs, the bad war on some drugs, all the poor persecuted people, lying government propaganda. Don't get started mate. And no blurting out about Mindy and Gupta smoking cones in her Porsche or how they hump like hares. My family is somewhat conservative. Booze is okay."

"Yeah, booze, which kills at a very high rate and has a strong link to violence is approved as a subject for polite conversation whereas entheogens that have death rates approaching zero, and which decrease violence, are taboo."

"Nobody knows what an entheogen is but yes, it's taboo."

"Pot, mushrooms, LSD, ecstasy."
"Taboo. Buddhism's okay. They'll be interested in that."
"Yes dear."

Della arrived to give us a lift to the rail platform at Waroona, on the way depositing Stubby at a home with the warning signs already posted on the fence. There he'd remain till Mary returned in six months. Francine bid him a loving farewell. I gave him a quick rub. He licked his friendly new keeper's shin. She squatted down to pat and chat. I love Stubby but was a tad nervous about the Pit Bull responsibility. We're off.

Once aboard, as I was the honorific guest, Francine kindly offered the window seat. The smells of the locomotive outside and passenger car within pleased me thoroughly. I extolled the virtues of railway travel to her as she fell asleep. The train, no youngster yet comfortable and warm, provided a most enjoyable ride with picturesque vaulting view of hilly countryside, forests alternating with grasslands and cropland punctuated with occasional homes and barns, cattle, sheep, and crows. Our mostly un-peopled route stretched to sleepy stops at Yarloop, Cookernup, Harvey, Brunswick Junction, and finally Bunburry where a little sis, Olivia, picked us up in an SUV.

After introductions Olivia and Frannie chattered catching up as I continued to survey the terrain we passed. Olivia took a detour to Ludlow to go by a thick endangered stand of tuart, full-foliaged trees with dull grey bark resembling the blue gum Eucalyptus we have in California. A hand-painted sign on the roadside beseeched us to help save these woods. Onward to Dunsborough, a favored Aussie beachside holiday destination where Olivia and her hubby Riley managed a cluster of time-share condos reserved this weekend for her kin and their canine. Both brothers and triple sisters were there with their spice and young children of various heights who ran around, wrestled, shrieked, laughed, crawled, and cried. The adults ambled, sat, hovered, and yakked. Big tight-woven Catholic family. A hardwood table was spread with crackers, cheeses, salami slices, sausages on sticks, apples, oranges, raw veggies, chips, dips, ice, and beverages squeezed, carbonated, fermented, and distilled. We partook.

Sitting on a couch, mom was quiet, not the outgoing positive matriarch I'd heard of, always providing, lively, taking care of everyone and everything. Her name's Meg. She greeted me softly with green eyes. Her aggressive internalized melanoma was the ever-present unspoken guest. Love and concern mixed in the room's atmosphere. A man with grey, curly hair entered through the sliding glass back door full-armed with firewood. I helped him place it by the hearth. He welcomed me. It was Frannie's pop, Jack. I could see goodwill in his eyes, feel sadness in his handshake.

The kids already have identified me as the weirdo in the house as I have made explosive popping noises with finger in cheek. "No," I told them in duck talk, "I'm not Donald Duck. I'm Davo Duck. I can articulate much better than Donald—with practice." After a while I have to tell them Davo Duck is asleep. It's unpleasant for me to talk that way for long. I wasn't trying to keep up with the vital info on the kids such as names and occupations, but we were doing fine with the random interactions. I did want to remember the adult monikers though. I can't look at each one of them and go, "Nice to meet you Riley. Tell me Riley..." etc., an old salesman's device. Soon, with a little reminding from Frannie, I'd pretty much gotten their names all down by creating an imaginary scene with mnemonic props like Jack on a beanstalk and Olivia wrapped around a giant toothpick floating in a martini.

Uncle James and I walked briskly on the beach. I tried not to let on that I could barely keep up. He used to be a world champion runner. Like Jack he's retired from a career with the State Electricity Commission. He's the philosopher of the group so we quickly fell into truth-seeking speculation. And one geography lesson. He asked me where I figured the sun came up. I pointed back toward the land since this was the West Coast. Nope, he said, we're on a peninsula facing east on a bay so broad as to hide the other shore. Later, on a solo saunter past a sandy beach to mottled rocky tide pools, the sun sinking behind hills seemed miscast.

With Dinner digesting, dishes drying, children sleeping, wind off the ocean blowing, the surviving adults surrounded a coffee table on three sides, a vigorous fire completing the form.

I was peppered with questions. How was my flight? I told them about getting the free round trip first class tickets. That reminded me of another guy I met who flew for free from Australia to the US. I bought an old Volvo from him back in about 1970. His name was something Fox. He asked if I recognized his name and I said no and he said he had stowed away in a cargo crate on a plane to fly himself back home from Australia. He got caught and made headlines all over the world. The papers called him something the Fox—like John the Fox. That's an old memory. I'd forgotten about him.

More questions. What's my impression of WA so far? Of course I love WA and Aussies. Whenever I'm with Aussies, I confided, I do have to deal with the consequences of my booze intake increasing a notch. Sort of like visiting back home Texas. That made them laugh.

"Davo keeps up," Frannie said. "Texans are like American Ozzies. I don't drink even as much as he thinks I do because he doesn't notice that he's drinking most of my drinks."

I confided I also drink more than all of my closest Texas friends—then downed my shot of scotch. Everyone laughed.

"I went to America," Frannie said, "To work for a family of Buddhists and I think, Oh good—I'm gonna be with spiritual people and I'll be purified. The husband used to be a Buddhist priest—lived in monasteries in Japan. They tell me another priest is comin' over and I meet David. By the time he leaves there's five more bottles of wine in the recycling bin. They drank like Ozzies the whole time."

"Oh, I'm sorry. It's true," I bowed my head in shame.

"That's alright," her father said. "You sound like some fine Catholic priests I've known."

"He's blushin'," Frannie said amidst the laughter. "Good. I thought you had no shame."

"So where you been on your trip?" Father asked, saving me from more public ridicule.

"Just Singapore and WA—after doin' some travelin' from California to Texas with my son Clay. Clay," I whined, "I miss Clay."

"I do too," said Frannie. "And I'm sure he misses you."

"He was so sad when we said goodbye at the airport in Dallas. We'd just had a great month together. It was a few weeks ago. I told him we'd see each other this December in Thailand. He said that's a long time. I told him yes, but you do it too when you grow up. Don't get so tied down to family and duty that you can't follow your dreams at least a little. And we'll be back together soon. He liked that. But still it was sad. And now I'm here," I said wiping the edge of my eyes.

"You came here just to visit our Frannie?"

"And you guys and whoever and whatever else I stumble on."

"I owed him after he'd been so kind showing me around. Otherwise I'd a told him to stay away."

"Couldn't have kept me out."

Frannie told about our trip through the Southwest. "Do you remember," she asked, "what I said when they wanted to know what I'd like for the trip I was about to go on with you?"

"Earplugs."

"Righto. He's got—what is it you've got?"

"Oh yes, It's true. I have an affliction."

"Which is?" her father asked.

"The love of hearing one's own voice."

"Yeah, you've got that bad," she said. "But he's paid for it with sweat. He worked like a slave at my house. You should see all he's done."

"You do a lot of work on your own home in California?" asked James.

"I used to, but now I just write songs and send them to Frannie," I said. "Hand me that guitar and I'll explain."

James handed me a guitar that had been leaning against the wall.

"Thank you. You guys can pick up the chorus to this song and sing it with me," I said. "Each verse is followed by the previous verse ending with the chorus so it piles up and gets longer and longer like in *Old McDonald Had a Farm*. You'll see as we go along." I couldn't tell whether that meant anything to them or not. "You go chorus, first verse, chorus, second verse, first verse, chorus and on and on like that." No matter. Enough talk. Had to start playing or I'd lose 'em.

—chorus

I got Nothin' to do but sit around singin' songs for you
I got nothin' to say but gushy stuff and memories.

The bills pile up, the dishes too
If I don't sing you a song I'm blue
Cause I got nothin' to do but sit around singin' songs for you
                    [always followed by chorus]

The grass grows high, my shoes ain't tied
Tons of trash outside, the clock's not right
                    [followed by prior verse as are all verses]

The fridge is foul, neighbors scowl
The dog she howls, the cat he growls

Clothes all dirty, house ain't purty
What ain't got dust got mold or rust

Dunsborough

The phone's alright but the plants have died
Lectricity's cut, the gas is shut

My agent calls, the auto's stalled
The toilet's stuck, the bathtub's yuck

My ex-wife calls, nother ex-wife calls
Ex girlfriend calls, mother sister call
Nother ex calls, nother ex calls
Nother ex calls, nother ex calls, nother ex calls
                    [include these two lines last time only]
Repo man hauls, child he bawls
Apples fall, the landlord calls

Earthquake strikes, tornado skies
Towns on fire, angry mob outside

Everyone could remember the chorus and since each prior verse repeated there was a learning curve there. By the end in which the whole thing is sung from end to beginning, the house was shaking. I quit while I was ahead, something that took me decades to learn—I used to keep playing till the last person had left.

I walked into town alone in the late afternoon on the second day in Dunsborough, letting Frannie and her family have some time without me. Stopped at a coffee shop with tables out on the sidewalk. Sat most pleased reading and sipping a latte. Fell into a chat with an older couple—which means older than me—late sixties I'd say. The topic was, of all things, a sculptor from Northern California whom I didn't know of—Hobart Brown. This guy sounded out of the ordinary. He lives part time in Margaret River and is involved with a kinetic sculpture race that happens once a year in the States. I told them how weird it was I had to go to WA to hear about this. It sounded like something I'd be interested in—sculptures that are also human powered vehicles. The couple had even gone to California to see the parade and said they had a grand time. Well thanks a lot and g'day and they're off to a winery—something like Lou Anne's. It sounded familiar.

Then I thought I heard my name. Looked around. Nope.

Back to the notebook. Saw three suggestions from Mike who'd driven me all over Singapore one afternoon: "Indiana Tea House, Perth Mint," and—there it is—"Margaret River—best Australian wine." Interesting. I've already been to the former—I knew I'd heard that somewhere too. And now Margaret River—where we meet Gupta and Mindy tomorrow. One down Mike, and the second one on the way.

I heard my name and looked around. Hmm. Just my imagination I supposed. My brain at times spins words into similar sounds, especially my name. It happens to me more when I travel, especially in foreign tongue lands. It just happened in Dunsborough, which is a bit foreign of tongue. It's the type of thing that can easily occur when one is high or paranoid but also to me when I'm sanely strolling down the street. Sometimes I hear whole sentences that seem to include my name, like "David's got the bag of rutabagas" or the more sinister, "Be sure not to tell David about it." This day I just heard my name. Then I heard it again. I looked around. Oh well, I've had lots of strange things happen to me.

I heard it again and turned my head. I was sure this time it was really my name I heard, but there are a lot of Davids in this world—maybe a mother calling her child. I kept writing notes.

Then someone did something no one should ever do to me. I felt a hideous stabbing electrical shock in my lower back ribs. Instantly I hurled around in my chair striking out and knocked someone back surprised and off balance. Good lord, it's Mindy!

"Oh god, Mindy, I'm sorry."

"You're a quick one!" she said regaining her bearings, one hand holding the edge of the table I'd thrust her into.

"Sorry. But please don't ever do that to me—I can't take it."

"I won't. Sorry. Just sayin' hi."

"Hi," and then, "Mindy!" and then "Gupta! Where'd you guys come from?"

"Remember? We're meeting at Margaret River tomorrow. Just stumbled into ya on the way down," Mindy said.

"Oh yes. Frannie's borrowing her sister's van. She was waiting to hear from you. You want to come visit?"

"No—we don't want to intrude."

"It'd be alright."

"Rather not."

"I'm sorry about hitting you but I have a condition—or something."

"A lot of people are ticklish," she said.

"No. Uh. Listen—I never met anyone who has it as bad as me. It's worse than ticklish and I'm that too but this is much worse—it's like getting shocked by electricity. It's painful and triggers an immediate unconscious reaction. It's happened all my life. I can't help but strike out. I apologize."

"Okay. Me too. And I'll not do it again. I promise."

It's true. I was holding an umbrella once in the Zen Center's grocery store and a woman I know came up from behind me and grabbed my ribs. I used to be a tennis player and I instantly hopped back and knocked her to the ground with a full two-handed backhand umbrella. Something like this happens now and then and frequently I get little shocks that make me shudder by barely brushing against someone or something.

After we'd recovered from our altercation, I offered to buy them lattes but they were fasting—just drinking water all day. I asked if they'd turned into ascetics and they just laughed.

We agreed to meet noon tomorrow at the winery with the sculpture exhibit the couple told me about, Lou Anne's. Mindy said she'd never heard of it, but there are a lot of new wineries popping up.

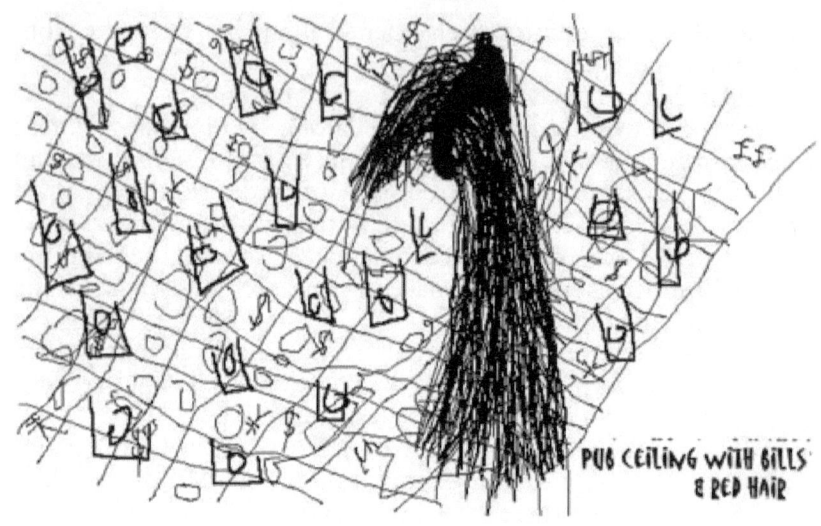

PUB CEILING WITH BILLS & RED HAIR

CHAPTER 9
MARGARET RIVER

Meet we did.

"I see you found it," I said, walking up to Mindy and Gupta on the lawn in front of Leeuwin Estate.

"Despite the name change," said Gupta.

"I should have known," Mindy said.

"Lovely," said Frannie looking out over the vineyards.

"You said it," Gupta echoed. "Gorgeous rolling hills of green with natural gatherings of trees abounding that beckon us to venture hither."

"Well my golly, that's a mouthful. It does look inviting. Think we can go for a walk here?" I said.

"I know we can. We camped in those trees over there," he said with a distant smile.

"Is that alright?"

"It's off their property."

"Oh—you sneaked out there and hid out. Looks doable."

"It was."

"He's acting a bit mysterious," I said to Frannie.

"Still loony from love I guess," she stage whispered.

"And you look tired Gupta—you both look tired. But you are

82

especially beautiful Mindy," I said. She had on a tight brown sweater and pants with a few leaves and dirt stuck on them and a green scarf covering her red hair that would otherwise be flowing down to her waist. "Yes, tired but radiant."

"Ah, you're just sayin' that," she said demurely.

"No I'm not," I answered adamantly.

"Well somebody did," she chimed in looking around. And then she removed her scarf.

"Something's different," I said.

"Mindy! Your hair! Ah, you look great in short hair." Francine went in to inspect. "I cut mine a couple of years ago. It's so much more free that way. Looks like an artistic job. Hmm."

"Gupta did it last night."

"Could maybe use a little touch up here and there. I can do that."

"Got scissors?"

"Yes I do by chance."

"After the tasting."

In we went. The girls looked at the wine list, Gupta sat in front of the stone fireplace, I scanned the brochures. This place has evidently gone to extremes to make the bestest wine they could. Robert Mondavi, the senior wine guru from where I live, helped them to get it going. He chose the site back in '75. It's organic or some of it is. Won a lot of prizes. Expensive too. The restaurant looked pricey. I got a brochure for Kelly who's a wine salesman and wondered if he sells Leeuwin or would like to know about it.

Tasting time. Frannie was careful not to drink too much. Mindy too. They take that seriously here and have a punishing .08 limit like in California. Gupta and I don't hold back and taste eight different wines—Sibling Shiraz, two Chardonnays, a Riesling, their Sauvignon Blanc Semillon, Cabernet Sauvignon, and then two more Chardonnays. The Chardonnays were especially delicious. Oh yes—we had one at the Indiana Tea House. Not the expensive one at sixty bucks a bottle. I bought the cheaper of them for Frannie.

Gupta asked if anyone still stomps on grapes to make wine and the woman behind the bar said for home stock, but not here. He said he'd like to and I told him to come visit and I'll introduce him to an old Italian I know who makes wine that way in Monterey County. Mindy and Frannie agree we should do that ourselves and started talking about how to plan for it, which I doubted would come to fruition. They got some more bottles we'd pick up after going downstairs to the gallery, which features leading Australian artists, especially paintings for the Leeuwin Artist Series, their premium wines.

We found a whole room for Hobart Brown's humorous and endearing sculpture—fascinating brass, copper, and steel creations. My favorite was the copper bus that's big enough to get, say... cats in. The lady there said all of Brown's recent sales were in Australia, not Humboldt County where he lives. He's from Ferndale way up north but with the same telephone area code I have. Ferndale's where they have the kinetic race. It's by the Lost Coast just south of Oregon. Big pot growing area.

Mindy and Frannie with scissors in hand took a walk into the vineyards on a sanctioned path as opposed to the wilderness where the amorous couple spent the prior night. Gupta and I walked another way. He whispered furtively that they'd taken mushrooms the day before. His first time.

"I friggin' loved the trip we had. It friggin' blew my mind. Actually, she friggin' blew my mind."

"What friggin' happened?"

"Mindy had never had it before either. She has a friend who grows them. They were Psilocybe cubensis, reputed to be the best. We went through a tour, looked around, sneaked off to the woods beyond the vineyard by the main house, and spread out a blanket over the ground that was slightly wet. It had rained the day before. We ate the mushrooms—three and a half grams each, a big dose— and waited. After about an hour she was saying it didn't affect her and she was joking she's going to demand her money back. She got quiet and stared for a while then, talking slower and looking around her, she whispered, 'The colors, the colors.'"

Gupta gazed into the distance. He said she kept saying, "The colors," and he repeated "the colors" in agreement.

"They're so bright," she said.

"Yeah," he agreed.

Then it came over them strongly, a feeling of wholeness and euphoria welling up. They looked around and reached around, crawled around, inspected the leaves, the dirt, the trunk of a tree.

"It was a fantastic experience," he said, "It was important. It opened up an astonishing dimension. But when I tell it, it sounds so silly. I mean—actual tree hugging."

"Yeah—most media would use your description as an excuse for ridiculing you, supporting the law that throws you in jail, takes your home from you, takes your children away."

"I don't have any children."

"See. I told you."

"Yeah, that shouldn't be illegal. Horrors. No. Making that illegal is the crime."

"They don't go arresting people who get crazy drunk or roll on the floor in churches. It's a private thing that should not be denied you. But some people love to persecute others for any reason they can dream up. That's the evil drug we must kick—persecution addiction."

"Okay, I've got your message. You're right but your time's up," he said, and went on describing their trip.

They hung out in the same spot for the heavy part of the experience, the first couple of hours. After being so fascinated with their surroundings they discovered each other and realized the other was a most magnificent being. They made love and Gupta said he could not possibly describe how serene and subtle it was. He said he felt as if they had bonded forever.

Then the next stage of their trip began. Mindy's spunk surfaced and she decided to run off naked. Gupta wasn't in as uninhibited a mood as she and had a keen desire that they not be discovered. He picked up their clothes and followed her as she ran down the hill into the vineyards. She saw a house and wanted to go in and visit. He begged her not to do that and said it was surely a house for staff at the estate and they wouldn't take well to being bothered by naked, euphoric trespassers. She soon forgot that and was babbling on about how she wanted to run all the way to the ocean and jump in and swim to Perth.

Mindy ran away then on the damp path back into the woods—a relief to Gupta. She went ahead of him as he walked on alone for a while catching his breath. Then surprise! Mindy jumped back around a corner, her naked skin covered in slimy, glistening clay head to toe. She crouched with hands outstretched and tongue fully extended roaring threateningly like a wild cat about to attack, her eyes shining out fiercely from surrounding dark clay. He almost fainted at first, then fell down laughing in the wet grass. She jumped him, growled, and chewed on his hip. He rolled over, picked her up, half-carried her to a little hillock where they sat. They remained there for a couple of hours quietly glued to the scenery till the sun went down. It was still winter and they were naked and content, grooving in 50 degree Fahrenheit air.

When it was dark Gupta and Mindy returned to the place where they'd left their back packs. They wiped themselves with towels, put on their clothes, and sat on their blanket. He opened up their sleeping bags and lay them out on a tarp. Mindy was running her hands through her long red hair and said she wanted to cut it. He said that would be a shame.

She said, "I want to cut my hair now!" Gupta suggested tomorrow and she said fiercely, "Find some scissors and cut it now or I'll burn it off!" She looked around. "Where's my lighter?"

"Okay, okay, okay. Give me a minute. Unless you brought scissors we don't have them."

"I'll burn it off then," she repeated looking for the lighter.

"Stop. Stop. Let's go down and we'll find some scissors."

Gupta went to the winery looking for scissors but they were closed. A watchman came out and said there weren't any scissors around. He kept an eye on them as they got into her car and drove off. A convenience store didn't have scissors either. They ended up in a pub drinking with Mindy announcing to everyone there how terrific the mushrooms were. She's so charming the clientele ignored the legal aspect, appreciated the entertainment, bought them drinks, and there was prattle and laughter. Gupta finally got some scissors from the bartender and cut Mindy's hair with a dozen fellow customers cheering. It was one of those places with all the local and foreign currency on the ceiling. The bartender stood on a stool, which Gupta held steady, and tacked her long red locks up with the dollars, franks, dinars, and pounds. Gupta and Mindy played pool and drank and back and forthed it with the gang till closing time and then the bartender kept a few of them in and they drank and talked more. The adventurous couple got back to their sleeping bags at about four in the morning and slept till ten.

The four of us sat on a hill overlooking the grape-less vineyard. Gupta was strumming Mindy's guitar, Mindy's very nice guitar. "What is it?" I asked, looking it over respectfully.

"It's an Ellis," she said. "Made in Perth."

"What can you do with it?" I said.

"How about this?" Gupta said and sang ...

Once upon a place
I first saw your lovely face
Oh yes we met by what they call as chance
And I sighed, sweet lady, may I have this dance

And we danced and danced and

Danced and danced and danced
And we danced and danced and
Danced and danced and danced
With your dancing eyes and smile and feet and hands
We danced and danced and danced and danced
And danced and danced and
Danced and danced and danced.

Love like this of what we're made
Wouldn't take no stock in trade
So come to me and join our hands
Kindly lady, may I have this dance

And we'll dance and dance and
Dance and dance and dance
And we'll dance and dance and
Dance and dance and dance
With your dancing hips and breasts and dress and glance
We'll dance and dance and dance and dance
And dance and dance and
Dance and dance and dance.

Once upon a place
I first saw your lovely face
Oh yes we met by what they call as chance
And I sighed, sweet lady, may I have this dance

He sang "and we danced and danced" over and over and wailed with the chords making his voice sound like a howling violin.

On the way back to Dunsborough Frannie and I talked about Gupta and Mindy's mushroom trip.

"They're following the way of Dionysus," I said.

"The god of wine."

"And religious ecstasy."

"And what are we following?"

"A bit more of Apollo in the mix—light and music and order."

"I'd never think of myself as that—or you."

"Human history can be seen as a struggle between Dionysus and Apollo. Greek theater was dominated by this theme. There's been tons written on it. Nietzsche made a big deal out of it."

"It's the balance that's important isn't it?"

"Sure. But you got to be left to have your times of imbalance like our buddies are going through."

"It's all imbalance, don't you think?" she said and looked at me with a slight smile.

The next morning there were goodbyes and hugging with Frannie's family. I bid farewell to the sisters and brothers, calling each by name. I shook James and Jack's hands and told them how great it had been to meet the family and how much I appreciated Francine. Jack said with touching sincerity, "We are so proud of her." I paused for a moment with Francine's mother. She told me she had an old friend in India, a Catholic priest, and, handing me a piece of paper with his name and address, suggested if I get his way maybe I could look him up and say hi for her. I said sure and kissed her hand. We looked at each other briefly but long enough to connect. Olivia drove Francine and me back to the rail platform. Francine was quiet on the train. Della would pick us up at the platform where she dropped us off. I gazed out the window at Australian grasslands, Australian trees, Australian sky, Australian heart and hurt.

RUSTY BEDHEAD GATE

CHAPTER 10
APOLLO ROUNDUP

Frannie, being the lighter by half, climbed up and caulked the seam between her house and patio roof. I skillfully supervised while leaning on her neighbor Sal's ladder. Back inside I put a check in a box on the fridge by the line that reads "fix roof."

"That's enough Apollo," she said. "Let's leave now, get there early, do our laundry in Freo."

"Agreed."

We had plans to meet Gupta and Mindy in Fremantle the following day, from there to go to an island called Rottnest. After that I'd stay in a hostel in Freo and she'd go visit her parents before returning home. We'd see each other again, but not for awhile. We only had three days left so we decided to get on the road right away. Enough work. We'd already spent a couple of days plumbing, hammering, pliering, and insulating the attic. What a job that had been, especially because of ex Banger's unsolicited and inebriated assistance. He came in drunk, insisted on helping, and ended up falling through the ceiling. What a mess.

"Grab our stuff and eat on the road," I said.

"Alright."

"To rat island."

"Freo first."

Now we could be off. Frannie started getting our food ready while I gathered the clothes.

"Look," I said, "I'll wash 'em now while we eat and get ready. We can dry them in Freo."

Her washer is in a hut out back, a packed little hut. I stood there with the overflowing basket of dirty laundry wondering where to put it down. What are shovels and paint cans and old clothes and two-by-fours, and who knows what else doing in there, I thought— and three old tires leaning on the wall outside?

The first time I'd done laundry here, I'd loaded the washer and added laundry soap, but it hadn't turned on. Frannie came up and said the electricity didn't work and told me to run an extension cord, which I did—from the guest room over the door through the corner of the kitchen, to the ante-room, out the back door, down the steps, across the patio, along the walk and into the laundry hut. So this time I did the same but, unlike before, there was no Stubby to come over and sniff the line where it ran along the cement.

Just then Sparky came by, which is what Francine called electricians. I'd asked him at the pub if he'd advise us how to get juice in the laundry hut and storage sheds, the latter to facilitate the transition into an art studio. He looked at the pipe coming down from the house into the ground that came back up at the laundry hut and went into the wall halfway up and saw there was an outlet in the wall inside and asked what's wrong with it and she told him it didn't work. He said he could fix that but she needs more juice brought in from the street and a new panel for the studio in the garage. He said if she digs the ditch he'll do the rest for $600. Sounds reasonable. After he'd left, I walked over to the laundry hut, just on a hunch, took the cord from the back of the washer, and plugged it into the wall. "Come here Frannie," I called as the washer started humming.

"Gosh, I never tried it," she said. "I just believed the people I bought the house from. Maybe I misunderstood them. I thought they said the electricity doesn't work here."

"Maybe it's this light switch they were talking about," I said.

"Yeah, it doesn't turn off. Have to screw the bulb in and out."

We ate mangos and smelly cheese. The clothes weren't yet done so we took a walk in the bush. She got into all the neat rocks on the way and said how excellent they'd look around a fire pit. We lugged a couple of stones back and she went to the storage shed and got a shovel and started digging.

The laundry was done but I suggested I might as well hang it up—at least for a while—so we could do the fire pit. She nodded. Clothes all hung. We discussed how wide the pit should be—about four feet. She carefully placed the rough, pitted rocks, some reddish, some blackish at the edge.

"Well, we've gone this far. I might as well get some more stones," I said, opened the gate, and sped off into the woods with a wheelbarrow. Two hours later the hole was dug—about a foot deep—and was ringed with a handsome assortment of volcanic and granite rock. We panted in mild exhaustion and smiled at the day's latest accomplishment. It was getting dark.

"Should we go now?" she said.

"It's a shame to go without breaking the fire pit in."

"Maybe you're too tired from all the rock hauling."

"Nope, but maybe you're too tired from all the digging."

"Naw," she said. "But maybe it's time to go."

"A song to urge you to stay," I said, ran inside, and got the guitar.

Hey diddle lonely one
Stay till the light is gone
Sit here in the dark
Underneath the stars

When the day comes to end
You'll be beside your friends
Love you as you are
Underneath the stars

Hm mm mm mm mm mm
Hm mm mm mm mm mm

Painted in evening hues
Dimming with fading views
Leaving only the heart
Underneath the stars
Underneath the stars

"How'd you know I was lonely," she said.

"It's just the way the song goes," I answered.

"I miss my mom."

That night Mars was at its closest ever in some enormous length of time and we took our gazes off the flames rising from the fire pit that did function perfectly, and looked up near the edge of the sky at the red god of war who still seemed pretty far away.

"An astrology article I just read in the Mandurah paper," I said, "claimed Mars is a channel to help you to be who you want to be. It magnifies your potential."

"Okay. I'll be me here now."

"Good. Me too—be me—not you."

Frannie got a coffee can from the back patio, took out a couple of chains with cotton balls on the ends, soaked them in kerosene, lit them, and danced around the fire with her own twin fireballs spinning.

Breakfast at the still smoldering fire pit, strong coffee with hot milk. Frannie packed the tent up and put it in the trunk of the Mazda while I took down the clothes from the line. We were going camping on an island. We get flashlight and matches and what else? A couple of books and her string-challenged guitar. We're all ready to go, but I had an idea for the side gate by the driveway, the entrance most used. My plan was to build a funky new gate out of branches.

"I have an idea too," she said and went to her storage shed. At the back wall she picked up an exceedingly rusted object. She'd found it in the bush and said it was once an ornate head board for a small bed, really rusted—rusted through in parts, just the right size. After a trip to the general store, where we purchased hinges, we hammered and reshaped them so they'd suit our purpose and soon she had a new gate of corroding iron swirls that swung eloquently. We celebrated by conducting a ceremony wherein she approached the gate and opened it for the first time.

"One small step for a girl," she said, "one beautiful addition to Dwellingup."

"One more gate!" I pronounced. "Come around back."

"Maybe we should go?" she asked.

"What appears to be procrastination from one point of view," I said with a grave tone, "is revealed from another as the march of progress."

"That sounds too important to argue with," she admitted.

There was a grate, a square meter of galvanized rods that looked like one side of a cage. It was propped against the opening to the firewood shed so Stubby couldn't get out when he was there, the shed being wide open in back to the alley. We had a spare set of hinges and, after some finagling, got it secured to where it was swinging nicely.

Now it was time to go for sure we agreed.

But there *was* that unsatisfactory side to the firewood shed by the fire pit. There were two long sections of corrugated metal leaning up against it, again so dogs couldn't get in or out. It needed to come up to the standard of the rest of her estate. She went and got one of the old tires and leaned it against the end. I got another for the other end and she got the last one for the middle. I asked if she had any spray paint and soon we were drawing the outline of a van on the side of the wall with three wheel wells around the tires. Last she added a top-hat sporting driver.

I got my rolling backpack suitcase packed and she her backpack. We were ready to go but she decided to make some sandwiches— haven't we been here before? Oh yes, yesterday—and while she did that I got the fireplace and water heater loaded and ready to light for her solo return and swept out the ante-room and picked up a few last out-of-place items from the yard—a board by the fence, a length of rope in front. We documented all our handiwork with a throw-away camera and were off.

"Finally," she said as we pulled out of the drive.

"That was one long goodbye. Man you are really game," I said. "It was great fun! We couldn't stop."

"What do you mean we?"

"You and me and Apollo."

"You turn Apollo into Dionysus. You're the most extreme person I've ever met," she said.

"Ah gee," I blush, "you're just sayin' that."

"No I'm not."

"Well someone did," I said looking around as we cruised past the jarrah rising high above the asphalt highway.

QUOKKA

CHAPTER 11
ROTTNEST

The first British seafarers who came to this island..." I read from a brochure.

"Thought these little beasties were rats," inserted Frannie.

"So it's called Rottnest—close enough for wenchin' poms," I concluded.

"Ferdinkum," she concurred.

Quokkas! Quokkas in their natural environs. They were all over and mulling around us with no concern. They've marsupial pouches in front, the women anyway, big feet, and they look like little wallabies, which I had yet to see in the natural. A quokka mother with a baby in the pouch sat nearby—hoping for some food I bet—but we're not to feed them. They are slow and helpless and have survived because there are no predators that can get to them on this island—except from the sky. You can't bring cats or dogs. It's quokka kingdom.

"They're so *cute*," said Mindy.

"Like fluffy little round balls," said Gupta.

"Some boys were arrested for playing soccer with one," said Frannie.

"That's terrible," Mindy moaned.

"No kidding," said Gupta, "to show soccer such disrespect!"

Mindy takes a swing. Gupta grabs her.

"You've got to close your tent up or they'll get in. They are rodents," I said. "The ranger warned me."

There was an eerie wail.

"And she said that the peacocks come around and leave their droppings everywhere. But they're so gorgeous and regal it's permitted."

We'd met in Fremantle and taken a morning ferry to Rottnest Island where no visitor cars are allowed. Frannie got me a senior citizen's ticket. I think she cheated. I was 58. I enjoyed getting a senior discount for the first time, but it did change my nickname for the cruise from Davo to Gramps.

"I had Rottnest in mind to go to when I arrived," I said. Tazi John had told me it was one of his favorite spots in WA. "And now here I am and, how nice, here we are, the four of us together again for two days. The girls from Perth and...and we're the..."

"The boys with girth," said Mindy.

"Ouch," said Gupta. "That hurts."

"It's cute," I said. "Like quokkas. We've but a tad extra. What's to hurt?"

"To be put in the same category as you. I'm not *that* girthy."

"Well, neither am I," I insisted.

Tents up and secured, we rented bikes and rode around the perimeter, watched the churning sea bash up onto rugged rocks to create rivulets and waterfalls that would fade to a trickle till the next big wave came in. We also waved—from a cliff at a school of migrating whales. There was clear blue and turquoise water and a secluded beach where we picnicked.

Periodically Gupta and Mindy would share her peace pipe. She'd take a big drag, hold it, and blow it into his mouth. Sometimes he'd blow it back into hers. Quite economical. Gupta tried to get me to join them but since Frannie didn't I didn't. Frannie says she gets higher not getting high than getting high. I agreed but said I thought that some entheogen use served an important initiatory purpose—helped one to wake up to higher states of consciousness. My readings have indicated they were traditionally and universally used that way and have only been prohibited by the state in resent times.

"The war on drugs, entheogens anyway, is the modern carryover of the Inquisition," I said. "They are nature's gift to show us there's more to life than what we think."

"The mushrooms sure showed me that," said Mindy.

"Indeed," agreed Gupta.

"And I've appreciated the few ecstasy trips I've had too," I said. Gupta said the mushrooms were ecstatic enough and he'd heard ecstasy could kill you. I said that people die on just about everything and that I thought the death rate around ecstasy was less than say, that for aspirin. He was also worried about the long term effects of ecstasy. I said I don't worry about that at all. He asked if it made holes in your brain as he'd seen on MTV. I said I thought most of the hype against ecstasy, including the stuff about holes in the brain, was pure malarkey, drug war lies. I said I thought it best for rare, careful use within a serious affectionate relationship and told him there are lots of therapists who have wanted to use it for couples therapy.

"But," I added, "to me E's a drug that is best the first time. It doesn't work to take it much. And I don't want to do it anymore. I've also heard it said to never take ecstasy with someone whom you wouldn't want to marry."

"I think that's true for mushrooms too," he said.

We turned wheels inland to outstretched green hills and stopped at a sign that explained there had once been a camp for rounded-up Aborigines on this field. We peddled further to a view of their graves. We came upon a cricket field being mowed and Frannie explained the rules of the game and it was so confusing I couldn't keep up. Gupta had learned about it from his father. Nearing the completion of our route, we crawled into a cave overlooking the mainland. Mindy brought out a pint of tequila, which we emptied as the ships sailed and motored by.

Frequently during the day we had come upon quokkas, always a treat. Back at camp I opened a bottle of red wine and watched the fearless little marsupials. One came under the picnic table and nudged my toes.

"Why haven't I ever heard of them?" I said. "We know all about koalas. School kids round the world should be as aware of quokkas as they are of koalas, and would if Teddy Roosevelt had known about them."

"Why do you say that?" Gupta asked.

"The origin of the teddy bear was that Roosevelt was taken with koalas."

"That's not right," he said.

"No, *you're* wrong," I said. "Think of teddy bears—they look just like koalas. I distinctly remember a grade school teacher of mine saying that. Fourth grade I think. Teddy bears are koalas."

"Nope," he said flatly.

"Sure they are. Frannie, Mindy—either of you know about teddy bears being modeled after koalas?"

"Sorry mate," said Frannie. Mindy shook her head.

"Face it," said Gupta. "You're poorly educated. Texas schools."

"Oh like Louisiana schools lead the nation?" I laughed.

"At least they don't teach us lies about koalas. It was an American bear cub that was the source of the teddy bear."

"Why do you say that?"

"I can't quite remember why. But I remember."

"Well that's not very convincing. Listen, Roosevelt went to Australia and became enamored with koalas and thus we have the teddy bear. Or maybe he saw one in a zoo."

"Nope."

"Okay. We've got to get to the bottom of this," I said.

We went to the park headquarters not far from our campsite to seek clarification, each of us sure we were about to defeat the other in a battle of trivia. The woman in the gift shop knew nothing. There was no Internet café. Finally, a ranger took pity on us and let us use his computer to go on the Internet.

How embarrassing. Gupta was right. Roosevelt refused to kill a leashed black bear cub in Mississippi while on an unsuccessful hunting trip sponsored by the Illinois Central Railroad. Think of that. Since he hadn't bagged any bears they brought him to a little one that was tied up and told him, here, you can kill this. Good lord. Anyway, he wouldn't do it. This story made it into the Washington Post followed by a political cartoon everyone saw. Roosevelt became known for his compassion (not always relegated by him to humans in times of war) and the little bear became his symbol. An East Coast couple who marketed dolls asked if they could name a stuffed baby bear doll after him. Roosevelt gave them permission. In 1903 both German and American versions of the teddy bear came out. And they looked like bears. In later years they started to resemble koalas more.

"Okay," I whispered, leaning back and looking through the door to make sure the ranger was occupied, "Let's see what we can find out about ecstasy."

"Clandestine research," Gupta chuckled, wickedly rubbing his hands together.

I type in "ecstasy death" on Google and follow a link. "Here we are."

"I'd get holes in my brain. I know it," he said.

"Here—there are occasional deaths—like from heatstroke—here a person who had asthma died after taking it and dancing all night and not drinking enough water. How's this? Same general death rate as going to dance parties to begin with—about one in 100,000."

"Maybe that's why Baptists are against dancing."

"Alcohol has a fifty times greater death rate than ecstasy."

"Well there are fifty times more people using it."

"No silly—death rate not death count. A person using alcohol has a fifty times greater chance of dying from it than a person using ecstasy. And here, look—tobacco is 200 times more likely. Poor smokers."

"That's cause there are more of them," he said.

"I'm gonna strangle you—why can't you get it that... oh, you're jerkin' my chain. Hey, look at this. Men who have taken ecstasy are 36% less likely to commit murder than those who haven't. And similar results for robbery and other crimes."

"They ought to arrest people who don't take it. Take ecstasy or go to jail. It's the law!" Gupta said in a deep soft voice.

"The only crime ecstasy users are more likely to commit is selling an illegal drug, like the libeled entheogens."

"Death's too good for 'em."

"Alexander Shulgin is the modern father of ecstasy. He lives in Berkeley."

"Surprise."

"Says it should be called 'empathy'. Hang on. Better not to take it more than once every four months—that's from the *Complete Book of Ecstasy*. Here we are—holes in the brain is... bogus. Told you! Oh—unless you get shot in the head by the cops for using it. Oh oh—here's an estimate of two deaths per 100,000 users. That's double what the other site said."

Gupta coughed self-consciously and I could hear the sound of the ranger's approaching footsteps. Quickly I closed the Netscape window. "Which is why quokkas are destined to become the international mascot for world peace," I turned around. "Oh, hello. And thank you so much."

"Find what you were looking for?"

"Yep."

When we got back to camp I had to tell the gals Gupta was right about the koalas and I was wrong. Through the evening he squeezed that little victory for every bit of glory he could. Frannie and Mindy ganged up with him and rubbed it in. Eventually, I've found, as Rimbaud, that everything we are taught is false.

"Maybe we could get your President Bush to come here and see the quokkas," Mindy said, "and then we could call them Georgie bears."

"And then people would come from the four corners of the globe to club them to death—cute or not," said Gupta.

As twilight gleamed through our little campground we listened to the curious crows, which Gupta called the disappointed crows. They had a distinctive call of four or so high and ascending notes he said sounded like Mindy about to have an orgasm and then, after a pause, a descending call resembling a plane going down—a sad finish after a hopeful beginning. This was the constant background music to our trip. They go "ah ah ah ah" ascending and then "ahhhhhhhhhh-hhhhhh" descending. Gupta imitated them with uncanny precision.

We put bangers and veggies on the grill at our campsite. It wasn't actually barbie as in bar-b-que season yet but we did it anyway. It was the only barbie I had down under, but I got the impression from all of the nostalgic comments I heard while there that almost everyone on that continent stands around the barbie with piles of meat and drinks beer in stubbies in warmer months.

"Somewhat like a lot of folks from Texas—not my family though," I said.

"That's why you're three bangers short of a barbie," said Frannie turning a banger over.

"Huh?" I said.

"Dropkick," said Mindy.

"I don't get it."

"Exactly," said Gupta. "You're hopeless."

"But cute," said Mindy.

"Oh, I get it. Teach me more," I said.

"Don't bother the babbler," said Frannie.

"I thought I was the babbler," I said.

"No—you're the wanker."

"That means 'masturbator'" said Gupta proudly.

"I'm the babbler," said Frannie, "babblin' brook rhymes with cook."

With our dinner of barbied Australian groceries, we drank another bottle of wine and then Gupta got out Frannie's guitar that he'd put new strings on back in Fremantle and sang a song suggestive of a healthy appetite.

—chorus

I lap it up babe—lap it up babe—lap it up
I lap it up babe—lap it up babe—lap it up
Lap it up babe—lap it up babe—lap it up
I lap it up babe—lap it up babe—lap it up
Oh oh—--—oh oh—so good

Like a kitty with the milk
Like his doggie on his toes
Like the spider with her silk
Like an elephant with its nose

(chorus)

Like the chillens with their cones
Like a Shop Vac with a spill
Like vultures on dem bones
Like a bee in a daffodil

(chorus)

"My turn," I said.
    "Can you do something shorter?" asked Gupta.
    "Sure. How about Nano Tune?"
    "Sounds short."
    "It is. Here goes." I picked up the guitar and stretched my arms out in front of me and hunched my shoulders repeatedly like Norton on the Honeymooners used to do, which drove Ralph nuts, and continued till it drove Gupta nuts.
    "Okay, okay, I got it," he said. "Someday—powie! To the moon!"
    "Good for you," I said.
    "Are you gonna play the song?" asked Mindy. "Or is this part of it?"
    "Okay, here goes."

Nano tune

"Well, go on," said Mindy.

"That was it," I said. "It's my shortest work—at one second."

Frannie fell asleep but the remaining three of us continued to party. We opened another bottle of wine and then, after more songs and yap, another, and then we went to the bar not far away and had a couple of drinks each while watching cricket on the telly, which still made no sense to me—the cricket, not the telly—but excited everyone else in the room. Gupta was staring at Mindy more than the telly. He wrote a poem for Mindy, on a napkin.

Mindy Mindy,
Terrifically
Splendifically
Wonderful
Blunderful
Under the sunderful
And the moonderoon
Your image in a spoon
As precious as
The galaxies
There in the skydaroo.
I lovely you.
Whoopta
Gupta

She kissed his cheek. We got another bottle of wine for Ron and walked out into the darkness.

Back in the tent we woke Frannie up by sitting around her drinking and talking loudly. I ruminated on Descartes' famous attempt to prove his own existence.

"I think therefore I am," I said. "Hmm. Let me think about that."

"How about I think therefore I think," said Gupta.

"We are on the same lave-wength," I said.

"How about I think therefore we need another drink?" he said drinking out of the bottle and passing it.

"Or how about, I drink, therefore I drink," I said taking a swig.

"Or, I think therefore there's an assumption of a self thinking," slurred Gupta.

"Good. Profound as heck. So I think I think I think I think," I double slurred.

"But that's just what you think."

"How about I don't think therefore I am not?" said Mindy.

"That's Buddhism," I said. "Or a slice of it. Katagiri said that. Eggscelent."

"Sorry, I don't know him," she said taking her turn at the bottle.

"It's the thought that counts," said Gupta.

"You think?" I asked.

"Did you say something?" mumbled Frannie half asleep.

After more of Ron's booze, Gupta started rambling on emotionally about what a great time he was having with us and how he loved Frannie and me, which he demonstrated with gushy hugs. Then he turned his slobbery attention to Mindy and declared how he loved Mindy as Romeo loved Juliet, as Anthony loved Cleopatra. I suggested he find role models with more life-affirming conclusions. He gazed at Mindy and went on about how much he loved her and how wonderful she was and how he'd do anything for her while Mindy slumped over and fell asleep on my sleeping bag lying next to Frannie. After an episode outside the tent in which my stomach reversed the usual order of things, I ended up next to Gupta in his tent, him telling me how much he loved Mindy and how wonderful she was and how he'd do anything for her as I slumped over and fell asleep.

The next morning, after Gupta regurgitated for a while, the four of us sat around barbie heat and drank coffee Frannie brewed. Gupta, Mindy, and I strained to piece together how the evening went, especially how it ended. Mindy remembered enough to tell Gupta he couldn't tell her how wonderful she was and all that for a while.

Taking the tent down was a lot harder than putting it up, not the usual order of difficulty. Depending on Frannie's superior non-poisoned state of mind and able supervision, we managed somehow with pounding heads to pack up and return our bikes. We then had nothing to lean on and had to crawl to the dock behind Frannie who was in revolting good spirits. As we rode the ferry to Fremantle I stared blankly at the waves. Gupta was nodding out. It was Mindy's turn to throw up. Once on shore Frannie went out shopping for mask material while we three drank a gallon of water, downed vitamins, and took detox naps in a room I got at the hostel.

Somewhat rejuvenated from slumber, Gupta and I made coffee downstairs in the hostel kitchen and swore never to drink again.

"Hey," I said, "I'd forgotten all about that guy who was tailing Mindy—or maybe both of you. Ever see him again?"

He peered right at me. "Ever see him again? Every time I turn around he's there, darting around a corner—I think."

"I didn't see him in Margaret River or Rottnest."

"I didn't either but he's there. He's here—or not far."

"He's made you a little paranoid."

"I don't know how much he's around. Maybe he only goes so far from Perth. It's disconcerting. I never had a tail before."

Wearily waving goodbye and muttering "Call me later," Gupta followed Mindy out to her car and they drove off to Perth. As they drove off I saw another car take off with a dark man at the wheel. I wondered if he was their Aboriginal tail. It happened so quickly I couldn't tell.

Francine returned. She hugged me and said we'd get together in a week. She left me with her guitar.

"Thanks for all the redecorating. You've been my Apollo," she said.

"Thanks for having me and showing me around," I responded uncreatively.

That was it. She was off to visit her mom and pop and to spend some time alone. I too was alone—with throbbing head—in Freo.

FREO
GALLOWS

CHAPTER 12
FREO

I leaned back in my chair amongst friendly young people in the Sunrise Hostel watching *Jackass: the Movie*. The antics of the guys in that flick made us howl and wince, me wincing more than the others as I'm of an earlier generation. A group of us went out together to a nightclub—Aussies, English, a Frenchwoman, a couple of German guys, an Indian and a South African joined in with the crush of other mainly young people holding drinks, downing drinks, buying drinks, dancing, talking, laughing. Don't meet many Americans.

The woman who runs the hostel had free drink cards. We drank freely. We found ourselves later in a bar where the only people dancing were women with women. "Poofer bar," an Aussie called it. I got to talking to a hefty Aboriginal woman and we ended up dancing till a heftier Aboriginal woman came up challenging me to a fight and I said I'm just being friendly and she said then I should buy them drinks which I did. When the drinks arrived she said I was free to leave. I did so, thinking Robert Crumb would surely enjoy drawing them.

Met a young Aussie guy at a pub our group wandered into. He asked where I'd been in Australia and I told him the last place was Rottnest. He related with a glow in his eyes about his trip to

Rottnest, how he and his friend started off with a six pack of beer before they got out of bed in Freo, how they drank on the ferry over, and how they then sat in a cave on the island, same cave as us maybe, with a bottle of scotch and got pissed till the sun went down and then stayed in the cave for days drinking till their brains ran out their ears. Didn't do anything or see anything except for some booze runs. And he said it as if it was the greatest experience of his life and the best possible way they could have spent their time. People here talk of getting pissed like it was opening Christmas presents. Even I can't keep up with them—not day after day. Being in Australia was often like visiting a fraternity house back in the sixties. A lot of the souvies play on the theme of getting drunk. Looking for a stubby holder to send home (I mail things home periodically when I travel so I won't have to carry them), all I could find were ones that said things like "I got pissed in Freo!" or, "I got pissed in Rottnest!" or, for variety, "Get pissed!" I'm not really a good party animal though. Eventually I lose interest.

Walking affects me in the opposite way—the more I do it, the more I want to. In Freo I walked morning to night to every sight I could find. The grey stone-walled prison, now closed for over a decade, had a row of examples of what the cells had looked like through the years—closet-sized rooms where murderers from Australia and loaf-of-bread thieves from England had been confined. Our tour group took turns going into one cell to admire an example of intriguing surreptitious Aboriginal art. Painting or drawing on the walls was forbidden but this inmate fooled them for years and created elaborate Aboriginal dot paintings, which he camouflaged with a primitive plaster concoction. The Ten Commandments was artistically rendered on the chapel wall with the sixth scribed as "do not murder" instead of "do not kill" because there was a gallows next door. It seemed like an important distinction, probably more to the administration than to the prisoner artist who made that mural. The gallows was the last stop on the tour. I looked down from the platform as our raconteur guide told chilling hangman anecdotes and I felt the ghosts of a hundred men swim by.

The maritime museum on Victoria Quay also had something hanging from the ceiling. It was Perth's Australia II, the racing yacht with the winged keel that won the America's Cup from the United States in 1983. There was another smaller sailboat thus suspended, the Parry Endeavour, the yacht that took lone yachtsman Jon Sanders around the world three times without stopping—once going west and twice east. Now he hangs out at the yacht club bar. I saw a video about his trip and it convinced me he was lucky to have survived the feat. I inspected the compact gear and comestibles he took along, asked a guard why he brought canned tuna, and was told there are no fish to eat in the vast stretches of deep ocean far from land and reefs. Really?

The submarine tour was the be-low point of my trip. I was certain, once we entered, that the dry-docked sub was on greased skids and had immediately plunged to the depths of the sea, the cramped capsule would never rise again, and our tour group would slowly suffocate before we were missed. There I was packed in a narrow steel cylinder stuffed with pipes and equipment and a dozen fellow tourists—feeling distinctly sardinish. How is it possible sixty-five men had lived in this tube so close to each other? Their bunks were tiny and stacked three high so it seemed to me the abdomens of all but the emaciated would touch the bunk above. The spaces for working, eating, and resting were so tight I couldn't see how they could move or stand—or stand it. The word claustrophobia took on palpable meaning. I wondered what type of men would choose to be in such a place. Baffled, I inquired if the crew was selected from especially short candidates. No—I learned from our guide the average height of these sub-surface sailors was not short. Surely men with mental and psychological make-ups far different from mine, beyond my imagining.

This horror tour rendered the prison, fresh in memory, far less threatening, even inviting. In comparison the gallows seemed preferable. I could feel panic right below the surface and invented a prayer for the moment, the endless moment, to help me to maintain sanity. And this wasn't an old sub from days when they were smaller, as I assumed, but one that had seen service into the seventies. I realized either this was a uniquely compact sub or every submarine movie I'd ever seen was a pernicious lie expanding the interior of the sub so there could be scenes of people standing around talking with lots of space between each other, of men working together with plenty of elbow room—so audiences wouldn't squirm in their seats or run from the theaters. The name alone was enough to frighten one—the HMS Ovens. Boy was I glad to get out of there.

I played pool with a guy from Holland and didn't shoot so straight but I heard a lot about the pot business and potency of the weed there. In the *Botany of Desire*, the author says the pot growers in Holland and California are doing the most creative botanical work in the world today. This Dutch guy went to cannabis conventions and tastings and I wondered how the latter could possibly be reliable. All I would be able to do is take one puff and then I'd lose my bearings. It's not like wine you can spit out, though you could try not to inhale—you'd still get high pretty soon. I guess that's the point. After the pool game, my Dutch acquaintance went off victorious to get seriously pissed on the legally available and far more dangerous local spirits.

I stayed and played a favorite by-myself nameless game wherein I call the shots as in straight pool but can't make any simple ones. They have to be combinations off banks or caroms, also once called billiards—off other balls. That's a satisfying way for me to play because I don't miss a lot of easy shots, which is what happens when I play regular pool.

Out on the street walking around looking at late night Aussies doing late night Aussie things such as staggering home or staggering into an after-hours club. I went into one, listened to the music, and had a Guinness. No matter what I sample, nothing pleases me in the beer realm like Guinness. I'm not really much of a beer drinker. I prefer wine. I like Irish whiskey and good Scotch too but they're so strong, better to stay away. I'd be happy to endorse Guinness. Guinness Stout—haven't found better on five continents.

Wandering back to the hostel in the empty street, I see an Aboriginal busker, street musician, who was preparing to sleep in a doorway. He'd done a great job of *Don't Be Cruel* earlier in the day. Everyone seemed to know him. People called him Rags, not a nickname indicating the opposite. I prodded him with a dollar to open up shop again and he got his guitar from its case and did a terrific job of another old Elvis song—*Blue Suede Shoes*. He beckoned me to sit on a blanket he brought out from his pack and offered me a cigarette. I accepted. He played some more.

"May I?" I inquired. He handed me the guitar and I played one that seemed in keeping with the style he was playing.

—chorus

Oh Francine, how do you do your do
Oh Francine, how do you do your do
Honey you're the best thing I ever knew

Met Francine about a quarter of five
Ozzie Queen at a black swan dive
Like pickin' up a wire that is live
Threw back her head and laughed at my jive

(chorus)

She stole my keys and ditched me as well
Said she wouldn't drive and drink that swill
Stopped for Maybelline at the top of the hill
Now I'm a runnin' after them women still

(chorus)

We talked. I learned a little about him and he some about me. It got cold. It was so late no one had walked by for an hour. We smoked more. As the smoke rose in the entryway where we nestled, he spoke in a hush tone, reached over to squeeze my shoulder, looked deeply into my eyes and beseeched, "Hear my story, how I came to be a lost and floating soul."

I just looked at him, unable to speak.

"There is a woman who came to Australia from far away," he began. "She was of the city, not the desert, but she went out to the desert and befriended some of my people. She had read about us. She had a story about my people in which she had an important role. She offered money if we would agree to tell her story. No one trusted her but some were interested in the money. A wise elder said that she was not a good person and warned of trouble. One by one her Aboriginal friends left her. Finally there was only me. She told me she was one of the great ones from the cross in the sky who took our form to come here to bring us back to the place from where we came. She told me to come with her. I went with her in her rented jeep to what she called a dreaming time place. It was just an apartment in a city. She made me give up all that was mine, all that was from my people, the little I wore, and she made me put it all in a box. She flipped a switch and crushed it. Then she put it in the trash. She gave me the clothes of the white people. She made me carry a wallet and put money in it and opened a bank account for me and gave me a credit card. I had to meet with white people and tell them her story. I had to give her massages. She made me sleep in her bed and bring her pleasure every night. She was not a woman I wanted to lie with. I told her to lie with a white man. She said I was a real person and all the white people were mutants. I was lonely and begged her to let me return to my people but she said she would hurt me with the power of the two-tongued lizard men. I was her prisoner. In time I realized I could not go back anyway because when I followed her I turned my back on my people. I became dependent on her. One day she was gone and then soon I had no money and the cards were no good and I had to live on the street. Now I am a ghost who has no dreams and sings the white people's songs. Thank you for letting me tell you my story."

I sat there for a while not saying anything. And then I asked if he'd ever seen her again.

"Yes," he said. "There." He pointed to a store across the street.

"You saw her over there?"

"In there."

"She was in that store?"

He led me across the street. It was a bookstore. "There she is," he said.

"Maybe her picture is in that book?" I guessed at his meaning.

"Yes—on the back of it."

I leaned forward to see the book he spoke of. I could barely make out the title. The book was named *Mutant Massage*.

A dharma heir and colleague of Tazi John's named Ross Bolleter started the Zen Group of Western Australia. John had given me Ross's number. I called him and we agreed to meet on Sunday when he wasn't in the studio recording. That got my interest. He said he continued to teach in New Zealand and Sydney, but had passed the mantle of the local group to a therapist named Ian who taught in Fremantle.

Ian and I met in a coffee shop. We covered a lot of Zen, American, and Aussie territory. Like a number of Zen teachers and students in America, Ian was a therapist. At my urging, he told me about Affect Psychology, the method he uses. My mind swam trying to keep up with it.

That was Tuesday. On Wednesday evening I walked in rain and wind that severely challenged my umbrella to a building near the maritime museum where Ian's group met once a week. I was in the habit of sitting zazen alone when I awoke in the morning, and it was pleasant to sit with a group on an evening—three forty minute periods with two brief walking periods in between. I like to meditate with small groups that tend to have a more humble vibe than the bigger ones. After the sitting was over, we went to another room, drank tea, and chatted. I signed a few of my books people had brought and two from the group's library. For a moment I was somebody, but then the meeting was over and, refusing ride offers, again I was out on the dark street alone in the calm sea air after a rain. And I was nobody again. Wherever I go, there I am not. I liked being nobody doing nothing special. It was the purpose of my trip—just to be here and to walk to there and take things and people in. Hello lamppost, my new friend.

But then one of the participants in the evening's meditation called out and caught up with me. We walked together back to the hostel and sat in the lobby talking. His name was Samo, short for Sam. He asked about what I was doing in WA and I went though a litany of sights I'd seen and told him briefly about Frannie, Mindy, and Gupta and how Gupta's quasi uncle had sent him here. I said I was enjoying Freo but maybe it was time to move on. He suggested I go to Northbridge in Perth and check out the scene there.

Samo's a therapist now and used to be a detective with the Perth police department. Perth is not far from Freo. He met Ian through their Affect Psychology connection. Samo was in his forties, soft-spoken, and had questions about the San Francisco Zen Center, especially Tassajara, the SFZC's remote mountain monastery. He wanted to go there for a year as a student. But he was also interested in studying with Tazi John who's in that area. I said he could do both or either—just had to arrange it ahead of time and get over there. John's group is the Pacific Zen Institute and they're a mellow group. But the SFZC has residential possibilities.

Samo told me more about Affect Psychology. There are nine affects, most with double names sort of indicating a sliding scale of meaning. There are two positive—joy/enjoyment and interest/excitement. Then there's the neutral surprise/startle. There are six negatives—disappointment/disillusion, fear/horror, anger/hate, disgust/dismell, contempt and shame. Dismell meant something like smell based revulsion.

"Affects," he said, "are biological responses to stimulus. After the affect follows the response, which is thinking and acting."

He suggested I find something in my experience we might apply it to. I tried to apply his system to the shock I feel when I'm grabbed from behind in the ribs or poked there. Most people don't invade your private space this way, but because I am the way I am some think understandably they have permission to kid with me like this. They have no way of knowing what it does to me, the electric shock. It's like I have a rare condition. But here we were focusing more on the reaction, which can be rage, especially if I'm grabbed or poked hard.

Rage as an affect is not directed, Samo told me. It just is. That's exactly how I felt. Also, it has a signature—it rises quickly but doesn't last long. Anger tends to simmer. The stimulus, affect, and response tend to happen so quickly we don't notice them as distinct. What we want to do, he said, is to watch the stimulus and affect closely so we can get a handle on the response. The stimulus would be the electric shock I feel when someone grabs me in the ribs from behind. Rage is the affect. As I remember it, the only time I ever got a handle on the response was when I was the host at the SFZC's restaurant, Greens. I'd be standing looking out over the floor and a customer, someone I knew well, would come up and poke me in the ribs and from the first I'd just let the shock go through me, didn't swing around and grab their hands and command them fiercely not to do that. I was motivated there to change the response. As soon as I was away from Greens, I lost that composed response. He said that was because the constraints of my sense of obligation toward customers had forced me not to allow an unacceptable response to happen. I had naturally, instantly isolated response from stimulus and affect. It would be possible to continue to do so in other settings. Oh I see. This gave me a way to work with it. Good. I thanked him.

"There's something I'd like to ask you about," I said. "Especially because you were a detective in the police department."

"Certainly."

"Well, like I told you, I came here with a guy named Gupta who's being shown around by his distant relative Mindy, and there's this guy we call 'the mysterious Aborigine' who is always following her around. She told us not to worry about it but her uncle Rudy who set Gupta up with her told us in so many words to make sure she's safe. Let's see—what am I asking? I don't know. It just seems sort of weird this guy spying on her."

"Intrigue," he said laughing. And then he cocked his head to the side and asked pointedly, "Rudy who?"

"Dugan."

Samo's demeanor shifted. He sat up and looked at me straight on. "From Melbourne?"

"Yes."

"Chunky guy? About seventy?"

"Yes."

"Balding?"

"Yes."

"Do you know who he is?"

"Nope. Sounds like you do."

He breathed out heavily. "He's the head of the biggest organized crime syndicate in Melbourne, hell, in Australia. He's a very dangerous person. You met him?"

"Yeah. In Singapore." I told Samo all about the meeting.

Samo told me to watch out. He was worried about me being involved with Mindy and Rudy. He said it might be best for me to leave the country. He really didn't like that Rudy expected me to keep an eye on Mindy and that I wasn't doing that. He looked at his watch. "Last train's leaving soon. Here," reaching in his wallet, "my card. Keep in touch. Call me anytime." He looked at his watch again. "Be careful," he said, shaking his head with concern, and was off.

SWAN BELLS TOWER x 3

CHAPTER 13
PERTH

Yes, I sell Leeuwin wines," wrote Kelly. "They compete with any-thing we've got here. Sounds like you had a crazy time there, or at least your friends did."

Since he's met Francine he can see her clearly in mind, but asked if there are any photos of Mindy and Gupta I can send. I was read-ing his email in an Internet café in Northbridge, the cultural and entertainment area of Perth, the happening part. So Kelly wants to know what the loving couple looks like. Let's see, both are so distinc-tive and photogenic. Mindy had made it easy for me to comply by emailing photos of the four of us she took with her digital camera while we were at The Maze and at Rottnest. I shot some of them off to Kelly with a CC to Clay amidst a detailed update of what I'd done—getting into the horrors of the submarine tour.

I wonder if before there were cameras people drew more, like pictures of where they were and the people they were with to send or show to their friends. I know there were more pictures in books. They probably also described the people in detail—what their faces looked like, the expressions, the nuances of mood, how heavy they were, how tall, what type of clothes they wore. Thank goodness there's no need for that now. Just a click of the mouse and they can see for themselves. On the other hand, I almost never use cameras. I hate to travel with them.

They detract from the view in two ways—thinking about the shots and worrying about losing the camera. I'll go look at some beautiful spot amongst tourists who are busy concentrating on camera angles so they can see it later. I hardly ever look at anything later, including photos of my children. But I also cheat. It's so easy these days to get fellow travelers to email me photos—so I can not look at them later.

A guy called Techo in the Internet cafe helped me with all this. He was sitting next to me fixing something on a computer. Inexplicably I was having an inexplicable problem. I didn't even understand if he did anything to solve it or if it just went away. It's too complicated and mysterious to try to figure out a lot of stuff with computers and software. If the problem goes away just be grateful. Techo was a trip. He had orange, spiked, stiff hair, tattoos on his arms, and a gold earring. He was quiet and steady, didn't smile but was kind. I liked him.

Aside from Ross Bolleter, there was Mai to look up in the Perth area. I called the number that little Malay lady had given me on the plane and she invited me over for dinner. I knew other people further off in that commonwealth country, that continent, that island, but Perth's too far far-flung to consider looking them up. It's as far away as if it were another nation. America's Cup skipper Dennis Conner called Perth "the most isolated city in the world." Perth's own tourist literature brags it's "the most remote regional capitol on the planet." That seems a little more accurate because there are all the other WA towns nearby and nobody seems to feel isolated—they have each other and they seem to like that.

Tazi John says when he's been there he's gotten the sense that, being so secluded, they've developed some odd disconnected traditions and methods of doing things. One example was a musician who had heard recordings of surf (I think) music and had figured out how to duplicate the sound on the guitar without ever having seen anyone else do it, so the way he held the guitar, strummed and fretted it, was unique, totally off the wall. There's an idea of things developing there independently. John also says Perthites are awfully friendly and informal, comparing them favorably to Sydneyans.

WAers do seem to share a sense of being off in a corner. I walked over to the home of Mai's kin and had dinner with them and later we went out to visit an aquarium and have dessert at a touristy wharf and there was a pole with signs pointing various directions with how many kilometers it was to the other big cities in Australia—4345 to Darwin, 6015 to Cairns in Queensland. Also to places like London, Tokyo, and Jakarta, which I saw was closer to Perth than Canberra, Australia's capital. And it was 3495 kilometers to Melbourne. Hmm. Melbourne. Wonder how Rudy is.

On the way to see Mai I took a stroll around lake Monger to admire the black swans and then headed off to my destination. I like getting to know places that way—even if it means trodding un-scenic byways through non descript commercial zones and into monotonous neighborhoods. To me everything is interesting—indeed, miraculous. I don't think that while I'm walking. I just amble on. People as well are each a miracle—they don't have to be entertaining or wise. I like them to be friendly if possible. These people were.

It was good being in a warm, inviting home, visiting with Mai—eating Malay food, and seeing the workshop of Daniel, her Aussie brother-in-law, an easy-going man somewhat older than his wife. In retirement from a government job, he makes commercial wood carvings on local themes. Back in the house Mai showed off some dolls she'd acquired. They didn't drink much—the people, not the dolls—a small glass of wine each. Good—I needed a break.

Let's see—what's her sister's name? What's she doing in the mental picture I made to help me remember her name? Singing to them. Sing—Bing, Ding, Bling, Zing. Heck—forgot the analogy, the association. Oh well, Wifey, Sis.

I mentioned at the dinner table that I wanted to visit the Swan Bells Tower in Perth and that hit a sore spot. Mai's sister and Daniel thought it was a big waste of money, money that could have been better spent on social programs. Like Mike in Singapore, they said the place to go was the Perth Mint. They planned to go there soon with Mai who was interested in the Mint shop where they sell commemorative coins and medallions, jewelry, and nuggets. I said I wouldn't be adding any such weight to my luggage this trip. My budget did, however, allow for some post cards. Maybe we can meet up there and go on the tour together?

They must have thought I was courting the Malaysian doll collector and I guess that can never be ruled out, but that wasn't on my mind. I was just saying hi. She's gone to college so our education levels were compatible. She brought up Christian mysticism again. But if she knew what a libertarian and often penniless hippie I was, I doubt she'd approve. We'll probably never see each other again—that's traveling. But maybe I'll look her up in KL. I don't know anyone else there. All my life there have been strong platonic relationships with women but I wonder how common that is in her part of Asia. Anyway, I get previews when I'm with women, previews that warn me of what could lie waiting in the future.

Like when I'm with a woman, if I find her attractive, I not only can visualize intimate and exciting recreational x-rated mental videos of us together, I immediately get previews of possible outcomes from trying to make that video come true. I look back on almost all my relationships with women fondly and I credit these prophetic fast-forwards somewhat for this (and having learned from my transgressions and miscalls). These at times ominous flashes have spared me grief.

I meet an attractive woman at a party and feel a tug. Internally I experience a precognition: "You didn't call me!" "You jerk! I hate you!"

Or, "I'm on my way over to make you dinner. I'm bringing a suitcase."

Or, "David, I'm pregnant!"

Or, "I didn't think AIDS was contagious!"

Sometimes a grotesque vision: "You and me growing old together, sipping Manishevits, the twenty cats, and my Lawrence Welk records."

Or just a wordless picture of being stuck in a relationship that is not rewarding where we really didn't have that much in common, and which is demanding in so many ways—but I had followed my genital tugs, a short-lived euphoric rush and got caught. This thought turns claustrophobic and I shake my shoulders a little as if I'm trying to throw off chains, the grabbing allure falls away, she becomes less appealing and I am careful how I relate. Saved.

These we could call red light previews. Sometimes though the mental preview of a member of the fair sex is a green light: go ahead—minimal problems predicted, or, go ahead—will be well worth the trouble, or, flashing green—go full steam ahead—will sacrifice all for. Yellow light previews are most tempting when under the influence of alcohol or following a long dry or lonely spell.

Anyway, Mai was just a friend and we had a good time and then I headed back. Ah, how nice being carefree and uncommitted, I thought as I sat in the evening air. Of course I'd be happy to roll over and play whatever for Frannie, but that's not an option so I don't really think about it. I did at first but it's not smart to obsess about the unobtainable. I prefer peace of mind. In a warm blanket of that peace I waited for the train that would carry me back to the Northbridge Hostel.

I sat up late and talked with Slim, the guy at the desk. He said since I liked to walk so much I should take the walk along the Swan River from Perth to Freo. I said I'd definitely do it. Ross's name came up in conversation. He had met Ross, told me to give him his regards when I went there. He said Ross was known all over Australia for live radio improvisational concerts done simultaneously with other musicians in other cities. He said all each would know was the starting and finishing time.

I enjoyed my tiny room with cot and chair. Like the hostel in Freo it's got a communal kitchen, pool table, and interesting travelers coming and going from all over the globe. Among the staff or the customers, someone will know where to go for whatever you're looking for—dancing, twelve-step meetings, a gym, bird watching. They had Internet-hooked computers that took coins, but Slim told me of the better deal down the street where I met Techo. He also pointed me to the cheapest phone cards. I could call home for a nickel a minute on the regular phone cards, but on the ones at the corner store that just printed out a pin number on the register receipt, I could call the United States for 1.3 cents a minute—78 cents an hour—so cheap the cost was no factor, just the time involved. I hardly used them at all, preferring email. Called my mother though who doesn't do email. She said my father, who died when I was eleven, would have loved to have been on this trip.

I talked to a traveler from Florida who went to a local clinic where she was seen without much of a wait. It didn't cost much either. This would be true for many places in the world. Nothing brings home the pathetic state of health care in the US like getting health care in another country. At least where I've been and heard of. I was in a national park in Washington state camping with Kelly and Clay and bought some firewood from the caretaker who lived in a trailer there. Somehow we got to talking about medicine or health care or whatever, which led him to say, "America has the best goddamn health care system in the world." I fear I got a little rude in my response. Right now I'd say the quickest solution to America's health care problems would be outsourcing. It's being done more than most people realize.

I'd talk to travelers from all over the world, mainly Europeans and Brits. Some Canadians. I didn't meet many travelers from the US. I don't know why. Maybe because lower-middle class Americans make less money. I stayed in cheap places frequented by students, but also by working class people, people who worked in convenience stores and drove taxis and could still afford to travel for three months, or six, or a year. Not so easy to do for Americans with those sorts of jobs.

Talking to folks in the hostel and around town, one thing that is distinctly different from when I've traveled before, is almost everyone has a negative opinion about our president. It's so embarrassing. Many people are downright disturbed by how he conducts US foreign policy. A lot of people brought it up right away when we met—not Aussies so much but Slim did. Only the Israelis tended to like Bush Jr. An American who'd lived in Argentina for many years summed it up when he said in his lifetime every American president up to Bush Jr. was popular in Argentina regardless of how right or left they were or even what wars they were fighting—Clinton, Bush Sr., Reagan, Carter, Ford, Nixon, Johnson, Kennedy—all popular. Junior not. That concurred with my experience of Japanese over the years and other folks on this trip. Junior just doesn't give foreigners the feeling he cares about them or their opinions or the future or that he knows anything about them or what he's doing. A German school teacher I was talking to said Bush seems like a guy in a bar who, in response to another drunk's attack, fuels the flames of anger, turning the whole place into one of those old Hollywood movie scenes where everyone's fighting each other and smashing chairs over each others' heads. He's seen around the world as ignorant and reckless. I was on my way to India eventually and picked up a Hindustani Times at a Perth newsstand and read a review of a book called *Jihad* that said Bush would be remembered for two things over there—greatly increasing the size and power of jihad, and ending 1300 years of Suni rule over the Shiites in Iraq thus paving the way for an Iran-Iraq Shiite front against Western hegemony. We'll see.

Slim told me no matter how bad we get the Aussie government will support the US. The reason goes back to the dominant role of the US in stopping the Japanese from conquering that part of the world. One of the Japanese plans called for exterminating the Aussies and turning that continent into another Japanese Island. They probably wouldn't have done it but better we didn't have to find out. The US is still Australia's ace in the hole in terms of defense. What, for instance, if their Muslim neighbor and third most populous country on earth, Indonesia, were to change its ways and become fundamentalist and bellicose? Australia would then need the US to protect them. So they support us with a few troops even when they think we're invading someone we shouldn't, even when they think we're nuts.

Tens of thousands of people were dying in Europe from a hellacious heat wave that August and there was some talk about that and about global warming and whether it was happening or not. Slim said like the US, Australia hadn't signed the Kyoto Protocol to reduce Greenhouse gasses even though it would allow them to increase their emissions—I think because they have so few people. I didn't understand why they didn't sign—industry pressure or US pressure I guess.

Local people seemed truly concerned about skin cancer and the hole in the ozone layer that protects us from ultra-violet rays. Australia has the highest rate of skin cancer in the world. They are also world leaders of getting out in the sun. There was a skin cancer prevention poster on a wall in the hostel with a kangaroo exhorting people to "Slip, Slop, Slap!" before going out into the sun. Slip on a shirt, slop on sunscreen, and slap on a hat.

There was plenty of talk in the hostel about the situation on the local streets. Gangs exist but know to leave innocents, tourists, and spending locals alone or the cops will come down on them like... um, like gangbusters. But beware of Aboriginal youth on petrol or other vapors—those deliriants can put them into unexamined states. Three fifteen year old Aboriginal girls just got busted for beating the tar out of a guy cutting late through a nearby park.

"Abo" was one diminutive not to be used. I'd heard it here and there without realizing there was anything wrong with it. It seemed strange a little word like that could have so much weight. I had to think of the N word to appreciate it. It has so much baggage I don't even like to write it down. Where I grew up, I considered anyone who used it to be ignorant and prejudiced. I can feel the history, hurt, and harm. Blacks can use it anyway they want but I've learned the hard way not to try to do that. So I eschewed the A abbreviation and stuck to the whole word, Aborigine.

On a drizzly day, after an inexpensive and satisfying Indian vegetarian meal at the Hare Krishna restaurant a block down from the hostel, Frannie's guitar in case in tow, I met Gupta at the hind-quarters of the main train station a block further down the street and over the tracks via pedestrian bridge. We were on our way to meet Ross Bolleter at his house.

Slim backed out at the last minute. Every time I'd seen him I'd reminded him about going to see Ross and he'd nodded and been agreeable. He was getting off just when I left and I asked if he was ready to go and he said sorry, he couldn't make it. He never meant to. I could tell. No big deal. It was just a tiny bit irritating. Gupta said Mindy did stuff like that too sometimes—agree till the end and then say no only when she had to.

On the back side of the station we ran into the Aboriginal buckster from Freo, the one I'd sat up with and who'd told me that incredible story. We listened to him for a song and dropped a bill in his hat. He didn't seem to remember me.

On the phone that morning Francine said she'd been sad and wanted to join us. Today she'd be in Mandurah but would try to break away and come for a while if she could. She said after Rottnest she had been some time at her parents and then gone back to Dwellingup. She'd spent the day before just walking in the bush and crying. That made me sad too and I urged her to come.

Gupta said Mindy had gone out the night before and had not come back. She'd called early in the evening and said she'd be a while and nothing since then. He said it made him real nervous—remembering Rudy's admonitions. "It got to me man. I really got scared. I mean, why did he make such a big deal about protecting her? And then she didn't come home. I think about that guy who follows her. I know she's a grown up and doesn't like to be tied down and is unpredictable and undependable... and let's see what else—a list of stuff like that. But I wish she'd call."

"Well, just to up the ante, Let me tell you about a conversation I had with a retired detective from the Perth police." And I told him what Samo had said about Rudy.

"Oh that's great. Well, it figures. I suspected something like this. Pretty obvious actually. God, he probably knows. I'll bet that Aboriginal guy has sent him film of her and me doing the dirty deed in beds, on floors—hell, in the park."

"In a public restroom," I added.

"We've been a snoop's dream. Mmmm. Dangerous huh?"

"Very dangerous he said. He suggested I consider leaving the country."

"Maybe we should," Gupta said. "Except then I'd just want to come back."

"Anyway, we could always be followed."

"Rudy kept telling you to keep an eye on us."

"Now wait. That was unreasonable. Anyway, she's probably okay."

"Now you're scaring me. Jeez. I wonder where she is."

"Well, she can't get hold of you now."

"Why did I have to fall for a gangster's niece?"

"Because you're a gangster's distant nephew."

Gupta groaned.

"Let's go to Ross's and call her from there," I said.

We traipsed under gray skies through a field wet with recent raindrops to streets that brought us to the brick house of Ross Bolleter who greeted us warmly and invited us into his modest living room, jam packed with two pianos—one of them looking rather worn, an accordion, a bass, and recording equipment. He's a solid bear of a guy with a beard and broad smile. The instruments, furniture, books and art in that room and the next attested to his duel roles as Zen teacher and musician.

"Pleased to meet you," I said. "I'm glad John gave me your number."

"Taswegian John," he said. "Ah, I haven't seen him in too long. How's he going?"

"Fine in general, but right now I'd say he was asleep."

Gupta had brought cheese and crackers and Ross opened some beer—Emu, obviously the pick of discriminating people. Ross started off by having me sign a couple of books. I said I was pleased as Judy (as in Punch and Judy)—showing off an Aussism I'd heard.

Gupta asked if he could use the phone and he called both Mindy's home and mobile numbers and left messages. He didn't look pleased. I told him to forget it—that we'd see her later. He still didn't look pleased.

Ross remembered Slim and said to return the greetings. He said Slim had been in the Australian left wing underground and had had to hide out for years. Tazi John ran in those circles—conspired, hid in them. I wondered if Slim might know him too.

Knock at the door. Ah, good. Frannie's arrived. She brought Simon with her. And more cheese and bread. And apples.

After lunch and repartee it was back to the living room where Ross played some cuts of the two CDs he was simultaneously working on in a studio. One was tango music, the other experimental, his fifth or so CD featuring ruined piano.

Ross explained there's ruined piano and devastated piano. A ruined piano would be one that had, for instance, been left outside for some years but was basically intact and, though not at all in tune, still made notes. A devastated instrument would more likely be decomposed and lying on the ground in a heap with rusted strings. He got into this particular artistic niche while on vacation with wife and kids a decade back. They stopped at a sheep station where he'd come across a piano in a field, broken down and falling apart. He had some microphones and a tape recorder with him, hooked them up, and played away on the wounded beast. The ranchers were perplexed yet permissive. A career was born.

Ross played both recorded and live piano and accordion music. I was right at home both with his charming, beautiful, heart-string pulling tango music, in which he multi-tracked piano and accordion and also with the intriguing ruined piano work. I'd been exposed to disparate musical traditions by my mother. In recent years a string quartet she composed was performed in Texas. When I was growing up she enlivened the house with classical music both solo and accompanied and played so much of the great music of the thirties, forties, and fifties—Cole Porter, Gershwin, Berlin, Kahn, Arlen. I ate it up. But she also exposed me to non standard music at times. I remember once she took me to a meeting of her music club to hear a prepared piano concert—that means the strings were messed with—for instance by having objects placed on them. A prepared piano technique Ross used was to place one or more balls on the strings that, when struck, would bounce them around. In high school I got into atonal and twelve tone music and then all sorts of wacko stuff through the years. So I was prepared for Ross's ruined piano.

I got out Frannie's guitar and Ross had a better one for Gupta. We played a few songs. Gupta was more helpful to me than I to him since he had a knack for lead. Ross played the accordion. He asked Frannie to woman, I mean girl the controls of his tape recorder. Simon seemed to be content just sitting in the corner listening and drawing pictures in his sketch book.

I did a number, derivative of Yun Men, the Zen master who is well-known among Zen folk for saying, "Every day is a good day."

Sittin' there is who you are
Be you bozo, be you star
On a cushion chair or fallen tree
Callin' to the fallin' in thee
Happy to be just who you are

—chorus

And as the mountain man say
Every day is a good day
Every day is a good day

Standin' up is gosh almight

Perth

Beyond the good and wrong the left and right
But any names like Buddha, Tao
Allah, God, Mind, Holy Cow now
Don't begin to cast light on your light

(chorus)

Lyin' down the run of day is over
There you are in dreams of streams and clover
Now you know why they say one way
Like the stars up in the sky they
Shine upon the branches and the boulders

(chorus)

Gupta took a more romantic turn, yet with an edge of realism. Ross followed him closely with understated accordion.

My babe—don't take no sass from me
Instead—she pours the glass for me
And my babe—she ain't mine

My babe—look in her eyes and see
She maybe—have a surprise for me
For to play with the shine

—interlude

She could dance with hunters or with reindeer
She could charm ole Satan on his knee
She could paint the moon or moon the painter
She could hug the sap right from a tree—could she

My babe—don't give me time of day
She ain't—got a watch anyway
She say—it's about that time

My babe—some sort of crook is she
The way—my babe she look at me
Tells me all I want to find

He repeated the interlude and the first verse and then it was...

Time to go. Ross gave us three CDs of his ruined piano music to divide amongst ourselves as we wished—*The Country of Here and Below, The Night Moves on Little Feet,* and *Piano Dreaming.* I took with me some of Ross's commentaries on old Chinese Zen stories including one by him called *Yun Men's Bright Light.* Wow. We're both Yun Men fans. Also some of his poetry, which would be included in a collection called All the Iron Night to be published in the following year. I glanced at one of them.

> *That sweet ring!*
> *It straightens the spine lifts off the roof unclenches*
> *the heart and as if that's not enough*
> *takes down the walls.*

Sound images indeed—bouncing off what Buddha had said after his great enlightenment. I slipped the material into my shoulder bag and, taking my turn at the door, gave Ross a hug. We agreed we'd try to get together again to do more music.

Francine gave Gupta and me a ride back to the hostel. On the way we dropped by Mindy's to make sure she wasn't there. Gupta called her mobile again. Francine and Simon had to get back to Mandurah to make pizza but they had a little time to come in the hostel and hang out. We went to the funky open air area out back, a place for lounging, smoking, pool and ping pong. A corrugated fiberglass roof protected us from light showers while amplifying the pitter patter. A couple of young Swedish women on a couch were deep in conversation. One of them nudged some tobacco and papers toward me when I showed interest. I rolled one up. Gupta was inside in a phone booth trying to get hold of Mindy. Francine got Simon to help her rack for a game of Eight-ball. Stripe solid stripe solid. Simon asked if I was coming back to Mandurah to play catch with him. I said I'd be there as soon as I got a little more sightseeing done in Perth. I didn't know really. Frannie still needed to have some space.

Gupta came back. He was agitated. Francine challenged him and me to play her and Simon. We told her to go ahead and break. I suggested we play that everything you sink counts—don't have to call anything. Agreed. Gupta said he still couldn't get hold of Mindy. Francine spread the balls pretty well but nothing went in. Simon applauded. Gupta nodded to me to go first. Said he wonders where the hell Mindy is—it's been too long. I missed an easy shot and told him not to worry—she's a big girl. But I was worried too. Simon knew more or less how to hold the cue. Francine suggested he try the ball I missed, which was on the lip of a pocket. Helped him line it up. Gupta said we've got to do something. Simon hit the cue ball hard off center so it careened sharply to a side bank, over to the opposite bank and back to barely tip the ball into the pocket.

"You're stripes," I said as Simon and Francine celebrated.

"Don't worry Gupta. She'll come home soon—when she wants. She's wild."

Simon hit the cue ball on the side again and it rolled to hide between the bank and two stripes.

"Wild? Really? Tell me. But we're still responsible for her," Gupta said.

"Your shot," I said.

He looked at it.

"There's nothing you can do," I said.

He looked at me.

"About the shot," I said.

He looked at the shot.

"About Mindy either. Enjoy the game. We'll call her again later."

Rather than make a safety play he tried a ridiculously difficult shot. "Do you forget what Rudy told us?" he said. "Do you forget who Rudy is?"

"I don't forget Rudy," I said. "I'm the one who told you."

"Have you noticed in the papers there's been more gang violence in Melbourne?"

"I have noticed. A killing just yesterday."

"Rudy's gonna get you," said Francine shooting one stripe into another that went in. She knew about Rudy from Mindy but had never taken it very seriously.

"Just what we need—feed his paranoia," I said as she and Simon celebrated.

"Good shot," said Gupta. "She sounded sort of stiff on the phone when I last talked to her—like there was something else happening."

Francine shot the other nearby stripe into the opposite side pocket. She and Simon celebrated.

"Good shot," said Gupta. "Like what if she's being held by that Aborigine and he told her what to say?"

"OK? What if? What can you do about it except wait?" I said.

Francine made another shot down the length of the table. Celebration.

"Good shot. We'd better do something," Gupta said.

Francine finally missed. My shot. "Where do you want to start?"

I missed the easy shot and left Simon with an easy shot. "Sorry."

"I don't know," Gupta said. "Good shot Simon."

Now Simon left Gupta with no shot again. Gupta and I kept getting nowhere both with pool and our conversation till all the stripes were gone and all the solids still on the table and Francine had a long shot at the eight ball. All quiet. She drew her cue back. A mobile rang. Francine put the cue down and reached into her pocket.

"Man, I think she's in—and thus we're also in—trouble," Gupta said.

Francine walked off, talked for a minute, returned, lined up the shot, and said, "That was Mindy. She wants us all to get together the day after tomorrow to go to the beach up north. Says she's waiting for you, Gupta."

She missed the shot. I missed. Simon missed the eight ball too. Gupta then ran the solids making one great shot after another but he just barely missed a difficult cut on the lone eight ball. Francine missed then I missed. Simon's turn. Long one. He shot without really looking at it. Bam! Gupta and I look at each other. Ball's in. Mindy's home.

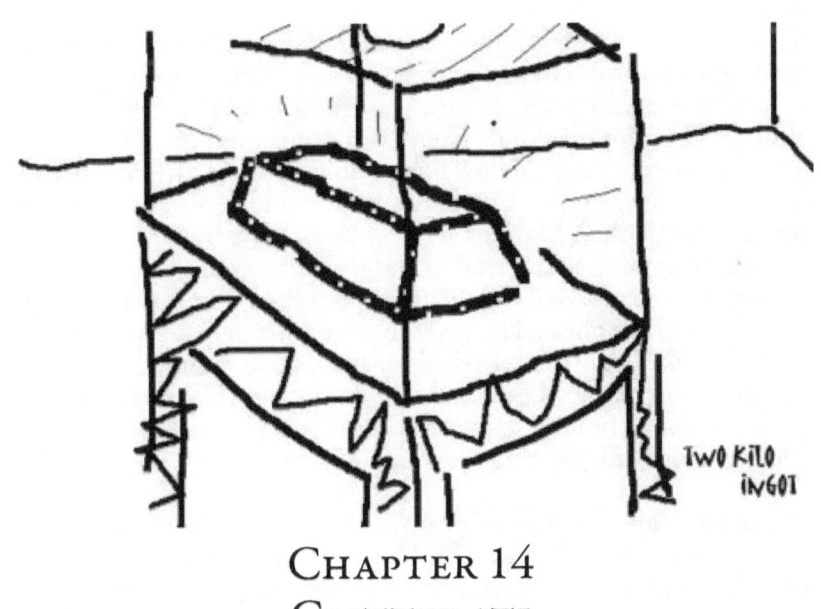

TWO KILO
INGOT

CHAPTER 14
GLITTERATI

I was feeling amorous. Hadn't glanced at a woman yet and felt that mutual zing that can lead to excited communication developing further. I walked the streets, my glances zeroing in on the females. This is the urge that propagates the race—and we humans don't just get it for a few weeks in the spring. Three drinks watching part of a soccer game lowered my standards—yellow light previews accepted. Little care about consequences. Still nothing two-way. I retreated to the Internet café to sink my lonely desire in cyberspace. Techo was there. We nodded. He suggests which computer I should use, keeping me clear of any that are slow or acting up. He pointed at a Mac. I'm mainly an inferior PC guy but online I can't tell the difference. Checked my email. Lots of spam. What am I gonna do about that? One of them hooks me in. A WA dating site. How'd they know I was here? Ah them cookies. Complete with photos—nothing risqué but in moments I was salivating. Love these Aussie women. One in particular grabbed my fantasy. Buxom, not too young, which means less trouble, pleasant smile, that hungry look. Yum yum. I shot off a brief response to her and hit the jackpot. She was online. Soon we were one-lining it back and forth. Nothing dirty. She's divorced, forty-nine, works in a government office, likes to dance—that's bad—I'm a terrible dancer. In an hour we're sitting in a pub talking.

She's nice. My whole body is tingling. Her whole body is sending inviting messages. Green light. My imagination was tying ribbons around the evening. My breath was getting short—I was literally panting. We kept drinking. Then I noticed something. Her personality started to change. Yellow light. Soon she was a different person. The softness was gone. She had a twitch and a distant stare. Bad reaction to alcohol. Maybe allergic. She needs a friend, not a lover. She was becoming both irritated and irritating and, most important, unattractive to me. Red light, flashing red light. She had flipped my switch to off. Boohoo. The bad vibes were palpable. I said I had to go. She looked confused. I asked for her phone number. I could see a desperation in the recesses of her eyes. Back at the hostel I tore the page out of my notebook and flushed it away—even though I'm a stickler about only putting toilet paper in toilets.

Standing at an observation point in King's Park looking out over the skyline of Perth. Waiting for Gupta whom I hadn't seen in a few days. It was mild for August, a warm winter day with occasional cool gusts from the river below. If in the sun, I took off my flannel shirt, if in the shade, re-donned it over the tee shirt. August down there is the equivalent of February in the Northern Hemisphere. Perth is 31 degrees latitude and on the ocean, comparable to San Diego, which could be just about like this in February. It does remind me of places in Southern California except for the colorful parrots that seem like they should be in tropics—I see them all around WA—them and what I thought were crows, but which a local woman informs me are Australian ravens. She said you can tell by their distinctive call. There were some of these ravens walking right up to me as I was talking to her. I was on a newly mowed lawn near the upside-down trees. That's what her children called them. She said they are boabs—the trees, not her children.

I entered the recently opened Lottery Federation Walkway and made a wish Francine wins one of their drawings. The walkway feeds into the pedestrian skyway at treetop level from which I gazed at the rows of dots moving against each other on the freeways and streets below—like an Aboriginal painting in motion. A cruise ship from Freo slid along the Swan River's estuary toward the Narrows Bridge that connects a southern peninsula with the Perth side. I wished to walk along that river to Freo. Sailboats were out but most wait for warmer days. I saw jet skis far enough away that their motors were barely audible. Admired an old brick building down by the river bank, the Swan Brewery according to the legend on a map on a stand beneath glass. I was standing there in the breeze thus when some young people came up to me. They looked college age.

"Excuse me sir," one said shyly.

"Yes."

"Are you enjoying your visit to the park?"

"Yes I am."

"And may I ask..."

"First," I interrupted, "where are you from?"

"South Korea."

"Oh. Where in South Korea?"

"We're all from Pusan."

"I like Pusan."

"You do? You know Pusan?"

I told them a few places I remembered in the south of South Korea and said every word of Korean I could remember, which took a few seconds. People love to hear that you know and appreciate anything about where they're from. So now they're all grinning broadly.

"Where are you from?"

"America." I hate to say that because there are so many countries in the two American continents, but that's what everyone says.

"We want to go to America."

"All together?" They laugh.

"What are you doing in Australia?" one asks me.

"I'm wandering around."

Smiling. Time for the big question. "Do you go to church?"

"Do I go to church?" I responded forcefully hand pressing on chest.

"Yes," the tallest one said as they all stepped back.

"Are you spies?" I look around.

"No."

"Okay. So, do I go to church?"

"Yes."

"That's a secret," I said.

"Why a secret?" the same young guy asked as giggles arose from his comrades.

"I can't tell you because it's a secret! And also because Jesus said to pray in a closet."

They don't know what to make of me.

"Do you believe in Jesus?"

"Depends on what you mean by Jesus."

"Jesus of the Bible, the son of god."

"You mean a male human being named Jesus?"

"Yes."

"My Jesus has no gender nor species. He is bigger than that. In fact he's so big he has no size. And no name and no gender and he's so big you should be very careful saying anything about him because everything we say is small."

They laughed and were intrigued. We talked for a while more about Jesus and they went away happy because I didn't tell them to go away and I took their pamphlet.

Then Gupta walked up.

"There you are Guppy."

"Davo."

"How goes it."

"It goes bad."

"Oh no. What?"

"Mindy broke up with me. Our love affair is over. She just wants to be friends."

"Oh I'm so sorry."

"It's not your fault. It's mine."

"I'm still sorry, I'm saddened."

"I told you she sounded different on the phone. I thought she was in trouble. It was me who was in trouble. I'm miserable."

"Ohhhh," I groan sympathetically.

"The brain's opiate receptors are treacherous when things don't go their way. I've been going through a lot of anguish. Can't get rid of it. What a crash. I just walk around and stare and can't forget her and even if I do there's this painful feeling and here I am in Australia alone and all I can think to do is leave."

"Don't leave. You still have me."

"Great." He kicked at the ground. "Your song's wrong. That Zen master's wrong."

"About?"

"Every day's not a good day. Today's not a good day."

"That's absolute—the god realm. This is relative—the people realm. Relative days can be bad."

"Just my luck."

"What can I do?" I asked.

"Nothing. I've been trying to meditate. Concentrating on the top chakra. Everything hurts. My third eye hurts."

"Takes time. It'll pass."

"Meanwhile time's slowed down."

"I know—the worse things are, the slower they pass."

"What do you do when you meditate?" he asked.

"When I meditate? Just follow my breath—or count the exhalations—or feel my feet as I walk and I say 'thank you' a lot or I just watch what's going on, just be there—that's the main one."

"I think I'll try following my breath. Need a change—maybe sneak up on the pain. I feel like I'm getting beaten up."

"Well, at least you're not turning to drugs and alcohol."

"That's a great idea. Let's go get a drink."

"Okay. But let's walk in the park some more first."

We walked. He talked.

"I've been blind. There've been all sorts of signs I refused to see." He laughed. "I'm so stupid. Really. It's been obvious she was losing interest. Yesterday when I got home we started to make out—I started it of course—and then she broke away and I followed her around and finally she said she didn't want to have a physical relationship with me anymore."

"Bad."

"Then she said she hadn't stayed out the night before last because she'd been too drunk to drive—it was because she'd been making love with an old boyfriend."

"That's terrible. What did you do?"

"I just stood there. Tried not to whimper. Then she said she was going over to his place again. I went to bed and slept for twelve hours—till I couldn't sleep anymore. She called this morning and told me not to be mad and that she still loved me and wanted me to stay there. And she still wants to go to the beach tomorrow with you and me and Frannie. She returned right before I left. I said stupid things like how I felt unattractive. She laughed and said baloney, said she'd had her heart broken plenty and it was just part of the game and we can still be friends and have fun. I guess I'll try. But I refused to meet the guy she was with. She wanted to bring him over. Can you believe that? I said I'd leave. We agreed to meet tonight at a pub in town to watch a game and then I can go back and sleep on her couch."

"Which rhymes with ouch."

"Righto."

"What game?"

"Fremantle versus Perth. Australian rules football. Come join us."

"Sure."

"Good—I need you there. Starts at six." He looked down digging his right shoe into the dirt and pushing it around. "She should love me," he said. "We really have a unique relationship. I never felt with anyone like I do with her. Not in a long time anyway. The strangest thing happened when I was leaving. Her neighbor and she were talking and the neighbor had a tabloid and she read Mindy her horoscope and it said her true love was near but she was in denial about it. I couldn't have paid that woman to make up anything better. But it didn't help."

I didn't feel jealous of him anymore. Whoops. I hadn't realized—just a little tiny bit jealous. I could see it as it went away. I was reminded of how romantic love is like a drug—unstable, undependable, emotionally risky—it can actually break your heart and kill you. Still legal though.

"You could do social work with those worse off to take your mind off your suffering. But that may be impractical right now. I bet the next best thing for you would be to keep moving," I said. "It's early but not early enough to take the walk to Freo."

"Walk to Freo? That's a long way."

"Well, I want to do it. Come with me."

"Maybe," he said.

"Anyway, today let's take the Historic Walk. I've got the map right here. First we can go down there to the Swan Bells Tower—see it?"

"Yeah. Okay. That sounds good. I've been there with Mindy. It's great."

"If you've been there, we could go to the museum by the train station. I could go back there. There's so much to see. I spent as much time watching them fix the roof as I did the displays."

"No, Swan Bells is good. I like them."

"Good. We've got a little time. Today they ring at noon."

A couple of ravens were calling from the nearby trees.

"There they are," he said, "the disappointed crows of WA."

"Correction—disappointed ravens, Australian ravens to be exact."

"These ravens are closer to American crows than what I think of as ravens. It's not exact. But—okay. Ravens. The disappointed ravens of WA. They were warning me about her. I should have listened. She was too good to be true. She says yes, but it can turn into a no. Ah ah ah ah—ahhhhhhhhhhhhhhhhhhhh," he imitated them perfectly—the high first notes and the descent—and then he said, "Yes yes yes yes yes—nooooooooooooooooooooooooooooo."

"Well Gupta, you're a liberated man again."

"Right. Hmm. That reminds me of something. Come this way."

He led me to a group of hippies and asked if he could borrow their guitar for a song. Wish granted. We sat with them. Gupta strummed.

I'm a free man, a free man baby
A free man, out of slavery
A free man, so sublime
A free man, a free mine I'm
Free—free, a free man, a free man baby.

Free like the bubble, floatin' light and round
Free like the Hubble, spaced out without sound
Free like the hobo, the whacko, or the clown
Free like the paraglider fore they splats the ground

I'm a free man, a free man baby
A free man, in the gravy
A free man, at this time
A free man, a free man I'm
Free—free, a free man, a free man baby

Free like the fluid, washin' in my spine
Free like the blood that flows inside my veins
Free like the oxygen I'm drinkin' all the time
Free like the freedom of the saint or the insane

Free man—a free man baby
Free man—don't mean maybe
Free man—freely playin'
Free man—I be sayin'
Free man—free man baby
Free man—free man baby

"You owe me five farthings say the bells of St Martins," Gupta recited bravely. It's from an old nursery rhyme he knew as a kid and here we are with those bells, which, along with some others specially cast for the occasion, were given to the city of Perth to commemorate Australia's two hundredth birthday.

"That's an awfully nice birthday gift," he said. "And some of them are so huge. I wonder how the parishioners of St. Martin-in-the-fields in London feel without their bells? I guess they still have god—or at least an idea of god."

"I guess they got some new ones. Ask the tour guide."

Before we could the bells started to ring. They're a marvel not only to hear but to watch.

The Swan Bells Tower is a striking building. It looks like an America's Cup type sail boat with huge stainless steel sails blowing full in the wind, a hundred foot glass spire housing the bells, rising off the deck. Like Daniel and his Malay wife had indicated, there was opposition to spending all the money to build it but I regard that as short-sighted. This building and these bells begin, continue, and augment a tradition, fertilizing their culture, creating such an interesting addition to the city that makes one's impression and experience more rich and positive. And it's fun. So much in our impression of a city or a building is in a few touches—Gaudi understood—add a flourish here, color there, some material to a wall, a rounded balcony—and it's warm and interesting and without, it can be depressing and boring.

The Swan Bells Tower can be considered a musical instrument, one of the largest in the world. The bells are hung for "change ringing," an old English method—no tunes, no random ringing. They swing them round to strike them in sets. A brochure we picked up on the way out read, "There are countless methods, each of which has a name, such as 'Plain Bob', 'Little Bob', 'Grandsire', 'Stedman', 'Cambridge Surprise' and so on, with the second part of the name indicating how many bells are being rung. 'Minimus' uses four bells, 'doubles' five, 'minor' six, 'triples' seven, 'major' eight, 'caters' nine, 'royal' ten, 'cinques' eleven and 'maximus' twelve. Hence 'Plain Bob Major' is rung on eight bells, and 'Plain Bob Maximus' on twelve."

"I've been meditating as we walk and I'm still miserable," Gupta mumbled as we stood way up on the observation platform.

"Give up then. You could jump."

"Might just get paralyzed. I'll keep trying."

"Oh—I know."

"What?"

"Affect psychology."

"What's that?"

"I don't really know, but I met a Zen teacher named Ian and a guy who sits with him named Samo who practice it. Samo helped me with that extreme reaction I have to being poked in the ribs." Gupta immediately made a threatening move. "Don't do it!" I called out. "Let's see. Disappointment is one of the affects. But I can't remember anything else like what you're supposed to do. Try just looking at it."

"Thanks a lot."

"We might get that drink. After all, you've given meditation a couple of hours. Obviously doesn't work."

"At least not when practiced while walking and talking with you."

"OK. Then try—the Walking Tour!" I said pulling the brochure out.

"Do you think it's because I'm a little overweight?"

"Probably so. How about a meat pie and the walking tour?"

"The Aussie hamburger. Sounds perfect. I think this time I'll get koala."

"Or quokka. Then we'll do the whole thing in order and number one is—here it is, straight down—Barrack Street for a few blocks—the Town Hall Center—built in 1870...hmm...by convicts."

"Weren't they all convicts?"

"Just our friends."

"Do we have to go inside every place?"

"As we choose—mainly just walk by I think. Except for number...number...nineteen—the Perth Mint. Let's do that last. There are twenty-three in all. Ah—I see the theme of the tour is the discovery of gold nearby in 1892. It's like San Francisco—built on gold—just forty-three years later."

Off we went.

"Any English here take a good look at something you've never seen before," said the Mint tour guide. It was an Olympic gold medal. That seemed a little mean. The Brits must have won some. They mainly do specialty coins—the Mint, not the Brits—the type Mai was interested in buying—commemoratives. There's all sorts of gold around—in the shop and on display. Silver too. They made a one kilo silver coin once, maybe the heaviest ever. There's a copy of the Hand of Fate Nugget, which weighed four hundred kilos. It was bought by the Golden Nugget in Las Vegas. There's a contraption at the Mint with which you can put something on a coin. The guide suggested, "This is your inheritance. Love, Mom and Dad." Our group followed him to the next room.

"Did you hear that Gupta? The guide says there are ten to twenty million dollars worth of gold here at any given time."

"I'd be satisfied with just a fraction of that. Doesn't seem like there's a lot of security either."

"Oh yeah. I guess they forgot about that."

The symbol of the Perth Mint is the black swan. The Mint is a handsome two story building made from limestone brought over from Rottnest Island. It was opened in 1899. The grounds in front are well tended though the roses were not in bloom. There's a room with a reconstructed 19th century miner's camp with life-size reddish brown dusty figures of the prospectors who made the big find. There are some scraggly short trees without any leaves that look more like dead gray branches stuck in the simulated reddish brown dusty ground.

"It's amazing they found this gold in the outback at a place with a brick wall and barred windows right next to it," Gupta noted. He further surveyed the scene. "Looks too dirty and difficult. I think I'd have let all the thousands of guys go for the gold like sperm rushing to the ovum—and stayed behind here in Perth and dealt in real estate."

We walked by bulletproof plate glass windows behind which employees spend their days putting gold, silver, and platinum through a workout. All we see now is gold. It does glitter. We follow it mesmerized as they cast it, roll it into strips, and anneal it, which the guide explains is a heating and cooling process to make the metal more malleable. It's re-rolled and then blank coins are punched. Excess metal is removed by an abrasive belt. We watched as the coins were weighed and sorted to determine which blanks are too fat, which are too skinny, and which are just right. Then there's the rimming in which the blanks are rolled between moving and stationary plates to achieve a milled edge. Then the coins are squished into their final form by huge presses. Time for a bath—the acid washing.

"That would wake one up," said Gupta.

The spray lacquering reduces tarnishing, then the coins are closely looked at by the demanding eyes of Mint inspectors.

We watched a parade of gold coins-to-be go by on a belt.

"Someday this will all be mine," said Gupta.

"You like," I said, "me like."

He asked the guide if there had ever been any robberies. No, but there had been one shot fired in the history of the place. A guard got himself in the foot.

The last part of the tour was called the Pour and was held in the original Melthouse, now a room at the far end of the Mint. We sat on mini-bleachers behind a wooden fence as in a courtroom. There, while keeping up a snappy banter, an employee melted a gold brick and made a new one out of it. He started off the demonstration by saying, if the fire alarm sounds, go out the emergency exit at the far end of the room opposite the entrance. We all looked that way. He stood before a brick wall while behind us was more bullet proof glass and a view of the busy workers and their gleaming coins.

Our latest guide informed us the gloves he donned were, like his shirt, made of one hundred percent wool, not one hundred percent effective. "I have to get into and out of the furnace quickly or they'll catch on fire," he said. He put on an apron of wool on the inside and reflective Kevlar on the outside—same as bulletproof vests. It looked like foil. Then he pulled a mask over his face—like what welder's wear.

"Gold melts at 1063 degrees centigrade," he said. "It takes one minute to get the gold from the furnace to the cast iron table." While he waited for that minute to conclude, he passed on more tidbits about this process. "There are lifting tongues and pouring tongues. These are lifting tongues," and he picked up the crucible. He said it takes thirty seconds for the gold to go from liquid to solid. "Already it's gone down to 1200."

The gold looked like melting butter. There was a momentary green glow. Gupta was transfixed. The guide changed to ordinary leather gloves.

"Now it's 800 degrees and has become solid."

He passed it around below our noses on a paddle and said to look out—if it falls on you it'll set your skin on fire. Everyone pushed back an inch. He picked the brick up. It lit his glove. He put the brick into water creating steam. He said they've made the same bar thirty-six times a week for eight years. The gold bar had gone cold. He picked it up and said he couldn't pass it around. It's worth a hundred and ten thousand dollars Australian.

"About seventy thousand US," whispered Gupta.

"Hmm. Or," I'm cogitating, "seventy one thousand five hundred. Or, if we carry it one more decimal point..."

"Shut up."

"Yes sir."

"Look," Gupta said, "There's the opening. That thing's just sitting there and it's cooled off. Hmm. They wouldn't miss it. We just have to distract him for a few seconds."

The tour was over. Gupta and I went through a hall to a small display room. In the middle of the room there was an ingot in Plexiglas one could reach in and try to lift. It was 400 ounces of refined gold—11.36 kilos—size of a brick. With effort I barely lifted it. Gupta had a better time of it.

"What are you writing now?" he asked.

"There —May 25th, 1945—just three months and sixteen days after I was born."

"What do mean?"

"That 1063 centigrade converts to 1945.4 Fahrenheit."

"What? What are you talking about?"

"The melting point of gold is 1063 centigrade which converts to 1945.4 Fahrenheit. I can remember that because 1945 is the year I was born and May 25th I figure is point four into the year."

"That's not important. What's important is extracting this brick."

We tried to figure out how to get it out.

"Freeze the Plexiglas then hit it with a hammer," said Gupta.

"You're working all this out to the last detail," I said.

"Hey, could I borrow your pen and notebook," he said.

"Why?" I asked.

"I want to go through that pour tour again and take notes. The next one starts pretty soon.."

"Okay. It was fun."

And it was fun again.

"Dinner time," said Gupta.

There's a restaurant across from the Mint. We stood on the corner and read the sign. It said "Japanese take-away" on one side, "Hot and Cold" on the other, and "Wasabi" in the middle.

"Strange," I said. "Why would a Japanese restaurant advertise wasabi?"

"That's the super-hot green stuff you mix soy sauce with, right?" said Gupta.

"Right. They call it Japanese horse radish but it's made from an herb."

"First time I tried it I thought it was avocado dip and put a big glob on a cracker. Thought I was gonna die," he said.

"That is a trip. I did the same thing once. What I remember is that all my tear ducts opened and my nose ran. It instantly made my face into a cascade. Quite cleansing. There was a guy on Jackass who snorted it. I think that would be going a tad far."

"Maybe we could distract the guard at the Mint with a wasabi spray in his eyes—and then grab the gold brick."

"Good idea. Oh, I see," I said looking at the sign. "Wasabi is the name of the restaurant."

We sat down at a table with sighs of relief. We'd been walking and standing all day. But now things had slowed down and there was nothing to distract him. Gupta had time to remember his fate.

"You look sad again," I said.

"Nobody likes me, everybody hates me, I'm gonna eat some ... wasabi."

"Time for that drink," I said. "How about sake to drown your sorrows."

"Sake and then... suicide by wasabi."

I thought about that word—wasabi. I played with it. "Wasabi. Wa sabi. Wabi-sabi."

"Wabi-sabi?" he said.

"That's a key Japanese concept of beauty, which incorporates loneliness and sadness, impermanence. Sabishi is sad. Wabishi is lonely and, I think, a sense of—of can't be comforted."

"Wasabi means that?"

"No—I'm just looking at the word and taking it apart. It's reminding me of wabi-sabi and how those words are appropriate now you're sitting here sad and lonely and since I am a compassionate person who feels your pain I too am sad and lonely in a sort of beautiful way. Wabi-sabi."

"Wabi-sabi," he repeated, "the unobtainability of the object of desire?"

"Something like that I guess."

"The sweet sadness of life and the bitter fruit of loss?"

"You've got it. And there's another reading on wasabi I just got. WA as in Western Australia. Wa-sabi—the sadness of Western Australia. The sadness of WA. The sadness of wandering around. There—in the distance can you hear the call of the disappointed ravens of WA, of wasabi."

With mutual melancholy we silently sipped sake while waiting for sushi and wasabi.

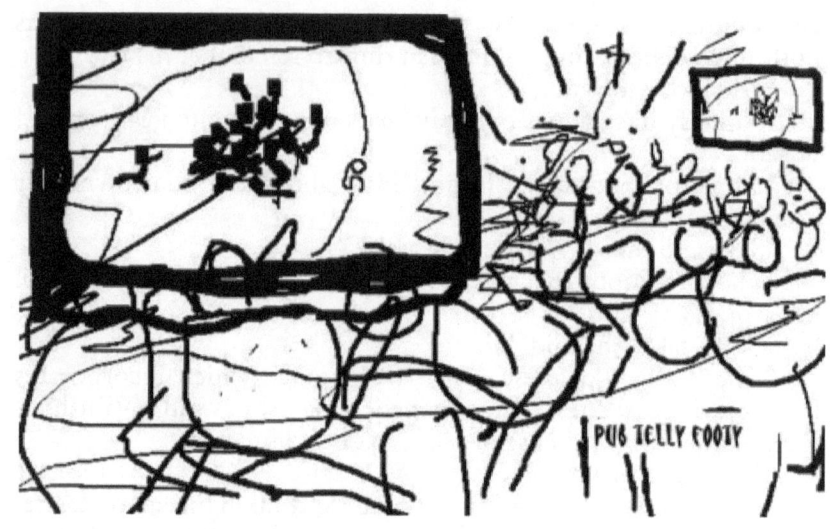

PUB TELLY FOOTY

CHAPTER 15
CRAWLIN'

A good hundred people were on their feet yelling. Mindy was one of them. It was a tense moment in the game of footy being played between Perth and Freo. The patrons of the downtown Perth pub seemed to be evenly divided between the two teams, which, along with the closeness of the competition, made for a dynamic evening. Gupta and I were enjoying the game, the crowd, and Mindy's lively participation. We were also enjoying the fish and chips and the Guinness Stout of which we each consumed four pints—a gallon between us. Wow.

I've watched many American football games, mostly cheering for the Forty-niners. In the States I can just say football for American football, but not anywhere else. Everywhere else football means what we call soccer. In WA I saw footy which is Australian rules football, soccer, rugby, and an American football game on Satellite. Soccer is meditative and flowing with precious few scores. It impresses and somewhat puzzles me it's so dominant worldwide. Rugby is wild and rugged with no etymological connection to that word. The head-butting of rugby should stop immediately if only for my sake—I worry terribly they're going to break their necks. Footy is full on, as they say, and fun. American football seems, by comparison, a mite heady. The players seem to spend most of their time talking and waiting around. Those other games don't stop much and I got used to that. But regardless of what people say, I hold that American football is the most violent and dangerous. Aussies and Brits who've experienced it know that. But American football is so brutal and bruising I think a change of rules must be made. I explained my suggested modifications after the footy match was over. It was close and exciting but I didn't know who won.

"I love these games," I said. "I like to watch them for inspiration. I think that's why I used to watch American football—for fun but also for inspiration."

"Inspiring like smashing your head into a wall," said Gupta.

"No, really. When I'm on some project like a book or something, I feel like those guys getting up off the field to keep giving it their all, play after play. Don't give up—keep smashing on. Something like that. But I've come to think it's time for a change."

"Like?"

"Like American football must eliminate the huddle," I said.

"How will they know what to do?"

"They do no-huddle now."

"But not all the time."

"They'll adjust."

"But the players are so exhausted that they've got to rest," said Gupta.

"They can still put in a hundred percent. They'll just be staggering like boxers and therefore those goliaths won't be able to charge into each other at the same high speeds. You know what those quarterbacks have got coming at them? It's murder. Concussions are standard."

"Some of those linemen do seem to have the lust to kill."

"Of course. So the rules have to be changed to channel this aggression with less damage to the pros, the collegians, the kids in school. But even with no huddles at all I still think it would be too brutal, so I've got another change in mind—a soft rubbery field. The traditional grass fields are too hard but Astroturf is murder."

"I don't know if America is ready for your vision of American football yet," said Gupta.

"That won't stop me. Did that stop Socrates? Marx? Martin Luther King?"

"Good analogies."

"Now you've got your no-huddle game and your soft rubbery field. There's one more addition."

"Suits of armor?"

"Close."

"I give up."

"Thick foam uniforms. That would do it."

"I get the image of what football would look like if it were played on the moon."

"Yes—that's right."

"Wouldn't it be boring?"

"Why? It would be easier to follow and the most skilled team would still win. The players would live longer, not lying awake at night in pain for the rest of their lives and football stadiums would be less like Roman coliseums."

"OK. That's your plan. Now you want to hear mine?"

"You have a plan for American football?"

"No. For the Perth Mint."

"A better way to strike the coins?"

"A better way to distribute the gold."

Then Gupta got off on his plan. How to rob the Perth Mint. He said when the man picked the gold ingot out of the water and put it on the ledge, we'd set off a smoke bomb that would trigger the fire alarm and send people rushing out the emergency exit that had just been pointed out to them. Just then he'd spray the man's face with a wasabi mixture, open his coat up unleashing a mechanical arm that would spring out, grab the ingot and retract it to his bosom where he'd cover it with his coat before anyone could notice. I'd spray the Plexiglas container with something that froze it, smash it with a hammer and grab that gold brick. Then we'd walk out with the others and disappear into the street.

"Whataya think?"

"Foolproof," I said.

Mindy and I had only nodded hello and yelled unintelligible comments at each other in the din of the game. Now that the place had calmed down she asked what I'd been up to since she last waved goodbye squinting through a hangover in Freo. I ran through a list of highlights. She said I'd seen more of Freo and Perth than her.

That's common to hear. I remember I had a friend I'd see at tennis tournaments when I was a kid. He lived in San Antonio just a couple of blocks from the Alamo and had never been inside. Like people in New York City who haven't been to the Statue of Liberty.

I told her I wanted to get out of the city more. Like on the way to Freo Francine had taken me to a regional park where we had a leisurely walk by crowds of flowering plants, crossed wooden bridges over a rocky creek, sat for a spell to see the sun slink down behind a distant hill.

"Sounds delightful," said Mindy.

"It was great except the park closed at sunset and her car was locked inside the gate. I had to take some of the fence apart so we could drive around it over an area newly planted with darling little purple flowers. I felt like the biker whom in '66 I saw purposely destroy a wide beautifully designed bed in front of the Conservatory of Flowers in San Francisco's Golden Gate Park. He just drove up off the street onto the lawn full of picnickers and Sunday strollers and plowed into the exquisite display of beauty, skidded around gouging the crap out of it in front of a horrified throng of people who had been enjoying a lovely spring day."

"That's so destructive and immature," said Mindy.

"Sounds great," said Gupta.

"Yeah. It was impressive," I agreed, "but bad."

So we got to making another list of parks and places out from the city. Gupta had a brochure with a map that helped. Mindy said she'd be happy to drive us wherever we wanted. We already had the plan to go to the beach the next day.

"It's winter," she said, "but the ocean temperature here only varies by two degrees year-round. Burns Beach is just a short ways to the north. We could go further up to Two Rocks. There's transplanted koala up there."

"From where?" I asked.

"Eastern Australia."

I wondered if they say E-A there but, before I could bring it up, Mindy asked if I knew what koala meant. I didn't.

"'No water' in Aborigine. They get all their water from a particular type of Eucalyptus leaf."

"Oh, like teddy bears," I said.

Gupta chortled.

Mindy got us back on topic, suggesting Araluen Botanic Park south of Perth and John Forrest National Park to the east, which I thought would rightly be called John Forrest National Forest. There was a contemplative Catholic monastery I wanted to visit and a Vipassana Center. Vipassana is insight meditation as practiced by the early Buddhists. The center was probably connected to a teacher from Thailand or Burma. She said we could look at a map tomorrow and figure it all out. I asked about how we'd three fit in her Porsche and she said she'd get the SUV.

"Whose is that?"

"It's really my uncle's but he leaves it here. I'll make a call to hold it. Ah heck," she said, "left me mobile in the car. No matter. Now it's time for pub-crawlin'!"

"Oh—oh," Gupta said. "What is that?"

"We'll go from pub to pub," said Mindy, "and get so pissed we'll have to start crawlin' to get to the next one."

Walking over to Northbridge, Mindy pointed to her car. "There she is. Good. Now you don't have to depend on me to remember. And here are the keys so you don't have to wrestle them from me. And we can always take a taxi home and get 'er tomorrow."

At the hostel I get a sports coat from my room. Mindy said I might need it to get into some of the clubs.

"You know what surprises me about the youth hostels where I've been?" said Gupta as we walked out.

"No, what does surprise you about the youth hostels where you've been, Gupta?" I said.

"I always expect them to be full of angry kids, but there are people of all ages and they are generally good-natured."

"Death is too good for you," I sneered at him.

I let them go into the first joint without me so I could do my email before the night got crazier. I sent Kelly and Clay a rambling missive on what was happening including a bit about the Mint tour and Gupta's plan to rob it. Told Clay to go to his atlas or the Internet to locate all these places Mindy had mentioned. I doubted he'd actually do it—maybe when I get back we'll do it together. Kelly had a comment on my mega-ticklish problem. He said he'd had a similar extreme reaction and had been cured by getting grabbed all the time doing martial arts. The type he practiced was bruising. I pictured my body being flung about like a Raggedy Andy doll and thought I'd continue investigating Affect Psychology.

I was talking to Techo when Mindy and Gupta came in to get me. I asked him to come with us and he agreed. He's the strong silent type not to mention a little freaky looking and it always surprises me when he's friendly and open.

"Glad you're on our side," said Gupta sizing Techo up as we walked out. "Looks like rain," he added.

"Good," said Mindy. "I want to get soaked."

We went up to a noisy crowded place, Gupta snapping his fingers saying "It's happening, baby." But it happened they wouldn't let

Techo in because he had a tee shirt on. My long sleeve shirt with collar passed their dress code so he got in by wearing my sports coat. The place was crammed with people drinking, dancing, talking and a constant thump, thump, thump of a bass drum. Techo's head started bobbing to the beat.

"Techo does techno," Gupta said in a radio tone.

There was an Aboriginal woman passed out on the floor by the bar. The staff didn't do anything about it. Nor customers. People just went around or stepped over her. Sad.

Mindy met a couple she knew and we all huddled together and talked loudly to be heard above the din. The male half of this couple commented on all the sexy women. I concurred. The woman with him said there were a lot of attractive men around too. "Like him," she said looking at Techo who smiled. Ah—there—he can smile.

"Yeah," her guy said, "Isn't it a shame that the more sex a man gets the heartier a fellow he's regarded, whereas if a woman is aggressively promiscuous people call her a slut."

"What's the problem with that?" Mindy asked.

"It's not right. Women just trying to enjoy life, shouldn't be called a slut."

"I'm a slut. I don't care. I'll shag anybody. I like being a slut. Call me a slut."

That left him tongue tied. Gupta looked down as she went on like this. It was painful. Finally he leaned over to her and whispered sotto voce, "You won't either. It's not true. I know."

She whispered back, "Don't be hurt. I do love you. Here." And she gave him a big kiss and, as she did, her eyes got wide. I looked in the direction she was facing and saw her mysterious Aboriginal shadow staring our way.

"Oh no," she said, Pulling away from Gupta.

"Was it that bad?" he said.

"Not you—him," she said, pointing with her eyes.

"Damnit," said Gupta "I'm gonna..."

"Let's get out of here," Mindy said pulling him in the other direction. He grunted in anger but gave in to her.

It was raining outside. "Follow me," she said to us and darted down the street and into a busy pub and through to the rear, to the alley and into another back door through a kitchen where Chinese cooks watched us blankly.

"Sorry Mr. Wong," she said to a man in a suit standing just inside the dining room of the fancy place.

"That's fine Mindy. Hurry back," he said as Gupta, Techo, and I followed her out onto the next street then into a jazz club where we took a booth in a dark corner on a second floor balcony. A waitress came over and we ordered, panting. Mindy, Gupta, and I downed shots of tequila. Techo drank a Coke and smoked cigarettes. I bummed one then I bummed another.

Gupta, now somewhat tipsy, told Techo about his plan to rob the Perth Mint and asked if Techo could add some of his computer skills to the job, possibly jamming the burglar alarm. Techo got a kick out of it.

Mindy said she needed to get some fresh air so we took a walk— out the back again and down the sidewalk into a residential neighborhood. We wandered around the streets in a gentle rain until we were back in a commercial zone. We were cold and wet but no one complained. I could see the lights of the entertainment district a few blocks ahead of us.

"We're not doing much crawling but we're sure staggering a lot," I said.

"Let's smoke a cone," Mindy said, as she sat down in a darkened store-front and lit her pipe. We joined her. She was going on about how much she loved being out in the rain, out on the streets.

"I wanna stay here. Why do I live in a house?" she asked in a distant rapid slightly crazed voice. "I want to sleep here! This is good enough. This is all I need. Think I'll move here. Don't need more than this. You guys can go on and leave me here."

"Adrian Quist," said Techo.

"Rhymes with pissed," I noted. "I'm quite Quisted myself."

"Me too," said Gupta with his tongue hanging out.

We sat in the cubby and smoked.

"I'm going to walk all the way home," Mindy said jumping up and spinning around. "I'm going to dance all the way home! You take a cab home. I'll go by myself." She went on like that musically and quirkily spinning and dancing down the street.

We three stood up slowly, keeping our eyes on her.

"She's going the right direction," I said.

Mindy started singing out.

I'm a I'm a slut—I'm a I'm a slut
There—I like the sound—as I'm spinning round
La la la la la La la la la la
How I prance and strut—tell ya tell ya what
I'm a I'm a slut—I'm a I'm a slut

"How tragic," Gupta said, watching her spin down the street, "I've been in anguish over a lost treasure that, should I acquire, would still not be something I could possess."

I'm a I'm a slut—I'm a I'm a slut
Dancing round the street—on my slutty feet
La la la la la La la la la la
But I'm not for sale—mine is free love tail
I'm a I'm a slut—I'm a I'm a slut

"Look at her—no one can possess her. She's a free spirit. But still I cannot let go."

I'm a I'm a slut—I'm a I'm a slut
Free from your constructs—free from all the shuck
La la la la la La la la la la
Hey there boys! Guess what? You're not the only ones!
I'm a I'm a slut—I'm a I'm a slut

Her voice echoed through the shadowy canyon of dark buildings.

Mindy was blithely singing and twirling through the intersection. An occasional car was passing. We stood on the glistening asphalt, her rapt and ambling audience.

La la la la la La la la la la
I'm a I'm a slut—I'm a I'm a slut
La la la la la La la la la la
I'm a I'm a slut—I'm a I'm a slut

Suddenly, there was the sound of an engine roaring in approach. A long black automobile sped up from the side street on the right and screeched to a stop between Mindy and us. It hovered there. We couldn't see what was happening. Its engine gunned. Then it blasted off wheels spinning and shot straight ahead down the cross street out of sight.

The three of us stood silently, numbed, peering intently down the black, wet street toward the lights of Northbridge. Something was terribly wrong, terribly songless. Mindy wasn't in the picture. Mindy was not to be seen or heard. Mindy was in that vehicle speeding off into the distance. Mindy had been taken away.

PART TWO
THE TREASURE HUNT

iMPROMTU MEETING

CHAPTER 16
DESPERATE MEETING

It's here, it's here, it's here somewhere! Somewhere, gotta be some-where!" I stammered loudly while frantically going through my shoulder-bag.

"Keep it down," said Gupta. "It's two in the morning."

He and Techo stood at the door to my tiny room at the hostel. The examined and rejected receipts, notes, brochures, stubs, and cards were in a pile on the floor. I shook the bag upside down. Nothing more. Next I dumped my dirty laundry and started going through it.

"Got it," I said, picking a business card out of a shirt pocket. "Sam Collins. Ah good—he wrote his home number on it."

We didn't know what the heck to do. Gupta and I did not want to call the cops, not yet. If there was any chance of us getting Mindy back before Rudy found out, then we might live to see our native land again. I wanted to get Samo's take on it. He didn't object to a two a.m. call and an immediate rendezvous when I started off by saying Mindy had just been kidnapped.

Samo drove up to the hostel and parked his Tercel behind Te-cho's dark blue fifty-five Chevy—leaving plenty of room because Te-cho was also behind it—getting a jacket out of his trunk. 'Bout time.

Even in the midst of a dilemma, it made me cold to look at him in a damp tee shirt in this chilly night air. He'd given me my jacket back long before. I stood up from a sidewalk bench, shook hands with Samo, thanked him for coming, and said a quick, "Techo, Samo." I dialed the evening's code on the front door. We went inside and up stairs to the communal kitchen. Gupta had coffee ready. He thanked Samo for coming. Samo didn't drink coffee. There were tea bags and hot water. Milk, sugar. A couple of hostel guests were making a wee hours snack. Not much talk. Kitchen sounds mainly—clinking and clacking. Cups filled. Ready. We went into the empty computer room. Door closed.

Then Gupta and I were talking on top of each other excitedly about what happened and how we have no idea what happened and what could have happened to Mindy and how Rudy would kill us and if we don't tell him maybe he'd kill us for that. Samo suggested we drink our coffee and just be quiet for a moment. Techo was already quiet. Samo had us tell everything we knew one at a time. Gupta went first, then Techo had some minimal comments, and then I went through the events of the evening. We described the guy who had been following Mindy—Aborigine, not fat, not thin, maybe in his mid twenties, short hair, dressed in jeans, a brown flannel shirt, tennis shoes.

"What about the fact that there wasn't a scream?" I asked.

"Could mean she knew 'em," said Samo.

"We know who did it—the Aborigine," said Gupta.

"We don't know that for sure," said Samo.

"Okay—but he's the only suspect, right?" I asked.

"Not really."

"What do you mean?"

"Just hang on. We'll see."

"He could have put his hand over her mouth before she had a chance to yell," I said.

"She's not the screaming type," said Gupta. "I think even if it was strangers kidnapping her she'd not be afraid. If she had time to scream she'd be likely to use it to ask the guy if he wants to smoke a cone."

"Now Gupta," I said.

"You know her," he said. "She's outrageous. Do you remember what she was singing at the time?"

"I'm a slut," I said. "Sorry Samo, left that part out. Nice tune too."

Samo asked if we noticed anything more about the car.

"It was big and black and went by in a flash," I said. "It slid up to her—on our side so we couldn't see her—and sped off—all in a few seconds."

"Like a big old car," said Gupta.

"It was like from gangster movies," I said.

"It had some brown wide trim down the side," said Gupta.

"Memories change details," said Samo. "You might think it looks like an old car from a gangster movie when it was just a big black Mercedes touring car."

"It happened so fast," said Gupta, "it could have been anything."

"It was a La Salle Hearse—carved panel—I'd guess about 1937."

We all turned to look at Techo.

"Good morning. Good morning. Time to get up." It was Samo.

I got up from the couch in the TV room and greeted him in a blur. Rubbing my eyes I trudged out to the hall. Checked on Techo—still asleep in my bed. When I returned, bladder empty, face splashed, Samo was sitting at the kitchen table. Soon Gupta was pouring coffee and hot water for tea again—and buttering toast. I looked at the clock on the wall above the sink. I'd slept about three hours. We'd talked till five. Samo had told us to get some sleep then so we could function. Now other guests of the hostel were crowding around us making breakfast, coffee, tea.

"Samo's been working on this all night," said Gupta.

"You haven't slept?" I asked.

"Nope."

"And you got up early," I said to Gupta.

"I got something on my mind," he said.

"Where can we meet?" Samo asked.

People online in the computer room. No one in the TV room yet.

"You guys slept in here?" Samo asked.

"Yep," Gupta said.

"No covers?"

"Nope. We were drunk and beat and it wasn't that cold," I said.

"You didn't seem drunk," said Samo. "Adrenalin."

"Yeah, I'm fine, but I can still feel what we drank," said Gupta.

"I'm ready to do whatever," I said.

"What about Techo?" Samo asked.

"Let him sleep," I said. "This isn't really his problem. And if he takes it on he can still sleep now."

"Here's what's happening as I see it," said Samo. "You guys have gotten yourselves in the middle of a gang war."

"Oh, great. Love the opening," said Gupta.

"There have been so many gang killings in Melbourne. Two new ones this week. Mindy's Uncle Rudy is the head of one of the gangs. Bobby Fenster is the head of the other gang. Fenster collects vintage cars. I don't see a La Salle registered to him or to any of his businesses but that might show up with further digging. There's enough for the police to question him on this."

"But if the police go to him then Rudy will know," I said.

"Look," Gupta said. "I think we should be clear about this. We don't want Rudy to know, but Mindy's more important than us. You're in charge, Samo."

"Yeah," I said. "Anytime you think it's to her definite advantage to bring the cops in, then of course, do it. But we want to try to get her back without Rudy knowing if possible."

"Sure. And this might not be foul play."

"Right," I said. "We're not positive of that."

"Do they attack each other's families?" asked Gupta. "I didn't think they did that."

"No, you're right. They don't," said Samo. "But there are three reasons why Fenster might have made an exception here." He paused to pick up a piece of toast. He chewed for a moment. "First, Fenster's favorite Lieutenant was killed a few months ago. The guy was like a son to him. That might have broken the family rule as far as Fenster was concerned. *If* he's behind it, he *might* have kidnapped Mindy as payback, but maybe to help negotiate an end to killing, maybe to trade her for someone or something."

"A trade followed by a double murder of two insignificant tourists," said Gupta.

"Rudy probably doesn't know anything yet. We still have time," said Samo.

"Second?" I asked.

"Second—Fenster's got no family other than his wife. She's almost always at home and when she goes out she's well-guarded. So there's not the usual conditions for fear of retaliation."

"Where is this son of a bitch?" asked Gupta. "I'll go get Mindy from him. It's my fault she was taken and my life's not worth anything with her kidnapped anyway."

"Hold on there," said Samo.

"It doesn't make sense to me," I said. "It's something that could get him in a lot of trouble with Rudy or the law—or both. Why would he do it? What's to gain?"

"Leverage over Rudy you idiot," said Gupta.

"Yes," Samo said, "but it would be like having a tiger by the tail. If Rudy knew Fenster had Mindy then at some point Fenster would pay. He might have it on Rudy at first, but either she'd come back alive in which case Rudy would get revenge, or she'd not, in which case Rudy would be unstoppable. But anyway, we're just going in circles because it doesn't really make good strategic sense. But," he added looking at me, "it doesn't have to make sense for him to do it. That brings us to number three."

"Oh—third?" I said.

"Third," said Samo. "Yeah—third and most important. Fenster is nuts. Let's say highly eccentric. And unpredictable. I know guys who've been following him for years. They say nothing would surprise them. He's done some brazen things in the past."

"Like what?" Gupta asked.

"Well, nobody could prove it but we all know he engineered the theft of Phar Lap out of the Museum Victoria in Melbourne some years back."

"Phar Lap?" I asked.

"A whole stuffed horse," Samo nodded. "It wasn't just any stuffed horse either but Phar Lap."

"And who's Phar Lap?" I asked again.

"How can you not know? Don't they teach you anything in America?"

"Sorry."

"Phar Lap was a racehorse, a national hero. Phar Lap won every important race in Australia back in the early thirties and then the Agua Caliente Handicap, the prize of American horse racing back then. There was nothing in any museum in Australia as important as Phar Lap in Melbourne. One day they went to work and Phar Lap was gone. The museum managed to keep it out of the papers. They just put up a notice that said Phar Lap was temporarily undergoing remedial taxidermy. Refused to bring the police into it because the culprits said there would be no trace of the body left to recover if the museum didn't do exactly as it was told. The museum could not afford to lose Phar Lap. They paid the ransom. That's the type of crazy thing that guy's capable of. And it's also why I think, if it was Fenster who took Mindy, that she hasn't been harmed—just used."

"If she's being used," I said, "then Rudy will know soon—because what else could she be used for other than... than something having to do with him? We've got to act fast."

"What about the Aborigine?" Gupta asked.

"I don't know," said Samo. "Maybe he's working for them. Maybe he did it. But I think Fenster at least should be checked out."

"How do we do that?" asked Gupta.

"Fenster's at his place southwest of Dunsborough now. He's down there with his wife and some of his crew. I know this sounds crazy and dangerous but maybe somebody should go talk to him, ask him if he knows anything. Just confront him or appeal to him."

Gupta jumped up. "I'm going. I'm going down there and I'm gonna tell..."

"Maybe I should go," Techo said. We all turned to the door. "But could I have some coffee first?"

"I'll get it," I said.

"Would a third party, a neutral party like me be better?" said Techo when I returned.

"Maybe so," said Samo looking at Techo, "but he's sort of conservative in his tastes—if you know what I mean."

"Or what about you and me going?" Techo asked Samo. "Surely he wouldn't mess with you."

"I can't do that," said Samo. "I still consult with the police. They'd have to know if I went. And they can't know officially, not yet."

"I want to go," said Gupta. "I'm not afraid."

"I don't know. You gotta calm down."

"Gupta and me," I said.

"Hmm," Samo groaned and rubbed his head.

"Let us go," I said, "Gupta and me."

"Please, please," said Gupta. "I'll be cool."

"That may just be the best," Samo admitted. "She's your friend. You're outsiders. He likely won't hurt you... probably. And he likes to meet people. He reads a lot. He's a real talker that Fenster, otherwise known as Waxo for wax prolific. Rhymes with Max as in Mad Max. Remember that mad part—anything can happen."

"How do we find him?" I asked.

"I've got that," said Samo.

"I could drive and wait outside," said Techo.

"No need," said Gupta throwing a set of keys up in the air and jangling them upon their return to his hand. "We've got Mindy's Porsche. You can give us a ride to it though."

"Take showers first and put on clean clothes." Samo said. "Look as presentable as you can. Fenster's a stickler for form."

"Everything of mine is back at Mindy's," said Gupta.

"Well go there."

"It all needs to be cleaned."

"You can wear something of David's," said Samo.

"Thanks a lot," said Gupta.

"The baggy look is in," I said.

"Or buy something on the way," Samo suggested.

Before long we were getting into Techo's Chevy. He gunned the engine.

"You've got my mobile number," said Samo. "Call anytime."

"Right here," I said patting my shirt pocket, "and here," tapping my head. "We'll be in touch."

"Good luck," he said, "and be careful what you say. He's not only crazy, he's sensitive—can take offense—and he's brutal. They're all brutal." He paused, looking down. "I hope I'm not making a mistake—letting you go like this."

BOOKSHELF DOORWAY W/ WOG BALL

CHAPTER 17
FENSTER

Eight"

"What are you talking about?" said Gupta.

"The countdown," I answered.

"What?" Gupta asked.

"Today's—uh—Thursday the 21st. And the 29th when we have the dinner date at nine with Rudy is a Friday. It's just about three so that's eight days and six hours. If the 29th is zero in the countdown, then today is eight. Is that clear?"

"How could you be thinking about that at a time like this? We're here to meet a dangerous gangster to get Mindy back—it's a life and death thing."

"And we have eight days to do it in. Hey—at least I left it at whole numbers."

"Okay," said Gupta impatiently. "Look—we've already blown enough time getting here."

"You needed clean clothes. We had to clean up and eat. We're here."

"Okay. I think I could be hanging from a cliff and need your concentrated attention to save me, and you'd be trying to compute the speed I'd be traveling when I hit."

"Multitasking."

"Ok. I'll humor you. We've got eight days. Now let's go."

We looked at each other, opened the doors to the Porsche, stepped out, closed the doors, tucked in our shirts, and walked up to a gatehouse gulping. The massive wrought iron gate was closed. Fancy metalwork at the top was in the form of a horse's head with mane. A high brick wall ran in each direction from the gate and what looked to be two strands of electrified wire ran along the top. I counted three security cameras.

A man in the gatehouse put down a newspaper and looked up at us with suspicion.

"You got an appointment?"

"No," said Gupta. "But we've got business."

"You gotta make an appointment first."

"Is Mr. Fenster in?" I asked.

"Gotta have an appointment."

"Tell him we're acquaintances of Rudy and Mindy and we come in peace," I said.

Gupta leaned over and whispered, "Come in peace? That's American Indian movie talk not gangster movie talk."

The man looked at us long and steady and told us to take a walk back to the car where he could see us and to wait there.

A few moments later he called us back as the gate swung open slowly with a creaking sound.

"Wait inside," he said.

"Try a little WD40 on that gate," said Gupta.

A golf cart with plaid awning roof pulled up and we got in. There was another serious guy inside. The cart zipped along an asphalt drive, no house in sight, a row of what are surely a variety of Eucalyptus on the left and a high hedge on the right.

"To the theater," said Gupta. "And step on it. The show's about to begin."

No response.

"We're even. I compute—you wisecrack," I said.

"Do these guys remind you of cops?" Gupta spoke softly toward my ear. "So friggin' serious and they look at you like you're guilty of something. I've got a cousin in New Orleans who's a cop and even he relates to me like that."

"And those guys have a higher crime rate than anyone," I added.

"Well, almost anyone," Gupta countered.

"Whose is higher?"

"Gangsters."

The cart rolled around a circular drive to the entrance of a large colonial style beachfront house. There was a polished old red roadster parked in front—like something from the twenties. Gupta and
I looked at it and each other. Two sinister seeming men stood by
the front door, one short and the other tall. I said hi and they paid
no attention. We were met and escorted inside by an elderly gray
haired man with wisps of stringy hair on his eyebrows and ears. He
introduced himself as Stan. As we went in Gupta said a big obvious
"Hi!" with a wide waving gesture to the sinister men. He stopped
like a statue when they didn't respond. I told him to come on. Inside
he asked Stan, who had already displayed some social grace, if these
are Mr. Fenster's goons. Stan said not to mind the "Twins," that they
keep quiet.

"Like the Queen's guard?" asked Gupta.

"Like the Coldstream Guard, yes," said Stan. He sounded English.

"The Twins, eh? Goony Twins," Gupta said.

"In case you need to identify them," explained Stan, "the short
one is Halffoot and the tall one is called Shorts."

"Why Halffoot?" Gupta asked.

"He had an accident and lost part of his left foot," Stan said.

"What sort of accident?"

Stan shrugged and ushered us into a spacious library with a log
fire flittering in a stone fireplace.

I looked around. It was an eyeful, had a traditional atmosphere
with dark wood, paintings and photos and memorabilia on the
walls, Persian rugs, overstuffed chairs. The most noticeable item was
a large stuffed crocodile.

"Do many Australians have stuffed crocodiles?" I asked.

"Oh no."

"What's that about?"

"It's just an old friend," Stan said.

"And there's a soccer ball," Gupta said reaching up.

"Better leave it," said Stan. "It's his prize wog ball," which he explained is what a soccer ball is called when it's used for rugby instead
of a proper footy.

So many books. "Doesn't he live in Melbourne? Is this his country home? This is his second library?"

"He has more time to read and relax here," Stan said and asked
us what refreshment we'd like. We agreed on hot tea with milk. He
told us to feel free to look around in the library, pointed to a door

that leads to a WC, and said firmly to stay within those bounds.

Gupta adjusted his bifocals, picked up a magazine, and settled back in one of two overstuffed chairs on either side of an intricately carved jade chess set on a low table.

I snooped around with the books. Tons of literature I could see. A lot of old stuff. I picked out a book with a leather cover.

"Oh, it's Thomas Hardy. *Far from the Madding Crowd.*"

"Isn't that maddening?"

"Maybe to some sexists. It was feminist for the times I believe. He was a foe of Victorianism, a defender of the working class."

"No you idiot. Maddening instead of madding."

"Obviously an error. I'll send him a note about it. Oh yes—my high school English teacher said he was a fatalist. As I remember, he tied everything together so completely it was ridiculous. But it's not a bad way to tell a story. Life's not that way though. It's full of loose ends."

"You're proof of that."

One area was packed with all the big names in Western philosophy like Socrates and Kant. There was a set of the Great Books. Being there made me want to read them all at once till I remembered that whenever I'd tried to actually read that much I never got very far. Just couldn't keep my interest up. It was such a relief to find Zen when I was young and realize I didn't have to read all that stuff. Zen's not anti-intellectual but it did give me something beyond words to work with.

Speak of the devil, I was surprised to find some books on Eastern thought—the *Upanishads* and *Bhagavad-Gita*, Zoroastrianism, Sufism, and Buddhism, lots of Buddhism—some old sutras from the Pali, *The Tibetan Book of Living and Dying, the Life of Milarepa, Cutting Through Spiritual Materialism* by Trungpa and Trungpa's *Shambhala: Sacred Path of the Warrior*. And there was Zen—translations by Blofield, Tanahashi, Taigen Dan Leighten, the Cleary brothers. Next to them were books by Van der Wetering, Pirsig, and Ken Wilber.

"Wow! Hey Gupta, he has Tazi John's book, *The Light Inside the Dark!*"

"I've read one of these books," Gupta said coming over and picking it out of the shelf. "*Manual of Zen Buddhism* by D.T. Suzuki. I thought at first that it was about an Hispanic guy who became a Zen master."

"Wow," I said, "*On Bear's Head*, a compilation of Philip Whalen's poetry. He became a priest in my lineage. I took Frannie with me to visit him at a hospice a couple of years before he died. While I talked to Philip she held the hand of a sad old Japanese man in the next bed."

There were many books on Chinese and Japanese martial arts. Several others by D.T. Suzuki. I told Gupta D.T. Suzuki wrote something like fifty books in English and about the same number in Japanese about Zen and Mahayana Buddhism and about Jodo Shin Buddhism. Especially as he got older he felt the self-power of Zen needed to be tempered with the other-power of Shin. Some Japanese had told me Shin was like Christianity in that you ask Amida Buddha to save you. It was said to be praying Buddhism—please help me. Then Shinran came along and made Jodo Shin, grateful Buddhism—thanks I'm already saved, already enlightened. D.T. Suzuki's last words, last public words anyway, were "Thank you, thank you." I said I like that approach and sometimes I say "thank you," as a mantra.

"Thank you to what?" Gupta asked.

"Just thank you," I said. "No subject, no object."

"What's the 'you' in 'thank you' stand for?"

"I don't know. Maybe I should just say 'thanks.'"

"Yeah, that's what your book's called. You're just advertising."

"Buy it now," I said.

"Maybe you should say 'thank Gupta.'"

"Yes, thank you."

"You're welcome. Hey—I'm going to go around chanting, 'You're welcome.'"

"I don't see Suzuki Roshi's *Zen Mind, Beginner's Mind,*" I mumbled.

"That was your teacher?"

"Right—Shunryu Suzuki. When people would get them confused, people who didn't know Suzuki in Japan is like Smith in America, he'd say D.T. was the big Suzuki and he was the little one."

"And then there's the Suzuki violin method," Gupta said. "He's the middle sized one."

"Hey Gupta. Here's an obscure one you'll appreciate—Leonard Koren's *Wabi-sabi: for Artists, Designers, Poets, and Philosophers.* Remember—wabi sabi—sadness and loneliness—sort of."

"Oh yeah. Wasabi, the restaurant—WA sadness—the disappointed ravens—it all fits together. God man, I'd forgotten I was unhappy until you just reminded me."

"He says a lot of good things about wabi-sabi. Here—Japanese don't define it—they feel it—it's central to their culture—it could be called the 'Zen of things'. I want to stay here. I want to reread this."

He can't possibly have read all these books—not and be a crook. But I guess that's not true. After reviewing in a flash all the Buddhists I've known, I am reminded you get a wide sampling of the human animal there.

I find a book on mazes and labyrinths and take it over to an easy chair under a floor lamp. "I'll look at pictures while you read cartoons," I said, noting Gupta was into a New Yorker.

The door opened. It's our tea. And shortbread! Thank you Stan. We sit and sip and chew. I thumb through the mazes and labyrinths.

After a while another door opened, one that was hidden by books. A man stepped into the room. He's thin, bald on top, and older than I'd imagined though I don't know why I'd imagined—maybe seventy. He walked up to us and said, "I'm Bobby Fenster. Welcome. Call me Bobby."

We introduced ourselves. He inquired about us straightaway. How was your trip? Fine. Do you need to rest? No. From America? Yes. Where? Gupta answered first.

"New Orleans? It's not bad for America," said Fenster. He said he was there once—in a hurricane.

I told him I was too, that I danced in it with my girlfriend. When Gupta said he's in real estate, Fenster asked him about the market in New Orleans. Gupta said his job involves mortgages nationwide. Phone work. Mainly entails looking at formulas and credit ratings and hunting around for lenders who'll take his clients on. But, he said he keeps up somewhat with New Orleans real estate. He thinks it's a market to be careful with though. He suggested to reverse the usual advice. When asked by Fenster what the usual advice is, he said, "Buy low, sell high."

"And why would that not apply in the Big Easy?" Fenster asked.

"In New Orleans you want to buy high and sell low," he said. Fenster looked perplexed.

"He's talking about elevation," I said. "Sea level and levies. There's a Randy Newman song about it."

"I don't know who that is, but it sounds like good advice," said Fenster smiling.

He asked where I live and I said north of San Francisco.

"San Francisco? Worst god damn place in America! It's over-rated. The people there are bums."

I told him that's why I live north of it and made a mental note not to invite him over.

He launched into a monologue on how San Francisco is where they killed Phar Lap. Phar Lap, Phar Lap, where'd I heard that I wondered—till he went on, saying, "Greatest athlete in the history of Australia." Oh yes, Phar Lap was the Australian race horse whose stuffed body had been stolen from the Melbourne museum—by Fenster according to Samo. Fenster had a lot to say about this animal. Phar Lap, the wonder horse, the prize of Australia. Phar Lap, whose name means 'lightning' in Thai, had won 37 of the 51 races of his career. Then he died mysteriously—in San Francisco. Fenster was convinced Phar Lap was done in by Mafia. As he went on praising Phar Lap and cursing San Francisco, I noticed a photo and painting of the horse on the wall near a framed headline of his American victory.

Fenster asked what I do there and before I could answer, Gupta said I kill horses for the Mafia. That drew a not-funny glare that transformed to raised eyebrows when Gupta said I'm a writer. I corrected to say I have written some with lots of help from skilled editors who made up for my lack of ability—and killed my darlings. He asked me what I write about and I said I've done a few books that relate to Japanese Zen coming to the West. He didn't recognize the titles, asked me to send him the books. He was ready to give me money on the spot. I said I don't sell books, don't keep extra ones. He can order them online, better yet, order them from the local independent bookstore. This man was not all bad. He wants to buy my books.

Some people want me to give them a book even if they have no prior interest in the subject. They think I get train loads of them for free. An acquaintance who has a seat on the stock exchange asked me for a book and I said oh gee I don't have any—I'd have to go out and buy you one. He said good. I said, oh you don't want to buy one? And he said no, that he liked to get them as gifts from the authors. I said I understood and asked him for a stock certificate. He looked at me like, are you kidding? But I don't get mad when people do this because I must confess that before I had published a book, I asked writers to give me their books. I had a friend who was giving me lots of free advice on software use. He'd published a big expensive book on batch files for DOS and I got him to give me one. At some point I realized what a foul thing I'd done and have tried to make it up to him since then.

I told Fenster he might like reading one of the books of lectures by my teacher, Shunryu Suzuki.

"What did he teach?"

"Hard to say. He emphasized practice, what we do, over what we say."

"So what did he do then?" Fenster asked? "Sit on his butt?"

"Yeah, he did that. But mainly I'd say he was tough on himself—and lenient with others."

"Sounds like a chickenshit."

"You nailed him."

"So how do you like Australia?" Fenster asked us.

"It's great," said Gupta, "especially the women, especially one woman, one woman who..."

"I love it," I said interrupting him. "I think the people here are great."

"I think that guru Rajneesh had the Aussies pegged pretty well," said Fenster. "You know of him?"

"Sure. What'd he say?"

"That Aussies are friendly, nice, insipid, boring, bland, uninspired and uninspiring. They'll put you to sleep when they open their mouths. All they want to do is drink and lie on the beach and stand around their barbies. The most useless, tedious, dull, dreary, monotonous, hopeless excuse for human beings on earth."

"Well," I said, "Rajneesh put every nationality down. It was like a running joke he used to encourage people to let go of their attachment to national identity."

"He was spot on with Australia."

"Goodness, that's not very patriotic of you."

"I'm from New Zealand."

"So why are you here?"

"Business."

"What about Phar Lap? He's Australian."

"He's a kiwi as well."

"Kiwi?" said Gupta.

"You don't know much," said Fenster.

"New Zealander," I said.

"That's not an important thing to know," said Gupta.

"You don't know what's important," said Fenster.

"Submit, Gupta," I said to him to stop a potential quarrel.

Fenster asked if I've practiced Buddhism and I said I came to the San Francisco Zen Center when I was twenty-one and have been a sort of bumbling practitioner since then. Gupta had to add I'm an admitted failure. Fenster got out of me that I was ordained as a priest though

I told him my robes are all in storage now. He laughed—kind of wickedly—as if he were trying to convey that he sees through me.

"If there's time," he said, "I'll teach you what all that is really about."

"Oh good. Thank you," I said.

I told Fenster I've been admiring his books and the room in general. He asked if I've read a lot of them. I told him I'm not a good reader but I've read some of them and into more of them. He asked if I've noticed the altars. I hadn't noticed. He took me to an alcove with a foot high Buddha statue—Thai maybe—a candle, ashes in a cup for incense, dried flowers in a vase—smart, don't have to change them, and a photo of the Dalai Lama with what looked to me like a Western Tibetan nun. He suggested I light the candle and offer some incense so I did. I told him I don't even have an altar. He said I should have an Islamic alter then—they're empty—no icons. He had one, a beautiful little ornate tile alcove in the wall by the fireplace.

Fenster was interesting but odd and intimidating. While we talked he looked us in the eye—whichever one of us he was talking to—looked without blinking and stood close moving in on our space, smiling and saying strange things. Strange things like, "Do you think you can cut off someone's head without generating bad karma?"

Without hesitation I answered, "I don't know. I don't know anything about karma." I noticed a Japanese sword hanging on the wall behind him and added, "but I don't think that would be a very nice thing to do."

"Nice?" he responded with contempt. "Life isn't nice, it's real. Now tell me—If I cut off someone's head will I have bad karma?"

"I guess, but it depends on the circumstance, the moment. I don't really know."

"Sure you know. You're a writer. You write on Buddhism. You're a priest."

"That means nothing. None of that means anything. I don't know more than anyone else. Asking me about truth is like taking a blind deaf mute primitive from the jungle, putting him on a New York Subway, and asking him to explain what just happened."

"Aren't you being a little overly modest?"

"It's worse than that," said Gupta. "It would be like asking the blind, deaf mute primitive to then create a coffee table book on the New York Subway system complete with schematics on the cars, engines, track system, electrical system, essay on the history of transportation...."

"Belt up," said Fenster interrupting him. Back to me. "Is karma like god's judgment?"

"Well, I think that the actual truth behind the words is the same, but the Hindus and Buddhists don't use that metaphor—karma doesn't indicate judgment, especially from an outside being or force. It's cause and effect, balancing."

"I didn't think you knew anything about truth."

"I don't."

"Yeah, he doesn't," Gupta said.

"Zip it."

"Look—you're demanding an answer so I'm doing my best even though I don't know."

"If I kill someone will I be killed in a later life?"

"That's a mechanical way of looking at it. That's for simplistic stories. To me the way it works is a mystery. There's nothing predictable—but as Dogen says—you know Dogen?"

"The Japanese master?"

"Yes."

"Not really."

"You've got a book of translations from the Shobogenzo up there."

"He's difficult—profound, poetic. I've never read more than a paragraph at a time of that book."

"Dogen says that you might see people who do bad things prospering and people who are virtuous suffering, but not to worry, that karma is as inescapable as one's shadow. See—he didn't try to specify how it works. It's life—it flows like water, blows like air. To think we know how it works is just arrogance."

"So I can cut off someone's head?"

"Better to stay on the safe side. What about giving them a hat instead?"

"What if they're spreading malicious rumors about me? What if they're breaking the rules of the Buddha, the precepts? What if they're trying to take what's mine? What if they're trying to kill me? What if they kill my friend, my dearest friend?" he said with his teeth gritting.

Wow. "Well," I said, "those do sound like issues you'd have to deal with. But do you think decapitation is the wisest course of action?"

"Didn't the samurai learn how to swing their swords through people with no thought and therefore no karma?"

"I was never into the whole martial arts thing," I said. "Maybe theoretically what you say's true. Maybe some people can do that. I don't know. It's not my life. It's like asking me about deep sea diving."

"It's my favorite part of Oriental thought."

"Deep sea diving?" said Gupta.

He paid no attention and went on. "You haven't read the Art of War?"

"I've read it, but I don't remember anything I can think of. Anyway, I'm a wimp. I didn't go into the army. I helped people to stay out instead. I don't hunt. I never liked contact sports. I've never been in a fight. I believe in surrender. All the men in my family have been like this."

"You don't believe in defending yourself or your country?"

"I believe in defending all beings. I've done a bit of environmental and peace work. I went into a monastery instead of the army. I think that helps to defend the country too."

"In what way?"

"In ways I'm still learning but I'd say one thing is by not turning to violence, and another is learning not to live by lies."

"Who tells lies?"

"We lie to ourselves."

"Who? Me?"

Samo's admonition to be careful what I said came back to me. "I can't speak for others. I don't know what's happening in their minds. I can only say that I lie."

"You lie? You're a liar? You're lying to me? You're not a man of your word?"

"You're getting the relative and absolute mixed up."

"So you don't lie?"

"I try to tell the truth but whatever I say about the absolute I fear is not true."

"So who lies about the absolute?"

Throwing Samo to the winds, "How about everyone including you and me."

"I thought you only knew about yourself."

"It's a hunch."

He laughed. Relief. It's exhausting to talk to him.

We beat around the Buddhist BS bush for a while longer. Gupta was obviously getting impatient. Finally Fenster said, "So you know Rudy?"

"Yes, we know Rudy," answered Gupta. "I thought you'd never ask. And we know Mindy. And we want to know where Mindy is."

"Where Mindy is?" Fenster asked. "Is she lost?"

"She's been kidnapped," he said, "And we want her back right now!" He was speaking too strongly.

I barged in. "We thought that you might be able to help us find her."

"Why did you think that? How could I help?"

"By letting her go," said Gupta.

"What on earth makes you think *I* have her?"

"Who else?"

"You're from America. Your friend gets lost and you come here. Why here? Why me? Who told you what?"

"Looked it up on the Internet," said Gupta.

"A Buddhist friend who's worked with missing people suggested we come here," I said. "He said you were an old friend of the family and might be able to help."

"That's true," Fenster said. "I am an old friend of the family."

"So where's Mindy?" said Gupta.

"Let me look into it for you. Maybe I can find out."

Fenster noted it was getting toward sunset and said we could meet again at dinner, assuring Gupta he would make some calls and see what he could find out about Mindy. This seemed to satisfy Gupta for the time being. Fenster had Stan show us to our rooms.

"Have a Captain Cook," said Stan pushing the curtain aside. I knew what he meant and walked over. The sky and ocean were sharing stunning layers of marvelous reds and yellows. He asked if I wished to do email, opened a cabinet revealing a keyboard and large flat screen monitor. He added that when it's turned on it's automatically online. Dinner would be in forty minutes and he'd call for us.

Gupta came over. "He's like Dracula," he said.

"Who? Stan? I think he's nice."

"No, you idiot! Fenster! He looks like Dracula and that's a Dracula door he came into the library through. The guy gives me the creeps."

"Good taste though," I said.

"A well-appointed room," Gupta nodded. "Top drawer."

I opened the top drawer of the bureau. "A sweater. Good call." Gupta walked to the window. I went online and was pleased to see Kelly had already sent me a new email telling about a mushroom foray he was organizing. I bragged to Gupta about how Kelly is an amateur mycologist and was pleased Gupta did not make the usual comment about getting high. That's what people think of when I mention Kelly's into mushrooms—psychedelics—that or getting

169

poisoned. Actually, I was the same way until Kelly became a mushroom hunter and I learned there was a whole world of people out there utterly fascinated with mushrooms who are into them for more than getting high or poisoned. They're like birders—pure, not anthropomorphic or greedy in their passion. I brought Kelly and Clay up to date with one small omission—not getting into the kidnapping and gangster thing. That left the weather and... let's see... I told them some of the slang I'd learned and how a lot of it bounces off rhymes—like "have a Captain Cook look."

Gupta sat at the window watching the ocean and sky further marbleize and darken.

GUESTROOM
SUNSET VIEW

CHAPTER 18
STEEL METAPHORS

Over a dinner of poached fish, baked potato, asparagus, and French bread, Fenster said he'd put some feelers out for Mindy. Maybe tomorrow he'd know something. "You have your rooms already. There's a pool out back and a spa. They're popular in America. There's no closing time. Go jump in the waves. There's a putting green. Enjoy yourselves. Library's open too."

Okay. We accepted. Didn't have much choice.

"If she's been the victim of foul play," he said, "I might be able to help you get her back—as long as she's intact. But I know this young woman and she's quite capable of running off on her own—even of making it look like she was taken—just for the sport of it."

"Mr. Fenster," I begin.

"Please, call me Bobby."

"Bobby, if you can help us to get Mindy back it would mean so much to us and to others. We care about her and we know that Rudy cares about her a great deal. We also know that you and Rudy do not care about each other these days, but we'd like to see you put an end to your animosity. A lot of people would be happier and healthier and, I'm sure, wealthier if that happened. One way to accomplish this would be to help free Mindy who is innocent, a family member. She's not involved with business. If she's someone's

171

prisoner please help us to set her free. If she's just playing around, having fun, then help us to find that out. I appeal to you as a man of wisdom and compassion."

He kept an eye on me and nodded seriously. I couldn't believe these words were coming out of my mouth and I was talking gangster business with a gangster. Where did it come from? I guess from the gangster movies I'd seen plus a slight Aussie twist. I was informed by Al Pacino and Frannie.

It was just the three of us in a big dining room at one end of a long table. Stan served heavenly cabernet. The talk turned to wine, which helped to soften the vibes between Gupta and Bobby. Eventually Gupta said he was wiped out and declined dessert and amontillado. He begged off to go to bed. Fenster suggested a little after dinner music first, assuring Gupta it would put him in a state of mind conducive to deep, peaceful sleep.

He asked Gupta if he's ever listened to Joan Sutherland. Gupta said he knows her name and thinks so. I said I'd heard her live. My mother's been on the opera board in Fort Worth forever and she took me to Dallas when I was fifteen to hear Joan Sutherland—before she was famous—Ms. Sutherland, not my mother. I was used to sleeping through the first half of the operas and just spacing out the rest, but Joan Sutherland kept me wide awake. It was indeed memorable. Fenster gasped softly and said that was her American debut.

Gupta said, "Oh—I thought she was a folk singer," which elicited a contemptuous scowl from Fenster.

"Her last American performance was in Dallas as well," Fenster said. "You didn't happen to make that did you?"

"No, but my mother did. I was in Japan."

"You obviously come from good stock."

Gupta rolled his eyes.

Fenster opened a cabinet and picked up a CD. "Here she is in *Lucia di Lammermoor*, which set her career in motion." Soon Joan Sutherland's rich, expressive voice filled the room. He listened shaking his head reverently for a few moments. "Listen to this woman— she's a genius. She had a natural gift greater than anyone else who's ever lived or who will ever live —a divine gift." Joan Sutherland continued singing and Fenster leaned back and listened. Then he sat up and said, "I've got a magnificent Doberman named Mars. He loves Joan Sutherland. He comes over and I play it for him and he sits and listens to her. Hear that voice! Every time you hear it, it's like it was being sung for the first time. She is the best. She's the greatest there ever was and that ever will be."

Gupta was starting to nod and not in agreement. Finally Joan Sutherland came to a stopping point. Fenster let Gupta go to his room. Fenster urged him to sleep as long as he wanted. Gupta said goodnight to Fenster coldly and then neutrally to me, looking deeply into me with eyes that telegraphed to find out what I could.

I found out a lot—but not about Mindy. As Fenster and I sipped sherry, he told me about himself, being terribly forthcoming. Let's see. He came from New Zealand when he was sixteen. He'd escaped poverty and an abusive immigrant German father. He started off running bets to get by and then got into selling stolen goods. Naturally he came to be known as Fenster the Fence, his first moniker. He saved enough to get a strip joint in Melbourne by the time he was in his early twenties. Then he bought a funeral home. "That opened up a lot of possibilities for me," he said with a note of fondness in his voice, "And I ended up with a little chain of funeral homes... with..." he paused with a distant gaze and a slight smile of pleasure, "with crematoriums." He turned to me. "Cremation is best, don't you think?"

"It's actually what I'm used to—though considering the number of people on earth, air pollution, and global warming, maybe a simple burial with the loved one wrapped in a sheet with a tree planted on top would be more environmentally sound. There's an English society promoting that."

"Nonsense," he scoffed. "Didn't Buddha say monks shouldn't break the earth? Better to increase the intensity and thoroughness of the incineration—scrubbers on the stacks and so forth."

"That would be good," I said.

I assumed he has dipped his beak more recently into illicit avenues of income enhancement, but he only mentioned legit stuff, relegating all illegal activities to his youth. He said he'd invested some in the Aussie and New Zealand film industries and in one Hollywood film, *The Usual Suspects*, on the condition that a prominent character be named after him.

Recently, he revealed, leaning over and whispering, he has gotten deeper into the flesh business with porno sites on the Internet. "Whatever can be done out there," he said, leaning back and making a sweeping gesture, "can be done better in a computer. But I still got the strip joint in Melbourne. If you come there you'd like it. It's got class."

He kept drinking. Me too. We were off the amontillado and onto the Irish whiskey. That was good. I can only drink so much sweet stuff like sherry, even the good stuff.

He said it wasn't the martial arts that got him interested in Buddhism. It was an Aussie woman named Robina who had become a Tibetan Buddhist nun. "Not just a nun—more like one of their teachers. She wears the purple robes and shaved her head."

"Maybe a Rimpoche," I said.

"Yeah, that's it." He said she has a program for working with prisoners in Australia and with men on death row in countries like America that have the death penalty. He knows someone Robina ordained in an Australian prison. But he didn't want to get further into that and brushed it off saying everyone had a friend who'd gotten into trouble—like he was a normal law abiding citizen. That was her picture with the Dali Lama by the Buddhist altar. He'd heard her speak in Melbourne and said he has a movie on her made by her son. It tells about how she went from being a tough street kid in Melbourne to becoming a Black Panther in New York City, then an angry man-hating feminist, and then a student of a Tibetan lama in New York, and finally a Buddhist nun and teacher. Now she travels all over the world for her prison project.

"She's celibate," he said. She used to be wild. She told a story about some guys wanting to rape her and she just pulled off her panties, lay down in their car, and asked who's first? And that scared 'em off. Then somehow he got into talking about the pure quality of the vaginas of celibate nuns and segued into the smell of Joan Sutherland's nether regions, which he was sure were atomized with heavenly perfume.

He guided me to a walk-in closet, and what had he collected in there but costumes Sutherland had worn in different operas. With a creepy smile he invited me to smell the crotch area of a petticoat. I felt obligated to do so and said it had a delightful aroma though I exaggerated to please him. Then he had me feel the material of one dress and inspect the layered ruffles of another. He seemed hypnotized by the texture and I remembered Aldous Huxley's comments on the feel and gaze of folds of cloth leading to transcendent states of mind.

He, Fenster—not Huxley—took me into a room with a number of computers, scanners, printers, and such. On the walls were expansive landscape and seascape paintings. There was a young guy working away. "This is Sid," Bobby said, "from Sydney." If that's so, why isn't it Syd? I said hi. Sid turned around and smiled. There was a five count Rubric's cube on his desk. Fenster said Sid runs the porn sights with Mel from Melbourne where they're headquartered.

"But it doesn't matter where they are physically located," he said, "they're still always working together."

"With Cy," Sid said, "from Cyberspace."

"Sid's my boy," said Fenster. "He's added a whole new dimension to my life in the realms of both business and leisure."

He had Sid show me some games he'd created. I've not been into computer games since the Ms. Pac-Man days, but I was happy to see what Sid was up to. We went into an adjoining room with a wide screen, very wide—like ten feet. There were comfortable purple corduroy seats with keyboards, earphones, joysticks, steering wheels, and mice awaiting the sitter. Fenster said the room's for movies or games or even working on the sites. Sid put up an image on the screen with many little jagged pieces, a jigsaw puzzle. He had me try it for a minute, moving the pieces with a mouse, and then I saw "auto-solve," hit that, and watched it piece itself together with a surprise unfolding as it did so—a delectable young lady immodestly attired—only toenail polish. He showed me games that worked with moving objects and revealed videos that lead to coital sequences to the extent to which one could solve some problems. Fenster said the next step would be in the area of inter-active virtual reality. He said in Melbourne he had a lab where technicians were working on a suit within a surrounding sensory cocoon that would give one the sensation that the virtual object of desire was actually touching one and touching in any way one can be touched.

"Actually I got this idea first from an old James Bond film," he said. "There's a lot of others working on it all over the world. It's gonna get so good your brain won't know the difference."

Good lord, that's just what I don't need, I thought. Sounds like a trip you might never come back from.

They showed me puzzles that got more and more complicated—word jumbles, sliding block, and Rubric, which I'd heard of and new names such as tanedra, plainim, and chain-reaction. I told them I can't do them—it's just not in me. I have friends who've been into puzzles. There's a guy at Zen Center who can solve the word jumbles in the newspaper almost as fast as the answers can be said. I'd be sitting there with cobwebs between the paper and me. Fenster asked if I play chess and I said I don't like to—just not my trip. I used to play bridge but I'm too scatterbrained for it. But I read bridge. I try to read a bridge column every day. More if I can. Why don't I play it then he wanted to know? I get confused and it's stressful. Do you ask people who read detective novels why they aren't detectives? And why would somebody watch porno instead of being with a real live person?

"A lot of people are frustrated," he said. "It's not as easy as finding a bridge partner. And we're making it closer to the real thing every day."

"You're doing this because you care," I said. He ignored it.

"You liked that book on mazes and labyrinths in the library," said Fenster. Hey, I didn't tell him that. "Show David some of our cyber mazes."

Sid showed me a selection of mazes on the screen and I agreed to try one in the form of a traditional hedge. I chose intermediate difficulty because I didn't want it to take too long. It was fairly extensive and complicated, constructed so one couldn't see inside except where one was—not like looking down on a rat's maze. Using Gupta's method I bore to the right with my joystick and, sure enough, got through it fairly quickly.

"Well done," said Fenster.

"A wall follower," said Sid. "That's the best way for simple mazes."

"A wall follower?" I thought I was going to amaze them and they immediately had a box to put it in. "Simple maze? What other kinds of mazes are there?"

"Many," said Sid. "That was a two dimensional maze." He brought up a graphic of a three dimensional maze. It was like the 2D but with different levels. "You can wall follow this too if you treat up as northeast and down as southwest. And then you can get into higher dimensions and hyper-dimensions and there are a lot of other factors, which come into play in conceptual mazes."

Good lord. I felt like a kindergartener visiting a college—not that I've ever let that hold me back. Asked them if they knew of the Maze near Perth. Sid had heard of it but Fenster hadn't. I told him when we get Mindy back and I have time to mess around again I'll take him there. Ha ha. Sure. I told them about a project Gupta had in mind to build a maze with hedges in planters on wheels so the maze can be reordered at will.

"Hey, that'd be good," said Fenster. "You could let someone go in and then close it off. Nothing would work. Wall followers would go crazy. Keep that in mind, Sid."

Back in the library Fenster poured Irish whiskey and we talked. He was getting a little sloshed, a little slosheder I should say, and started lecturing me who was getting sloshedest. "The only type of Buddhism that really works is the way of the warrior, the samurai kind," he said. "It's real. It's about life and death. We've got enemies and we've got friends. We're good to our friends and we pull our swords when we meet our enemies. We've just got to learn how to do it without anger. We've got to be clear about it. These people that go meditate in temples all the time think they're getting all enlightened. Let's see how enlightened they are when I cut their heads off."

Uh oh—there's that idea again.

He went on and on and started to repeat himself. He put down Buddhist priests as phony hypocrites and said they should be whacked. "They build empires so they can sit around and do nothing, get soft. It would be alright if they made samurais out of their students but they don't. They make weakling devotees out of them."

I asked him if he's had any actual experience with any Buddhists this impression is based on and he said he's met a few and can tell by what he's read in books. He told me how lucky I am to have run into him, that I could have gone my whole life wandering about in sissy Buddhism like a chicken with my head cut off—just can't seem to shake that metaphor. But now he's going to enlighten me as to what's really real about Buddhism—the ability to fight and kill (and maim I guess) without reaping bad karma. And who should be his idol in all this? The man whom he calls "the first samurai and a great Buddhist?" None other than the warrior mounted on a horse in a painting on the back wall of the library. He asked if I know who it is.

"A Chinese or a Mongol warrior?" I guess.

"The great Mongol warrior—Genghis Khan."

"Oh."

He then delivered a lecture about the greatness of Genghis Khan. "When you hear the name of Genghis Khan," he said, "you might have an image of a ruthless barbarian with hordes destroying all in their path through overwhelming numbers. Not so. He conquered with inferior numbers through superior tactics. He was a great genius. He grew up in chaos—the tribes were independent and always attacking each other. His brilliant idea was to change the game. Rather than hit and run it was unite or perish. Those who joined prospered. The Empire expanded and eventually spread into Russia, Eastern Europe, India, and China. Kahn developed a sophisticated legal code. Those who didn't want to go along with him met the sword. Khan's army would kill every living being—all the people and all the animals—the babies, the dogs, the ducks—in a merciless, orgiastic blood fest."

Fenster especially enjoyed detailing these mass murder sprees and said sometimes at night he awoke and lay in bed looking out the window at the stars and could remember riding into battle, into massacres with Khan, wailing out their petrifying battle cry and holding high sharpened spikes that bore the severed heads of their victims. Entranced, with eyes rolling slightly back into his head, he spoke nostalgically of spending whole days severing heads, gathering them into great piles, and then affixing them to the poles to be used in the charge.

"You haven't gotten to the 'great Buddhist' part," I said. "Where does that come in?"

"Don't you see?" he said. "This man transformed the world. Where there was chaos he brought order, where there was crime, he brought law. At the height of his empire it was said a virgin could walk without fear for eight thousand miles carrying a bag of gold.

"And it wasn't just that. Khan also believed in freedom of religion. He stopped the Muslims from spreading their religion by the sword and he did this by being stronger. Where Khan ruled, Muslims, Jews, Christians, Buddhists, Taoists, Zoroastrians, Hindus, you name it—they lived together in peace. None could tell the other what to believe or to do. He preferred Buddhism and kept a Buddhist monk at his side through all the years to advise him and sometimes, I admit, to hold him back."

Fenster went on about Khan, action and non action, life and death, form and emptiness, and enlightenment, which he thought he knew quite well. He made an observation in the course of his rants I thought about, lying under warm covers after I managed to escape and get to bed. "One thing a good student and a good teacher have in common," he said, "is they only deal in questions they both know the answer to. The answer comes first, then the question." That's something to think about. I don't know. Hmm. Wonder where he picked that up?

So I'd met Fenster's four heroes—two women and two men, yin and yang, each of them represented on his walls among the books. There was Genghis Khan—the sword of order, Robina—the compassionate, Joan Sutherland—the artist become one with the muse, and Phar Lap—the ideal athlete dying young. To him they walked on the earth and soared in the heavens, each demonstrating a noble form and power he fairly worshiped. I feared his expression of their inspiration. I feared his rationalizations of any position. I feared he was one capable of making great errors of judgment, arrogantly confusing form and emptiness, where one takes a teaching for spirit and tries to apply it to the world—and vice versa. His take on things made me shiver. It seemed he could confuse mass murder with wisdom, war with peace. I feared he might make the Mansonian mis-

take, the grand delusion of so many rulers, conquerors, revolution-
aries, and do-gooders, the Blues Brothers' calling card which reads,
"We're on a mission from god."

This concern of mine had come up more or less. I guess a drunk-
en comment I made had put an end to the evening's lecture. I stand
by the content. It was the lack of discretion that was drunken. Fenster had gone to the wall and taken down the sword. It was a fine
looking specimen with a carved handle, a little shorter than some
of the Japanese swords I'd seen. He held it up. "This is the sword
that cuts through delusion. It's the two-sided sword of wisdom and
compassion."

"No," I said, "the sword of wisdom and compassion you couldn't
find in the material world if you looked forever. You're making the
mistake that fundamentalists make, that movie makers make—taking the metaphors literally. It's Taliban Buddhism. The swordless
sword of Buddhism cuts both ways—wisdom and compassion. That
sword is just a sharp hunk of metal."

Fenster looked at me with rage in his eyes. "Someday you
may find a hunk of metal cuts deeper than your insipid ideas," he
growled. A menacing exhalation, then with finality, "Goodnight!"
He departed the room by the doorway in the bookshelves, turned
before disappearing and said, "And if you write about me, I'll... sue
you!"

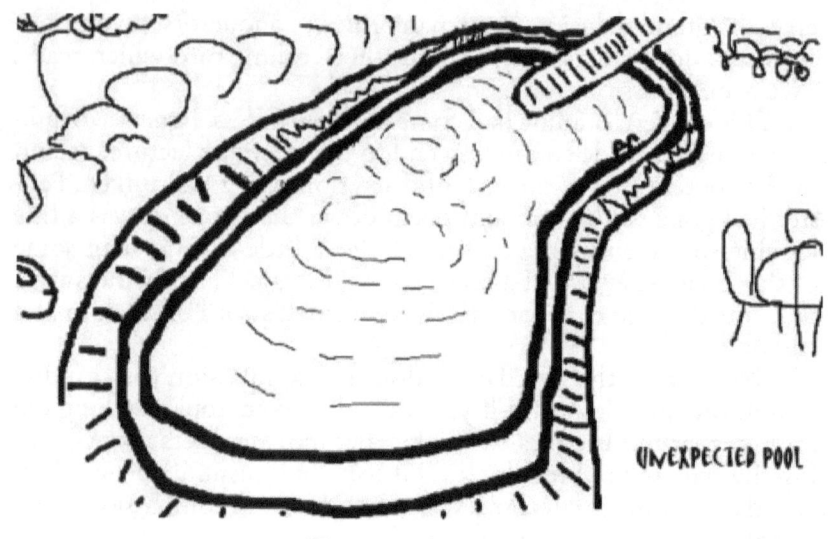

UNEXPECTED POOL

CHAPTER 19
HIDING

A voice was calling my name in the dark. I shook my head. A figure came up to my bed.

"Who is it? Can I help you?"

"It's me stupid—Gupta."

"Oh. Goodnight Gupta. Nice seeing you." I roll over.

"Get up. Get up. I want to look around."

"What? Huh?"

"Get up. Come on."

"Are you sure?" I said.

"Hey—while you're having fun with that villain, would you please try to remember that our friend Mindy has been kidnapped and may be in great danger and that you and I are also in great danger if she's not back soon?"

"Wouldn't we be more effective after a good night's sleep? Be energetic in the morning and ready to roll?"

"Except there may be something for us to find here. What if *she's* here?"

We sneaked downstairs and prowled around opening doors slowly, peeking in, using the handy compact flashlights that were thoughtfully supplied with our rooms. The only sign of life in the house was coming from the area where Sid works. We entered a back room and found two empty beds.

"What are we doing entering rooms in his house?" I asked. "Mindy wouldn't be in his house. You know who would—Fenster and his wife, Sid, or Stan, or those two guys."

There was a shed nearby without any windows. Nope—just tools. There was a garage with eight wide doors. We peeked in a window and saw a new Mercedes sedan. Next was an old racing car, the type that's cylindrical with thin front tires with spokes. The rest were hard to see. Not a place to keep someone though. We heard Joan Sutherland's voice coming from the house and sneaked over into some bushes. Through a window we saw Fenster in the computer room. Gupta's jaw dropped.

"He's wearing a dress," he whispered.

"Yes. It's one of Joan Sutherland's," I answered. "It's gorgeous too, though I don't think he quite fills it out."

"Yuck," said Gupta.

Fenster was lip-synching an aria, dramatically gesturing before an imaginary audience. Gupta nudged me, pointed to Fenster, stuck his tongue out of the side of his mouth, crossed his eyes, and twirled his finger round by his temple in the universal sign of insanity. We continued squatting in the dirt clods watching Fenster do his Joan Sutherland. Her aria ended and he walked across the room. Sid was at a computer. They talked. Interesting working relationship. We tried to hear what they were saying but couldn't—the orchestra still going in the background.

Gupta squeezed my arm tightly. I glanced up at him. With a frightened look on his face he nodded to the side. I turned to see what he was nodding at. Oh-oh. A Doberman was sitting on the grass staring at us from outside the bushes. We moved slowly to the side. It started to growl. We stopped. It stopped. We started to move again and it growled again.

"Just don't move and everything will be alright," came a voice. I looked to the side. There was a face looking straight at us. It was Shorts, his index finger pressed against his lips. Something soft was over my mouth with a hand pressing on it hard. Must be the short one, I thought as I fell into his arms and faded away.

I wake up with a headache. Ouch. I wonder where I am. Earth. Um-hmm. Uh—Australia. Francine—no. Gupta. Mindy... Mindy oh yes. Uh-oh—we're at the gangster's place, Fenster. Went looking around. The bushes. Doberman. My back hurts. What is this? Can't move. Can't speak. I'm gagged—and blindfolded—and tied up. I hurt all over. Ropes—ropes are tight. There's someone pressing on me. It must be Gupta. Oh yeah—we were caught in the bushes looking in on Fenster and Sid. There, I've figured everything out. This feels awful. What can I do? Guess I should wake Gupta up. Why? Why not get some sleep even in this state. Probably won't be able to do anything anyway. I hear voices—and footsteps. A door opens.

"They're still out."

"How you want to do it?"

"I want to stab them."

"Drown 'em."

"Too much trouble. Lemme stab them. It'll just take a few times each."

"Just hold 'em down under the water till they stop wiggling and then take them to Amenity."

"I want to stab them. Come on."

"Too messy. We could just put plastic bags over their heads."

"Okay. But that's not fair. I never get to stab anyone anymore."

"Are there any plastic bags in here?"

"I don't know. Let's look."

I started breathing hard. I felt a shaking. It was Gupta next to me. The men were looking around for plastic bags, Gupta's shaking got worse.

"Maybe in the car."

"OK. Let's look in the car."

As soon as they're gone Gupta and I were thrashing about rolling over each other, bruising ourselves on whatever it was we hit up against.

"God damnit! There's no bags here either! Maybe over in the trash," came one of the men's voices from outside.

Gupta was rubbing on something going back and forth fast. I stayed still. I heard him suck in a lot of air and breathe in and out heavily—then his whispering voice.

"Got it! Rubbed the duct tape off. Jeez, my mouth's bleeding like crazy. I'm gonna try to reach my hands and pull the rope or bite it—so don't do anything. Yoga, do your thing."

I grunted softly. We sure didn't want to alert the Goony Twins. I assumed it was them. Gupta struggled and twisted. I could feel it but I didn't know if he was making any progress. My pants were wet. Our backs were pressed together and then he twisted us so I was face down on the wood floor. He was mashing me in. I didn't complain.

"Got it!" he exclaimed but not too loud.

I lay there.

"Come on baby, come on baby, come on baby!" he encouraged himself.

I felt a loosening. "Ouch!" I talked! He tore off my duct tape.

In a moment we were free of our bindings. There was a window in back. Gupta crawled over and slowly opened it. It creaked, terrifying me. He stuck his head out and looked left and right and crawled out. I followed. It was getting light. We could see the beach behind us. We crawled across sand with splotches of grass for a ways then into and through bushes and were up and running as fast as we could away from the cabin. Neither of us said a word. We just ran the other way in terror—away from the beach weaving around trees and bushes. I slowed down and then we stopped.

"Not as young as you, gotta catch my breath," I panted. "I peed in my pants."

"I did too. At least I didn't..."

"Me either."

"Where the heck do you think we are?" asked Gupta.

"I don't know but I suspect near Fenster's place. We want to get away from that beach and that cabin and Fenster's house."

"Yes, yes, yes. And away from the Goony Twins. Let's go."

We ran again. He held back so we could stay together. We ran and ran and ran then charged through some dense bushes and went flying right into... into water! With one resounding splash after another. It was a swimming pool. Like wind-up toys we just keep moving our arms and legs till we'd swum to the other side, crawled up, and shaken ourselves off.

"Whata we do now?" asked Gupta. "Knock on the door here or keep going?"

A woman wearing a white apron stirring something in a wide green bowl came out the back door of the expansive white wood home and looked at us with astonishment. Before she could react we're running up to her pleading for help.

"Hold on boys," she said. "Hold on. Now what can I do for you? Oh my gosh!" she exclaimed, looking at Gupta's mouth, "you're bleeding terribly. Let me get something for that."

Gupta spoke. "There are gangsters trying to kill us. We just escaped from them. Call the police."

"No, no, don't call the police," I said. "Do you have a phone we can use? They've got our car. We've got to get out of here. Maybe you could give us a ride."

"There are gangsters who want to kill us," said Gupta. "They may come looking for us here."

"Slow down now," she said. "Why don't you just come inside and let me clean up this cut and dry your clothes. Nobody's going to find you here."

A few moments later we were sitting in warm dry robes drinking orange juice and the nice woman was taking our cloths off to a drier. She had thoroughly cleaned his lip and put a large band-aid on it.

"At least we washed the pee out of our clothes," Gupta said when she was gone.

We sat and watched the sky and surrounding area brighten up. The woman returned with a tray of plates with scrambled eggs, Canadian bacon, toast, and marmalade. After placing the tray on the table, she carefully checked Gupta's lip.

"That's most kind of you," he said.

"My husband's coming in a minute and he'll take care of you. Don't worry about a thing. He knows the police around here well. I've got to run along now."

"Thank you very much ma'am," I said with relief and wondering if they say ma'am in Australia.

She went down the spacious hallway. It looked familiar—like something in some movie I guess—or a country club I've been in.

"A pleasant change of venue," said Gupta

"Better service too," I said.

"That's uncanny," Gupta said looking out toward the backyard.

"What," I answered pouring us more coffee.

"The sun's rising from the direction we came from."

"So?"

"We came from the beach."

"The last time I was near here, in Dunsborough with Frannie, there was a bay. Fenster's home is just on the bay."

"No—While you were online last night I watched the sun go down through your bedroom window, which faced the beach. You saw it. Fenster's home was on the sunset beach, on the West."

"Oh yeah. Well, I don't know—we're in Australia—everything's upside down here right? Or maybe it's a sort of mass hysterical dyslexic thing where our brains are getting it backwards because we've been traumatized. I don't know—I'm confused."

"Let's see," said Gupta, "if the sun's coming up from that way, then it went down from the other..."

There was the sound of footsteps, footsteps coming down some stairs. We turned away from the back yard to face the interior.

Thoughts raced. Her husband was coming. Good. Those guys are surely looking for us. Wonder what we're going to do. Our wallets are back at Fenster's along with the car keys and the car. Does this guy know Fenster or know of him? Probably don't want to call the police. Or do we?

"Let's stand up," said Gupta. "It's more polite don't you think? Especially since we're in bathrobes."

We stood up. A Doberman ran out toward us growling softly. Gupta and I tensed. The man came into view. We froze with horror. The dog kept growling.

"Don't worry about Mars," he said.

"It's Fenster!" Letting out big whoops Gupta and I spun around and tore out toward the back door only to come sliding to a stop in front of the Goony Twins who were standing by the exit looking at us menacingly. Trapped. We turned around.

"Good morning Bobby," I said to break the silence.

"Good morning. You've finished your breakfast?"

"I think we're finished period," said Gupta.

"Oh don't worry. Sit back down. Everything's fine. I see you finally got to use the pool."

"The water was just right," I said.

"What the hell is going on?" said Gupta.

"I think I may have a clue that could lead you to Mindy." He looked at Gupta. "It's okay. Don't worry."

"Don't worry?!" said Gupta. "They were gonna stab us, drown us, suffocate us, kill us, turn us into lifeless corpses."

"That's a tautology," I said. "Just corpses alone would do. By definition they're lifeless."

Gupta turned to me in anguish. "No! You've gotta stop doing that!"

Fenster intervened. "They were angry because you were snooping around. That's not showing proper manners for house guests."

Gupta just emitted frustrated pre-verbal utterances.

"It's also not being the perfect host to murder your guests," I offered, "even if they do break some rules of decorum."

"Well, the boys have to have some fun."

"Fun! I almost gagged on my—on my gag," said Gupta. "David probably almost had a heart attack."

"I'm sorry. It gets awfully tedious around here for them. And that's unfortunate about your wound there," he said looking out at the pool.

He gestured to the Goony Twins and they went away.

"We ran away from the beach," Gupta said, "and now we're back at your place, which is on the beach."

"We boomeranged!" I said. "How appropriate."

"Not quite," said Fenster. He took us to an observation deck on his roof where there was a serious guy with binoculars. In front of us was the ocean and in back we could see the bay over the trees. We could barely see land way far off beyond through a mist.

"You're on a little peninsula," he said.

"I thought we were running east," said Gupta "and we were running west."

Little did I know I'd be tested when Francine's Uncle James had pointed this out.

Fenster's wife brought us our dry clothes. He invited us back down to his library if invite is the right word. We met him there correctly attired a few moments later.

"I've got a clue," Fenster said. "Follow it and it may lead you to Mindy...eventually."

"What do you mean, 'a clue' and 'eventually?'" Gupta asked rather hotheadedly.

"You know where she is?" I said.

"Bear with me," he said. "I just want you to go on a little treasure hunt. She is a treasure isn't she?"

"What sort of friggin' game are you trying to play while Mindy's life may be at..."

"Silence!" Fenster demanded. "I'll start you off with an easy clue."

"Tell us now, right now, where..."

"If you want to see her again..." Fenster interrupted. Gupta got quiet. "Good. If... if... then you'll pay attention, close attention, to the clue I have when I'm ready to give it to you. You'll find the answer in this room and then you'll go."

"Okay—what is it?" Gupta asked resigned.

"But first, let's listen to an angel sing," Fenster said to him. He pressed "play." I motioned for Gupta to sit down drilling my eyes into him to convey to him that he must cool off and go with this guy's flow because this guy's in charge.

Joan Sutherland came on. It was rather soothing and beautiful once I gave in to it and sank back in my leather-bound overstuffed chair.

"My Doberman, Mars," Fenster said to Gupta, leaning over, "he comes in when I put on Joan Sutherland and he loves her. He sits and listens to her attentively each time." Fenster gestured and, as he said, there was Mars sitting by the door.

"Oh yes," said Gupta. "Charming dog."

"Silence. Hear that voice? Every time you hear it, it's like it was being sung for the first time. She is the best. She's the greatest there ever was and ever will be. She's got a divine gift."

It sounded familiar.

Finally Joan Sutherland's concert was over.

"Well, thanks a lot," said Gupta. "Can we have that information on Mindy now?"

"Did you see the sword on the wall?" Fenster asked him.

"Yes I did," Gupta answered. "But can we..."

"I talked with your so-called Buddhist friend about it last night but he doesn't respect it. His Buddhism is unmanly."

"Now, now," I said scolding him.

He ignored me. "You're ancestors are in the great tradition of the Bhagavad-Gita, the holy scripture in which Krishna instructs Arjuna in the meaning of god, ethics, and warfare. Arjuna's got David's problem—he's a namby-pamby who doesn't think it's right to go to war—especially against his cousins. Krishna sets him straight. Do your duty. Kill or be killed."

"I've read it," said Gupta. "It's not quite the emphasis I'd...."

"Genghis Khan had that manly spiritual practice. He cleansed the world with that spirit and with the blood of the weak and undisciplined. He cut through delusion and he cut through those in his way. The Japanese knew Buddhism and fighting could be compatible. They could swing the sword and be Buddha."

"Yeah, brainwashed kids—and they killed a bunch of you guys," I said.

"That's beside the point now. They could take life or give their own as easily as the petals of a dandelion are blown into the wind. Now they may have lost that spirit."

"And they lost two million people to that spirit," I said. "They had propaganda like that in the thirties and forties. I think you should read Brian Victoria's Zen at War to balance your philosophy."

"It's not just the Japanese Buddhists who can cut off heads without breaking their vows," Fenster went on ignoring me. "Three Tibetan monks were found beheaded in Dharamsala at the Dalai Lama's temple as part of an ongoing argument over whether a particular deity should be recognized."

"That's not Buddhism to me. It's just violence," I said.

"You have a lot to learn young man."

"Well, that's half-flattering."

"You may have to learn it the hard way—the hard steel way," he said, gritting his teeth on the metallic word. "You didn't seem to learn anything last night. You squandered your opportunity and so you must pay."

"You certainly have some interesting opinions about Buddhism," I said.

"They aren't opinions. They're the immutable truth."

"Jeez man," said Gupta, "How about the information on Mindy please? You guys are driving me crazy."

"You're hopeless," said Fenster looking at Gupta. "It would not be bad karma to slice a sword through your neck."

"Fine," said Gupta. "But how about telling us about Mindy first?"

"Yes. It's time for the clue," Fenster said, pulling out an envelope from his jacket's inside pocket and placing it on the table. "I'm going away now. It's been a mixed pleasure meeting you both. If you have any spine and any sense you'll find your precious darling. If you don't, I fear you'll never see her again. It's alright either way. Nothing is born and nothing dies. We are living in a cosmic dream in which the fittest survive a moment longer and the fools are cut to pieces a moment earlier. Good day gentlemen."

With that, Fenster departed through the bookshelf door.

"I think he's getting his Buddhism mixed up with his Darwin," I said. "His understanding of karma—well that's the type that gets you turned into a fox. He's mixing his levels."

"A fox?"

"Yes, there's an old Chinese story of a priest named Hyakujo— in Japanese that is—who thought he was beyond karma and so he turned into a fox. You see, one day..."

"David! Shut up! Don't think about foxes! It doesn't matter! He's crazy! Hell, you're crazy too!" Gupta stammered as he opened the envelope. "This is what matters!"

There was a piece of paper inside. Gupta held it up to the light. I crowded in. It read:

An uninhabited place is one without greed, anger, or delusion.

A moment of silence.

"Now what the hell does that mean?" asked Gupta.

"Let's see," I said, "let's see. Well, he's got these themes here at the house—Phar Lap, Joan Sutherland, Robina, and Genghis Khan and the Japanese sword. Maybe it's something to do with one of them."

"My mind's a blank," Gupta said.

I sat down. Gupta sat down. I looked at the chess set for a connection. Gupta looked at the crocodile. A clock on the wall ticked. We kept turning to the piece of paper.

An uninhabited place is one without greed, anger, or delusion.

"It's Buddhism," I said after some thought. "Maybe Zen. It could mean a hermit's hut, a place where one meditates. The uninhabited place means a place or a person with no self—realizing emptiness—when you drop an idea of self you are free of the three poisons—greed, anger, and delusion."

"That's too philosophical. Uninhabited. Uninhabited. Where is there a place that no one lives?"

"I think it may be early Chinese." I looked at the shelves.

Gupta started to look around. "Where is it no one lives? Where no one goes? How about the WC? Nobody lives in there." He went in.

I looked around for a book that might have that sort of message. Gupta came back out.

"I searched thoroughly."

We thought and thought and looked and looked and sat and sat and looked and looked again.

"I don't like this," said Gupta. "We're getting nowhere. Look how much time has passed."

"Where is it that nobody goes at all?" I said.

"Like in the fire?" he said walking to the fireplace and looking on the stone shelf above.

"No body, no being, no sentient being."

"No Buddha," Gupta said perfunctorily.

"No Buddha! That's it!"

I rush to the Islamic altar near the fireplace and pick up a book right next to it. "Red Pine's *The Zen Teaching of Bodhidharma!*" I exclaim. "Right next to the Islamic altar with no Buddha, no Allah, no Mohammed, no idols, no icons—where no one lives! He didn't even want to put the book on the altar out of respect so he put it on the shelf right next to it. Here's an envelope! On page fifty-three. And look—here's that quote: *An uninhabited place is one without greed, anger, or delusion.* And he said it was easy. Interesting that he chose that particular..."

"We don't need to think about that damn quote anymore!" shouted Gupta. "Let's get on with it! What's next? Read what's in the envelope! Let's find Mindy!"

PARKED AT FENSTER'S GATE

CHAPTER 20
SEEKING

*So you turned pine needles and found these planted seeds.
Congratulations. Now thrust through three blades above
where one lives in leaf of glass and sneeze this which hales
from the very first. If you can't swallow it, then think about
what it is.*

Gupta and I stared at the piece of paper. Nothing.

"Good lord," I said. "I guess the first one *was* easy."

"Where is that son of a..."

"Forget it man. We don't have any choice. Don't waste our time
with anger. Okay?"

"OK. Let's go," he said.

Sid appeared just then with our wallets and keys.

I said good morning to him and he smiled. I asked where Stan
was and he said Stan had a day off. The golf cart with plaid awning
and serious driver was waiting.

"How'd you get this job?" I asked Sid.

"Met an associate of Bobby's in prison."

"What were you in for?"

"Hacking."

"Oh. Do you know who Robina is?"

"Sure. She came regularly to my prison. I told Bobby about her."

"Why can't the others be as nice as you and Stan?" said Gupta.

"Takes all kinds," said Sid. "But I wouldn't recommend testing Stan or me."

Zooming out of there in the Porsche, I suggested to Gupta that since we didn't know where we were going it probably wouldn't be necessary to risk getting a ticket speeding to get there. And we might be going in the wrong direction.

He complied. "This car wants to be driven fast though."

"Seven," I said.

"Seven?"

"Seven as in seven, six, five, four, three, two, one, zero, bang you're dead."

"Oh yes. Do you have to remind me?"

We mulled over the new clue. I tried to find some connection to Fenster's heroes but nothing came to me. "This is a treasure hunt, Gupta. The guy has put us on a treasure hunt. I can't believe it."

"He is so demented. When this is over I'm going to go back and... and..."

"And get your head cut off. How about forgetting the revenge for now and let's concentrate on the hunt."

I took out the small envelope and opened up the note again. "Nice paper—a lot of cloth in it."

"Would you stop that!"

"Okay. Okay. Let me read the whole thing over again first. *So you turned pine needles.*"

"Pine needles are just pine leaves."

"Sure. Double meaning—pages and Red Pine. So that means we turned the pages of Red Pine's book. *And found these planted seeds,* which must mean that the following are the clues, the seeds that are planted. And *congratulations.* So all that we can put on a shelf for now. It just says 'good going and here's the next clue.' Agreed?"

"Agreed," Gupta said driving onward. "Dunsborough is the next town."

"Check on gas."

"Gas in Dunsborough."

"And thanks for not looking at me while we're talking."

"Why would I do that? I've got to watch the road."

"It's what they do in movies. It drives me crazy. If those scenes were accurate there'd be all sorts of bloody accidents in the films and they'd never get to advance the plot. You can't look away for more than a second safely."

"I don't want to look at you anyway. You're not that attractive."

"I think they do that cause they've found it's too boring, not good cinema to have one person looking straight ahead concentrating with frequent quick glances at the rear and side view mirrors when they're supposed to be engaging and involved in snappy banter."

"Fascinating—now why don't you snap back at that clue."

"Okay. So this part is the clue: *Now thrust through three blades above where one lives in leaf of glass and sneeze this which hales from the very first. If you can't swallow it, then think about what it is.* What could that mean?"

"That's impenetrable. I'll drive—you solve riddle."

"Thrust through three blades. Stab with three knives? Three forks in a river? In a road. Maybe there are three forks in the road somewhere but I can't look at the map while you're driving or I'll get sick. Reading this clue has taken me to my limit."

"Inner ear inheritance," said Gupta.

"Yep. But Kelly can read continually even on windy roads—so it skipped a generation."

"Fascinating again, but he's not here. We'll look at the map when we stop. Let's keep going. Three forks is only one remote possibility and we can stop and think about it if we come to a place like that," Gupta said staring straight ahead.

We did come to a place like that. Gupta pulled into a gas station that was at a fork in the road with a smaller road to the side. We figured it could be seen as three forks. There was a store there where we got some snacks.

"Oh no," said Gupta. "Look at this." He picked up a tabloid with a headline reading, "More Death in Melbourne." Inside there was a photo of a dead man lying in a pool of blood.

"Black and white blood looks scarier than in color," I said.

"That could be us, man," said Gupta. "It gives me the chills. And these guys are probably getting killed by Rudy and Fenster's boys just for being members of the other side. Maybe they haven't even done anything that bad. But we've done something bad. We've lost Mindy. We might even get tortured before they kill us."

"It *is* frightening," I said. "All the more reason to get on the trail of this clue."

"Which road do we take?" he said.

"I don't know. Let's look at the clue again."

"Three... three... Okay—let's go to the next. Above where one lives," I read.

"*Above where one lives.* Where does one live? In a house? In an apartment? Above a house," he says.

"Overhouse. Outhouse."

"What's the name of that place where Frannie lives? Dwelling?" he scratches his head.

"Dwellingup! Dwellingup! Above where one lives!"

"Which way to Dwellingup?"

"Davo! Guppy!"

"Why hi there!" I said.

Hug for each of us.

"What are you doing here?"

"Just happened to be in the neighborhood," said Gupta.

"Frannie! Am I glad to see you!" I said.

"Come on in. How's Mindy? What's new? What happened to your mouth Guppy?"

"Hmm—we'll get to that."

"We've got some catching up to do," I said. And then, looking down. "What are you wearing on your wrists?"

Frannie had been having a hard time. She'd been sad about her mother. Her vacation wasn't over but she didn't want to play. She'd been staying alone making necklaces and bracelets and hanging decorations with lots of little tiny beads and stones and stuff to sell at crafts fairs but the repetitive detail work had gotten to her—carpel tunnel syndrome. At first I was worried she'd cut her wrists. But that's not like her. She's not a complainer so I didn't even know she had the carpel tunnel. She'd moved to working with larger objects and paint, activity that uses her hands and wrists in different ways. There was paper hanging up to dry she'd just pressed the night before.

"Used the lint you brought," she said. "Getting ready to do more."

While letting her in on what had happened to Mindy and the frightening peculiarities of our visit with Fenster, Gupta and I scarfed up the leftovers in her fridge. Then we slept for a couple of hours. We were exhausted but couldn't sleep long with Mindy's dilemma pressing on us. Frannie had been cogitating on the conundrum. She'd written it up on the door to her refrigerator.

She had a line going through "above where one lives" and had written "In Dwellingup" over it so that it read: *Now thrust through three blades in Dwellingup in leaf of glass and sneeze this which hales from the very first. If you can't swallow it, then think about what it is.*

"How did he know about Dwellingup?" I wonder aloud.

"I know," said Gupta. "Remember that first night when the four of us were at the pub and Mindy and Frannie started listing all the things we should see. There was Dwellingup and stuff near here on it. Maybe they took the list from the bathroom wastebasket."

"Oh yeah, you didn't want it after it had fallen on the floor below the urinals. Maybe they were watching Mindy and picked it up."

"With latex gloves I would think."

"Well, let's see. Maybe that will help. What from around here would be on that list. I don't have it. It's with my stuff at the hostel. It's with my email on the Internet, which you don't have here. But I'll remember."

"Three blades, leaf of glass, sneeze, from the very first, can't swallow it," Frannie said, going over the parts.

"Leaf of glass sounds like a book," Gupta said. "Whitman. The last one was a book. Got *Leaves of Grass* by Walt Whitman?"

"No. But the library might. It's tiny though," said Frannie.

"What's 'from the very first?'" Gupta said.

"Adam and Eve," I said.

"Aborigines," said Frannie.

"Yes!" Gupta and I said simultaneously.

Striking and superscripting again we now have: *Now thrust through three blades in Dwellingup in leaf of glass and sneeze this which hales from the Aborigines. If you can't swallow it, then think about what it is.*

"A book on the Aborigines," I said. "What about *Voices of the First Day?* Where would that be? Library again. Bookstore. Or maybe in the museum."

"Maybe so, but there are also Aboriginal blades—knives, axe heads and spears in the Dwellingup Museum," Frannie said. "Maybe three of them together."

"The Dwellingup Museum was on the list," I said.

"We're on an anthropological quest," said Frannie, "and we wish to see 'three aboriginal blades.' Do you have anything like that here? Blades, knives, axes? Anything of that sort?"

There were a few aboriginal odds and ends but nothing that filled the bill.

"Wait a minute," said Gupta. "Three blades. Blades can be the sections of a leaf."

194

She gasped.

"It's not that big a deal," I said.

"The Forest Heritage Centre!" she said excitedly. "That was on the list too!"

"Thrust through," said Gupta as we paid our admission. "It doesn't mean there are blades thrusting through something but that we go into the blades, the sections of the building are built like a leaf."

"In leaf of glass—that's the display cases. There's something in one of them."

He read the clue again.

Now go into the Forest Heritage Centre in Dwellingup to a display case... *and sneeze this which hales from the Aborigines. If you can't swallow it, then think about what it is.*

"Now what can you sneeze if you can't swallow?" I asked.

"I know," said Frannie and we followed her running. A guard coughed as a warning.

"The snotty gobble!" she said arriving at a case. "The Aborigines used it for chewing gum. You sneeze snot and it's not considered nice to swallow it—or gum."

"And to 'think about what it is,' is to chew on it," I said, "which is what we do with gum."

There it was for the second time—a little sample of the curiously named plant in the glass case. "Weird," I said, "this place was on the list we made at the pub in Perth, but not the snotty gobble. Yet, Fenster chose the one thing that struck me most here."

"So where's the next clue?" Gupta wants to lift the display case glass and look under the snotty gobble but there's the guard at the end of the room. Frannie drops her brochure and while stooping to pick it up looks under the case. She reaches her hand in and tugs. I hear the faint sound of tape being pulled as she fake coughs loudly and voila! An envelope is in her hand.

"Who should open it?" she asked politely.

"Well you of course," I said. "You won it."

She does so as we press in. "Lovely paper," she said unfolding it.

"See," I said to Gupta who is not to be distracted.

And then she reads:

A man falls in love with a woman not just because of her beauty or learning but because of the tenderness she gives to frivolous things.

"Horrors!" cried Gupta. "Where the hell would that take us? We've got to find Mindy right away! She'll be dead or Rudy's gonna have us killed by the time we get through this joker's treasure hunt!"

"Cool off," I said to him. "You're disturbing the guard. It's not going to be impossible. It's going to be something around here. Let's go."

"Horrors! Horrors!" Gupta kept saying as we filed out.

"Thank you sir," I nodded to the attendant as he eyed us suspiciously.

Back at Frannie's we couldn't get anywhere with the clue.

"Let's forget it for a while," she said. "That's what I do when I want to find something."

"Let our subconscious mull it over for a while," I said.

"I like that," she said. "Our subconscious, not our subconsciouses."

"Well I don't know if it's singular or plural," I said.

"Or both or neither," she added.

"And I don't know if it's the subconscious or the psyche or brain or mind or angels or what," I said.

"Leave it alone and it will come home," she offered.

"Wagging its punch line behind it," Gupta completed.

"I don't know what's happening but I always ask for help," I said.

"By saying thank you," Gupta added.

"That's right Let me illustrate that with a song." I picked up the guitar. "It's called…"

"Lemme guess," said Gupta. "Thank you."

"Nope. It's called *Francine*."

"That's sweet," said Frannie when I was done.

"I played it for an Aboriginal buckster in Freo late the other night. That's what he said too."

"Sounds more like Mindy than Frannie," Gupta said.

"We're one and the same," said Francine.

"Not to me," sighed Gupta. "Nero fiddled while Rome burned. We sit around and sing while Mindy languishes."

"Sing another," said Frannie. "The muse will find Mindy for us."

I played a song called *Thank You*.

"I knew it," said Gupta lying down.

"Gimme the words to that last song, will ya?" Frannie asked.

"See you in my nightmares," Gupta whispered turning over on his side.

Continuing to pursue the method of discovering through forgetting, he falls asleep. Frannie gets a blanket and gently lays it over him. She suggests I take a nap in the guest room, Mary's room. I remove my shoes and get on the bed. She puts a blanket over me.

"Don't need so much cover inside here anymore," she said.

"Yes, it's getting warmer."

"No, that's not what I mean. The house is warmer because of the insulation in the attic—thank you very much."

"Oh yeah—and the ceiling here. It looks great," I said gazing up at it. "If you're into funky."

Semi-woke to—what is it?—sounds like a little helicopter. It's still light outside. Usually know the approximate time even half awake. Hmm. Say, five—an hour before sunset. Ah. Bed soft. Interesting ceiling—crudely textured swaths of plaster fixing the rupture that came at the finale of the insulation madness. Reminiscing. In Mandurah the salesman's head shook—you can't get all that insulation in your Mazda. Squeeze in trunk, shove in back, and Frannie waved triumphantly driving off with me pinned under two rolls sharing the front seat. Back home we unloaded the insulation, which puffed up beside the dwarfed car. Neighbor Sal said we'd found the circus clowns' secret. At my urging, Frannie tacks a Do Not Disturb sign on the front door. We don gloves, respirators, goggles, and up she goes with mat knife, trouble light to hang, torch in hand. I hand up, she pulls up, fluffy unrolled bats. She works from the cramped edges, big me from the peak. Silent teamwork. Time passes. We're three quarters done. A distant sound tugs—it's the doorbell. We ignore it for a while but it won't stop. Descending. Open door. Banger, beer bottles bulging in coat pockets inside and out staggers in and urges we join him to torch black boys in the bush. What? Frannie explains black boys are tarry grassy trees like Joshua Trees and they go up whoosh! Don't do that, we say. We gotta work. Bad boy insists on helping. While he's WCing she whispers how he lay around drunk and stoned for a year and a half and now wants to help. I say no, but she says a softhearted yes. He does okay for a while in the attic helping stuff the stuff between the joists, but approaching the finish line he loses balance—whaa! crash!—through the ceiling to the first floor. Light streams up into attic. Down-laddering into the guest room. He's okay. Hit the bed's mattress dead center. Luck o' the drunk. It's a mess. Sheet of rock hanging, battered, broken, white bits 'n' dust all over bed, dresser, floor. Poor Banger's mortified. She says it's okay but time to go. I say all jobs have goof ups. He leaves with his tail between his legs. We turn in. Getting' that gypsum board fastened to rock hard jarrah joists next day was a bitch. Bent screws and broke screws from neighbor Sal, bent and broken nails from craft room. Finally pre-drilled for thick nails from hardware nook in general store. Respect for WA carpenters cemented. Plaster of Paris spread with kitchen spatula over first-aid-box gauze sealed up unions and cracks. And now there's a healed ceiling with character holding in the attic's thick coat of fiberglass and we're all toasty warm, me in bed gazing up remembering, smiling. End of nostalgia. Leaving foggy here and then for back to planet Dwellingup here and now. Whirring in my ears. Hmm. She's blending up stuff to make more paper, humming. Pretty. Sad. She sings.

Take this lint and add it to
A basket of the shredded news
Blend with water, flowers, and glue
Oh Mama—I'm losin' you

Here's a bead that I forgot
To string before I tied the knot
I'll put it in the bauble box
Oh Mama—I'm losin' you

Take the kettle—water's hot
Earl Grey's waiting in the pot
Set the cream out, sugar, and cups
Oh Mama—I'm losin' you
Oh Mama—I'm losin' you

I wander into the kitchen rubbing my eyes. Hers are red. Paper hangs to dry on string running over our heads. I hold her and we stand there for a moment and let the sadness soak in.

"I thought you said you didn't use glue making paper," I broke the silence.

"It rhymed," she said softly.

On the fridge I see the clue I was supposed to be solving in my sleep instead of remembering Banger stumbling through the ceiling. *A man falls in love with a woman not just because of her beauty or learning but because of the tenderness she gives to frivolous things.*

"This clue could have something to do with you, I think," I said.

"Me?"

"Yeah, your art. I appreciate all the little things you do. Banger does. Now Gupta does. I don't know. Any of your art downtown here in a shop?"

"Yeah. Are you saying it's frivolous?"

I walked into the living room where Gupta lay sleeping on a couch. A fire was going in the iron stove. "Let's go check it out. He can guard the fire."

Thirty minutes later we're back. "That's weird. It's something I've read. I know that quote."

"Me too," she said. "I read it recently—I can't remember."

"I can't think of anything from the list. I want to look at all the books here," I said.

"What's that gonna help?"

"I don't know. What else can I do? I think this one's from a book. I'm turning over every stone. It might help me think."

I went to the bookcase in her bedroom and squatted down. "Let's see. You've got your tarot books, some poetry. Don't rule anything out. I've given you a few—the *Botany of Desire*. You've got my old Lin Yutang Tao translations I left here."

"The worn one you said you wanted to read one last time tearing out the pages as you finish them?"

"Yeah. Let's see. What else is there?" Some fantasy, crafts, a few novels. "Nah. Not one of these. Frivolous things? Where would I start? Where else are books? I think it's here—either in a frivolous thing or in a book."

"You're not gonna find a clue in here. They don't know anything about my place. They haven't been in here—I hope."

"I might find something that leads me to the clue. Anyway, I'm desperate. We have to go forward. Any books in the bathroom? No. God—maybe it's in the crafts room, the repository for frivolous things." I opened the door.

"Look what I found on the table out on the patio," she said holding up a book. "I'm sorry. I forgot. That's not good for it to be outside. You sent me this last year. I was readin' it yesterday."

It was Tazi John's *The Light Inside the Dark*. I started thumbing through it.

"I like his Zen," she said. "It's got a lot of warmth. Yours is so much nothing—no me, no you, no here, no there. His has got people and the world and feelings."

"He's a soul-man," I said continuing to look—and somewhat hurt at her estimation of my soulless Buddhism.

Frannie poured me more coffee. "Let's move to tea after this," I said. "I'm gonna get the shakes and diarrhea if I have any more coffee."

"What kind of tea you want?" she asked.

"Bingo!"

"Don't have that."

"Frannie! Here it is! Page 129! *A man falls in love with a woman not just because of her beauty or learning but because of the tenderness she gives to frivolous things.*"

"Oh wonderful!"

"But wait—there's no note." I kept looking through the pages then went out to the patio where she found the book. Nothing. I went back inside dejected. Frannie wasn't there.

"This is impossible!" I call out so she can hear.

"Here it is!" came her voice from the front porch.

"What the hell?" I went running out.

"Page 129. That's my address."

She pulled a small envelope from behind the solid block with a "nine" painted on it. "One twenty-nine Marginata Cresent," I said. "Oh yeah."

Back at the kitchen table. We're sitting across from each other.

"You're finding everything," I said.

"I'm gonna be a private eye!"

She opened the note and then didn't read it to me and closed it. "One question."

"Okay."

"Who put this note there? Who put the one in the Forest Heritage Centre? Are they dangerous people? Who did it? What are they doing in my house?"

"Somebody who works for Fenster. But it looks like he didn't get in your house—just the back and front porches."

"There was a man here this morning. Out front. I forgot. He was dressed up. Formal. He asked where the cemetery was with the motorcycle engine. So I sent him down there. He was English."

"Did he," I started to ask and paused for a moment. "Did he have much hair?"

"Not much. And it was gray. But he looked like a mouse with his really long ear hair."

"Oh, then I know who left the clues."

"Who?"

"Stan—Fenster's butler. Fenster's English butler."

"An English butler?"

"Bobby Fenster's butler or valet. He's obviously putting the clues up."

"He seemed nice enough," she said, and again unfolded the piece of paper and looked at it. "This one's strange." She read it.

Not a cricket call, nor informer in need of bath, the void is, inside out, and under an old wet roof.

I repeated it while looking at the sheet upside down and knitting my brow. "Well, looks as if Stan went over to the cemetery. The inside of the motorcycle is there outside. It gets rained on—wet roof."

"There are crickets there," said Frannie.

We ran over and checked the plot with the motorcycle engine encased in glass but could find no clue anywhere near it.

I sat down on the edge of the gravestone. "Hear the crickets?" she said.

"Not a cricket call," I shook my head.

"Mozzies coming out too," she said whacking a mosquito.

"What now?"

"We'll think of something," Francine offered with an optimistic determination. She was definitely on the team. I was glad. And I was stumped. Discouraged. I feared it would take forever to figure this one out.

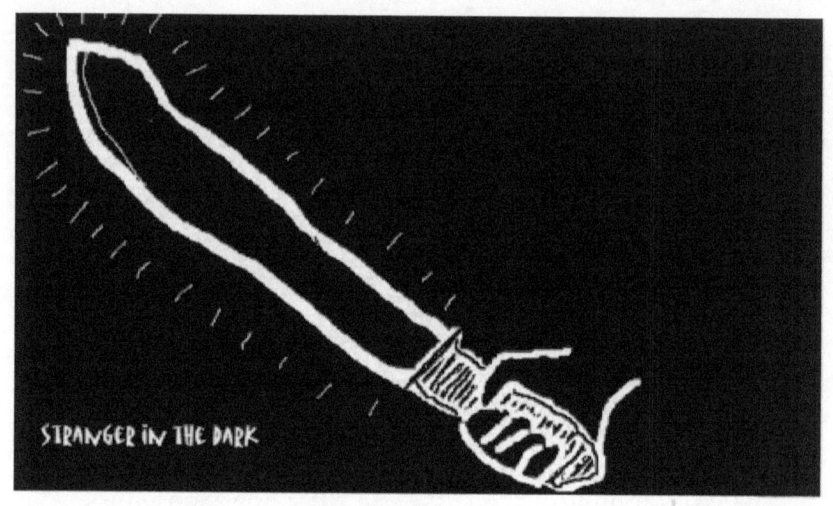

CHAPTER 21
ON ANON

"Oh Gupta, wake up and go to sleep," I speak the old line softly. "Time to get up." He opens his eyes. "There you are. We've got to go. But you can go back to sleep in the back seat of Frannie's car. We're taking both."

"Six," he mumbled.

"No, no—it's still seven. Just after dark on the 22nd."

"Seven?" puzzled Frannie.

"Seven days till we dine with Rudy."

"Let's get on it then," she said with a worried look.

We were on our way back to Rottnest via Freo. I had never driven a Porsche before. Glad it was an automatic cause I think a left-handed gear shift would throw me. It was fun, but it was drizzling so I didn't hot dog. Anyway, my mind was on quokkas. Frannie and I had figured out the clue walking back to the house. It was a quokka. All the clues so far were things I knew about—as Fenster had hinted.

Not a cricket call, nor informer in need of bath, the void is, inside out, and under an old wet roof.

It's not a cricket call—call rhymes with ball—cricket as in the game then—*not a cricket ball* leads to a soccer ball or *not a soccer ball*. Remember the boys who were arrested playing soccer with a quokka? *Nor informer in need of a bath*

202

was Not a dirty rat—that was cute. The first sailors were wrong. The quokka was not a rat. *The void* was the first thing we got—by looking void up in an old Thesaurus in Mary's room. Pocket or pouch were the words that did it. It stood for the marsupial pouch, not some empty, shining Hindu or Buddhist type cosmic void. *Inside out, and under an old wet roof* must mean that we should go back to the cave at Rottnest, which was wet when we were there. I start to see a commonality in the clues. It's not from the list in the pub. It's all stuff I'd written about to Kelly and Clay. He's definitely read my emails. How? Could Sid have gotten into them? I remembered going online from the computer in my bedroom at Fenster's. But not only the emails from that night—they got 'em going back. I felt as exposed as if I'd had the digital equivalent of unprotected anal intercourse with a promiscuous HIV positive Haitian hemophiliac intravenous drug user.

So we were on our way to Rottnest. We weren't going to wait for the ferry from Freo. Frannie was calling ahead on her mobile to charter a plane. Tazi John told me his only trip to Rottnest was on a single engine plane from Freo in a storm so heavy the ferries weren't running. He said it was hairy buffeting over to the runwayette and he was grateful when he stepped back down on terra firma. Glad he told me because that's where I got the idea for flying there and saving time. It was a little pricey but Gupta had the money from Rudy, which would go toward the cause.

I pondered the inside-out part of the clue. Could it indicate where at the cave on Rottnest the next clue was waiting? Like in something outside the cave that was usually inside like... a rock, no—a bottle of booze left behind? Drunk on the inside. Should be on the inside but it might be on the outside with the message in the bottle waiting for us to read—or for some hiker to stumble on if tonight we are brutally murdered mid-hunt for shirking our duty to guard Mindy.

Oh god, poor Mindy. How's she doing? Is she being abused? Is she alive? She could be incinerated in one of Fenster's crematoriums as he apparently was threatening to do to the stuffed body of that racehorse.

All of a sudden I was transfixed with a new image. Stuffed. The horse stuffed. Stuffed quokka. Inside out—insides out. Stuffed quokka in the Western Australian Museum near the central train station in Perth. Right under the spot where the roof leak was being fixed, the wet roof. I had mentioned it in an email to the boys cause I'm into construction and stood there watching them fixing it. I replayed the clue in my mind: *Not a cricket call, nor informer in need of bath, the void is, inside out, and under an old wet roof.* I started yelling as I drove along. We should go to Perth! Not Rottnest! It makes much more sense. Fenster's clues so far have been more or less nearby so the closer of the two choices seems to make more sense both from the point of view of likelihood of success and ease of checking it out.

But there's no way to get hold of them. Wait—yes there is. Frannie's got her mobile. I can stop and make a call. Hey! I replay what Mindy said at the pub where we saw the game on that last night together—she'd "Left me mobile in the car" before we went pub crawlin'. I am right now driving her car. I reach into the compartment in the middle just to my left—as I'm on the right—and there it is. It's dead. Found the charger that plugs into the lighter. Nifty.

All I've got to do is call Frannie now. Oh—messages. Wonder what's there.

The first message was from Gupta. It was pathetic and rambling. Oh there in spite of the grace of the Great Mistletoe go I. The next was from some guy much cockier and on the sauce, saying casually if she wanted to come by at any time he would be there. No name— just "It's me." The third started with "It's me" too. I wonder how many of them there are? "Bluey! I don't want to be a pest. I guess I am a pest. But I've changed. Give me a chance Bluey." Bluey? Wonder which night he was. Guess he struck out. There was a "Just callin' to say hi" from a woman. Then this: "Mindy—if you get this please call me now. My name is Samo and I'm a friend of Davo and Gupta. If however, it's Davo or Gupta listening to the message, please call me right away."

Samo answered with, "Can you talk?"

"Yeah, it's David. I'm driving Mindy's Porsche to Freo but I want to change and go to Perth but I need to get hold of Frannie for that and I'm not sure..."

"Davo, Davo, Davo—listen to me. Don't worry about that now. It's not a problem."

"Oh—okay, sorry."

"I've been checking up on things. That car Techo identified so positively as a La Salle hearse with the carved wood paneling?"

"Yeah, yeah, yeah."

"He even got the year right—1937."

"What do you mean he got it right? You found one?"

"Found the record of registration and listen—it's not registered to Bobby Fenster or to anyone connected to him."

"It's not?"

"No. It's registered to a Gelar Waters."

"Gelar. Gelar. I know that name. Who's that?"

"Mindy's legal name is Mindy Waters. It's her husband. I think she may have been kidnapped by her husband—or gone with him. But I don't know anything about him yet. Just found this out. I'll look into him tomorrow."

As my head spun out of control, I think it must have affected the car, or maybe I hit the brakes too hard or something, because the next thing I knew the Porsche was spinning on the wet road and I was just trying to stop it but there wasn't any traction. I cringed the cringe of a lifetime as it circled and I waited for a deafening crash or crunch or smash but there was just a soft slush and a moment of dizziness. I'd ended up on a grassy slope on the other side. Stars were twinkling in my field of vision—not real ones from the sky. I breathed a sigh of great big relief and muttered a thank you. And then I was mad at myself for being uncool and losing control. I heard my name being called—my Australian name—"Davo, Davo, Davo are you there?" Oh yes. I picked up the mobile from the floor.

"Hello again. Sorry."

"Are you okay?"

"Yes—I just made a little detour onto a grassy knoll. No snipers here though. I think I can get out—not of the car—pull the car away. Ah yes, here we go. Weee across the highway to the right side I mean the correct side."

"You're okay?"

"Yes. Just let me catch my breath."

"Take your time."

"Okay," I said trying to talk but still just catching my breath. Finally, "Back to Mindy's husband. Listen—I've got to think about this. I'm not sure what to do. You want to meet tomorrow morning?"

"Sure."

"How about at the museum when it opens, the natural science museum."

"Okay. Their snack shop opens at ten I think. Maybe nine. Whenever it opens."

"I'll be there."

"See you then."

I realized I didn't have Frannie's mobile number. Well, Freo's not that much out of the way. I was just driving and not listening to the radio or anything so I started listening to DAVO 58.5, my thought stream, and started to think maybe I could remember her number and it would be good if I could because what if she's reserved an airplane and is about to put a non-refundable deposit on it with a credit card. Then again, Samo might be able to get it. His number's in my phone now. I don't have most of my numbers on me. Left them at the hostel. Hostel—is my stuff safe? I bet they put it in the cage. Slim and I were getting along well and he seems like a thoughtful guy. Better go there tonight to make sure. It's the place to stay anyway.

Let's see—Frannie's mobile number—oh yes—it's 5555-5555. No, just kidding I said to myself chuckling. Eight numbers though. The first four numbers were something to do with her age—forwards and backwards as I remember. Her age last year—in 2002. That's two numbers—three and five—was it 3553? Maybe. Okay—I'll leave that. The next four I said I'd never forget. Oh yeah—the year Clay was born minus how old he was in the year his great grandmother died. I tried it. Didn't work. Kept messing around with the first four numbers till—she answered!

Gupta was awake and they were behind me a ways. I got all excited remembering why I wanted to call her and started telling her about the stuffed quokka, naturally having to let her in on the whole chain of thought starting with the image of Mindy in the crematorium and the stuffed horse and how we shouldn't go to Rottnest. And then I remembered who owned the horse—I mean the hearse—and started getting confused what to do and didn't want to talk more. We agreed to meet at the Northbridge Hostel which would take about forty minutes more.

Forty minutes. That's the length of a period of zazen that I'm used to. Good lord, I could use a little zazen. Deep sigh. Driving can be zazen. I should calm down and do driving zazen and appreciate this Porsche. Who knows if I'll ever have the opportunity again. Hands, wheel, road, breath, dark edges of scenery whizzing by, no one here but us skandas—form, feelings, perceptions, impulses, consciousness and I'm not so sure about them. Thoughts arise, each morphing into the next. I let them come and go one by one, not serving them tea as my old teacher once advised. I drive on without a care, without a name. After some kilometers had passed, I forgot I was doing zazen and started singing.

Fools together, fools together
Fools our whole life through
Fools together, fools together

Whatever it is that we do
There may be times that we are super duper smart
And others that we sail through
But usually we're foolishly fools
And fools together too

Fools together, fools together
Fools from head to toe
Fools together, fools together
Wherever it is that we go
There may be heroes, bodhisattvas, good hearts
And moments of clarity too
But usually we're foolishly fools
And fools together too
And fools together too.

I drove on—humming zazen.

"There's no need to go on this treasure hunt any more!" Gupta said strongly. "She's with her husband. She just dumped us and went off. The free spirit theory was the right one. This whole treasure hunt is just a stupid game Fenster's playing with us. And he's playing it because you got so involved with him. He just sees it as an opportunity to mess with your mind."

"You don't know that for sure," I said shaking my head.

We were at an Indonesian restaurant near the hostel, eating dinner, and trying to figure out what's what.

"What if her husband's working for this Fenster character?" Frannie said.

"There's her husband, the mysterious Aboriginal guy, and Fenster. Her husband could be working with either or both of them or neither or Rudy. We don't know," I said. "But it won't hurt to go tomorrow to the museum and meet Samo. And remember Fenster looks more honest now—maybe. He said he wasn't involved but could lead us to her. So if she's with her husband and it has nothing to do with Fenster and he just has some info on them, Fenster's clues might still lead us to her. We just don't know. We need to find her even if she's not in danger because Rudy will be furious if he finds out we've lost her."

"Yeah, I think so too," said Gupta. "Okay. We know her husband was involved but we don't know if he's friend or foe. I give up. That's enough for tonight. You must be exhausted man. Let's go to Mindy's. I've got two keys to it—hers and mine."

The hostel did have my stuff in the cage and Slim released it to me when I paid what was owed. Frannie was planning to go to her sister's where she stays a lot, but Gupta suggested we all stick together. Good idea.

I was really, really, really exhausted—hadn't slept much since...since a few days back. We opened the door to Mindy's and went in. I told Francine to go on and take the bed and Gupta and I would sleep on the couches like before. Maybe after a dip in the spa. Yes, a dip in the spa we all agreed. That'd put us to sleep deep.

We could see okay from street light coming in through the blinds in the living room, and I squinted rubbing my hands along the wall while saying, "Where's a switch?"

"Don't turn the light on," came a firm voice in the doorway to Mindy's bedroom. "Don't move." A silhouetted figure stood there holding something long, familiar, and worrisome.

"Maybe we're in the wrong house," Francine said. I was happy to hear her voice because it is female and so extremely non-threatening. She knew to speak for us.

"I've got a machete in my hand I'm prepared to use so just what are you doing here?"

"I'm Francine and this is David and Gupta and we're friends of Mindy's. We were planning on staying here but that's not necessary."

"Oh," and then a sigh of relief. "Oh sure. I know you guys. Sorry."

He did? Who was he? He was in a bathrobe—I could see that much. He turned the light on.

Gupta jumped and I went, "Oh my gosh!"

"You!" yelled Gupta.

It was Mindy's shadow, the mysterious Aborigine.

"Where's Mindy!?" Gupta said, right away in a demanding tone.

"I have no idea where she is. She ran away from me on Wednesday night—with you guys."

"What are you doing here?" said Gupta. "You know she doesn't want you around, man."

"I was waiting for her out there and she didn't come home so finally I just came in to get some sleep."

"Sleeping in her bed? Why have you been following her, man?" Gupta asked. "Why did she have to run away? Why do you keep bugging her. It's obvious she doesn't like it—or you. How did you get in? Where is she?"

"Can we all sit down and have some chamomile tea and cool off

208

and be chums and let things go slow and easy?" said Frannie.

"Yeah, Gupta. We've got time," I said. "Anyway, it's not him who took her—we don't think. Let's just sit down."

Gupta sat down. "And you can put the machete down now, please."

"Oh, sorry. Took her?"

"Yeah, Mindy's run off or maybe been kidnapped. But we know it wasn't you."

"Who?" he asked.

"Her husband," said Gupta.

"I'll check the fridge," said Frannie.

"There's beer in there. I'm gonna get dressed," our sort of quasi host said. "Her husband eh?"

"Yeah," said Gupta. "Either he nicked her or she just ran off with him. She was in a crazy mood—drunk and stoned and dancing and singing crazy stuff on the street."

"Sounds like her. Let me get dressed and we can talk about this," he said, turning and disbathrobing as he walked into the bedroom.

"Would you like a drink?" called out Frannie.

The Aborigine turned back around, walked a few steps into the living room and said, "Just juice for me."

Unselfconsciously he stood in full view and we three stared intently, obviously entranced by him in his tight white underwear. We couldn't help it. His dark brown muscular physique was compelling, but what held our attention firmly were the seven letters tattooed boldly across his chest spelling out the name Melinda.

"Oh my god," said Gupta.

"Ah... ah..." I uttered.

"And your name is Gelar," said Frannie, "Gelar Waters. I've heard about you from your wife, Mindy. Pleased to meet ya."

WA MUSEUM

CHAPTER 22
TEAMWORK

Upon realizing we were sharing company not only with the man who had been relentlessly following Mindy but with her husband as well, and that the two of them were indeed one, and considering the serious and unlikely events of the last few days, a good deal of query and explanation were called for. Gupta started off the investigation of Gelar with vigor and a damning presumption of guilt.

"What the hell have you done with Mindy?! Where is she?!"

"Nothing. I don't know. What are you talking about?"

"We saw her get snatched up by *your* hearse! Yours! Don't deny it!"

"Snatched up? What do you mean?"

"You know what I mean!"

"I don't! I want to know what's happening!"

We had each assumed the husband did it when we heard he owned the vehicle that was used to take her away. We'd seen it come and go and that was that. But one small phrase out of Gelar's mouth dismissed our lynch mob assurance as surely as the discharge of a flushing toilet.

"My hearse was stolen."

"Oh—I hadn't thought of that," said Gupta.

"Me either," I said.

"I wondered who'd kidnap someone with a rare collectible vehicle registered in their name," said Frannie. "I see now—they did it to point the blame at you. Any sign of it since then?"

"Nope. If it was any of the guys her uncle is involved with—or fighting with—it's probably been melted down by now. It was one of a kind considering its condition. But that's the furthest thing from my mind now. It's not flesh and blood one of a kind such as her. Kidnapped. Oh no." He sat down and put his head in his hands.

We were quiet for a while. We stared, a group non-think, waiting for the next thought to arise. Gelar drank his orange juice, Frannie and Gupta Emus, me a shot.

"So the treasure hunt is back on," said Gupta.

"Full on," I nod.

That in turn required a lengthy explanation for Gelar's sake, from the start in Singapore up to the moment we saw his tattoo, which brought him equally up to date and in the dark with us.

"But what about your following her all the time?" asked Gupta. "Are you pestering her?"

"Yes," Gelar said. "I admit it. I am obsessed with Bluey."

"Bluey?" Gupta asked.

"It's what I call her."

"Any reason why?" I asked.

"For her red hair, of course," clarified Frannie.

"I know you're hot for her," Gelar said looking at Gupta. "I have no problem with that. However much I'm trying to win her back, whatever competition we would have, that's not on my mind now."

"She got tired of me as a lover and regardless of how much I want her, it doesn't matter. Anyway, I'm just here on vacation, so I'm not really in the running," Gupta said.

"She got tired of me as well, of my dopin'," said Gelar. "I've been clean and sober now for a good while. I like it. I won't go back. But so far she isn't interested."

We asked Gelar what he knew of Rudy and Fenster. He said he knew Rudy well and knew of Waxo Fenster. Had heard the guy was crazy and from what he'd gathered tonight, those rumors were well founded.

"We thought you might be tailing her for one of them," I said.

Gelar squirmed a little.

"You were!" Frannie exclaimed.

"Don't tell her. I was. I am. I keep an eye on her for Rudy."

"Oh gosh, did you tell Rudy that I didn't stay with Gupta and Mindy?" I said.

"No—it's not like that. I don't report to him. Just look out for her. And I guess I get a little carried away."

A year before, Mindy had complained to Rudy Gelar was stalking her. Rudy could see Gelar's motives were innocent, was worried about Mindy so he offered Gelar financial support to watch over her even more. Gelar came with motivation and the ability to kick butt. He wouldn't carry a weapon—the machete was of course Mindy's. He was a little clumsy and obvious for surveillance, but it didn't matter because he had an excuse, being preoccupied with her.

"I failed miserably though," he said.

"Welcome to the club."

"So do you think we're justified," Gupta asked, "in fearing not only for Mindy but for ourselves at the hands of Rudy?"

"Yes."

We three guys looked at each other. We had a shared task to protect Mindy and an equally shared threat of reprisal for failure to do so, a failure which we'd only be able to hide for so much longer. I told Gelar about the dinner date we had with Rudy on the 29th.

"Today's the 22nd, Friday, so it's next Friday. We've got a week."

"He'll kill us," said Gelar. "He'll kill us all if she's been hurt."

"I knew it," said Gupta.

"But he seemed to be such a nice guy," I said.

"Yep—until you lose his niece," said Gupta.

"So, aside from Mindy, there are three of us in deep trouble until she's rescued," I said. "You're the only one not in danger Frannie."

"But we're all four committed to getting her back and we're all four sleepy," she said.

"I got to find out when the Western Australian Museum opens," I said.

"Nine," said Gelar.

"Okay—we have a nine o'clock appointment tomorrow morning at the museum with Samo," I said drying off from a soak in the spa. "I'm finally going to sleep. You come with us, okay?"

"Sure," said Gelar.

"I'm gonna call Techo and ask him to be there," said Gupta.

"Frannie should have the bedroom," Gelar offered magnanimously and then added, "I'll change the sheets."

"Nah," she said opening a cabinet by the door. "I got it."

We look at the two couches and three guys.

"And Davo sleeps next to me. We go camping. He's a pal. Like one of the gals."

"Maybe tonight you'll get lucky," said Gupta.

"Don't be juvenile," I said, sort of embarrassed.

"It's okay," said Frannie. "I'm an Ozzie. We like naughty talk."

Up early. Gupta and I did his yoga and my zazen together. Mindy has two sinks so we brushed together too. I broke the silence.

"Glide Dental Floss," I said, holding the product up to the mirror. "I treat it as carefully as my passport. I carry one in each bag when I travel—one in my suitcase and one in my shoulder bag. That way if one bag gets lost, I still have my Glide. Of course I can't carry two passports so I carry a copy in my shoulder bag. Glide, as indispensable when traveling as my passport."

"What the hell was that?" Gupta asked.

"I'm practicing product placement. But it's too wordy. Gotta get it down."

"You think you're in a movie?"

"Life product placement. I'm placing products in my life."

"Well, life is like a movie. Myself, I like this thick cottony stuff better. It's more abrasive."

"My teeth are too close together. Glide's the only thing that works for me that I've found. I hate hate hate to have dental floss stuck between my teeth. Glide," I returned to my ad holding it up again, "wherever oral hygiene products are sold."

"Remarkable," Gupta said, shaking his head. "You're insane."

"You must be insane in some way too."

"Yeah. I'm still miserable thinking about Mindy. Even though her life's in danger or she might even be dead, I can't stop wishing she would come back to me as a devoted lover."

"Samo can help," I said.

"The detective?"

"Just wait. I'll bring it up at the museum."

"Oh, by the way, six," he said.

"Beat me to it. Six it is."

"Six till dinner."

"Or six till death."

"Pleased to meet you mate," said Samo to Frannie.

"And this is our mystery guest," I said.

It was great to watch the look on Samo's face as I introduced him to Gelar Waters. We were at the museum coffee nook. There was a horrendous amount of catching up to do, and it was only two days prior we had been together at the hostel wondering what to do first.

"Oh, I want to ask you something I've asked before," I said. Samo Nods. "Okay. We're sure now that this is a kidnapping because Gelar's stolen hearse was used. Right?" More nods. "What sort of kidnapping is this? Don't kidnappers usually follow up kidnappings with notes that tell loved ones what to do? Where to leave the money and all? I think we'd have heard from Rudy if he'd been contacted."

Samo spoke. "Your visit with Fenster could have changed the whole thing. You were there quick. Hard to call. At this point Fenster could be playing with us and waiting himself to see what he's going to do. Remember, he's nuts."

"Hard to forget," said Gupta.

I asked Samo if, while Frannie and I were enjoying the displays, he might tell Gupta about the affect, as in Affect Psychology, of disappointment and what to do about it. Gupta said that was the furthest thing from his mind now. Gelar excused himself to check out some paintings. As I walked off I heard Samo saying disappointment was the response to a blocked expectation. Naturally. Wonder what he said next.

After Frannie and I got a little lost in a hall of beautiful, murdered, mounted butterflies, we went upstairs to a passageway between two large display halls. There it was—not in full lit view, but on a dusty dark shelf maybe twenty feet from where we stood—our stuffed quokka. We were on a walkway that ran next to a balcony overlooking the large room below from all four sides. There were shelves running around the walls holding stuffed mammals, birds, and reptiles that seemed to be stored more than exhibited. Three sides of the balcony were closed to the public. When I'd spent the morning at the museum a week before, I'd stopped there to watch some workers repair the ceiling where rainwater had damaged it and noticed the taxidermied quokka. Sure didn't imagine I'd be back to search through its pouch.

Of course I didn't know for sure if the next clue was there or not—but I'd touched on it in an email—"stuffed quokka on a shelf caught my eye"—so I was expecting it. There was a guard with his back to me standing across the way looking into another room. I dared not try to go past the wooden gate with the sign that read "Staff Only" as long as he was in my view. Frannie walked around to him without a word to me, said something, and in a moment he went off with her. I opened the gate and stole swiftly to the quokka, slipping my hand into it's pouch and there it was. Quickly I snatched the envelope and returned to the other side of the gate, closing it just as a guard walked in from the opening near me and called out, "That area's closed, sir." I thanked him and went to get Frannie.

Conversation stopped when we returned brimming with urgent priority.

"That was quick," Gupta noted.

"Let's open the envelope," said Frannie.

"Nice paper," said Samo eyeing it.

"My turn," I said, used a knife at the table, pulled out the message, and read the following to an attentive audience.

> *What started on cue by the first sign of the rise, flew to the let-down kingdom, and now in those bowels pecked, it hides where all the kings men are at loss.*

"What the hell was that?" Gelar looked stymied.

I leaned over toward him and said, with heavy drama in my voice, "Welcome to the treasure hunt." And then more humbly, "Anyone?"

We looked around at each other, everyone obviously hoping someone else had an idea as to what any part of it meant. Nope.

I showed Samo and Gelar the quokka clue and told them the other steps we'd climbed in the treasure hunt. Then we worked on the new riddle for an hour and a half. We solved it. But only after Techo arrived.

Gupta figured that *flew to the let-down kingdom* pointed to the disappointed ravens. He scratched his head. "Went to Rottnest? King's Park? There are ravens everywhere."

What started on cue—Samo said Cue is a town up north so we went with that and it held.

By the first sign of the rise—took a long time and the very abridged version of how we got there is rise is sunrise is sun. Frannie said the first sun sign is Aries. Gupta said Aries is a Latin species name for sheep. There are a lot of sheep stations up there. So we agreed on "What started at a sheep station near Cue."

We were at that point when Techo came in. We didn't fill him in on the big picture, just this clue.

"Remember to look for rhyming clues," I said as we resumed our sleuthing.

Techo didn't take long to tell us to look at the last word—*loss* rhymes with Ross. He put the parts together for us in greater relief. It was at a sheep station near Cue that Ross Bolleter first played ruined piano. Raven Kingdom leads to *Crow Country,* the name of a

CD Ross put out in 1999 that includes ruined piano music.

"Wait?" I said double-taking. "How do you know who Ross Bol-leter is?"

Turned out Techo was familiar with Ross's music and had worked as web master on an avant guard music site that featured Ross's work. They had some articles on Ross's CDs and concerts. And he knew I'd been to see Ross so he hadn't just pulled it out of a hat.

So we had quite a bit of it figured out: Ross's ruined piano music as heard on Crow Country started at a sheep station near Cue\ *And now in those bowels pecked*—inside the ruined piano played\ *it hides*—is the next clue\ *where all the kings men are at loss*—couldn't put something back together—what? A Ruined piano it seemed.

"Cue's a long way off," said Samo.

"Let's try Ross's first," I said. "*Where all the king's men at loss* may mean we can put things back together at Ross's. Who goes to Ross's?"

"You guys go," said Samo. "Gelar and Frannie and I can work some other angles. Okay?"

"Okay," said Frannie.

"You game Gelar?" Samo asked.

"I'm your man."

Before we left, Samo handed Techo a mobile that scrambles the conversation. "Phones of course can be bugged," he said. "Mobiles are easy to pick up on." Discussion amongst us we want to make sure was not overheard by the bad guys should be made on these secure mobiles. He had three others. He said the phones we used probably weren't bugged, it's a lot of trouble to go to, but judging by how much they knew about my emails and the gravity of the event, we couldn't take any chances. It's not like this treasure hunt was a just game. Even though it was wrapped in such a civilized cover, it felt more like a no-holds-barred death match.

CLAUSTRO-SUB-IC

CHAPTER 23
DUNDER

Thanks," I said, handing Techo back his mobile.

Ross didn't answer. I'd left a message. Gupta, Techo, and I went there anyway and rang the bell a few times. We could see his ruined piano through a small window in the front door. We knew we could get in but were hesitant to do so. We only wanted to look inside the broken beast for an envelope. Front door was locked but Techo said he could get inside in a minute.

"They didn't go inside Francine's," I said. "Why would they take that chance?"

"Exactly. Let's go around back," Gupta said.

Oh. In the back yard there were three pianos of the ruined variety. After a period of snooping around the dilapidated innards of this keyboard bone yard, Techo found an envelope.

"Let's get out of here before we open it," he said.

"Thanks Ross," I bowed to the house before entering Techo's souped-up Chevy.

In a coffee shop near the hostel, Gupta, Techo, and I opened the envelope and read the new clue. Hmmm. We scratched our heads and tossed the new conundrum around for a while. Frannie called

Techo on her mobile. She was on a
stake-out staring at the door of a big brick building. I told her what
we'd been doing.

"What does this one say?" she asked

"I'll spare you this one," I told her. "It's so cryptic. Well I guess
that's what they all are. We've deciphered enough of it to know
where to go, so Gupta and I are off to Freo."

I didn't want to say where this clue led. I didn't even want to
think about it for it brought us to the dreaded submarine at the Maritime Museum, but exactly where to look inside that nautical coffin,
we didn't know. The key word was "fell" and we couldn't figure out
what that word, or anything that rhymed with it might indicate. Techo had called a veteran friend with sub experience and searched the
web at the Internet café to try to hone in on where exactly we should
look, but no cigar.

Gupta and I grilled the sub guides. It was easy to do without
arousing suspicion—we just wanted to know where the bell was—or
something that rhymed with fell or was suggested by it. We went on
a tour and checked it out. My breath was shallow, my arms shook.
I wasn't much help. I was too involved with being buried alive. We
strayed during a couple of tours looking all over. It was a day-mare
for me. I didn't get acclimated. Like a bad acid trip—paranoid expanded consciousness—or should I say enhanced contracted consciousness—just an awful claustro-sub-ic feeling with panic on the
horizon every moment. Oh Mindy what I've suffered for you. Gupta teased me. It didn't bother him at all to be in there.

The imaginable horror happened. We had to stay behind on the
last tour. I shuddered as I heard the echoing clang of the fore and aft
hatches closing. Locked in that dreaded coffin for the night. We had
little flashlights and used them sparingly. We didn't know where to
look. We tried everything bell-like including the mock torpedoes.
We looked at every part that rhymed with fell we could think of:
well—where they got water from, cell—any little rooms, the brig
but we could find no brig, jell—lubricants—that took us just about
everywhere, yell—one thing we couldn't do but I cried and shook
a few times. In the course of following every lead we could think of
I imagine we looked at or touched just about every surface in the
whole sub. We kept moving. It was cold. It was dark. It was cramped
as could be.

At about two in the morning I was reaching my hand into an
almost inaccessible spot behind a cluster of pipes when I felt, not
the envelope I was seeking, but a bottle. Carefully I placed my fin-

gers around it and brought it back over and under pipes and around valves until I could place it on a surface and inspect it. "Bundaberg Rum" it read, and I found a date—1969. It was half full. Made in Brisbane with premium ingredients and their carefully guarded, ancient dunder. I cried again, this time with a single tear of joy. We drank the whole thing.

Sitting in the dark depths passing the bottle, Gupta said nothing. I said nothing. We'd given up for the night. We weren't freaking out—just sitting there resigned to our fates. The only sound was our breathing. Finally he broke the silence.

"I took her for granted. I was foolish. I wish I had it to do over. I could be with her in a way that made her want to stay with me. Maybe. Maybe I could have handled things differently." He paused. "Nah. Wishful thinking. There was nothing I could have done. All roads lead to this nothing. You're right. There is nothing."

"What about affect psychology? Did what Samo tell you help?"

"I can't remember. It has joined the nothing."

"I could use a little more nothing," I said, "And less of the coffin effect. And a warm blanket."

"And pillows."

As we lay there in the dark, Gupta started singing.

She's got her stars—I've got mine
Once was we were valentines
But now—we divide the universe

She's on her side—I'm on another
King and Queen of something or other
Who have split the cosmos

There's nothin' else in the ten directions
That's not either hers or mine

She's the southern—I'm the north
For whatever it is worth
Lord and Lady of all space and time

We've our poles and we've our spheres
Infinite and empty dears
Only Nirvana can join us

There ain't no answers to no quantum questions
That don't fall in his or hers

There it's counter—here it's clock
There it's glove and here ol' sock
Same dancing sunlight upon us

She's got her stars—I've got mine
Once was we were valentines
But now—we divide the universe

"I have an appropriate pocket song for the occasion," I said.

"Wail away."

There's no hope for us all
No hope for us all
We try so hard to do what we can
But there's no hope for us all

We slept cold and huddling for a few hours in a cramped steel nook where we were confident the first tour would pass us by without noticing. We followed them out at ten thirty, like refugees being released from a concentration camp. Once we were in the daylight, Gupta turned to me and said, "Five."

"Five indeed," I responded. "Sunday the 24th. And we're free. Oh lord, free, free at last." I kissed the sky.

"Free to die in five days," said Gupta.

Nevertheless, we stood in the sunlight gratefully absorbing the heat and feeling the expansiveness of just being on the earth without being confined. I felt a great pity for people who are incarcerated, a favorite pastime of my native land. With us it was just overnight. For so many it is a lifetime, and so many of them harmless victims of zealous fanaticism or just the old habit of putting others in cages.

But this comparative analysis of degrees of suffering didn't stop me from shuddering. What we'd gone through was for nothing. "God man," I said to Gupta. "That was so bad. It was hell."

"Hell!—that rhymes with fell!" he said.

Great. Hmm. Sounds like hull he pointed out. We looked around on the hull and then, Gupta saw a little bit of something white sticking out from the underside of one of the propellers—propel!

There was easy access as a scaffolding was up for some maintenance work. Gupta slipped over a chain, climbed up and yanked the envelope from under the propeller without worrying about anybody seeing him.

"It was outside," he said.

"Outside. Outside. That's too hard to guess," I said feebly. Propeller was the word.

"Let me look at that clue again," I said. Gupta reached into his pocket and dug it out. Then the problem was obvious. The word was feller, not fell. If we'd noticed that we might have figured out "the feller" rhymes with propeller. Part of the note had gotten wet from dew in the ruined piano—and some ink had run—or maybe Fenster had it done that way on purpose.

"Fenster set it up so we'd be likely to be buried alive in there all night," I said, "knowing from having access to my emails that it was the cruelest thing he could have done short of murdering family."

"Oh well," Gupta said. "Something to tell our grandchildren—if we live that long."

We staggered out of the Maritime Museum and got a room at the Sunrise Hostel where I'd stayed before. After cleaning up, we went out to a restaurant and ordered breakfast. When our plates had been taken away, slowly we opened the envelope and read the next riddle. We looked at each other puzzled, more puzzled than we had been by any other clue. Here's what it said:

What started on cue by the first sign of the rise, flew to the letdown kingdom, and now in those bowels pecked, it hides where all the kings men are at loss.

"What the hell?" Gupta said.

We went back to the hostel, slept for a few hours, took showers, put on clean clothes, got some tea and kangaroo pie—thank you kangaroo, and went back to the Porsche. I called Techo and told him we were coming, but was too dejected to say anything more.

"Do we have to go back to Ross's or does this mean we have to go to that sheep station near Cue? Or is it a mistake or what?" Gupta said.

"I don't think it's a mistake. It's a loop or a dead end. This is no ordinary treasure hunt. We're in a treasure hunt maze."

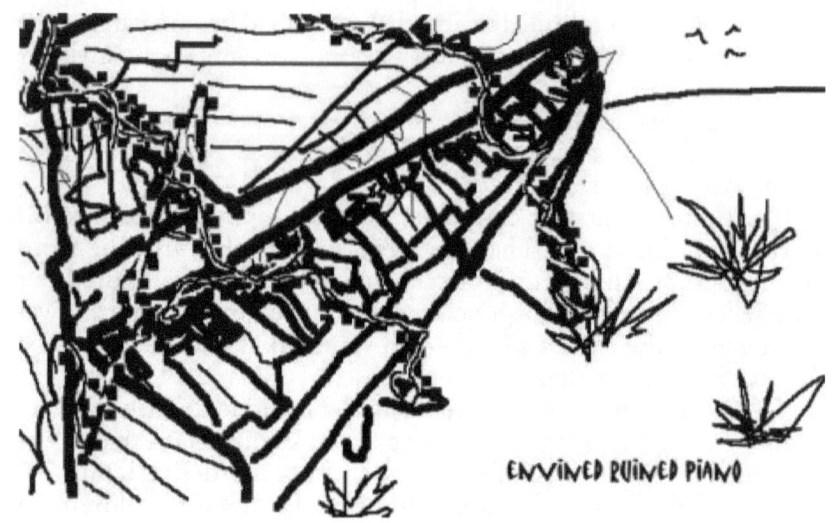

ENVINED RUINED PIANO

CHAPTER 24
KNOT CUTTING

Wire up the fingernail. Ouch. The thought of it was killing me but the actuality was causing Gupta to grit his teeth hard and suck in air. He was sitting on a piano stool clutching one hand with the other. A little drop of blood dripped from underneath his left fourth finger nail where a piano wire had abruptly entered.

It was late afternoon. Techo, Gupta, and I had been combing through Ross's ruined pianos—the ones in his back yard, the one inside his house, and lastly here the one at the studio where he's working on the two quite different experimental and tango CDs. I listen to Ross playing a piano accordion through the double pane glass. There's an engineer at a mixing console. They've been in the control room for a while. There's no one else here. They're intently listening to the tape to see what they think. The lovely tune was muffled, distant, no louder than Gupta's heavy breathing. I know this song and whisper so to Gupta. It's *El Desbande* by Astor Piazzolla, the great Argentine tango composer. Ross played it for us at his home—beautifully. I'm sitting right next to his accordion. They're not looking out here into the studio though. They're concentrating on the recording. They don't even know we're here—or that we were in his house. I figure it's better to break and enter in secret than to involve him in this somewhat extra-legal venture. He's a Zen teacher and musician with a reputation that might be tainted by association with riffraff like us—especially if this thing blows up. Anyway, we didn't find anything.

"Maybe we should go to the sheep station at Cue," I said as we sneaked toward the exit. "We'd have to fly. There's no time to drive."

"No. Enough," whispered Gupta fiercely. "That song—El Desbande means we should disband or rush away—not from each other but from the course of action we're taking. And this is a sign," he said holding up his finger. "It says no. No sticking your hands in pianos. No flying. No driving. We've got to get to the end of the treasure hunt and find Mindy."

"Well, that's the ring finger. It's a sign that you're having a problem with your love life. Have you considered counseling?"

"Oh boy are you psychic," he said. "No, I mean it. No more. No more running around."

"He's right," said Techo.

We walked out of the recording studio unnoticed and went around the corner to Techo's Chevy.

"Okay. I agree," I said. "Anyway, there was one clue in a ruined piano and that's probably all there will be. We just spent a couple of hours proving that. Cue's too far. But to review: *What started on cue by the first sign of the rise, flew to the let-down kingdom, and now in those bowels pecked, it hides where all the kings men are at loss.* The whole thing just means to look in a ruined piano somehow connected to Ross," I said.

"Or maybe it means we're sure to be at a loss in figuring out," said Gupta.

"So okay. It'll lead to... to something else. So it'll take a fresh approach, an unexpected definition... or something."

"Something like something's wrong," said Gupta. "We've got to take a radical turn."

"Cut through the Gideon Knot," I said.

"Cut through the Gordian Knot," Techo corrected.

"Oh. Yeah—let's channel Alexander the Great," I said, "and swing a sword right through this convoluted mess. I think Fenster would appreciate that."

"What?! You disgust me," Gupta said. "Speaking of that man with any degree of respect or sympathy—like you were trying to please him."

"We do want to please him," I said. "He's got something—someone—we want. Remember?"

"I'd rather just take her from him."

"That may happen, but until then, try 'please'. Thanks would be even better."

"Thanks!? You're nuts."

"Mindy first, revenge second. Getting Mindy will be the best revenge. Didn't your mother teach you to say 'please' to get things? Now just visualize Mindy back and, following the way of Shinran, say 'thank you' and our collective unconscious or subconscious or something will find her."

"Jeez. You're a religious fanatic. Let's go," he said shaking his head.

Back at Mindy's. Techo's at her computer.

"The submarine clue indicated the treasure hunt has loops, at least one loop, that takes us out of our way and brings us back to some point we've already been," I said. "So what else would that riddle lead to that isn't 650 kilometers away?"

"There's no time to keep doing this," Gupta said.

"Let's take a break and pray for something different to occur to us," I said.

"Oh no," said Gupta, "more prayers."

"Maybe Samo and the others have come up with something," Techo said. "He's supposed to call soon."

"Yeah," I said. "Techo—I want to check my email, okay?"

"Just don't write anything you wouldn't tell Fenster," he said.

"I can't think of anything they'd discover by me going online from here. I could even write them notes."

"Yeah," said Gupta. "Tell them to go cram it."

"First I must log on to the web site of my ISP."

"ISP?" Gupta puzzled. "Let's see—sounds like what the little round green thing in the pod answered when asked 'Who is you?' 'ISP.'"

"Internet Service Provider," I said, "is another less charming meaning."

Techo moved over. I sat down at the McIntosh, went on the Internet, logged on to Sonic.net's web site, and looked at my in-box. "It's a miracle! It worked! Thanks Techo, this is beautiful. There are only a few messages and no spam!"

"What are you talking about," asked Gupta.

"Techo told me to get a new email address and put an auto response on my old one that said to please resend your message to the new one. I was getting sixty spam a day. Spam doesn't read the forwarding message. Yea!"

"Neat," said Gupta. "But you really want to read your email now?"

"Hmm—nothing I need to read now. I'll get back to them. I got another idea." I Googled Ross Bolleter. "Ah, there's a fine-looking photo of him in his Zen robes. I looked around for a while and asked Techo, "What's that web site you worked on you said had stuff about Ross on it?"

"Yeah. Here." He leaned over me and typed the address in.

"See anything here that might help? Maybe something in that riddle that bounces off something in here?" I said. "How about *in the bowels?*"

"What about it meaning 'in the vowels,'" said Gupta.

"Yeah, could be pecking in the vowels but I still see it as the bowels, the innards of the ruined piano. Hey, there are ruined piano images on this site," I said. "Any interior views?"

"This photo shows the insides well," Techo said leaning down and putting his hand on the cursor. "You can see how screwed up some of the piano keys are and how the strings and action are fallen apart in there." He moved his cursor over the spot he was talking about. "Hey! What's that?"

"What?" I asked.

"A hot spot. The cursor arrow changed to a hand indicating a link in there."

"So what?" Gupta asked.

"So—I didn't put any links there."

"How about clicking on it?" Gupta said.

Techo's mobile rang. Samo reporting in. He, Gelar, and Frannie had been scoping out some businesses associated with Fenster in the area. Samo was going through records and notes, talking to cop friends, trying to figure out what property might be tied to Fenster through other names. Frannie was keeping an eye on a shop for women's clothing, browsing, going around back.

Gelar had been checking out a funeral home. Techo recognized the name—Amenity. I'd heard that name at Fenster's place—one of the Goony Twins mentioned taking Gupta's and my corpses to Amenity, an association that helped it to stick in memory. Samo said there were three branches of Fenster-owned Amenity Funeral Homes in WA—one here in Perth, one in Freo, and one in Dunsborough. Samo had some buddies keeping their eyes on the latter two—an ex-cop at one and an ex-con at the other. Gelar said Fenster had been in his office at the Perth site for a few hours. Techo said he'd done some work for a church that was next door to the Perth Amenity—set up their computer system, did their web site, and fixed up a big digital marquee in front to announce the Good News for everyone driving by. He said it's out by the airport.

I told Samo I had nothing to add other than to say we were still on an untamed dodo hunt but that we'd sort of given up running around though I didn't know what else we could do. I updated him on what was happening with our dead ends. He was clueless too. We agreed to check in with each other in a couple of hours.

Back to the computer. With Gupta and me looking on, Techo hit the link in the ruined piano image. It opened to the site for—oh my gosh—for The Maze.

"Why would that be here?" Techo said. "Someone planted a pop-up that goes to an amusement park site?"

"Techo, that's the place that Mindy took us to on our first day here."

Perplexed, we looked on. It was advertising a new maze, a seventh one that would be open soon, a special maze for "our foreign guests." I told Techo to try it out and it went to a page that said, "This maze site under construction. Take a nap and come back in an hour."

"What the hell is that about?" I said. I scrolled down for a phone number.

"That's odd," said Gupta. "But let's check on this."

Gupta called and asked if the new maze was open. "Maybe we should go there," he said waiting for an answer.

"What new maze?" the woman on the phone finally said. I could hear her voice.

Gupta told her about the seventh maze on their web site and she went away again and came back and said that their web site only promotes their six mazes.

"What the heck?" Gupta said after he'd hung up.

"Ditto," I said.

"Take their advice," said Techo. "You look beat."

"Whose advice?" I asked.

"Whoever's talkin' to you through the computer. They told you to take a nap for an hour. Good advice. You're both a little delirious. Rest up for a while. Let me look into this."

"I don't like them telling me what to do, but I can sleep," said Gupta plopping down on the couch.

"Me too." I reclined on the floor with a cushion under my head.

"Try the bedroom," said Techo.

"Too far," I said and was gone. I can sleep anywhere no trouble—a talent I've always had, and which was enhanced by sitting long hours of meditation.

An hour later cat nap over. Gupta and I got up and sipped from cups of strong tea Techo had brewed. Darjeeling with lemon. Techo said while we were sleeping he looked at the actual site of The Maze and it indeed has no seventh maze.

"The way this looks to me is that Fenster's tech guy..."

"Sid from Sydney," I said.

"...just copied their site, added the seventh maze ad to it and gave it a new temporary address with a link from Ross's ruined piano innards here—hacking it just for you."

"That's kind of him," I said. "But the seventh maze just says 'under construction.'"

"That was an hour ago. I think when we went there it hit an alarm on their end. Look at it now."

There's a blue screen with a strange phrase on it: *Beneficials of the lemon you want,* it reads. Below were six empty squares in two groups of three.

"It's the password to get in," said Techo. "Six characters."

"I don't want a lemon," said Gupta. "Except the lemon in my tea. Hey! They don't know about it do they? Come on—tell me that's a coincidence."

"It's a coincidence," said Techo.

"Or you're working for Fenster."

"They paid me to put the lemon in your tea. You caught me."

"They paid me not to tell you Gupta," I said. "But they said I could mention it in jest like I'm doing right now to further divert your suspicion."

"Stop it or I'll have to be straight-jacketed! I want this to end. I want Mindy back."

"And what's Mindy?" said Techo.

"Trouble," Said Gupta.

"What else?"

"I don't know...a girl?"

"She's a woman," said Techo.

"Okay. For once we can say woman."

"What are we looking for?"

"Tell me."

"A woman. But this is plural," Techo said.

"Lemon women," said Gupta.

"Women," I repeat. "*Beneficials of the women you want.* Need two sets of three letters each."

"Big tit?" said Gupta. "That fits."

Techo tried it and failed.

"Doesn't sound like Fenster to me," I said. "I think he's a mite prudish—despite his porno biz."

"Big fun?" Gupta continued. Didn't work.

"How about beneficials rhymes with... sacrificials," said Gupta.

"I don't care for that," I said.

"I don't either," said Gupta.

"Beneficial initials of the women you want," suggested Techo.

"Initials of the women you want!" I said excitedly. "That's what we're to put in the squares below."

A call to Gelar with Samo's help got Mindy's middle name. Alice. "Melinda Alice Waters. Or Dugan. MAD," said Gupta. "Sounds right. More than MAW. I'm mad about her and mad at her and she's mad as a hatter if that matters."

We added Frannie's initials forwards and backwards with both sets for Mindy but couldn't get anywhere.

"What other woman do we want?" I said. "What about that stewardess, Gupta?"

"Just know her first name. Uh—and I forgot it. What about your Malaysian friend."

"I don't think so."

"What's that story you're working on?" asked Gupta.

"I'm not working on any story."

"About your devoted dog who should be reborn as a woman?"

"Lola! Oh. She doesn't have three initials. With my last name it would be two."

We tried a few combos. Nope.

"What's the name of the story again?" Gupta said.

"It was just a joke, a curious idea."

"You mentioned it in an email?"

"Maybe."

"Okay the name of the story in the joke?"

"Lola, Come to Me as a Woman."

"Try Lola as woman, LAW" said Gupta.

Techo writes LAW MAD. It doesn't work. He tries LAW MAW. Nope. He reverses it. MAW LAW. MAD LAW.

Eureka! Flashing across the screen are the words, "Welcome Pilgrims! Do come in!"

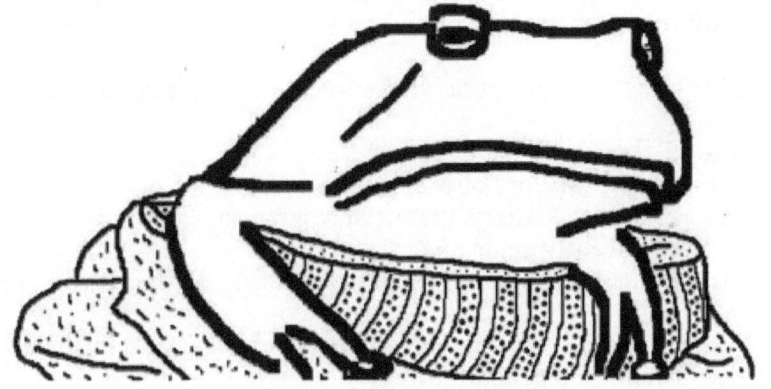

CHAPTER 25
AMAZING MAZE

And there it was—dazzling and awesome. With sound—Ross's tango music and then—Mindy's voice calling from a distance. That tore us up. We followed. There were so many streets, corridors, tunnels, buildings, rooms, and gardens where we'd been and almost been—easy to access with close up or sky view, obvious how to navigate, well-constructed. The clues we'd solved were there. But there were new questions and hints that led to new locations with hyperspace links that opened up other clues to other places, cyber places yet many familiar places—our WA universe on the screen.

We'd get blocked till we figured something out and then to new spots to get stuck again. A lot of it wasn't so difficult such as: *What the hippie and female Saudi adulterer had in common. They were* _____. This led to a bar called the Stoned Goose located in downtown Perth. But we didn't have to go to the real there to get the next clue. Some were based on old trick questions like this one: *An old Aussie term for angry is "as cross as a frog in a sock," and hungry can be "peckish." That's two words that end in GRY. But there are three words in our tongue, English. What's Oz slang for the third one?* I started trying to figure out a third word that ended in GRY, but Gupta had heard something similar before and knew it was a trick. The answer to that one was found when we ignored the first part

229

and reduced it to: *There are three words in our tongue, English and*
then answered, *What's Aussie for the third one?* In other words, what's Aussie slang for "English," the third of those three words?

"Frannie taught me that one," I said. "Wenchin' poms. Poms as in pomegranates."

"That's just one theory of what it means, what it comes from," said Techo.

"Really?" I said. "What else?"

"Abbreviation of Port of Melbourne where a lot of Brits landed. Prisoners of Her Majesty. Permit of Migration. There are others, most of them recently made up."

"I said pomegranates in an email so try it first. Right? If you can find any."

We then hunted for a pomegranate, which we found in the cyberspace Dwellingup general store.

A link on a box of that red fruit opened to a bad joke with a bad word: *Sounds like the Abo Buckster wants to return to where you met him last.*

"That's Outback," I realized right off and told Techo to take us to a place that sounds like that, namely out back behind the main Perth train station where Gupta and I had run into him on the way to Ross's. There he was. "Try his hat with the money in it," Gupta guessed. Called it. The cursor turned to a pointing hand at that spot. The next clue opened up with a click.

It read simply: *How far everyplace is from here.* That led to the sign near Mai's sister's home, the one at the wharf that had the distances from that spot to far off cities in Australia and elsewhere. That led to a clue in Mai's brother-in-law's workshop.

How did they have time to do all this? Must be made from something they were working on already. But there was so much that had to be specifically done for us—like Daniel's workshop. Places we went and wanted to go were laid out so we couldn't see much at once or what led to what—the passages would be hidden. But it was all there—the Forest Heritage Center, Frannie's home, Tazi John's book, the mazes at The Maze and the animals there from numbat to Double-wattled Cassowary. There was a lead to the motorcycle engine tombstone. There was a dead end at Frannie's behind her hibernating car's license plate that had the sequence 921 on it, the reverse of her address. From Ross's ruined piano innards, one could go to the sub and back or straight to the web site that led us here. It went all the way to Cue and who knows where from there. We didn't try because we were sure it was a dead end. The quokka clue led also to the cave on Rottnest to a message in a bottle lying in a bush just outside. That clue, which included "swing low sweet chariot," led to the gallows of the prison with a note at the bottom that brought one back to the cave—another dead end. We'd find links just putting the cursor down at random and go off on new tangents of the cyber-space treasure hunt.

"Isn't that cheating," I wondered aloud.

"Curse you," answered Gupta shaking his fist in my face.

We examined the riddles as they came up and solved them one by one. It was a lot easier in the computer because we could see what the choices were and hunt around quickly. And having Techo, who speaks Australian, was helpful at times such as when we went to the Swan Bells. We heard them ringing. There was a vender outside selling apples and pears. Techo said, "Apples and pairs—climb the stairs."

The marquee of a movie house featured Tom Hanks and Meg Ryan in *You've Got Mail*.

"Boilerplate formula romantic film," I said. "Silly. And charming."

"Check your mail," said Techo.

There was email from Kelly, Dennis, Tazi John, and Eihei Dogen. That's interesting—he's been dead since the mid thirteenth century. That's his posthumous title—which would be easy to get from the Tanahashi Dogen book in Fenster's library. The email Subject line read: *Today's profound quote.* The message simply read, "For today's profound quote, go to this link: http//:www.dogen-says.com.au." I hit that link and it opened up a site with the famous, for some Zen people, self-portrait of Dogen. Below the portrait was written, "What is your name?" I put the cursor in the box and wrote my name. A box opened that said "Wrong name."

"Forgot your name?" asked Gupta.

I tried it a few different ways. Didn't work.

"Try Tom Hanks," said Techo. "He's the one who had mail."

"Oh yeah." I tried that and Meg Ryan. She had mail too. "Ah heck."

"No wait," said Techo. "It wasn't Tom Hanks who got it. That's the actor's name."

"I sure don't know what the name of the character was," I said.

"IMDB," said Techo sliding over and typing.

"IMDB?" said Gupta. "Sounds like someone thinks they're a little yellow flying colonial insect with a sweet tooth and a stinger."

"Not quite," said Techo. "Internet Movie Data Base." He already had the movie up on the screen. He scrolled down to the cast. "Tom Hanks is... Joe Fox."

Back to dogensaysdotcomdotau. I write "Joe Fox" and yippee! Enter we do—to a screen with a checkered board, which we instantly recognize as a Scrabble board. An empty Scrabble board.

"Are we supposed to play Scrabble now?" asked Gupta angrily.

Techo tried his cursor on the screen. Nothing. He typed. Nothing. The tiles were poured from a cup, then turned letter side down.

"It's a video," said Techo. "All we can do is watch now."

That's what we did. Quietly we watched the game unfold word after word. The screen froze at one point.

"It's not finished," I said.

"That's what we've got to figure out," Techo said. "It's a word jumble. We can arrange the letters now as we figure the words out."

"Where's Greg now that we need him," I said referring to my Zen friend who solves these things at a glance.

We got a few words and then I solved it at a glance. "I see it. That's easy. It's a famous Dogen quote to take the backwards step that turns the light inward. Almost that."

In a while we had it. *Learn the backward step that turns your light inwardly.* More silence.

"That was quick for a change. Hey, we should high five sometimes," I said.

"Shut up," said Gupta.

"How about saying 'yes!' with our fists up the way they do in movies?" I demonstrate. "Yes!"

"Stop it. Do that when we get Mindy back," he said unmoved. "And by yourself. Focus. Think about what your pal Dogen has to say."

"Well, you said IMDB," I charged.

"A moment of weakness. Think Dogen now."

Techo and Gupta look to me for an interpretation of the Dogen quote.

"Hmm. I, I, I, I—let me think about it," I said. "It's famous." After a minute: "It's from the *Genjo Koan*, Dogen's most famous work." We went to Tanahashi's *Moon in a Dewdrop* on Amazon.com, opened the book so to speak, went to the *Genjo Koan*. It's not there. "It's in something else Dogen wrote." We searched for the phrase. It came up on the Berkeley Zen Center's web site. "Oh. It's from the *Fukanzazengi*, Dogen's instructions for zazen. My gaffe. Hey, it's word for word—it's their translation, their copyright." Nothing though. No links, no clues. "Let's just go on," I said. "*Learn the backward step that turns your light inwardly.* Another dead end."

We went back in the maze to downtown Perth. We were lost for a while and then picked up on another lead by putting the cursor over a piece of paper on the sidewalk. Need to enlarge. Turned the cursor into a magnifying glass. Click. It was a brochure from the Perth Mint. That's not hard to find. We went from room to room—gift shop, mining site, glass-walled hall to observe minting in action. The big ingot was sparkling in the Plexiglas case. The cursor would lift it. We went to the Pour Room. The ingot there was sitting cooling and shining in the same spot as in the real tour. On the audio Jimmy Cliff sang, "You Can Get It if You Really Want."

We went on. Once again, it seemed as if everything from all my emails was there—the Leeuwin winery kinetic sculpture, the pub with Mindy's hair hanging, the Indiana Tea House, the Hotham Valley Railway—wished I'd had a chance to ride it. And there were places I hadn't heard of Fenster obviously thought were must-see spots—the Kalbarri Coast with coral reefs, Ningaloo Marine Park, a picturesque town named Esperance, no night clubs or strip joints though.

"Go back to that Dogen quote," said Gupta.

"Yeah," said Techo. "I don't think we exhausted that."

"How can we *learn the backward step that turns our light inwardly?*" Gupta asked. "How about going to Fenster's library?"

Techo found the way—zooming up over WA, back down on Dunsborough and Fenster's estate, into his house, and to the library. We snooped but could detect nothing that responded with a hot spot in the books or the room. Weird thing was we did find a copy of the Berkeley ZC's *Fukanzazengi* lying on a table, magnified it and there was that quote highlighted—but no link.

We went further out the front door to the gate house. There's the roadster. Back to the swimming pool and yes—through the woods to the cabin the Goony Twins took our chloroformed or something ed limp bodies to. There was a plastic bag dispenser thoughtfully placed on the wall. But nothing in our attempts to go back or inward opened a door.

Return to the library. The Fukanzazengi on the table seemed to be just a reminder, a tease. The only hyperlinks in that room were highlights and background for Robina, Phar Lap, Genghis Khan, the Japanese sword, and Joan Sutherland. Her hyperlink also unleashed her voice, which was good for a while but which Techo could only get rid of by rebooting.

"They've been working on this every day," Techo said as the operating system started up again. "Building it, modifying it. It's massive."

"They're crazy," said Gupta. "I mean he's crazy, nuts, a sadist, a bully, a freak, a fanatic, a psychopath, a kidnapping crook, a nasty villain. He's bad, evil, malicious, crazy... "

"Now you're repeating yourself," I broke in.

"Unproductive," said Techo.

We went on and on and on through the treasure hunt maze. It got late but we didn't stop. At one point in the early morning I turned to Gupta and said bleary-eyed, "Four," and he said, "No, it's earlier than that." Then he paused and said, "Oh yes—four."

"Four what?" asked Techo.

"Four more days to live at the rate we're going," Gupta said. "And it's getting less funny and more frightening every day."

We took turns nodding out but no one lay down for long. I stepped outside to see the top of the red hydrogen ball of glowing sunrise. The next time I noticed, setting sun rays were streaking through the window. It was endless, really endless. At first the on-line maze was a great relief but we realized this too was getting us nowhere—and it was just a larger infinity in which to be lost and confused.

Frannie called. She'd been at a costume shop in Freo. Samo was looking at some video porn stores. They were going home to respective family. She wished us well.

Darkness. Gupta was ready to explode. We'd tried everything we could think of—like I talked to Techo about wall-following and asked if there were any way to apply that to this cyberspace maze. We couldn't figure anything out with that. I remembered something Sid said about another method to use on 2D mazes, which was to fill in the dead ends and loops but that didn't seem to help. It wasn't a simple maze.

"Once again we need to cut through that knot," I said. "Back to Dogen. Back. *Learn the backward step that turns your light inwardly.* It really sounds like good advice but how can it be applied? We went inward when we went to the web. How much more inward can we go. Or backward?"

"If we could just get to the bottom of this!" shouted Gupta.

"Good idea!" said Techo. He was lickety-split back in Fenster's library and put the cursor over that line in the text of the Fukanzazengi and clicked the mouse somewhere that changed the screen into bland, black on white irregular lines of words and symbols.

"HTML?" asked Gupta.

"Yes," I said. "Of course—the inward language the Internet is all done in. See—it's all just typed out. Well, let's read what's there and see what we come up with."

Gupta and I leaned over Techo peering at the computer screen.

"I'm not real used to it," I said. "I have a web site and I do a little HTML, but it's tedious for me. Mainly I work with WYSIWYG— What You See Is What You Get—with Front Page or Dream Weaver and don't see the HTML. Incidentally Gupta, those initials don't remind you of anything do they? Nothing about bees or pees?"

"What initials?"

"HTML."

"A blank. What's the acronym stand for? Happy The Many Lilliputians?"

"Haven't Thought My Liege," I said.

"High Time Mister Loony," he countered.

"He's The Most Lost," I said to Techo.

"Heavens, That's Most Ludicrous," Gupta trumped.

"Please look at it," said Techo impatiently. "Both of you."

"It's over our heads," I said.

"No—look at it," Techo said. "You might see something I don't."

Gupta and I looked closely at the formulas, words, letters, numbers, and symbols of the site. The whole Fukanzazengi was written out in regular English but there were embedded instructions in code as well that determine font, margins, colors. And nearby were all the more complicated codes for the images and sounds.

"What's that Hindi doing there?" Gupta said pointing.

"That doesn't do anything," said Techo. "It's for the people who were working with it and some of this must have been done in India. It's not a message to the computer, doesn't show up on the web page. It's probably a technical message from one Indian programmer for other Indian programmers. Nothing that applies now."

"They were working on this in India?" I asked.

"It was probably just scooped up accidentally when some web designer copied something he wanted to duplicate from a page on the web."

"That's not what it is," said Gupta.

"It's not?" Techo asked.

"No. It's for us."

"You can read that?" Techo says.

"My father made me learn Hindi when I was a kid."

"That's neat," I said.

"I had to worship the monkey god too."

"Oh that's terrible," said Techo.

"I still worship the monkey god."

"Yeah," I said swatting Techo. "Hanuman's a cosmic archetype."

"Whatever works," said Techo.

"Now listen to this," said Gupta, "Ha! I think you will like it."

"Read it!" I commanded.

He did. "*Take that walk... you've been wanting to go on... tomorrow.*"

"Hmm," Gupta looked at me. "It's a decidedly less cryptic message. But what walk would that be?"

"That can only mean the walk from Perth to Freo," I said, "along the Swan River that, as it said, I've been wanting to do. Remember? I wanted to go?"

"Oh yeah."

"But how do we know *our* tomorrow is the one intended in the message here?"

"Oh, it says the date—August 26th. Tomorrow. Even says 'leaving at 9 a.m. Check your calendar to see if you're free,'" said Gupta.

"Nine a.m. tomorrow," I said. "Oh great. Sleep. Rest."

"Sleep. Rest," echoed Gupta with relief.

"We're back in the real world. Turn off the computer, Techo. I think that may be the end of this... this amazing maze."

"We don't know that," said Gupta. "It might just start up again in some way. But I really, truly hope you're right. I'm going to go take a hot tub."

"Me too. Oh my gosh," I said. "I forgot. Ross is giving a concert in Freo tomorrow night. We're on the guest list—all of us. Remember? That's perfect. We'll get there and eat dinner and go to his show."

"Unless you're murdered on the way," said Gupta.

"So who should go with me on the walk? Both of you? Just me?"

"You two go," said Gupta. "I'll drive."

"Nope—you'll walk too," said Techo, "And I can't go. It says right here in English after that Hindi, 'Septics only.'"

"And that's uh, who?" questioned Gupta.

"You two," said Techo. "Septic tank—rhymes with yank."

SWAN RIVER
ESTUARY

CHAPTER 26
SWAN RIVER

I don't want to go on this walk," said Gupta. "I want to sleep. I want Mindy to just come back without me having to do anything." He rolled over and hid under the covers.

"We've slept a ton. You said no sticking your hands in pianos, no flying, and no driving, but you didn't say no walking. It'll be refreshing," I said, looking at a map I got at the tourist bureau. "It's twenty kilometers by car, but could be more like thirty walking by the river."

"Thirty! And I have to go?" he said.

"Yes. Get up. And Gupta?

"Yes?"

"Three."

"Three to go," said Gupta getting up.

"Three to go," I repeated.

"Three days till we have dinner with Rudy."

"Just the four of us."

"Yep—Rudy, you, me, and—Mindy. She'll be there," he said in a monotone staring straight ahead and putting on a shirt.

I went back outside and joined Samo whom I'd been talking with for a while. We didn't know what on the planet to expect from this assigned walk.

237

Snipers? I had a mobile set to vibrate in case there was an urgent development. Samo said he'd not be far if we needed him.

We took off from the base of the Swan Bells Tower heading down along the Swan River estuary on a wide walkway. Soon we would see actual swans on the other bank of the river after crossing Swan Bridge.

"Lot of swans," Gupta said, "black, white and titular. I just hope this isn't our swan song."

"I'm really glad to be finally doing this," I said as we went along a marsh. It was so good to just relax and walk. "This is my favorite thing to do. I much prefer it, for instance, to shivering in claustrophobic paranoia in a cramped metal marine coffin."

"Or frantically following psycho clues into oblivion."

It was a lovely walk and a warm day. We passed wetlands, marinas, and the backsides and front-sides of upscale homes, condos, and apartment buildings.

While Gupta went to pee in a clump of trees I sat on a bench next to a well-dressed gentleman, a Mr. Huxworthy, who was friendly and talkative. He lived nearby and had worked for thirty years in sewage disposal. This is an area in which I also have some experience, having been involved with Zen and nonZen rural and remote communities and homes. I was somewhat familiar with septic systems, outhouses, compost privies, and aeration of sewage. Mr. Huxworthy was currently involved in the Woodman Point wastewater treatment plant on the southern boundary of Perth. It disposes of primary sludge by two stage anaerobic digestion followed by drying on open sand beds, the results of which are then used as a soil conditioner, an admirable arrangement.

The solid waste disposal systems in Perth and the surrounding area are designed with the objective of preserving the purity of the Swan River. They are prepared for occasional huge rainfall that might flood the system and send impurities into the river. As a result, the sewer pipes are especially large and numerous. He said one could get lost down in that system.

Gupta returned from his minor waste disposal journey, found our conversation deadeningly boring, and said it was time to move on. So I bid Mr. Huxworthy good day, thanked him for, what was to me, a most invigorating discussion, and headed off with my fellow septic.

The sun was as high as it was going to get that day when we crossed a large bridge with heavy traffic. I was looking out over the wide expanse of the river at a cruise boat when Gupta clutched me.

"God! Don't get me on the ribs like that!" I said shoving him back.

"Sorry, touchy," he said. "I forgot. But something is worthy of your attention."

"Okay. I've recovered. What is it?"

He turned and gestured to a large billboard ahead of us, which read, "Hi Davo and Guppy! Hope you're enjoying your walk!" It was signed "The whole gang!"

"He's sure going to a lot of trouble for us," I said. "I'm beginning to feel that the strangers we pass are working for him."

"The people in the cars too," Gupta agreed.

"Even the disappointed ravens are reporting in," I said watching a few of them calling from high wires.

A man standing at a bus stop followed us with his eyes. Children playing ball stopped to observe. Everyone worked for Fenster.

Thankfully it was a beautiful day and the smell of the air and the wooded area we entered combed the paranoia from our thoughts—for a while.

We took a road that led to a dead end in a yacht club. We climbed up a steep embankment to the path above that we should have stayed on and at one point stopped to catch our, actually my, breath, and there, due to the steepness of the hill we climbed, not two feet in front of our faces, was a curious convex object planted into the ground. Was it an enormous dried flower with a multitude of desiccated petals? Was it a mushroom of sorts? A mottled stone? I started to feel it's texture when suddenly Gupta swatted my hand aside and I gasped, realizing it was a nest of bees. Cautiously we continued, hearts thumping, up and away from the hair-trigger hymenoptera bomb I'd almost absentmindedly triggered.

"Probably planted by one of Fenster's boys," said Gupta.

We passed through a park with an outdoor pavilion where people ate desserts, drank coffee and tea, and gazed through the trees to the river. I got cheese cake and tea and Gupta coffee and ice cream. The waitress told us our bill had been covered by a man who wished to remain anonymous. We looked around at the faces at the tables.

Continuing on we came to a bluff above the riverbank. There three Tibetan monks, easily identified by their maroon robes, caught my eye. They were sitting on a bench at an overlook, signs of Freo in the distant view.

"Let's go say hello," I said to Gupta. "Time for a rest anyway."

"Let's not," he said. "You should keep your eye on the prize."

"That would be 'eye on the pry', so let's pry."

"Ah Krishna," he mumbled.

As we approached the men of cloth, something about them seemed strange—the way they held themselves. I hailed them with a friendly "G'day." Two who had short hair kept their backs to me but the one in the middle with a shiny pate turned around. Oh! It was a woman, a Western woman. I could only tell she was a woman because her figure was too buxom for her maroon robes to hide. She was old, had a large nose, and there was something about that look in her eyes. I greeted her with a bow.

"Blessings to you," she said in a quivering voice. Was this the famed Robina? I'd seen that photo of her and couldn't quite remember.

"And the same to you," I responded. Gupta nodded.

"Enjoying your walk?"

"Yes," I said. "And what a lovely view here."

"Where are you from?"

"The States."

"Where have you been?"

"Just around WA."

"And you?" she asked Gupta.

"Same," he said looking away, not in a good mood.

"Have you heard the Swan Bells?"

"Yes—beautiful—to see as well as to listen to. In fact, we just walked from there."

"Oh—quite a stroll. And the Maze? Have you been to the Maze?"

"Yes! Not many people mention that! But we have been there and we loved it."

"Have you been to the Perth Mint?"

"Yes."

"Would you like to go back?"

"Probably don't have time."

"Oh, I think you should," she said with a lilt.

"Hey man," whispered Gupta, "Let's keep going."

"Hold on there," the nun said. "Would you do me a favor when you go back to the Mint?"

"I uh..."

"I'd like you to pick up a little something for me there."

"She's crazy man, let's go," Gupta said.

"Where do you live? I, I, I—if I go. What do you want?" I stammered, not wanting to be rude.

"Did you see the bar of gold they pour?"

"Yes."

"And the one in the clear case you lifted?"

"I lifted? Yes. I did lift it. But..."

"They would be nice to have."

"Which would you rather have, the 200 or the 400 ouncer?" I asked in jest.

"Both."

This was weird stuff for a Buddhist nun to be saying.

"You're not Robina are you?" I asked. No—couldn't be.

"Yes I am," she said. Wow. "And I'd be grateful for this contribution to my prison project. Let me play you some music while you think about it," she said and hit the play switch on a CD player sitting on the bench.

"What the hell are you talking about?" said Gupta angrily. "Let's go! We're not going to..."

"Gupta, be quiet and listen," I said, "listen to... Joan Sutherland." Joan Sutherland's voice rang out majestically.

"Joan Sutherland!?" cried Gupta. "What the hell is this. Oh my god. You're not... You're Fenster. You crazy son of a bitch!"

The other two monks turned around. It's the Goony Twins. They're practically snarling in their monk's garb.

"That's goddamn Fenster in drag man—and with a fake nose," Gupta said.

"I am *not* that man when I'm dressed in these robes! Now there is just Robina!"

"Just some friggin' nut," said Gupta.

The Twins lean forward and clench four fists.

We stagger back. "Be polite Gupta," I said nervously. "Robina. Ah—I admire your work in the prisons," I said to Fenster, uh to her, "A pleasure to meet you."

"Okay," said Gupta. "Nice to meet you. Let Mindy Go!"

"Listen to genius, you Hindustani piece of excrement. Listen to Joan Sutherland. She is the greatest ever. She had a divine gift."

"I'm not in the mood," said Gupta.

"You be quiet. Why even the noble Doberman Mars loves to hear her sing. He comes into the library or wherever her voice is playing and he just sits and listens. Every time we are blessed to hear her voice is like the first time we hear her. She is the best there ever was and the best there ever will be. Now listen and appreciate greatness."

"Have I heard that spiel before?" said Gupta. "It sort of gives you away."

"Silence!"

The Goony Twins stared at us to insure compliance. The short one was fingering a knife. At least it was short. A couple walking by with a child looked at us curiously, the five of us standing still and listening to Joan Sutherland's platinum voice soaring through to the treetops. After this aria was finished, Robina Fenster shut the CD off.

"It's been quite a trip," I said. "You have a complicated mind."

"A complicated sick mind," said Gupta. "A sick mind that..."

"Now now," I interrupted. "And you created an incredible task for us. It's been quite a trip. Now please, give us Mindy back."

"First take another trip to the Mint—except this time lighten their load a little."

"That would be awfully difficult," I said.

"It's your final task in the treasure hunt. Treasure for treasure."

"We've had enough of your games," shouted Gupta. "Give us Mindy!"

Fenster Robina stood up and pronounced shrilly, "I'm talking about bricks of the shiny Kalgoorlie! And, failing that, an equal serving of sausage and mash—rhymes with cash! One hundred plus two hundred is three hundred."

"We can't. Are you kidding. We can't do anything illegal like that—or dangerous, or come up with that much money," I said.

"Oh you'd be surprised what people can do if they're motivated enough."

"And if we fail?"

"Then you and your friends will be entering the next bardo, as the Tibetans say. Now listen to this:

Kali takes while Shiva gives,
With the smaller brick she lives.
With the bigger she and Fran.
With them both long live your clan."

Oh my god. Frannie. She is in danger. And what's that about the clan? It's not just Gupta and me anymore.

He-she reaches into his-her robe's sleeve, pulls out a large envelope and hands it to me. "I work on death row," Robina Fenster said. "Here are the condemned. I will ordain each one of them before they are executed."

"Why? You've got plenty of money!" I said.

"For my prison project!"

"Robina's prison project is to help people. She doesn't hurt people."

"Don't lecture me! I'll build my own prison! And you'll help me do it! That's why you'll do it! For that and to test you and punish you if you fail the test! It's a challenge! It's karma! Be up to it or reap the headless fruit of failure. Thanks to me you're going to see what sort of stuff you're made of! I'm not poured into the wimpy mold of your meditate-and-be-nice Buddhists. I'm from the blood and guts school of life and death, act or be acted on! Prepare to taste the sharp edge of fate! I was a punk and then a Black Panther and then a man-hater. Now I'm a muscular Buddhist you must fear!

Kali takes while Shiva gives,
With the smaller brick she lives.
With the bigger she and Fran.
With them both long live your clan."

"Couldn't you integrate a little more ahimsa?" I suggested. "You know ahimsa? Non-violence toward sentient beings? Not harming? That's Robina."

"You don't know Robina! She's a woman. Yours is girly Buddhism! Bring the bricks to me or for starters I'll go slicing through your friend's pretty soft neck! And then the rest of you! Halleluiah!"

"God, he's over the edge crazy for real," said Gupta. "Let's get outa here."

"If you two wish to be able to go back home with something connected to your shoulders, then dare to do what no one has done—rob the Perth Mint! Halleluiah!"

We're just standing there as if in a windstorm.

"Bring my treasure to the Amenity Funeral Home in Perth anytime night or day within three days—that's Friday by sunset or it's headset. Now have a nice walk! Halleluiah!"

As we walked quickly away, Fenster danced around in his robes wailing halleluiah while the Goony Twins' cold eyes followed us.

"That Hindu poem, the Christian Halleluiah, the Buddhist robes, old testament punishment, cultish threats," I said to Gupta. We rounded a bend and dashed off into the woods. "He sure mixes his metaphysics."

"And meta-forensics," Gupta replied.

Dusk was taking over for its brief interlude as we entered Freo. Suddenly I jumped and grabbed at my thigh. Oh, it was the mobile vibrating. Samo on the other end.

"What can I do for you?" I said.

"I think we know where Mindy is," he answered.

OLD SWAN BREWERY

CHAPTER 27
PLANNING DEPORTMENT

"Do you know this guy?" Samo said handing me some photos.

"Yes. I know him. That's Stan. He's Fenster's English valet and I bet, most trusted assistant."

"Right. He's been with Fenster for thirty years."

"He's the guy who planted the clues in Dwellingup and maybe everywhere else," I said. "He went to Frannie's door."

"He was at the Brewery," said Samo, "but he's not on the eight hour shift. That's these guys."

"Nope. Never saw them."

Samo was talking about the building that used to be the Swan Brewery below King's Park. There's a posh restaurant on one side, but on the other there's a section that hasn't been used for years. It's rented in the name of a freight company tied indirectly to Fenster.

"This one's Terrible Terry. He's mainly a clerk. Did time for fraud and for tax evasion. No violence in his history. This is Queenly from Queensland. Opposite story here. A number of assault arrests. Acquitted twice for murder. And this is Brandon Johnstone, called Johnno. He's a go-to guy. Odd jobs. Been in prison twice—for extortion and robbery. Acquitted for kidnapping a politician's prize dog in Melbourne."

245

I looked carefully at the photos. "So what do ya think?"

"If she's in there, I figure the best time to break her free is toward the end of a shift, but with plenty of time to get away before the next guy comes on. Johnno, the graveyard guy, looked more beat when he came out. But it may be better to attack in the afternoon when there's a lot of activity in the restaurant and everywhere else."

Samo and I were out front of an auditorium in Fremantle where Ross was doing a tango piano and accordion recital for a packed house consisting mainly of Argentine immigrants. Gupta was in there with Gelar and Techo. We were among a hundred or more people standing. Not Frannie though. She selflessly offered to stay on watch at the Brewery that night to look for more suspicious activity. Gupta and I had arrived at Freo in time to make our dinner date with Techo and Gelar before the concert. Samo came later. It was intermission and I wanted to say hi to Ross briefly but I couldn't get through to him because the hall was so packed. The fire marshal surely would have freaked—if he weren't Argentine.

I told Samo about the unorthodox meeting with Fenster and of his unreasonable demands. I said at dinner Gupta started talking about how we might have to rob the Mint and Gelar and Techo seemed to take it seriously. We needed to discourage them. Aside from being illegal it seemed to me to be impossible. Samo said he'd come over to Mindy's tonight after the concert so we could all talk about the situation and the plan to set Mindy free and that would keep their minds off trying to sneak those gold bricks out of the Mint. And once Mindy's free we can deal with Fenster. Hmm. Maybe *he* can.

I passed Samo a manila envelope with a color copy of the gift Fenster in Robina drag had bestowed on Gupta and me earlier that day. Gupta had made a copy for each of us before dinner. It was a collage made from photos of Mindy and the treasure hunt gang—Frannie, Gelar, Gupta, Samo, Techo, and me. The unique design aspect of this work of art was that the heads and bodies were separated and spread out without regard to each other. There was a background of familiar Perth sights. In the right top corner Genghis Khan sat on a horse in battle gear with my head on his spike. Samo took his copy and went back inside.

I saw a distinguished looking gentleman light up an American Spirit and politely solicited one. He was most willing and eager to chat. He was from Buenos Aires. I told him I'd spent part of a summer there almost forty years ago and had a wonderful time. I called him *Che*, which they call each other there. The women of his coun-

try, "especially one," I added, "had stolen my heart." He smiled widely. He went on and on about how special it was to have such a great
tango musician in WA. He said he played some tango on the piano—poorly. Much better, he said, to hear an accomplished pianist
like Ross Bolleter. I told him about my connection to Ross through
Zen and music and the man about flipped. He introduced himself
and gave me his card—Philippe Vargas. He was a banker. He suggested I come to a meeting of the tango club. Superior way to meet
women he pointed out. I said it sounded good to me. While he was
telling me about the spiritual dimension of tango, I watched Ross
climb out of a window onto the balcony of the performing hall. At
an appropriate moment I excused myself, caught up with Ross who
was being besieged by fans, and told him how splendid the concert
was. Similar to what everyone else was saying I suppose. I inquired
as to why he climbed out on the balcony. He was trying to get to the
loo. It was too crowded to move inside.

"Two" said Gupta as soon as he was done with his yoga. I was cross-
legged on the floor behind him, using a cushion from the couch.
　"Ah, good morning," I said. "Again you beat me to the count.
And yes, toodaloo it is—day after tomorrow." I uncross my legs.
　"Oh, pardon me master," he said, "I didn't mean to disturb your
Samadhi."
　"All is contained within this vast mind my son. Nothing on
heaven or earth can disturb it."
　"You may be tested soon." He looked at the clock on the wall
and jumped up. Ran into the bedroom and woke Gelar, then zipped
into the bathroom. Soon he was dressed, drinking coffee, gobbling
food. Gelar did the same.
　I asked Gelar what he knew about the painting on the wall. I'd
been around enough to know its intricate dot patterns are Aborigi-
nal or influenced by Aboriginal art.
　"You like it?" he said.
　"Oh yeah, I love it. I keep staring at it and at the boy with the
snake around him. It's part of his power. It's his spiritual friend. You
don't see snakes portrayed that way where I come from."
　"Good. Thanks," he said.
　"Oh, I see," I said. "The boy is you, a self-portrait."
　"The whole painting is me," he said going out the door with
Gupta.
　I knew where they were going—to meet Techo and then to the
Mint to do research for their robbery. Samo couldn't talk them com-

pletely out of it last night. I tried to dissuade Gupta and Gelar as well but Gupta just pointed to the collage he had mounted on the wall in the living room. He said if we get Mindy out first though, they wouldn't go through with it of course. We talked about how to come up with three hundred thousand dollars, the facsimile Fenster said he'd accept. Rudy could do it but forget that.

Techo went back to the web to see if there were any changes to the Treasure Hunt Maze only to find it gone. www.dogensays.com. au was gone as well. He couldn't find a trace. No hints, no evidence.

Last night late, after Samo departed, the would-be Mint thieves got to arguing about the Coriolis Effect. They kept flushing the toilet, running the tub, and I'd hear Gupta's exclamations of "See! See!" But it seemed not all his experiments went as hoped. It was still one of the unsolved mysteries. Aside from that, there hadn't been much playing around lately. Or drinking. That's understandable. We needed to be alert to keep up with developments and it was just two days till we all died at the hands of Fenster or Rudy or found out it's all just a big joke. But anyway, it was such a relief not to have to be following the treasure hunt in the real world or the webbed world. A small consolation while awaiting impending doom, the only constant of our recent history.

It was time for me to go too. I was going to relieve Samo on surveillance—keeping an eye on the Brewery till Frannie relieved me. I was to meet him at the restaurant at nine in the morning, well after the eight o'clock shift change. Fenster's guys didn't go near the swank eatery. They sneaked up, darted in the far door on the other side of the building, and disappeared quickly when they departed.

Samo came up to my table and sat down. "Somewhere in that building your Mindy may be," he said. "And if so, we're going to get her out. Soon. Better be soon. Everyone's getting exhausted—and a little nuts. Tomorrow afternoon. I hate to wait but I want to be sure. And the timing needs to be right."

The idea was for Samo and some of us to go in at about two in the afternoon. Frannie would stay in the bushes. If there was a problem Samo would hit a preset on his mobile that would vibrate hers. She was to listen in case he had something to say, but if he didn't, then she was to call the police on a special number. His old partner knew something was up and was prepared to send a force to the Brewery.

I told him how the boys set out early that morning to prepare for the heist contingency. Samo shook his head.

Early that evening Frannie came over. She was on her way to visit her parents who of course had no idea about her involvement in these clandestine activities. They thought I was a good influence. She wasn't wearing the wrist brace. She'd taken my place in mid afternoon in the bushes opposite the Brewery keeping an eye out and knitting a scarf that didn't exacerbate the carpel tunnels. Now Samo was there. And I was going in soon for the later night shift. Samo was going to take my place again in the early, early morning. Not long before we were to go in.

Frannie and I talked about guys. She needed a nice Aussie guy. I really like them all but some can be a little crude at times—and abusive. Like some Texans I've known. She said almost every night in Dwellingup there's a fight at the pub. Really? Those nice fellows? Yes.

I told her how impressed I was the night Banger insisted on assisting and crashed through the ceiling. Still she spoke to him with a gentle and kind voice. "It's exactly how Buddha told people to speak to each other," I said to her.

"He never told me that."

"Uh-huh. You're Miss Buddha."

"I'm Frannie."

"Same thing."

I've heard such extreme stories from Frannie about some of her friends and boyfriends. Like one she'd told me about Banger and Bud at a time when Banger was living with her. Frannie had just tidied up and they came in with a couple of bottles of Jack D. They were bleeding terribly, getting blood all over everything and she got her medicine kit and healing herbs and oils out and fixed them up. Banger had a tomahawk thrown at him and it went into his hand. She said tomahawk, by which I think she meant hatchet. Anyway, the guy who attacked him was known for chasing people he thought were on drugs. That's one reason he was still out there. If you only throw tomahawks at druggies you're much less likely to get arrested just about anywhere. Banger's friend Bud yelled at him from the street that they weren't on any drugs—just drinking—and threw a big rock at the house of the guy with the tomahawk in feeble revenge and the guy came out with a bat and broke Bud's arm. For an added visual, Banger had cracked his neck earlier and was wearing one of those thick, white supportive collars. Frannie had fixed them up as well as she could and they were meanwhile chugging the Jack D and getting deranged. Then Frannie said something Bud didn't like

249

and he slugged her. Banger said, "Settle down," and Bud pushed him back. Frannie tried to intervene and then Banger said to her, "You're coming between me and my mate," and threatened her with a backhand. She finally got Banger to go to sleep on the couch but then Bud staggered in from the kitchen and started trying to cut Banger's ear with a butter knife and Banger was so pissed he didn't even wake up. Frannie threw the butter knife out of the room and told Bud to go away. Banger woke up and said to Frannie, with irritation in his tone, "Steady on, mate." Finally both guys were asleep and she tidied the place again and cleaned up all the blood. The next morning the boys were just sore and went off to a clinic to tend to their wounds but they couldn't remember enough of the night before to apologize for it.

Although these wild buddies of hers were good hearted, at least when they weren't drunk, I felt she deserved better—someone gentle like she is who would be good to her. I said I know she loves her friends but in terms of a partner, she should be careful not to give her crystals to the hyenas.

I got the guitar, took out a folder of songs, and picked one to play. She leaned over to read it but I wouldn't let her, telling her you gotta have the music with them. So I sang it.

If you want to get a girl you gotta treat her mean
That's what they told me back in Abilene
Treat her mean, treat her mean
I'd rather treat you to a cup o' tea
Cause I—I just want to be good to you.

If you want a meltin' mama you gotta be cruel
That's what they told me back in high school
Gotta be cruel, gotta be cruel
Honey, I'd rather be your fool
Cause I—I just want to be good to you

Can't keep my cool none
Babbling on these days
Can't hide my love hon
Let me count the ways

They'll beg for more if you act real cold
That's what I was often told
Act real cold, act real cold

I'd rather melt before you on the floor
Cause I—I just want to be good to you

If you want to be the boss use strategy
That's what the studs all said to me
Strategy, strategy
I'd rather surrender unconditionally
Cause I—I just want to be good to you

I repeated the first verse and put the guitar down.

"That's sweet of ya," she said.

The Mint-robbing trio returned discussing details of their caper plan. Frannie tried to talk the boys out of even considering it, but forceful persuasion is not her forte. Gupta repeated that until Mindy is out they'd keep planning and he said they were getting it down tight. He said their escapade isn't set till the day after tomorrow at one—zero day—a whole day after we planned to have Mindy out and almost five hours before the sunset deadline for delivery of the goods or putting our heads on the chopping block.

The three conspirators had spent their day at the Mint going on tours and plotting the particulars of their scheme. Gupta had drawn detailed sketches of the rooms they would be in. I asked him why he didn't just take photos and he said there was a rule against that. They returned to the Mint four times, each in different disguises so they wouldn't be recognized. They bought false mustaches and wigs, wore suits and overalls, changing clothes for each tour. Techo put on long sleeves to hide his tattoos, stored his gold earring, dyed his hair black, and lost his spike. I bet it just made the guards notice them more. They're distinctive. Seemed like putting a wig on a turkey and trying to walk it out of a Thanksgiving feast.

At first they had the idea of getting locked in at closing time a la submarina, but Techo said there were all sorts of precautions to make sure that didn't happen and more security after hours than when open. Their plan is for after lunchtime when people are the most tired. Just at the point the tour was about over and the poured gold brick has been cooled in the vat of water and placed on the ledge, Techo is to set off several smoke bombs that will obliterate visibility and trigger the fire alarm. At the same time a CD player with a super powerful micro-speaker he'll have planted under a bench in the demonstration room will blast Ross's ruined piano

251

music sped up insanely—at an ear-splitting volume that will further confuse and encourage everyone to flee as quickly as possible. There will be pandemonium. Techo will split as soon as the smoke bombs and noise attack commence. At that moment Gelar will whip out a can of Super Cold 134 and spray the Plexiglas with a minus fifty-two Celsius stream. Then he'll whack it hard with a hammer, which will shatter the Plexiglas to smithereens. Gupta is to sit on the front row left during the demonstration. He will hop the railing, go around, grab the cooled gold ingot, and, wearing heavy gloves, slip it into a special padded pocket in his overcoat—just in case it's not as cool as the guide had indicated. Techo nixed the nifty accordion grabber and the wasabi spray idea has been replaced with pepper spray to be used only if necessary. The gold ingots are not too heavy to carry. The big one is twenty-five pounds and the small one-half that. Gelar and Gupta will take the emergency exit with the crowd and run to the side street where Techo will be waiting with his getaway Chevy revved up. Afterwards he'll paint it a cherry red. Techo has already accessed the Mint's computer and security systems and the police communications system and planted programs in them that will activate just before the anointed tour, deactivating and scrambling those systems, plus a program to make all the traffic lights green for the getaway route and red behind them so they'd be difficult to follow. They will drive straightaway to the Amenity Funeral Home to deliver the precious booty and retrieve Mindy.

I said it sounds like they've covered everything except knowing how much time they'll do in Australian prisons. Meanwhile, I announced I had calculated minus fifty-two Celsius is a little over minus sixty-one Fahrenheit. Next I'd start trying to figure out where Celsius and Fahrenheit meet. Techo and Gelar looked at me confused. Gupta advised them to ignore me.

They attended to details, getting everything ready, going through their choreographed moves. Techo handed out ear plugs and gloves and went on his laptop checking the programs to aid and confuse. Gelar sprayed a Plexiglas box with Super Cold 134 and then hit it with a heavy ball peen hammer. It shattered. He had a new big can and a small backup can if he needed it. Gupta put Mindy's mobile phone charger in Techo's car so he could communicate—couldn't use Samo's phones on this gig. He read the instructions that came with the pepper spray, their only weapon. Tested one container out back, emptying the whole thing and getting some in his eye, which made him stagger howling into the bathroom. Good thing he'd read the instructions, which said to wash with mild soap to cut the oil if that happened.

I was preparing to go to the Brewery for the night. The partners in crime were discussing who should sleep where. Techo's staying for the night. They're arguing over whose turn it was to sleep in the bed. I said if the Three Stooges could sleep together then they could too. It was a big bed. But of course, I pointed out, the Three Stooges left their clothes and shoes on.

"Minus forty," I called out from the door.

"What?" said Gupta.

"Fahrenheit and Celsius meet at minus forty."

"Commit yourself as soon as you can," he called out.

"Techo does look more like Curly now," I added, and went off without knowing how the boys solved their bedding dilemma.

Sitting in a clearing behind the bushes and keeping an eye on the door, where the thugs supposedly watching Mindy would come and go, presented a new difficulty—trying to stay awake. I learned the meaning of sleeping with one eye open—like being in the monastery but with a greater sense of urgency. Actually, this sense of urgency is exactly what some spiritual teachers try to instill in the minds of their students. It's not unrelated to the stillness and concentration found by hunters and warriors. Life and death is the great matter— as the wise of old have said. Heck, as Fenster said, and which was apparent as I stared at the door below and wondered who's inside— and if I'd be going in there.

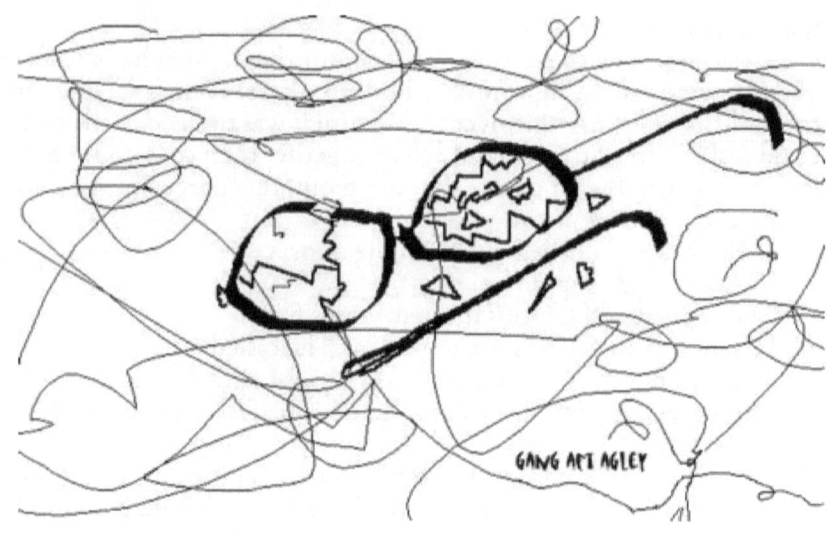

GANG ART AGLEY

Chapter 28
Deminted

Oneness," I said as I entered Mindy's front door in the early morning.

"Once upon a time," Gupta echoed poetically.

"One fine day till we dine... or die."

"Dine on or be dined on."

"May it be dine with—with Rudy and you and... "

"And Mindy."

"And aside from that," I said, "what are your plans for today"

"Our plans are to be concentrated and prepared."

"And, oh doomed one, has this looming threat concentrated the mind wonderfully?"

"Indeed it has. We are getting it down to Pentium precision. And how was the Brewery watch?"

"Uneventful. Samo came back at about seven thirty in the morning. We watched Queenly go into the far door but Johnno didn't come out. No big deal. Samo's gonna stay there till we all show up at about one. He says we can take on two of them if we have to but Johnno will surely be gone by then."

"Why wait?"

"It has to do with timing and assuring back-up from the police if we need it. He's had to arrange that on the sly without really saying directly what's happening. He's cautious. He's patient. He wants it done right."

"We should just go in and do it. This is no time for waiting around."

"Samo's in charge. It'll happen soon enough."

"It'd better be sooner than later or Plan B is impleminted. One way or the other we'll succeed."

"Gang aft agley," I muttered.

"The gang what?"

"Gang aft agley."

"I don't get it."

"It's what Robert Burns said happens to the best schemes of mice and men."

"The poet? He said that the best laid plans of mice and men often go astray."

"Nope. That's the way it's come down. But what he wrote was, 'The best laid schemes o' Mice an' Men\ Gang aft agley\ An' lea'e us nought but grief an' pain\ For promis'd joy!'"

"A pessimist. Blind mice and careless men don't prepare well. We've got Plan A and Plan B. We'll show him."

The phone rang, Mindy's phone. Gupta answered it casually. He tensed up and sat straight. "Yes sir," he said and then, "She's out shopping. Yes it is a little early for shopping but she wanted to meet with a friend and you know women, young women especially. Heck, who knows when she'll get back."

He listened for a moment.

"Nervous? No! Not at all! Yes, he's here. Sure. Yeah, his friend Frannie is here too. Well, they're out as well. Uh. Well, how about..." Gupta stopped mid-sentence. He looked at me with his mouth open and slowly put the receiver down.

"Who the heck was that?" I said.

"Arg..."

"Are you okay? Do you need a Heimlich maneuver or something?"

"Ra, ro, ru..."

"Yes?"

"Ruuuudy!" he said with fear and trembling.

"Confirming dinner tomorrow?"

"No. No dinner tomorrow."

"That's great! Man, that let's us off the hook—for now, huh?"

"No. Not at all. Quite the opposite. He said we'd have dinner—

t-t-t-tonight at Jessica's—instead of tomorrow! And then he hung up."

Silence.

"What are we gonna do?!" Gupta said with a pathetic look on his face.

"We're gonna do it to it, that's what," I said. "Where's a secure mobile?"

The phone rang again. Gupta answered again. He listened, said nothing, and hung up. He looked at me.

I leaned over and looked at him. "What was that?"

"I think I can repeat it exactly," he said, and then taking on the nasty nasal tone of voice I'd grown to despise, "Genghis Kahn here. Can't wait till tomorrow. Sorry. New schedule. Bring your contribution by sunset tonight. Meanwhile I'll be sharpening my sword."

"The phone is tapped," I said. "Gosh, I'd a thought Rudy would have covered that. Guess there's not usually anything going on through this one he needs to hide."

"Fenster knows," said Gupta. "He knows about everything. We're doomed."

"But we've been careful not to talk about our plans on that phone," I said. "Remember? We haven't mentioned what we know—about the Mint or the Brewery or Mindy or anything. All that's been on the secure mobile phones. Lets just hope he doesn't have one of those taps that can hear the room through a hung up phone."

"That can be done?"

"Yep. But let's assume he doesn't do that, cause if he does we'll be going into a trap."

"Okay, please don't be listening Waxo," Gupta says looking at the phone. Then he looks back at me. "Correction. Zero."

"Ooh. Ground zero," I respond.

"Dinner tonight."

"Seafood dinner."

"With Rudy, you, me..."

"And Mindy," I add optimistically.

"And Frannie—he invited her too."

And then Gupta started to scream.

Awakened by Gupta's distressed vocalizing, Techo and Gelar came walking into the room, the former rubbing his eyes, the latter his crotch. Gupta had calmed down and was now sitting and staring ahead. I was staring ahead too.

"Change of plan. I gotta call Samo," I said.

Techo passed me his mobile. I called Samo and told him the

news. He sighed. Said for me to come on and, okay—bring everyone now. We'd meet at the restaurant. He said the night shifter never
came out. He'd call Frannie.

"If Mindy's there," Gupta said, "we'd better go get her out right
now. If she's not out soon, we go to the Mint."

"It's happening," I said. "Let's go."

Soon Gupta and Gelar were ready to go, but not Techo. "Techo!
get off that computer! We gotta go." Gupta called out with irritation.

"Just a sec!"

Twenty minutes later we were all at the Brewery restaurant except for Frannie who was on watch just above us and over some.
Samo wanted only Gupta and me to go in with him. Us? We're
not qualified—not like Techo or Gelar. They're tough as nails and
Ozzie nails can penetrate jarrah. Gupta could get his glasses broken.
I could freeze with fear. But I didn't want to say anything. Samo's the
trusted sergeant. Gelar and Techo are to stay at a table in the restaurant while Frannie stays in the brush with the phone waiting for an
emergency call that could be the signal for her to send the boys—or
to contact the police. Oh I see. He's leaving the number two and
three ranking soldiers behind to save us if need be. But Samo intends
to take care of anything difficult by himself.

Off we go. Samo's got a gun. Guns scare me. I can see that guns
scare Gupta too—at least this one. Samo's at the door. Gupta and I
are behind him. The door's locked. It takes Samo about ten seconds
to get it open and with almost no noise. We walk quietly down a
dark hall using sunlight reflected from windows at the end to guide
us. The doors to the rooms also have opaque glass windows so we're
not trying any. We're looking for light and listening for anything. In
the back of the old brick building we ascend stairs to the next floor.
Light and sound from a room. Approaching slowly. Samo motions,
whispers to us to let him go in by himself and then to follow when
he calls. Abruptly he throws open the door and rushes in gun pointed. We hear him say, "On the floor." And then, "Come on in." That
was quick.

There's a man on the floor face down with his arms spread out.
There's another man tied to a chair who is gagged. His eyes are wide.
Samo keeps his distance from them and tells Gupta to watch the
hall, me to frisk the guy on the floor. I say I don't know how. Samo
said to just feel around for something hard and rest assured, his John
Thomas won't be. I find nothing. I glance quickly around the room.
There are some dried flowers in a vase, a bookcase filled with books,

a table with water and glasses and a phone, some flat rectangular mats with cushions on them, a couple of chairs, a poster of a Tibetan temple on the wall, a photo of Robina, another of Phar Lap, another of Joan Sutherland, another of Genghis Khan, two samurai swords on the wall, and a Buddha statue on a little table behind a candle and incense burner sans incense—but no Mindy.

"Looks like Fenster was the interior decorator," I said.

I recognize the man on the floor as Johnno, the one on the midnight shift, and the one in the chair is Queenly, his replacement.

"Where's Mindy?" asks Gupta strongly from the door.

Johnno shakes his head.

Samo ungags Queenly in the chair.

"Where's Mindy?" Gupta repeats.

"Who?" said Queenly.

"Who? The woman you kidnapped for Fenster, the woman you've been hiding!"

"Let me do the talking," said Samo. "Was there a woman in here?"

"No."

He repeats the question to Johnno.

"No woman," he said.

"Then what are you two doing here?"

"Today?" asked Queenly.

"Yes. And yesterday and the day before that."

"Well, we were practicing this. Would you let him get up and untie me?"

Johnno sticks his head up to see if that's okay.

"No," said Samo. "Practicing what?"

"Tying each other up and seeing how long it takes us to get out," said Queenly.

"What have you three blokes been doing here on eight hour shifts?"

"Meditating and doin' the moves and stuff," said Queenly.

"Meditating?" repeats Samo. "Moves?"

"Yeah," said Johnno on the floor. "Waxo has us come here to meditate and do martial arts. It's part of his training. And other stuff."

"And what was Stan doing here?" I asked.

"Checking up on us, of course. Making sure we're on schedule. We've been doing it solo but now we're supposed to overlap our shifts to practice tying each other up and other things. Fenster calls it our practice. There's these Asian exercises too we do with and without swords. I can get the list if you want. And pictures of the moves we go through."

"What about Mindy?" barked Gupta. "You've got to know where she is!"

Both men looked at him dumbfounded.

"I'm sorry," said Johnno. "Who is she?"

"What's this about?" said Queenly.

Samo picked up his phone, said something pre-arranged quickly to Frannie, then turned to me. "They're coming over here to go through the building with you and Gupta. I'll stay with these two till you're done."

Downstairs, I let Frannie, Techo, and Gelar in. It took us twenty minutes. No Mindy anywhere.

Gupta, Gelar, and Techo sped off in Techo's car leaving Samo, Frannie, and me wondering what to do. We decided they must have gone back to Mindy's to prepare for the Mint job so we raced there to talk them out of it. They weren't there.

"They can't have gone to the Mint!" Frannie said. "Don't they have to prepare?"

"I think they were prepared," I said. "Everything was in Techo's car ready to go and now I remember him lagging behind when we were in a rush to get to the Brewery. I bet he was setting the programs for the Mint security systems and traffic signals—so he could activate them with a phone call. Look—it's not long till noon, till the next pour! Come on let's go!"

"Good luck," said Samo. "I can't get near that. Anyway, I've got to figure out where Mindy is." He got in his car and was off.

We were off in Mindy's Porsche, Frannie at the wheel. We rush up to the ticket booth at the Mint. The clock behind the attendant reads 11:55. Frannie steps to the front of the line, saying, "Let me buy yours for you," and while the couple there was trying to figure out what was happening, she gets a bunch of tickets, handing all but two back to those whom she cut in front of. We rush into the Mint and then to the back where the pour is about to begin. On the way I bump into a small woman.

"Excuse me," I say.

She turns around. "Oh hello David."

"Mai! Daniel! And... Mai's sister! Hello. So good to see you."

"We finally made it here," she said.

"Let's meet after the pour. I must go stop it, I mean see it, uh... and catch someone before they leave. See you in a jail—I mean a jiff."

And I squeeze my way past them.

At the pour room I can see Techo, now fairly straight looking, standing by the doorway to the side hall that leads to the small display room with the bigger gold ingot in the Plexiglas box. I see Gelar in there. I wave frantically at him but he's not looking my way. I wave to Techo but he's staring intensely at the guide. There are some punk kids who have taken the front left seats where Gupta wanted to be. Instead he sits in front of the pour spot near the right end. The wild hair and sloppy clothes of the punk kids are in stark contrast to the reserved appearance of the rest of the demonstration crowd. The punk kids are acting up a bit. Security keeps a close eye on them. I stand on my tiptoes and can see Frannie trying to move toward Gupta. Gelar's in the corner of my eye through the hall in the next room. He's trying to inch toward the center, but it's so crowded he can't move anymore. Neither can I.

The demonstration starts. The demo man gets into his rap, throwing in the same humorous comments with the same timing as before so everyone chuckles on cue. He pours the brick into the mold while prattling away data I had once found interesting, now just disturbing. Gelar is in the other room standing behind a group of people crowded around the Plexiglas box with the gold ingot in it, pushing in on them excusing himself. He's got gloves on. Now the boys don't seem so confident. Sweat beads on foreheads and hands tremble. The ingot is placed on the paddle to be passed almost red hot before the seated and standing group. I wave to Techo again and whisper "hi" loudly. He sees me and makes the "shush" sign and hits something with his hand. He looks down alarmed.

Boom!!! Boom!!! What? Oh my god! The smoke bombs go off! Go off too early! Accordion tango music shrieks madly! Thick smoke billows swiftly into the air! The fire alarm screams! The security alarm screams! People scream. The demonstrator is startled, slips forward and the dreadfully hot gold ingot falls from the paddle bouncing off Gupta's forearm instantly incinerating his sleeve. He screams in pain falling to the floor as his arm sizzles. Gelar's struggling to get the cap off the can of Super Cold 134. Gupta is on the ground screaming. Techo looks around confused but can't see anything much through the smoke. Gelar finally gets the cap off, the people who were in his way are pressing coughing through the smoke toward the emergency exit sign that can be seen as a red glow. Gelar sprays the Plexiglas, which fogs up with super-frozen crystals. He pulls out the hammer and strikes it with all he's got. Nothing breaks. He sprays it again and hits it again. Again, nothing.

Guards go chasing the punk kids out the front exit pushing through a throng of panicked tourists. Gelar uses his spray can up then hits the frozen case again with all the strength he can muster. It holds. Everyone's eyes are watering. The demo man leans over Gupta in the smoke with great concern but keeps one foot stepped over the gold bar crunching on Gupta's glasses on the floor afraid someone else will get burned because there's almost no visibility and people are hysterical and coughing in the din of other sounds. A guard at the doorway yells at Gelar to go out the emergency exit, not being able to make out the frost covered Plexiglas, the spray can, or his hammer in the smoke-filled room. Gelar drops the can and the hammer, and runs to join Techo standing over Gupta who continues to scream in pain. A guard asks them to leave, strangely polite in the chaos. They do. Sirens are heard, the room empties of tourists, fills with firemen, policemen and medics. Gupta is taken off in a stretcher, groaning and coughing. A flash illuminates his face as he's loaded into an ambulance. Techo runs up and asks the driver which hospital they're going to. He and Gelar run to find his Chevy booted. "Should have paid off those parking tickets," he mutters. The traffic lights are all flashing green except for the intended escape route Techo notices with disappointment—it's flashing red. Cars are banging into each other, honking horns can be heard from all directions.

CHAPTER 29
LUCKING

Like surprised unfortunates unexpectedly swept away by a tsunami and deposited in new environs, Frannie, and I stumbled along teary-eyed and coughing with a puzzled assortment of teary-eyed and coughing fellow tossed tourists on the lawn outside the Mint. There we collided with Mai and party. The fact that we were still panting and dazed didn't stop me from introducing Frannie to them. I was upstaged mid-intro by a loud noise and our heads turned toward the oscillating *whoop whoop whoop* of a siren as it cranked up and an ambulance tore off, its Doppler effect bouncing back in ever diminishing waves.

Excitedly we all jabbered about how amazed and puzzled we were at what we'd just experienced. Our side had to fake half of the bepuzzlement because we knew a great deal about what had just happened. But actually, we didn't really know what the heck had just happened either so it wasn't that hard to fake. After sitting on the grass for a couple of moments, catching our breath, and regaining our composure, we entered into small talk. Frannie said I already know more people in WA than she. She asked Mai where she got the gold pendant. At the Mint gift shop. "Where'd you get that lovely bracelet?" Mai asked. Frannie had made it. Mai said they had come to the Mint from a sumptuous brunch at the Swan Brewery. I was just starting to tell her we had probably passed right by each other there when Techo and Gelar came running over from the street asking for a ride to the hospital. Oh goodness. We'd better go. We have an injured friend. As we ran off I apologized, called out I'd phone. Waved goodbye to Mai and hers who seemed amused at us as we sped off piled in the Porsche looking, I imagine, like four kangaroos in a tea cup.

At the hospital Frannie was on her mobile talking to Samo. I was sitting in the emergency waiting room with Techo and Gelar, two hang-dog lucky reprobates. Gazing at them, a duo of impressions swept into each other like waves colliding—one, a crushing sense of their miserable failure, though failure against formidable odds—as if they were dejected amateur ball players heads down in the locker room who'd just been humiliated by a bruising team. Second was an aura of miraculous good fortune one might feel being in the presence of survivors of an airplane crash. Everything had gone wrong—but no one got in trouble or badly injured. Another of Gupta's howls came piercing through from the emergency room. Not mortally injured, anyway.

A couple of detectives questioned Gupta and the rest of us and we all just said we had no idea what happened—there was just, all of a sudden, a lot of smoke and noise and yelling and here we are. They thanked us and went off.

A doctor finally emerged from the double swinging doors. She told us Gupta's okay. He'd been moved to a room upstairs. We took the elevator. I told a buxom blond nurse we're all close relatives of Gupta's, making an effort to keep my gaze elevated. She eyed us, possibly considering the range of skin colors and accents involved, before leading us into Gupta's room. Techo kept an eye on her. Gupta's arm was badly burned, she said, but it's been cleaned, treated with anti-biotic ointment, and wrapped.

"He is in a good deal of pain," she said.

"It's not a good deal. It's a bad one," mumbled Gupta.

"The analgesics are beginning to take effect," the nurse continued.

"And I'd advise giving me pain killers as well," Gupta suggested in a blurred whisper.

"Hi Guppy," said Frannie. "Hang in there. We're with you mate."

We surrounded Gupta's bed. He gazed up at us gritting his teeth and looking a little dreamy. His arms were on top of the sheet, the right one covered in white bandaging. Frannie leaned down and placed a kiss on it as gently as the touch of a butterfly landing. Gupta was breathing heavily. The nurse said the pain is good, the sign of a second degree burn. That ingot could have easily given him deep third degree burns right through the nerves, she said. No nerves, no pain. That would be much worse and would necessitate skin grafting. She asked him when he got the cut on his lip and the blood under the fingernail and I answered he fell down the Swan Bells stairs. She showed us a paper bag on a table that contained his clothes, shoes, wallet, heavy gloves, and earplugs. I pulled out the flannel shirt with right sleeve sporting a gaping hole with charred edges.

The nurse's beeper beeped and she went down the hall with Techo's eyes following her. She was sending some reporters away, telling them the patient wouldn't be able to see them until tomorrow.

I told Gupta how lucky the three of them had been—not to have gotten caught. He whispered he wants more luck. He wants a happy ending and then said something I don't catch. "Hmm?"

"He said he fears the only happy endings are in massage parlors," said Frannie.

He groaned. He was fading, looking distressed and we knew why.

"Mindy," he mumbled. "Mindy, we failed you. We didn't get the gold. Now, we need three hundred thousand dollars. At least it's Australian dollars."

"Your sense of humor is hangin' in there," Frannie said.

"It's not humor. It's horror. Fenster's waiting and Rudy's coming in a few hours." He looked at me and sadly said, "Zero minus, minus?"

I spied a wall clock. "It's one fifty-one," I said—not trusting my natural sense of the time for fine tuning as important as this.

"Mindy is still kidnapped and in danger and we'll have to tell Rudy." His slurred words were getting hard to understand. "Call the police. Call Rudy. We should have told Rudy from the first. This has all been a big... Go save her. Mindy. Three hundred thousand dollars—Mindy, three hundred thousand dollars—Mindy, three hundred..."

"I'm gonna call the funeral home and ask for more time. Maybe I'll go there. I think Fenster's there—appeal to him directly. And Frannie said Samo has got some ideas," I said, pretending Frannie had said that Samo has got some ideas. He was on his way so it was close to true but Gupta's morphine took over anyway and his eyes glazed over. We left him, for the time being, out of it, moaning, mumbling about Mindy and three hundred thousand dollars, his mantra for the time being.

We met Samo out in front of the building. Immediately the talk went to how long we had till he brought in the police. His friend in the force was ready to move. He said it's not the first time they've been on call for a family to change its mind in a kidnapping.

"What time is sunset?" I asked. "Fenster said to bring the money by sunset."

Techo got a paper from a nearby stand and checked. "Five fif-ty-seven," he said.

It was three minutes past two. Almost four hours. We agreed to spend one more hour looking for alternatives.

"Let's brainstorm," I said.

We sat on the steps and I stared at a raven that circled us and flew to the entrance to a bank down the street.

"I haven't had time to tell you I hardly recognized you this morn-ing," said Frannie to Techo. "And," she added, "how handsome you look with your new hairdo."

Back in the hospital room, Gupta lay quietly passed out. The door opened and two men in suits entered with the nurse whose beeper went off so she did too. One of the men wore thick glasses and the other had thin ones.

"He looks okay," said the man with thick glasses. "Sleeping like a baby. The nurse says he'll be out of here tomorrow. He'll be fine."

"She also said it's a severe injury that will take a long time to heal. This is serious. Don't kid yourself. You're the director of the Mint and can't afford to underestimate the potential this case has for a catastrophically high award."

"I guess that's the arm that was burned," the director said.

"Yes," said the other with condescension, "the arm that is not wrapped," here he slightly lifted Gupta's left arm, "would be the arm that wasn't burned, whereas the arm that is wrapped with bandages," he pointed, "would be the one that was burned."

The director lifted the bandaged right arm a little to examine it.

Gupta's eyes opened and he groaned pitifully. The director dropped his arm in fright and Gupta shrieked louder and more piti-fully.

The nurse stuck her head in, "What's happening in here? Is he alright? Are you alright sir?"

Gupta groaned softly and lay there.

"Have you talked to him yet?" she asked.

"We're just about to," said the man with thin glasses.

Her beeper went off again and she departed.

Gupta mumbled, "Mindy—three hundred thousand dollars," so softly and incoherently the men didn't notice.

"Maybe it was carelessness on his part," said the director.

"Mindy—three hundred thousand dollars," Gupta groaned again below the radar.

The lawyer pulled the director aside and whispered firmly, "Him careless? Sitting in his seat where he was supposed to be and your employee drops an 800 degree gold ingot on his arm? Carelessness is the right word—gross carelessness—and not his. Now you start thinking about a settlement right now and forget about shifting the blame—or get another lawyer."

As they talked, Gupta continued to repeat softly, "Mindy—three hundred thousand dollars."

"Well let's ask him—he seems to be awake." He moved in closer to Gupta. "Who do you think is responsible for your injury sir?"

"Mindy..."

"He said 'the Mint.' I heard him clearly. He thinks the Mint is responsible," said the lawyer. "Now stop that approach."

"What do you think he'd settle for?" asked the director.

"Three hundred thousand dollars."

"Did you hear that?" asked the lawyer.

"Hear what?"

"Mindy—three hundred thousand dollars."

"There, he said it again. Listen."

"Mindy—three hundred thousand dollars."

"Is that what you think is fair?" asked the lawyer.

"Mindy—three hundred thousand dollars."

"Look," said the lawyer, "He keeps saying the Mint and three hundred thousand dollars. He's clearly thought about this while he's lying there."

"What do you think?" asked the director, and then, leaning over Gupta again. "Would you settle for one hundred thousand?"

"Mindy—three hundred thousand dollars."

"Two hundred thousand?"

"Mindy—three hundred thousand dollars."

"Okay," interrupted the lawyer. "We've got a deal." And then quietly to the director. "He's not budging. You'd better run with this. He's obviously delirious and doesn't really know what's happening now. But that's clearly what he wants. If a lawyer gets a hold of him they could go for a million or more. I've got a form here that will

266

do." He pulled out a piece of paper from his briefcase. "Just add the date and the amount and his name. What's his name?"

"It's on his chart here—Jackie Gupta."

"Jackie Gupta and three hundred," he wrote on the paper. "There we are."

"Sir, are you prepared to sign this?" the lawyer said to Gupta who was still mumbling the same line. "Sir!"

Gupta looked up.

"Sir, are you prepared to sign this agreement to settle with the Perth Mint for three hundred thousand dollars?"

"Mindy—three hundred thousand dollars."

"Yes—that's right. With the Mint for three hundred thousand dollars."

"Huh?" said Gupta coming to.

"Just sign here. Can you see?"

"No. Glasses."

"Here use mine," said the director.

"Ahhh," said Gupta throwing them off with his left hand.

"Too strong," said the lawyer putting his own on Gupta.

Gupta looked at the paper, read a few words, then nodded off.

"Wake up, sir." The lawyer picked up his left hand. "Are you right handed?"

"Right handed?"

"Oh it doesn't matter," said the lawyer, and he helped guide Gupta's left hand to sign. "Good. Good." He picked the paper up and handed it to the director. "Now you sign it."

The nurse walked in. She was conscripted as a witness and signed it. Her beeper went off and she left. The lawyer whipped out a blank check, made it out, the director signed it, and the lawyer placed it in Gupta's left hand.

"Here. We'll give you a copy of the agreement later today."

They departed.

Gupta looked at the check. His brow furrowed. As he dropped off to sleep again he pulled the check and his arm under the covers, rolled onto his left side and was silent.

Techo had gone off with Samo to check out the Brewery one more time—just to be sure. Frannie, Gelar, and I went back to Gupta's room and were by his side when he woke up. Frannie asked him how his arm was. He started moaning and crying about Mindy and then told us haltingly, "Dreamed... check... my hand... three hundred... check... to get Mindy... back."

"I think I understood him," I said. "He's delirious."

"It would be a good dream to come true," said Frannie.

Gupta slowly pulled his hand out from under the covers. In his grip was a rectangular piece of paper. We all three moved in and peered. It was a government check signed by the director of the Perth Mint and it was for $300,000. After a moment of making sure we were seeing what we were seeing and convincing Gupta it wasn't an opiated dream, we realized there was no time to think about it, wonder about it, rejoice about it—we had to get him out of there and to a bank to cash that check right away. The clock on the wall said 3:32.

"I don't think Fenster would take a third party check," I said. "What time do the banks close?"

"It's Thursday," said Frannie. "At four."

Gupta wasn't supposed to leave. We didn't want to cause any commotion and I don't think he'd have been considered aware enough to discharge himself. We slid him out of the bed and Gelar into it. We had Gelar roll over on his side and covered him. Carefully as we could, we put on Gupta's clothes including the shirt with the burned hole in it. I rolled back the sleeve. He only cried out at a moderate decibel level a few times. We stuffed his hospital gown into the bag and we were off—the poor fellow staggering with me propping him up by his left side, Frannie protecting the right. We breezily chattered to each other and him hoping to make the fact we were dragging a drugged and delirious un-checked-out patient less obvious. We were as careful as possible not to bump his arm not just because we didn't want to hurt him but also because we didn't want him loudly vocalizing exclamations of pain and thus drawing attention to us. Stealthily we passed doctors, nurses, orderlies, administrators, patients, and guests and they passed us as well, all too busy to notice anything. We probably could have dragged a corpse out of there.

I was gonna get that money one way or another. But I wasn't thinking about it. I was channeling something, maybe just my own moxie, but I could feel it rising and telling me what to do, deciding what to do. We trudged to the nearby bank propping up groaning Gupta between us. It was the only one we had time to make it to before closing. It was an awful lot of cash we wanted but it was the headquarters of a big bank. As Frannie and I trudged with Gupta toward the door like some six-legged animal, a long-haired vender selling hand made jewelry on the sidewalk came over to help us up the steps. As we walked up to the door the guard was just locking it. I yelled. He saw me. I begged. He pointed to his watch. I pointed to Gupta's bandaged arm and that did it for some illogical reason. The guard opened the door. Frannie and I dragged the half-conscious Gupta to the teller. Soon we were at the door of a vice president. I told Frannie I'd take it from there. I plopped Gupta into a chair and told the startled bank officer what I wanted. I showed him the check and Gupta's passport, which he always carried thank goodness. Gupta was falling over on me. The vice president told me with discomfort they can't just cash this check on the spot. I insisted, saying it's a government cashier's check signed by the director of the Mint. It's as good as cash. I suggested he call him. We need it now. The VP called the President in.

The President listened to the VP's account of what we wanted and was about to launch into his reasons why they can't do it when he got a better look at me and exclaimed, "Ross Bolleter's friend! What an honor! Please come into my office! I've been wanting to see you again!"

Good lord. It's that man from Ross's concert. Oh yes, I remembered his name. "Good to see you again Mr. Vargas," I said. "I'm sorry my friend, Mr. Gupta, is in such poor condition. He had an accident at the Mint."

"Oh yes, I heard," he said. "An American was injured in some terrorist attack. A shame those Muslims got away. I'm so sorry this has happened to you, Mr. Gupta. It is most unfortunate. Please come have a seat in my office."

"Thank you," I said, dragged Gupta in, and deposited him in a chair where he slumped over.

"The last time I saw you, you were talking with Ross Bolleter on the balcony of the Fremantle Performance Hall. What a glorious concert. I wrote to my good friend Robert Duvall about it and suggested we stage another concert so Robert can hear Ross Bolleter's magnificent interpretation of Astor Piazzolla's music. Robert is a consummate tango dancer."

"I've read that."

"Since then I've been trying to play the piano more but I am not talented."

"I'm sure you're being overly modest," I said.

"And I've purchased some of Mr. Bolleter's ruined piano CDs. Most curious. Not melodic at all but strange and otherworldly. I could never be so original."

He served us strong, good coffee. I actually got Gupta to take some sips, thinking it might help to get him somewhat mobile—he slumped over again. Mr. Vargas asked if I knew when Ross's next concert would be, opened a window wider, and lit up an American Spirit after asking permission. I not only gave him permission but requested one for myself, which he was happy to provide. Gupta was leaning over drooling. I took a tissue from Vargas's desk and wiped the dribble from his face—Gupta's, not Mr. Vargas's. Vargas went on about Ross and tango meanwhile not paying any attention to Gupta. Finally Vargas asked about the money. I explained to him briefly this was a matter of life and death that I could not discuss and urged him to call the Mint to talk to the director to make sure the check was good. Vargas said that would not be necessary, that Ross's friend's word is good enough, the check is a cashier's check, the VP would have to call anyway to get the cash—company policy. Of course they'd cash it. But it would still take a day.

"I must explain the exact situation then so you can understand the urgency involved," I said in a hushed tone leaning in closer to Vargas. He leaned in closer to me.

"I can't say exactly who we're working with, Mr. Vargas, but Mr. Gupta and I were in the process of apprehending those terrorists at the Mint when they caused that great commotion, wounded Mr. Gupta, and got away." I leaned over closer to him and lowered my voice. "Can you be trusted with top secret, classified information known only to Australian and American intelligence operatives, something you can never tell anyone?"

He nodded gravely with furrowed brow and wide eyes.

"You might think that, being clandestine agents in covert work of such extreme importance, that we have unlimited amounts of cash at our fingertips, but we are still constrained by bureaucratic red tape." I looked at him with a disgusted scowl and he shook his head with angry sympathy. I continued. "It would take us at least a day to get this money from our sources. Mr. Vargas, those evil-doers are holding Ross Bolleter. Now, they are demanding the $300,000 Mr. Gupta received from the Mint in return for Mr. Bolleter's release. They want it by sunset today or... or.... Mr. Vargas, do it for Ross, do it for Australia..." I breathed heavily. "Do it for tango!"

"Mission accomplished," I told Frannie who was waiting at the door to the bank with the helpful jewelry craftsman when we exited. I quickly thanked him for his assistance and told her Gupta and I would go right away to the funeral home. I refused to let her come. Too dangerous. No room anyway. Don't like having the Porsche over-booked. It was parked right in front of us. She gave me directions. It was way out by the airport. She said she'd go back and get Gelar out of the hospital.

Gupta was regaining consciousness. As we drove off he asked me the time. I looked at his watch and told him it was four fifty, one hour and seven minutes before sunset. Plenty of time.

"Go to airport," he said.

"What for?"

"Locker."

"I get it. Good idea. You're more aware than I thought."

Traffic was at a standstill. The lights were so screwed up they'd been turned off. Cars took turns at intersections. We saw the aftermaths of fender-benders. I pulled over to the side, rode up on the sidewalk, back to the street, sidewalk again, over to the wrong side of the street, and in this cavalier manner, made better time, hoping the police were too busy to notice.

"Gupta, you got change for ten dollars?" I asked. "The large lockers are ten dollars but medium is all we need and it's six."

He looked at me with disgust through slitted lids. "Speed, not money stupid. You more out of it than me."

"Good. You're beginning to speak so I can understand you."

A moment later I hurriedly got back to the Porsche. "Okay, we splurged with large." I slammed the door.

"Ahhh!" He groaned in pain.

"Sorry."

"Firk you."

We sped off with only a key as ransom.

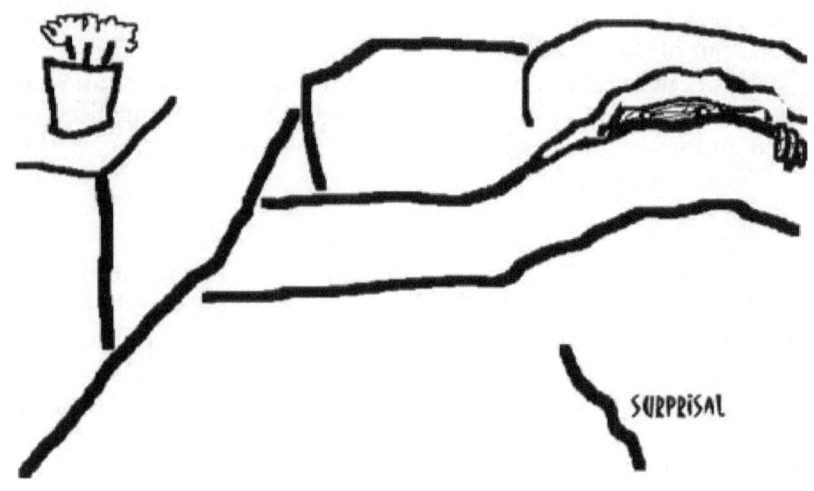

CHAPTER 30
SURPRISAL

Back at the hospital, Gelar was doing his duty, lying on his side covered, and cruising in dreamtime just under the radar of consciousness.

The door opened. Footsteps. A hand gently on his head. A woman's voice softly, musically called, "Wake up, wake up, wake up sleeping prince, wake up little boy, wake up wounded Romeo, wake up, wake up."

Gelar pulled the covers slowly down so his eyes alone were exposed. They opened wide and he gasped as the voice continued, "Oh there you are you poor dear. How are you? Are you in pain?"

Gelar shot up and exclaimed, "Bluey! Bluey!"

Mindy leaped back. "Gelly! What are *you* doing here!"

"I'm... I'm pretending to be Gupta. You're free!"

"This is the ultimate in stalking!" She was in new clothes and had an Ahern's High Fashion shopping bag in her hand.

"Bluey! Where have you been? Have you just been shopping?"

"Only for the last couple of hours. Before that I was a prisoner."

"You were!"

"I sure as hell was. You *like* that?"

"No. No. I Like you free. You escaped?"

272

"Yes, I did—but I didn't escape you Gelly!"

"I'm not stalking you honey. I'm helping to find you."

"In there? You were looking for me under the covers?"

"Bluey I can't explain everything right now. There's too much to tell and I'm too... I thought they were going to kill you. But you're safe now." He started crying. "We have all been working together to find you and we tried to pay off Fenster but it failed and Gupta's arm was badly burned..."

"I saw his face on a TV screen in the copy shop just down the street. He was in an ambulance. Something about an accident at the Mint. I ran over here to find out what hospital he was in and lucked out. I mean I thought I lucked out. But where is he? What's this all about?"

Frannie walked in, gasped excitedly, ran up, and hugged Mindy saying, "Oh how wonderful! Where've you been? What happened?!"

"I escaped from my kidnappers."

"Where were you?"

"In a room in the Swan Brewery where I was being held by Fenster's boys."

"You *were* there," said Gelar.

"You knew?"

"How'd you get away?" Frannie asked.

"One of the kidnappers let me go."

"You just walked out?"

"Yeah. Well, there's more to it than that, but yeah. I walked over to the restaurant and sat down with some people. Threw them a little off kilter at first but then we got on fine. They ended up giving me a ride downtown."

"I'm so glad to see you," said Gelar. "So glad." And he whimpered a little.

"We're so happy you're free," said Frannie hugging her again. "We were worried to death and doing everything imaginable to find you. Actually—much more than you could imagine. We were there at the Brewery. A bunch of us. Anyway, we've been on your case round the clock for a week."

"That's kind of you."

"You've been shopping?" said Frannie looking at Mindy's shopping bag and new beige pants and chocolate brown silk blouse.

"I was a mess. I had them drop me at Ahern's where I have an account. Took a shower and threw away the clothes I came in with. Now what were you saying, Gelly? About Fenster and Guppy?" She turned to Frannie. "I saw Guppy on the telly bein' loaded into an ambulance. That's how I came here. And then I find Gelly! I still don't get it."

"Well," said Gelar, "what happened was..."

Samo and Techo walk in.

"Samo! Techo!" said Frannie. "This is my mate Samo and this is my mate Techo," she said to Mindy, "and this," she paused, "is my mate Melinda otherwise known as Mindy. Mindy's free!" she said with a broad grin. "She was kidnapped and she escaped!"

"A miracle!" exclaimed Samo. "How fortunate. So good to meet you and see you're free."

"Give him a hug," said Frannie. "He's been workin' night and day to find you and free you. And Techo too."

Mindy hugged Samo then Techo who were both dazed by the news. "I don't know what you've been up to but I appreciate it," she said.

Samo got right into checking on Mindy's condition. Was she hurt anywhere? Was she in shock? Should she be examined by a doctor?

"I think that mainly I need some exercise," she said. "I've had plenty of rest and I've been fed alright. Not the restaurant food though. Fast food. Awful. Why didn't they get me good food from the restaurant there. I couldn't believe it when I got out and found it in the same building."

"They sure let you dress nicely," said Samo.

"Just got this stuff. I was all dirty and sweaty a couple of hours ago."

A man with a suit walked in, the lawyer from the Mint. "Excuse me," he said. "I just wanted to make sure Mr. Gupta was doing alright." He approached the bed. "And to give him a copy of the agreement he signed." He handed it to Gelar. "Um—Mr. Gupta?"

"Yes. Thank you."

The lawyer handed it over hesitantly, walked slowly toward the door, turned around looking quizzically at Gelar.

"He looks terrible after he's slept," said Frannie. "I don't recognize him in the morning."

"I don't know what's happening either," said Mindy shaking her head.

The lawyer managed a confused smile and left.

"Now who was he again?" said Mindy.

"He's from the Mint," said Frannie. "It's about the money they gave Gupta."

"The Mint gave Gupta money?" asked Samo.

"I haven't been able to get hold of you," said Frannie.

"Techo and my mobiles were both down. My fault."

"The Mint gave money to Guppy?" said Mindy.

"How much?" said Samo.

"Enough to pay Fenster," said Frannie. "Three Hundred thousand dollars."

"Pay Fenster?" asked Mindy.

"Well where's Gupta? Where's Davo?" asked Samo.

Frannie gasped. "Davo and Guppy! They've got the money and they're on the way to Amenity to give it to Fenster! We've got to stop them!"

Techo's head jerked. He went out.

"We've got to get to them right now!" said Samo. "Call them! He's got Mindy's mobile."

"Ah—I'll call them up on mine," said Frannie. There was a silent pause. Then she was talking rapidly. "Gupta! Gupta! Pick up the phone! Pick up the phone! Oh you can't hear! Mindy's out! Don't give them that money! Don't give them the money! Mindy's free! She got out!" She hangs up. "It was just a message. I just left a message. I'll try again." She held the phone to her ear and put it back in her pocket. "Not answering. What should we do!?"

"We should rush to the funeral home," said Samo.

Everyone poured out of the room.

"Come on Techo! Get off that computer! Let's go," called Samo. "We're not gonna wait for you. Gotta get to Amenity now!"

"I'm comin'!"

"What's this about money again?" asked Mindy as they ran down the hall.

"The ransom money—three hundred thousand dollars!" said Gelar.

"For me?"

"Yes," said Frannie. "Well, for Fenster for you."

"That's very flattering. Though I could see more—even a million. But how'd you get $300,000?" she panted trotting.

"I don't know much more than you," said Frannie as they quickly descended stairs. "I think the Mint gave it to Guppy for burnin' his arm. He cashed it at the bank down the street. We've got to stop them from payin',"

"But he'll just kill us all then won't he?" asked Gelar as they exited to the street and piled into Samo's car.

"Mindy's free," said Samo. "He just lost his shield."

"He'll still want to kill us," yelled Gelar over the engine roar.

Techo caught up and jumped in the back seat as the Volvo sped off.

"Kill you?" said Mindy.

"Yes," said Gelar. "Fenster has been threatening all of us. With beheading no less. You too."

"He's not going to behead anyone, or be a danger to any of us anymore," Mindy said reaching into her shopping bag. "I got the goods on him here. Evidence to tie him up with a long string of crimes."

"We should back that disk up," said Techo.

"I've already got it all backed up on disk and hard copied and waiting to be distributed to media and the authorities if anything happens to me or to anyone. A friend at the copy shop is prepared to act if I don't get back to him before long. And if lightning strikes him, I left it with my friend at Ahern's. "

"How'd you get all that?" asked Samo as they sped along.

"I turned the charm a little on one of the fellows watching me."

"On Johnno," said Samo nodding.

"On Johnno," she agrees.

"No! No Bluey! Not one of those gangsters!" cried Gelar.

"Johnno was cute. He's waitin' for me to run off with him and I feel a little bad about that."

"No! Sleeping with the enemy!"

"I'm alive too!"

"Where were you?" asked Samo.

"In the empty part of the Swan Brewery."

"We looked everywhere," said Frannie.

"It was a sort of hidden room. You wouldn't have found it."

"What time did you get out?"

"Before noon."

Samo hit his head with one hand. "They fooled us." He made a sharp turn with the other.

Mindy asked Samo who fooled them? He explained.

"Oh," she said. "Johnno had Queenly tied up but I was still waiting for him to give me the goods on Fenster. I wondered what all that racket was about. I was close but I thought at the time it was just them and some of Fenster's other men arguing. I was almost out of there but Johnno was insecure and needed a little more reassuring I really loved him and would meet him later to run off. I feel bad I won't be there."

"No, no," said Gelar holding his head with his hands.

"What did they tell you?" Mindy asked Samo.

"That they were practicing tying each other up and getting loose and the reason they were coming and going in shifts was Fenster made them meditate and do some sort of martial arts and stuff."

"Fenster does make them do all that—or try to. They complained a lot—having to cross their legs in the Buddha room. They didn't know if you guys were with the cops or what and Johnno couldn't believe you left them there with Queenly still tied. Johnno just put the gag back on as soon as you were out. He was laughing when he came back to me. So that was you. It wasn't long after that he gave me the disk and stuff and let me go. Trusting soul."

"We were that close," said Samo. "That's terrible."

"It's a day for screw-ups," said Techo. "I even put on the wrong music."

"If you'd saved me then I wouldn't have had the goods on Fenster," said Mindy. "Johnno had it hidden where you probably wouldn't have found it."

"If there were only some way we could tell Davo and Gupta!" said Frannie.

"There's a chance the boys will find out," said Techo.

"Why don't you call Fenster," said Frannie, "and tell him we got the goods on him and not to take that money or harm them and maybe we'll leave him alone?"

"Maybe better to surprise him. With Mindy out, I'll call my buddy at the station and have them come on over as well. I'm eager to see what you got on Fenster, Mindy—minus your own case, which would mean trouble for you and the boys with Rudy. Right?"

"Oh yeah, we don't want him to know about this. It wouldn't be worth what'd hit the fan. It's all in here," she said and pulled a large envelope out of the shopping bag. There was a photo of a white wooden building on the face of it with Amenity Funeral Home written across the top. She stuck it in front of him.

"That's where we're going," said Samo.

"Amenity," said Mindy. "I used to go there when I was a kid. Back when Rudy and Fenster were on better terms. They have a crematorium in back Fenster's fond of. Uh-oh. We'd better hurry."

CHAPTER 31
AMENITY LOST

"Damnit," Gupta mumbled, "the mobile's battery is out and the charger's in Techo's car."

"Booted car."

"No!"

"Yeah. Makes for a slow getaway. But why phone anyone? What's there to talk about anyway?" I said as we pulled into the parking lot of the funeral home.

"Jeez, Is there anything we did right?"

"Yes, get second degree burns. Otherwise it's all *gang aft agley*."

"You have a point—you and Robert Burns."

"It's going to blow Fenster's mind when he finds out we have the money," I said. "Though he won't be pleased we don't have it—on us that is."

"Well, we have to see Mindy first," said Gupta. "No Mindy, no money."

Gupta was getting pretty conscious. And mobile. We exited the car and walked toward the entrance of the white wood building with its wide porch, columns, and portico, through which runs the circular driveway lined with—trees.

"Are these Eucalyptus, Mr. Biology?" I asked. Gupta nodded.

Across the street were offices. On one side was a parking lot and on the other side the sun was setting, setting behind a church.

"Man," Gupta said, "we're just making it—look at that sun going down."

"We're five minutes early," I said. "Got time to burn, time for the sunset to burn."

It did make an impressive scene, the scarlet daylight's end behind the church, the church with a huge electronic sign that read GIVE THANKS UNTO GOD FOR HIS GIFT TO YOU OF JESUS, HIS ONLY BEGOTTEN SON. Gupta looked at it squinting and shook his head.

"Thank you," I said.

"What are you saying 'thank you' about?" he asked.

"Thanks for Christ consciousness, 'utterly divine mind' as Pseudo Dionysius says, the only begotten son of god, god, which is the incomprehensible absolute, and thanks that we've gotten this far."

"How the hell can you think about stuff like that at a time like this?" he said.

"We should always be grateful," I said. "that we're divine, to be alive, to be breathing this great air, under this beautiful blue sky, paying a jumbo ransom."

"We're close to death, might not be breathing in a while, the air has exhaust in it, the sky gives us skin cancer, my arm's killing me, the morphine's wearing off, we're giving a fortune to a gangster who might cut our heads off for fun, we're terrified. You're crazy."

"How about 'thank you to Hanuman? It's all just words that point to immediate reality."

"Shut up."

The sign went blank and then changed to read, "MINDY IS FREE!" Unfortunately, we didn't learn that till later. Gupta and I were looking straight ahead at the front door of the funeral home as we walked and when he turned to look at me he was facing the wrong direction and when I turned to look at him a tree had come to obscure the new message on the sign.

A couple of men came out on the porch and watched us approach. One was tall and one was short.

"Recognize them?" I asked.

"It's the Goony Twins," said Gupta. "Are you grateful to see them?"

"It's not really gratitude for anything in particular, actually—ultimately it's gratitude that we are already Buddha or one with god, Brahma, something like that," I said.

"One with the Goony Twins."

"Good day, gentlemen," I said. "We have something for your boss." I looked at Gupta's watch. "We have arrived here three minutes before sunset. Please tell him that."

They just stared at us. And then Halffoot stared over our heads and then Shorts stared around our heads.

"Now pay attention," I said. "We have something for Bobby."

"Uh, come in," said Halffoot.

"Why are they staring over there?" said Gupta turning around. "Oh—reading the inspirational message from the church? Hmm. Ah, there's a new one, a shorter one. Can't quite make it out anymore. Need my glasses. But they're on the floor of the Mint. That's where I lost them getting, in a roundabout way, the treasure Bobby is waiting for." He smiled impishly at the Goony Twins who were not amused.

"A new inspirational message?" I turn around to look at the sign again. "Well, let me see," I said. "I can't see it. Sun's in my eyes. No matter. I can make up my own. How about, "From the first, not a thing exists." That's, uh. I forget. Some early Chinese teacher. Maybe Hui Neng. I can see it doesn't speak to you, to either of you. Hmm. So how should we proceed?"

They grabbed us.

"Ahhhh! My arm!" shouted Gupta as we're dragged inside.

"What a pleasure. We didn't know you'd be here," I said.

Fenster was sitting behind a polished wood desk. "I know you didn't get the gold. It's on the telly. Flubbed attempt—by punks. I gotta hand that part to you. But anyway, where's the money?"

"We've got it," I said.

"You've got the money?" said Fenster. "How much?"

"Oh you mean like is it enough to cover the small gold ingot, which would save Mindy, or the one to save Frannie as well, or the sum of the two to save us all. Or, as you so poetically put it

Kali takes while Shiva gives,
With the smaller brick she lives.
With the bigger she and Fran.
With them both long live your clan."

"Yes, yes, that's what I mean. How much means how much."

"The sum of the two. Three hundred K."

"Give it to me."

"We didn't bring it," said Gupta gently rubbing his arm. "We want to see Mindy first."

Fenster scowled at us. He looked at the Goony Twins and nodded toward the parking lot. They departed. Fenster served us some tea. Nice of him. Behind Fenster was a photo of Phar Lap with his keeper. I commented on it. Fenster said nothing. I complimented the artistry of the row of nice little capped pots behind him. "Crematory urns," he corrected, smiling unpleasantly. Gupta asked him what the hell was happening. Fenster just glared at Gupta. Finally Shorts came in and shook his head.

"Okay—it's not in the car either. Where is it?"

Gupta looked out the window, "Hey what the hell—you've destroyed Mindy's car." The doors, the hood, and the trunk were torn off with contents spread around—spare tire, seats, carpet, engine parts. "What the hell, man," said Gupta.

"The loot," said Fenster. "The bullion substitute."

"Just give us Mindy and you get the money." Gupta looked at me in a strange way and then fell over on the floor. I started to say something to Fenster but I got dizzy.

"My head hurts," I said.

"Mine too," moaned Gupta.

"This seems familiar."

"Oh heck. Can't move."

"Me either."

"Waking up tied together. Yes, I seem to remember that," he said.

"Except we're tied down on something this time."

"I think he gave us that date rape drug in our tea," he said.

"But that could get him that ugly guy as a roommate for five years," I remembered.

"I think the date's with Fenster."

"Unfortunately."

"Where are we?" Gupta asked.

"Let's see. Tile walls over there and," I crane my head up, "that looks like a furnace in front. I think this is a... a crematorium."

We looked at each other and in unison let out an anguished cry of, "Ahhhhhh!"

"Don't you think it's about time Samo and the gang showed up?" Gupta asked as we twitched and turned. "They're coming!" he yelled. "Our friends are coming!"

"Yeah, maybe so. I hope they hurry up. I can't get anything untied."

"We didn't really make any appointment with them did we?"

"No, we just ran off here. Make a mental note not to do that next time," I said. "Need an exit strategy."

Suddenly there was the intensely amplified echoing sound of a woman's voice with a full orchestra behind her. Joan Sutherland never sounded so frightening. The door opened and we heard jangling. Then in front of us appeared Fenster dressed in some ancient oriental combat gear. We stared at him in terror as Sutherland backed him up. He strutted around us for a while until her vocal level came down to the point where Fenster could be heard.

"Listen to her sing. She's divinely inspired, the best there ever was and will ever be. If this is to be the last thing you hear, you're fortunate. Why my Doberman, Mars, he comes running to hear Joan Sutherland...."

"Maybe cause you feed him then Mr. Pavlov?" groaned Gupta.

"Silence!"

"And who the hell are you this time?" moaned Gupta.

"I am Genghis Khan, slayer of multitudes." He pulled a sword and swung it over his head, his eyes bulging. Then he let out a blood curdling shriek that was most effective in reducing Gupta and me to quivering marmalade.

"This is the sword that cuts both ways!" He looked at me with wild eyes that made me regret having corrected his understanding. "It cuts through delusion and it cuts through your neck!"

"You can stop with delusion," I said.

"Where is my treasure!?" he yelled dramatically. "It's the treasure or the furnace!"

"No Mindy, No money!" Gupta yelled back.

"All who yield to Khan's law live. Those who deny it die!"

"No Mindy! No money!" Gupta repeated.

"Maybe we could modify that demand," I suggested.

"No! Keep a unified front!"

"Maybe there's a compromise in this," I meekly offered.

"No compromise!" grunted Gupta.

"No compromise!" howled Fenster Kahn.

"See, we've got some agreement there to build on," I said.

"The money or the flame!" cried Fenster.

"Why resort to an oven?," challenged Gupta. "What ever happened to cutting our heads off? And how convenient! There's a sword right there!"

"Hey Gupta, Please!" I yelled.

"The sword is too quick, too merciful for you!"

He left the room and with a burst, high flames were spitting out in all directions in the furnace ahead. I yelled, "Okay! We'll tell! We'll tell!"

"It's my money and no money no Mindy! I mean no Mindy no money!" Gupta craned his neck up and looked at the furnace. "OK! Let's talk!"

But Fenster was gone and Sutherland and her orchestra were getting louder again as the flames rose higher.

Another door opened and the Goony Twins threw someone else in. He was familiar. Oh—it's the guy who was on the floor in the Brewery—Johnno. Now he's on the floor of the crematorium.

"What are you doing here?" I asked him loudly through the music.

"Mindy's waiting for me!" he yelled, looking at the fire in the furnace and swallowing hard. "She's waiting for me and I'm not going to be there! She'll think I've betrayed her!"

"What?" said Gupta. "What's that about?"

"Come over and untie us!" I cried.

He's obviously been beaten. He's trying to get up.

The slab we are on starts to move slowly, very slowly toward the flame. "I guess we held our position a bit too firmly," I yell at Gupta.

"Are you grateful now?" Gupta retorts.

"To the end," I said, and then we both started yelling. As we're yelling and proceeding toward the furnace we wriggled like crazy.

Johnno was crawling across the floor toward us.

"I've got a hand free," Gupta said.

"How's that going to help us?" I asked. "I guess you can wave goodbye."

Johnno was up on his knees getting closer. We kept yelling and moving toward the flame that was getting hotter, especially on our feet, very especially on Gupta's feet because he's taller than me and we were tied onto the slab with our heads even.

"It's burning my feet! It's not funny! It's burning my feet!"

"I feel it! I feel it! Get over here quick and untie us!" I urge Johnno.

Gupta reaches down under the slab with his left hand and pushes in as far as he can. He's found a moving part, jabs a finger in. There's a hideous crunch followed in a nano-second by Gupta's yelling louder than ever. It stops.

Gupta's screaming about his finger and screaming about his feet. His shoes are smoking. Johnno pulls himself up to us. He loosens a belt that holds in our feet. We instantly pull our knees up.

"Thank god," said Gupta. "And thank you Johnno."

"My pleasure, mate."

He unties us all the way. I get off. Gupta's finger was stuck in a cog or something. With a muffled whimper he jerks it out. A splash of blood follows. He jumps down as the slab enters further into the flame.

"They forget I work here," said Johnno picking a key off the trim above the door.

With our newfound ally, we go as fast as we can out into a hall. Both Johnno and Gupta are limping with me in between them helping. Blood squirts from Gupta's index finger. There's a door to the outside at the end. We hobble frantically toward it, open it, exit into the outside world with a clear view of MINDY IS FREE! on the sign of the church. We look at it with amazement.

"Mindy is free?" I say with disbelief.

"Mindy is free!" repeats Gupta and we start running toward the sign, him passing me up while emitting gasps of pain.

"I know," said Johnno, who's running with a limp alongside. "I set her free."

"You did?" said Gupta. "That's nice of you."

"Wish we'd known that earlier," I said.

"Now let's get far from here," said Gupta.

We'd gone a good ten meters when the Goony Twins jumped out from behind two trees with drawn guns that squashed our hopes. They lead us back to the building, within which Joan Sutherland was still singing grandly.

Just before we got to the door, Halffoot stopped. "Hey, do you notice that?"

"Joan Sutherland singing?" I guessed.

"Yeah," said Shorts with what sounded like genuine concern. He picked up Gupta's hand and inspected the bleeding finger.

"I didn't know you cared," Gupta said.

"I don't," said Shorts. He turned to Halffoot. "Wash it off in the faucet out here. I'll be back in a minute."

He came back just as he said and wiped off Gupta's finger, put cotton over it, and wrapped it carefully and tightly with medical tape. Gupta groaned at this new pain and we looked at each other perplexed.

As Halffoot pushed us into the building we saw Shorts carefully wiping up the trails of drips Gupta left behind.

"Sorry about the mess," Gupta said.

"You have a nice, domestic quality," I said to Shorts as he wiped up the last drop and inspected the floor. "And you're thorough."

"Shut your trap," he said.

"You think we weren't watching?" Fenster said, still dressed as Genghis Khan. He glanced quickly at Gupta's finger and looked away. He looked at Gupta's arm, the scab on his lip, and his burned shoes. "You seem terribly accident prone."

"You missed the place where he stuck the piano wire up his finger," I said.

"You're stupid," Gupta said to me and then to Fenster, "And you're a bad man."

"Good and bad are relative," said Fenster. "To pick and choose between them is to fall into endless confusion."

"You're forgetting *sila*," I said.

"Mushy morality," said Fenster.

"That's a start," I said. "Now go deeper."

"It's useless without the treasure," he said. "Give me my treasure and then I'll be a good man."

"We don't have to give you anything now," said Gupta. "Mindy's free. "

"What makes you think so?" said Fenster.

"Everybody knows. It's even on the church's sign over there," I said.

Fenster looked over toward the church. "Bugger me dead!" he exclaimed. "How the hell?" He turned to me. "Give me the money or I'll have you both and all your friends beheaded. How's that?"

"We'll give you the money!" I said. "If you're going to let us go."

"No David! He can't kill us or our friends or any of us. If Mindy's free then the cops must be looking for Fenster for kidnapping!"

"Oh, yeah!" I said turning to Fenster. "Let us go and we won't make things worse on you."

"Nice try," he said. "But Mindy's not going to go to the cops. What would she say? What proof does she have of anything? Rudy wouldn't approve. And I know for a fact you two would be far better off without him knowing."

"Not any more," I said. "She will tell Rudy. Rudy's gonna get you. Let us go now and we'll tell him to go easy on you."

"Your friend's right," Fenster said. "You're an imbecile. Look. Give me the money or I'll kill you. End of discussion."

"Gee, he seems convincing to me," I said to Gupta nervously. "I know it's your money but how about reconsidering?"

"Let's talk to Mindy first," said Gupta. "That sign and this guy saying he let her free could all be staged by Fenster."

"I believe it," I said. "I mean I believe she's free."

"Yes," said Fenster snarling at Johnno, "That weak doomed traitor let her wrap him around her little prick-probing finger to escape. He let her go earlier today."

"Prick?" said Gupta. He turned to Johnno. "She didn't..."

"We fell in love."

"I can't believe it!" Gupta stared at the sky.

"It was love at first sight—when I snatched her off the street that night, she just looked at me and smiled. And then... she kissed me."

"No!" exclaimed Gupta, "She *did* come on to her kidnappers and from the very first!"

"Just to me. Queenly was driving. She never cared for him or Terrible Terry."

"Silence!" said Fenster.

"Bobby, I believe you," I said. "Mindy's free."

"Yes, I'm convinced too." said Gupta shaking his head in—belief. "But don't give him the money."

"*I'm* telling the truth, but *you're* lying. You're bluffing! You have nothing!" said Fenster.

"No, we do have the money—nearby. We just wanted to make sure Mindy was safe before we gave it to you," I said. "Now she's safe and so you can have it. Naturally, we'd rather not give it to you—I can think of other uses for it—but, that aside, your actual conditions were that if we provide you with both gold ingots or $300,000, that we would *all* be off your hit list."

"It might be worth $300,000 to me to watch you burn!"

"No, no, no—we had a deal," I said. "That's not fair! No incineration! No decapitation! That's not right! That's not honorable! Genghis Khan wouldn't go back on his word! We went through that exhausting, and highly inventive, treasure hunt and we brought you the treasure before sunset even after you changed the deadline this morning. We have brought you the treasure, not the attractive and heavy gold ingots that you would have preferred I grant you, but the agreed equivalent in cash—actually, it's a little less than the cash value of the gold but it will save you the trouble of fencing it—even though you *are* Fenster the Fence."

"Stay on subject you idiot," said Gupta.

"Nah—you don't have it so you burn," said Fenster.

"We brought you the key," I said, pulling the key out of my pocket and holding it up to him. "And the money's nearby. Since we didn't know Mindy was free, it was only right that we just brought the key. You would have done the same thing. Genghis Khan would have approved. He was fair. He lived by law. He was a man of his word."

"Yeah," said Johnno.

"Silence!" said Fenster. "*You* are definitely going into the inferno."

"No—he's one of us now so the 300,000 should cover him too," I added feebly trying to save the poor schmuck.

"Forget it—he's mine." Fenster looked at me. "Okay, Boys, lock 'em up. I know this key," he said. "It's to a locker at the airport—over by Virgin Blue. Right?"

"Right," I nod. "The number's on it."

"It's not yours to give," said Gupta. "Give me the key. It's mine."

"Shutup. If my treasure is there you two go free," he said snatching the key, "and if it's not, you all three end up compactly settled in your own little cozy urns that will sit on a shelf in my special mausoleum of revenge." He walked off and left us with the Goony Twins.

"Where's the cavalry?" whined Gupta.

"I don't know," I bemoaned sympathetically. "I do wish they'd drop by."

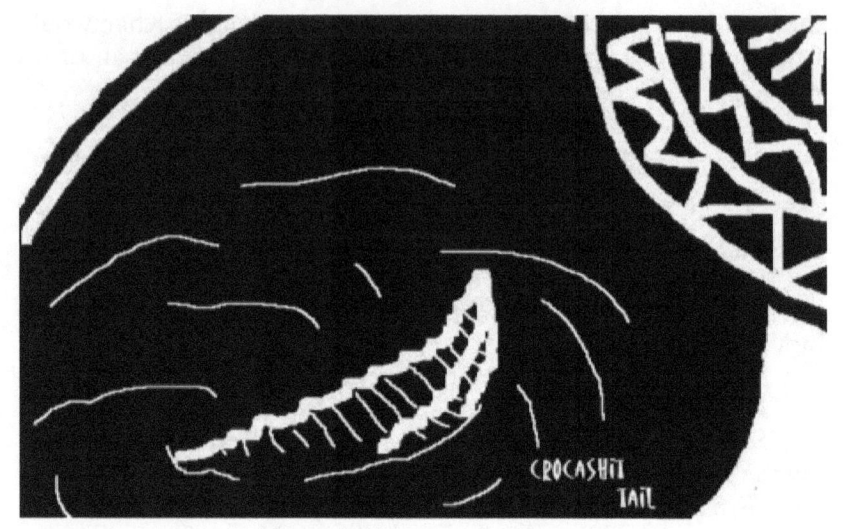

CROCASHIT
TAIL

CHAPTER 32
CROCASHIT

The steel door slammed shut with trailing echo. We could hear the lock clicking with finality.

"You gave away my $300,000."

"It was just three hundred Australian."

"Whatever—you gave it away."

"I'm just buying us time. Needed to give him something to do rather than cook us. Anyway, let's think about getting out of here."

We're trapped in a room with no other door, no windows. Gupta optimistically went to check the door out. Knob wouldn't turn. He found some stiff wire on a shelf and stuck it in the keyhole.

"Forget it," said Johnno. "I know this place. We're in the boiler room. You'll never get through that door. But the Twins shouldn't have put us in here. They weren't thinking straight." He went to the corner behind the boiler. "Fenster meant for them to put us back in the crematorium. Maybe they didn't cause there was still blood on the floor in there."

"What does that matter?" I asked.

"We just have to move this cabinet," Johnno said, opening its tall, gray metal door.

"We're going to rearrange the furniture?" asked Gupta.

"Hang on," said Johnno, as he removed a tool box and threw some heavy items to the floor. "Here, gimme a hand."

"Nothing else to do," Gupta shrugged. I told him just watch and helped Johnno to push the cabinet to the side. When we'd slid it over a ways, the edge of some iron disk was exposed.

"What's that?" I grunted as we kept pushing.

"A way outa here, that's what," Johnno said and then the whole circle was in view.

"A manhole cover!" Gupta exclaimed. "Pardon my negativity."

Johnno picked up the crowbar and started to pry it open. "Let's get out before they realize their mistake."

"Where does it go?"

"This leads to the Perth sewer system. Fenster built this access as an escape route. He chose this lot to build the funeral home because it was right next to one of the large tunnels. We can get far away before we go back up into the daylight. They'll never find us in there. It's a big mess with all sorts of pipes running this way and that all over Perth."

Gupta and I looked at each other with distress and yelled in unison, "No!"

"Uh-uh," I negated, shaking my head.

"Not another maze," Gupta concurred.

"You go without us," I said.

"Are you kidding?" Johnno said.

"Oh, maybe," I said. "Give us a minute to adjust." I'd been more enthusiastic about the complex sewer system discussing it with Mr. Huxworthy on the bench by the Swan River. "I don't know if I can take it. What do you think Gupta? He'll get the money and be happy and come back and let us go. Even if we escape he can always find us."

"Yeah, but on the other hand, he might be in a bad mood—or a crazy one. And this might be our chance."

"Good point. And what if he finally decides to cook us or really cut off our heads? It *would* be good to have some distance between us. Give him time to count to ten."

"There actually is a good reason to consider not going down there," Johnno said.

"What could that possibly be—other than us going crazy from getting lost in another puzzle?" Gupta asked with keen interest.

"Crocashit."

"What?" we both said.

"There's a croc down there. We call him Crocashit."

"A croc!" we exclaimed.

"Croc as in man-eating, reptilian crocodile?" I said.

"Yeah," said Johnno. "That's the one."

"What's a crocodile doing down there?" Gupta asked shaking his head with a combination of disbelief and intense disappointment.

"Fenster put him there to get people who tried to sneak in here," Johnno said over the unpleasant sound of metal scraping on cement as he pushed the heavy cover aside. "And to put the chomp on those who tried to follow him in an escape." He went to the cabinet and grabbed a chain. "And he's got an escape all figured out—with a get-away car in a garage."

"How do you know that beast is down there?" I asked. "What's to stop it from running off?"

"There's bars with a gate. He can't get through—unless he figures out the combination." Johnno dropped his legs down into the hole and kept hold of the crowbar and chain as he started to descend. "Grab me a torch from up there would you. There's another for you."

I handed him a flashlight and kept the other.

"If you want to come you'd better come with me now. I know how to open the gate. Of course you might figure it out. It's a kinda brainteaser."

"No!" said Gupta, "No! Not a puzzle to escape a crocodile on the way out into a maze. Horrors! That's crazy. That's unnecessary! That's sadistic! That's masochistic! That's hellish! That's not real!"

Johnno nodded. "That's Fenster. You gotta turn the handle to the right while pulling back on it, then to the left, then push and back to the right—or is it uh... It's pretty simple, but actually, I'd better be there. Poor Halffoot got confused one day and the croc got him and he got his new name. Before that he was just plain Don. Well, that was actually another croc—that one died and got stuffed."

"Oh. I know where it is," I said. "So that's what happened to the other half of Halffoot's foot—wow. But how does he live down there? The croc, not Half-foot. It's gotta eat more than half a foot. And you have to push that cabinet over every time you want to feed it?"

"The access from the boss's office is the one that's used. This one's just a back-up. When he's here he feeds it. Otherwise, one of us does."

"What does it get fed?" Gupta asked cringing. We looked at each other with dread.

"Mainly chickens. Come on now! We don't off that many blokes.

And people would leave evidence—like bones and blood and hair and stuff. There's nothin' like that burner out there for leavin' no trace. Which reminds me—I gotta go."

"Is Crocashit a big croc?" I asked, inching toward the gaping hole.

"He's enormous," Johnno answered. "Would Fenster go half-way? Get the bolt cutter and the big monkey wrench so you can whack it and hold it off with me."

"I haven't been in Australia very long," I said, "and I haven't warmed up to crocodiles yet. I gotta think."

"I gotta go," Johnno said. "I want to get a head start before they come after me. And come to think of it, that combination won't work for you cause I'm gonna override it so if you want to come you've gotta come with me. Mindy's waiting. Thanks to you I'm not gonna disappoint her. Here I come Mindy!" And with that he went down.

"Well," I said, looking at Gupta "Should we go? It would be nice to be free and see Mindy and so forth."

"Yeah, right. I think the meeting with the crocodile is more like-ly."

"We could learn croc control real quick. And there'd be three of us."

"But why? Why?" Gupta said with exasperation. "Why would Fenster do that? Why? I want to get out of here but I don't want to be eaten by a giant lizard! I don't want this crazy man running my life anymore! Why would he put that creature down there? He's nuts! He's crazy! I don't wanna!" He was jumping up and down—rather awkwardly due to his injured soles. "I just want to walk out of here! I want to go back to the hospital bed with the nice men who give me money. Not die by crocodile!"

"I'm sure Johnno knows how to control it," I said grabbing the heavy tools for Gupta and me to use in what seemed would be a gladiatorial manner. I placed one foot down to the first rung of the ladder.

Then Johnno's amplified voice came shooting up from below. "No you don't! No you don't you Crocashit! Get away from me you son of a dinosaur!"

We gasped as we heard sounds of clanging and smashing mixed with Johnno's fierce yelling. And then it became eerily quiet below. Gupta and I waited for the next sound. Nothing. We waited more. Then relief as Johnno called out for us to come down—that he was on the other side of the gate and it would lock shut when he let it go.

"Darn," I said. "We shouldn't have hesitated. Now there are two of us instead of three with that thing." I started to climb down.

"Wait," said Gupta. "Hear that?"

"What?" I said peering back up into the room.

"Shhh," he motioned and put his hand behind his ear.

I heard something faint, then louder.

I stammered indecisively. Gupta looked from the door to the sewer and Crocashit access. More sound from outside.

"Someone's calling our names," he said.

"Go on! Go on!" I yelled down at Johnno and, as I heard the gate clang shut and the chain rattle, I caught in the faint light and shadows below—the sight of a thick tail swinging through the shallow water by the gate. I shivered, then turned to the door. More yelling. "Calling our names?" I bit at a fingernail. "Coming to bake us or save us from the slicing pendulum?"

"Save us! Save us!" cried Gupta.

The sound of people came from the hall. They were indeed yelling our names. We stood there frozen.

"Hey," said Gupta, "They're callin' 'Davo' and 'Gupta!' It's the cavalry!—I hope!"

We yelled back hoping it was the right thing to do. Then someone was trying to get in. The door opened and Gupta and I watched immobile and clutching each other as Samo entered followed by Gelar and then a policeman—there were more outside the door. A perfect storm-sized wave of relief washed over Gupta and me as once more we were in the midst of our Aussie mates plus official uniformed protectors. Gupta seized the nearest body, Gelar's, and hugged him crying out, "It's about time!" Then he moaned in pain as he'd forgotten his wounded arm.

I put down the flashlight and pipe wrench and looked on with amazement. "Very good to see you. I won't need these now."

The policeman, seeing we were okay, joined with others out in the hall.

"We came as quick as we could," said Samo. "We got held up. We were here a little before the cops—quizzing the receptionist. Just as the cops got here, Fenster and two of his cronies ran from their car by the front door into his office. He was dressed in some unusual costume and was carrying a briefcase and a sword. And boy do we have the goods on him. That guy who thinks Mindy's gonna run off with him gave her enough evidence to keep the prosecutors busy for years."

"Johnno was just with us. Fenster was gonna cremate him but he got away. Who got what on Fenster?" I asked.

"Mindy got it from Johnno—murder, fraud, theft, child porn, date rape drug dealing, tax evasion, smuggling, and more. No charge for kidnapping her though—we're keeping Mindy out of this so nobody gets in trouble with Uncle Rudy. The boys have got Fenster and his twins trapped in his office. My mate in the department is negotiating with them now. Not with him—he won't talk—with one of his men. They've got him cold. Fenster's not going anywhere."

"Oh yes he is!" cried Gupta.

"Uh oh," I said. "The sewer!"

"The sewer?" asked Samo most baffled.

"This way," I said, picking up the flashlight and turning its beam toward the opening. "He can get down there from his office."

Samo and Gelar came over and peered into the darkness. Just then a furious cry came from down below and then Fenster's undeniable voice yelling, "No! No! No!" with the rattling of chains.

Fenster wasn't getting away. He was still going "No!" over and over as I shined the light and Samo and I stuck our heads down into the hole. Still dressed like Genghis Khan, he was holding off the croc with his sword and pulling at a chain on the gate. That's what the chain Johnno grabbed was for—I hadn't noticed the lock. He'd made it so no one, not even Fenster, could follow. Good boy. Samo yelled down at Fenster to give up and come up. Fenster rattled the chain a few more times in vain and waded to the ladder while keeping a blade on the croc. Samo told him to leave the sword below and then gave him a hand as he climbed out in full Genghis Kahn regalia.

"My goodness. You going to a costume ball?" asked Samo.

Fenster smiled, thanked Samo politely for the assist, brushed himself off, and quickly pulled a pistol.

"All of you in front of me with your hands up. Now. Don't hesitate. Good. Good. Continue being obedient and I won't use this on you. Close that door and lock it," he said to Gupta. "Don't hesitate!" Gupta did so. Fenster nodded toward me. "Go to the cabinet and get the key to that lock—it's hanging on the inside of the door. If that one's not there, there's one taped to the bottom of the bottom shelf. Try something and I'll shoot you all."

"Balls up!" Samo cursed himself as I moved to the cabinet. "I should have been prepared for that. Sorry. How unprofessional of me."

"We've all been tripping up today," said Gupta. "It's in the stars."

"It's in your moronic brains," said Fenster. "Which will soon be on this floor if I don't get that key now."

The top key wasn't there. I found the other one under the bottom shelf, tore the tape off it, and, as I reached over to hand it to Fenster, Gupta stuck his arm out with something pointed at Fenster's eyes—the pepper spray!—and pressed it. Nothing happened. He pressed it again. Unflinching, Fenster glared at Gupta with a scowl, gun pointed in his face. Gupta shook the bottle next to his ear.

"Damn it. I brought the one I practiced with. It's empty." He threw it down. "Not our day."

"I almost shot you then," said Fenster. "I should have. You're just such a loser I didn't have to. But I think I will anyway."

"Just take your key and go," I said putting the key in Fenster's weaponless hand.

"After I shoot your friend. Not in panic. Not in anger. It's just. It's mercy killing. And maybe I won't stop there."

"Think of Robina," I said.

Fenster cocked the pistol.

Suddenly there was a hissing noise. I looked to see Fenster's hand and gun turn bright white. He screamed in agony as Gelar continued to spray Fenster's hand with Super Cold 134, the little spare can he'd not used at the Mint.

"Don't touch it," Gelar warned as he took Fenster, paralyzed with pain, lay him on the floor and gently placed a foot on his arm above the crystalline frost. "Better not take it from him yet," he said. "Might break his wrist. And it would burn anyway."

Samo opened the door. Several policemen came rushing in. Samo told them what was up with Fenster's hand. Gupta filled a bucket with cold water from a spigot by the boiler and poured it on the frozen area. Fenster screamed. Samo removed the pistol.

"Good to hear an expression of pain that's not coming from me," Gupta said.

As he spoke the cops started to carry agonizing Fenster out of the room.

"Can I breath a sigh of relief now?" I said.

"Definitely," said Samo.

"What's that?" asked Gelar shining the flashlight into the abyss.

"There's a sword and a crowbar," I said. "Oh yes, and a huge crocodile."

"Oh, a croc. I see its tail and now it just brought it's head up. Big. Really big. What's it doing there?"

"It's one of Fenster's goons," said Gupta.

"Looks like a briefcase by that grate," Gelar said.

I went over and looked in. "That's the $300,000," I said. "Oh yeah. Forgot about that. That's Gupta's. But right now it belongs to a huge crocodile that is between us and it."

Without hesitating, Gelar climbed down the ladder while making a strange whistling sound, waded in the knee deep water right up to Crocashit with his hand in the air between the croc's eyes, walked around it, reached over and picked up the bag from a ledge, reversed his movements, and climbed back up. And Crocashit just acted like he was the guy's pet.

"Where'd you learn that?" I said, astonished.

"From my father."

"How's your finger?" I asked Gupta, walking down the hall.

"Still mangled and throbbing, but nicely wrapped," he responded, holding it up. "And they cleaned it so thoroughly. Puzzling."

"And your arm?"

"It hurts too—more deeply," he said not holding it up.

"And you're limping," said Samo.

"Oh just a little burn."

He looked at Gupta's shoes and then to mine. Both pairs were charred on the bottom—Gupta's worse. "Blimey man!" Samo said. "Looks like you guys had a close call."

"Seconds away from reducing to ashes," I said. "But Gupta was in the lead."

"He's accident prone, huh?" said Samo laughing. "Where do you hurt worse?"

"The damaged body parts take turns sending pain signals."

"What time is it?" I said. "I mean, exactly. I know it's after eight." Gupta held his wristwatch up to me.

"We've got less than an hour till dinner," I said.

"You can make it," said Samo. "Mindy and Frannie are waiting for you guys outside."

"Mindy!?" exclaimed Gupta. "She's here?"

"Excellent," I said. What service."

"Wonderful," chimed in Gupta. And then, turning his head, "What's that racket?"

There was a lot of noise coming from up front. When we walked through the door to the lobby, it was filled with people overwhelming the receptionist who had been overwhelmed as it was—with policemen. And these people were saying strange things like "Where's the beer? Where's the beef?"

In the midst of the crowd, Mindy and Frannie met us with hugs and tears and we met them with the same. Gupta just started sobbing when he saw Mindy. We went through the ever-increasing throng in the parking lot till we saw Techo waiting by his car. People continued streaming in and were even bumping into us. It was then I saw behind Techo that the sign at the church had been changed to read: FREE BEER AND BARBIE AT AMENITY FUNERAL HOME!!

"How'd you do that? This is amazing."

"When we got here, I told the receptionist I was tech support," he said. "You like the message there huh? Thought we might need some reinforcements."

"How do you do that?" I asked again.

"I set the program for that sign up in their computer. Always leave a back door for maintenance I can get to on the web. Let's get outa here," he said, "Before there's so much traffic we can't move."

"How'd you get your car so quickly?" I asked.

"Samo made a call. They delivered it here. Did it without a key."

"What about Mindy's Porsche?" Gupta asked.

"It's taken care of," she said pointing to a tow truck.

"The Goony Twins should have to pick up the pieces," said Gupta. "They made the mess."

"I think they can't function so well in handcuffs," I said looking back at the entrance where they were being escorted out by the police.

Mindy grabbed Gelar and pulled him to come with us. "Come on Gelly, you've earned a meal," she said. "You too Techo."

Techo shook his head. "No thanks. I'll just drive you."

"Me neither," said Gelar.

"Rudy'll be happy to see you."

"But I'm a mess. I smell. I can't go anywhere," he said.

"I smell so bad I can smell myself," I said.

"I smell like blood, sweat, and tears" said Gupta. "And not metaphorically."

"We're stopping by a men's store on the way," said Mindy. "I've already ordered the clothes and it's all set out and waiting for you to put on—underwear, shoes, and all. They got a shower and razors and I know men can shower, shave, and dress in five minutes—and that's about how much time you'll have. And Frannie and I will help you Gupta so don't worry about keeping up. They'll have glasses too."

Samo waved goodbye. Techo maneuvered his vintage Chevy

slowly through the people and cars coming towards us. I looked back from the front seat and smiled to see Mindy and Frannie squeezed between Gupta and Gelar. Ahh, Mindy was out of danger. We all were.

That was the end of the thrills and threats. And after that no mandatory mazes, predatory puzzles, nor stupefying treasure hunts. We had our treasure—the girl from Perth, the girls from Perth, our mates from Perth. And Gupta had that briefcase—and its contents.

1937 LASALLE HEARSE

CHAPTER 33
PARTY TO CRIME

You like the wine? That's a dynamite Margaret River Chardonnay." Rudy sat surrounded by five relieved and resting reprobates. Without waiting for a response, he continued his praise. "This golden nectar is one of Australia's very best which means of course about the best in the world." The man was jovial, enjoying his role as magnanimous host to his niece, her estranged hubby, distant nephew, and their pals. We were all enjoying his company as well. He loves to help others satiate themselves, encourages splurging on his largess. Good to be on his good side.

"Hey!" said Mindy who then playfully hit Gupta on the head with her napkin.

"Yep, she's real and really here," said pincher Gupta to me.

"You're supposed to pinch yourself to see if you're dreaming!" she scolded.   Gupta and I were superlatively pleased and goofing. When Rudy's head was turned we made faces that conveyed subtle messages like, "We're here! We're alive! Mindy's here! Miracles happen! There is a supernatural power protecting us!" We were gaga.

Rudy's sun-glassed man Stevo was stationed at a nearby table sipping coffee, scanning the other customers and front door. I think he was a little extra nervous because Rudy wasn't sitting with his back to a wall. Rudy wanted us to have a view of the river.

"Is this the best or what?" Rudy went on.

"Excellent," I said.

"Better than best," said Gupta.

Gelar nodded drinking a non alcoholic wine. "Extraordinary. Better than any grape juice I ever had."

"It's not fermented," said Rudy, "so I pity you. You quit drinkin' too?" he said to Mindy.

"I'm thinkin' about it," she said. "Actually, not thinkin' about it—just not doin' it for a while. Thinkin' is what I had some time to do a lot of recently and decided I spent too many nights blotto—nights that were adding up to years. But don't let me stop ya."

"You're supposed to be the wild one honey," said Rudy. "Well god bless ya. And now there's more Leeuwin for the rest of us."

"We had a nice little visit to that winery, didn't we?" said Mindy, holding up the bottle and looking at the fine art on the label.

"Yeah, it was good," I said.

"Beautiful countryside," said Frannie.

"Oh yes—it was quite enjoyable," said Gupta.

"Better than that," Mindy said. "I'd say it was... ecstatic."

"We should have more contact with our American relatives," Rudy said. He lifted his glass, "A toast to our..."

There was a bright flash, as a waiter at the next table took a photo of a smiling birthday party of six. Instantly Stevo was out of his chair and had snatched the camera from the waiter's hand.

"It's okay," Rudy said to him. "It's a good day. There's no harm. Let 'em have it. It's okay," he spoke in a sort of "down boy" tone.

Slowly Stevo gave the camera back to the frightened waiter and returned to his perch. The birthday party-goers were stunned.

"Put their meal on my tab," said Rudy, then looking over at them with his glass raised, "Happy Birthday. Enjoy." They slowly raised their glasses, smiled, drank, and then gradually went back to laughing and talking among one another.

"Now where were we," he said. "Oh yes, to our American family."

For over a week none of us had much more than what food-on-the-go we could grab. That night we munched and wolfed like starved Kookaburras. The dinner was lavish and transcendently savory—thanks to Jessica's brilliant cooks, Bodhisattvic lobsters, and selfless crabs. Just being there at that table was like a dream—the sort of heavenly reward suicide bombers might expect to be reborn into, minus the seventy-two virgins.

Rudy asked what we'd done all August.

"Oh, nothing newsworthy," said Mindy. "Except for Guppy earlier today. We just traipsed about here and there. Let's see, we went to The Maze and got lost."

"Gupta's a maze savant," said Frannie. "He and Davo love conundrums."

"And we went to the Indiana Tea House," I said changing the subject.

"Rottnest," interjected Gupta. "The quokkas. Loved the quokkas."

"The whole experience was like—hmmm—one big treasure hunt," Frannie said fearlessly.

"What treasure did you like best?" asked Rudy.

"The Ozzies of WA," I said. "So friendly and loose—and, maybe like me, some of them are a little tiny bit deranged."

Rudy smiled and grabbed my arm playfully. "What else you got to say about us?"

"I have a toast," I said standing up. "They say the Eskimos have all these words for snow—sixty-five or two hundred—changes depending on the source. As with so much we're taught, it's not true. Its an Arctic myth. But what is actually a true anthropological fact is that the Ozzies have an uncountable number of words for, well for Schindlered, blind, blotto, pissed, Brahms and Liszt as well as Adrian Quist gutful of piss, mental, as full as a goog, canned, cot face, shit-faced, slaughtered, sloshed, soused, sizzled, stonkered, Molly the monk drunk! So a toast to our toasted hosts, the venerable boozin' Ozzies, good mates who love a good time and who, unlike my ancestors, didn't let the Puritans overrun their shores and spoil the party!"

Customers at the tables on both sides of us cheered with raised glasses as well.

"Where'd you get that?" asked Gupta.

"I been writin' 'em down in me wee notebook," I said.

"When have you had the time to memorize it?" he asked.

"While you were drunk on Mindy," I whispered.

Gupta scribbled something down and quickly handed it to Mindy while Rudy was at the loo. She read it out loud.

Dear Mindy
My friendy,
I'm stupid.
'Twas Cupid

Made me do it.
I Intuit.
Love, Guppy
Dumb puppy

She smiled broadly and kissed him on the cheek.

"Did anyone ever tell you that you were accident prone?" said Rudy laughing.

"You're the first," said Gupta with a forced smile.

Gupta's bandaged and unbandaged wounds were an inescapable topic of conversation. All passed as results of the searing gold ingot incident that had been at the top of the news all day featuring that still shot of Gupta as he was rolled delirious into the ambulance. It was spread wide across the front page of next morning's early addition, already out, and which Rudy held up for all to see.

"Aside from that, Mr. Gupta, how did you enjoy the Mint?" Rudy asked loudly, and leaned back guffawing.

Gupta needed more professional care. Back to his hospital bed and an overnight. Arm inspected and redressed, finger and feet attended to. The morning was spent largely in talking to members of the press making up all sorts of crap. When the curvaceous nurse from the day before came on duty she was puzzled by the new wounds as she didn't realize Gupta had ever left. Techo dropped by to see how Gupta was doing and paid a bit of attention to her as well. Frannie got instructions on how to tend to Gupta's wounds and we took off for Dwellingup where he was to rest up before our departure. He needed a place to repair including from injuries resulting from his madness with Mindy whom Gelar had gone home with after dinner. Frannie said I should take it easy too and I did sleep a lot the first night, but the next day I was obsessed with the idea of cleaning up and organizing three areas we hadn't gotten to before—the laundry hut, the storage shed, and her cluttered, jam-packed art room behind the kitchen.

We got going with the latter—pulling its innards out—the paints, brushes, canvases, poster board, bottles of glue, bags of glitter, clay, wood, stones, normal tools and curious apparatus, books, pieces of junk, unnamable objects, half filled coffee cups, a vacant wasp nest. After a proper cleaning, throwing up additional shelving, dividing stuff into want and don't want, give and take, here and there, this and that, a painting to give to Sal and his old dog next door, it was all done and we stood proudly and surveyed our handi-work. On to the laundry room. It was all work and all play.

We took a break in the late afternoon and walked to the pub to graze on Emu with the local stock. Went shopping together and our rich friend Gupta bought the groceries but Frannie insisted on paying for her own lotto ticket, saying he shouldn't have to support her gambling habit. He knew it was bought in hopes of helping her friends in Mandurah. He bought her another ticket for good luck. I pointed out that by not buying a lotto ticket I got to keep the cost of the ticket and had the same chance as her of winning—if you round off the odds to the nearest ten thousandth.

Gupta spent a goodly amount of time reading on the rattan couch in the patio out back. His job was to heal, he was doing it splendidly, and the aches and pains had decidedly subsided. He didn't like the pain killers they gave him at the hospital so the bottle just sat there all lonely till Banger came by for a visit. Once Gupta got up to assist a couple of intriguing women of the woods who came down the dirt access road out back in a rusty old truck pulling a cart. They picked up the trash, recyclables, and sellable stuff gathered from all the or-ganizing. Frannie paid them with *objets d'art*.

Two dreams came true on the last day there. We rode the Hotham Valley Railway and saw wallabies at sunset hopping along their way. That night we three sat at a blaze under the stars round the ring of volcanic rock. Frannie did another fire dance. We looked at the Southern Cross and its neighbors not seen by us up above down under.

Gupta and I took turns playing the guitar. Here's one I sang.

Looking up above tonight—at the spread of brightening stars
Hints of wonder that recite—how wonderful you are
I love you for your eyes on me—I loved you from the start
But in the end I love you friend—for you are pure of heart

Walkin' down the street alone—dog on leash that's trailin' free
Kickin' long a bouncing stone—where once you walked with me
I love you for your gentleness—I love you for your warts
But in the end I love you friend—for you are pure of heart

Pen on paper light from lamp—stomach's growlin' goes unheard
Late and tired dear here I am—a wrappin' up these words
I love you for your mischief—I love you for your art
But why I still hold to this torch—is you are pure of heart

But why I still hold to this torch—is you are pure of heart

We left early the next morning. Freddy was sleeping in the bed on the porch. Hmm. Never met him.

On the way to Perth we visited Simon and he joined us in a game of catch. All Gupta could do was chase the ball and kick it back to one of us. Then we played a game where we'd give Simon a subject and he'd draw it. He was quick. I got a 1937 LaSalle Hearse on Google Image search and he whipped one right out. He did about forty sketches including one of Frannie and friends saying g'bye to Gupta and me at the airport down a long hallway.

Hours before takeoff. Party down. While a cool and versatile quartet serenaded us with rock, swing, jazz, and country tunes, the treasure hunt gang surrounded a nightclub table, celebrating our monumental and accidental success. Bonded and bound, in high spirits to be all together for surely this one last time. Moving around the table, there's Techo, Samo, Gelar, Mindy, Gupta, Frannie, and me. The first hour of the gala was ours with more mates invited following that. With the minute hand creeping close to the top, Frannie excused herself, saying she'd be back in a jiff. As soon as she was gone, Gupta announced he'd something to bring up quickly before the others arrived.

Mai came in about the time our little private chat was over. She asked what we were all huddled together about and I said it was a secret. Mindy jumped up, ran to her, and they hugged. It turns out they'd met at the restaurant at the Swan Brewery just after Mindy escaped. It was Mai and family who had given Mindy sanctuary at their table and a ride into the center of town. The blonde nurse from the hospital joined Techo. I'd invited Ian but he had to be with his Freo zazen group. Slim from the Northbridge Hostel came with a French woman who was staying there. Frannie came back in with her new friend Gecko, the fellow whom she'd met selling his crafts in front of the bank, the president of which arrived as well—Vargas. He was all blown away to be at a party with Ross. Ross wasn't there yet though. I knew he probably wouldn't make it because he was in the studio recording and we'd already seen each other earlier—had lunch at a Chinese restaurant in Northbridge. I had assured Vargas that Ross would be forever grateful for his role in sparing him from the grips of the terrorists, but reminded him he could never mention it for reasons of international security. He nodded in utmost seriousness. I introduced bachelor Vargas to single Mai. It turned out she was also interested in tango dancing. Maybe he'll like her dolls and she'll end up living here near her sister.

In terms of coupling, Mindy'd definitely softened up to Gelar. They had the vibes of a new item more than a failed marriage. Gelar, who'd always been fairly quiet, got down on his knees before Mindy, opened up his shirt revealing the tattoo he'd acquired on his chest years before, and dramatically stated for all to hear, "Oh Bluey, take me back! See—I love you always! It's still there branded on my heart. Melinda! And I'll never find another Melinda like you. You're the best of 'em all!" She grabbed him and they smooched uninhibited before a roomful of eyes and sighs.

"Love a public pash," said Frannie.

"It's for the best," said Gupta smiling bravely.

After Samo's wife arrived, Gupta and I were the only unmatched ones in our troop.

"Well, we've still got each other," I said.

"Oh great," he responded unimpressed.

I made up for my singularity by bringing over a funny older woman I'd been flirting playfully with at the bar. Can't remember her name but recall she was retired from a company that made pies out of marsupials.

Gupta was staggering around talking to people. He had no date so he played cupid. There was a fellow he got to chatting with who was upset because his boyfriend was mad at him. During a break, Gupta went into a huddle with the band. When they came back on, they said there was going to be a special song sung by a patron of the club. Gupta picked the mike out of the stand using his less wounded left hand with wrapped finger, and softly spoke in a dramatic deep voice. "Frank, this is a special song dedicated to you from Trenton." At a table near the front, one man looked at another. The band struck up a few bars and Gupta belted out *John Belushi Butt*. Afterwards the two men embraced and all clientele burst into applause.

"And now," Gupta said, "a little something for the one who is responsible for bringing us all together. And with sincere congratulations to Gelar for winning her back," he proceeded to whip out a thumping rock 'n roll song that went:

A walkin' downtown, at a corner I found myself
Talkin' to that girl from Perth
There was a warm breeze, my darn knees about
Buckled to that girl from Perth
She took me drivin' in the country, sunny, bumpy

It was somethin'
Now I'm standin' alone, hand on the phone
Thinkin' 'bout that girl from Perth

Those looks sorta started when our pals parted
Talkin' 'bout that girl from Perth
In the woods, on the shore, on the dance floor I'ze
Stalkin' that girl from Perth
Walkin' down the city street with her yin yang tattoo
An' her bare feet
Then I'ze sittin' here workin' on my second beer
Drinkin' to that girl from Perth

She'll be in Queensland, hair full of sand
Sun on that girl from Perth
Or in Darwin town, she'll burn it down
Look out for that girl from Perth
I'll jet through the astral stream
To get to that rascal of my dreams
Now I'm drivin' along, high on a song
Singin' 'bout that girl from Perth

"Astounding song," I said to Gupta as he sat down amidst enthusiastic applause from the besotted patrons as well as the band.

"Couldn't have done it without you," he said.

"A song for me. Thank you my hero," and Mindy gave him a kiss.

"You guys sure have similar styles," said Frannie.

"Only superficially," said Gupta, "and I'm better. Davo's terrible to play with. He has a bad sense of rhythm. He speeds up and slows down. He gets things discombobulated. But he's got his good points."

"We got a song from this guy," said Mindy hitting me on the head. "It's for all of you." She jumped up on the stage and grabbed the microphone. Frannie joined her and they sang, starting off a *cappella*, the band gradually joining in.

There's a time to grieve, a time to groan
A time to say I can't make it on my own
But oh, there's a time it is known
To say thank you

There's a place to sigh, a place to cry

A place to sit and wonder why
But oh, there's a place in this life
To say thank you

Here come the boys
Makin' all their noise
The gals get them to lay down their toys
To rejoice to rejoice to rejoice

There's a mind that is lonely, a mind in pain
A mind that somehow makes it through the day
But oh, there's a mind on the way
That says thank you
Thank you

We stood outside the nightclub in a light drizzle. Gupta and I were bidding last farewells to the fellow revelers not coming to the airport—principal among them, Samo and Techo. Ross had not shown up. Too bad. I wanted to say bye to him. Vargas was even more disappointed. One unexpected visitor was the Aboriginal buckster whom I saw sitting unobtrusively on some nearby stairs. He'd been there all evening. He wouldn't come in so we'd had a dinner sent out to him. Gelar went down the block for the La Salle hearse. It had been found on a side street not far from where he'd last parked it. Not a scratch.

Between the hugs and slugs, the friendly put-downs and pulling up of embarrassing memories, Gupta and I shared the limelight with some guys just a few meters away who were struggling with the task of holding ropes, lowering a piano from a balcony on the second, third, wow, way up on the fourth floor of the building. A truck had backed up to the sidewalk and was prepared to be loaded with what they told us was a Steinway grand. It was wrapped up to protect it from scratches and the elements, tied with thick ropes, hanging from two large pulleys protruding from the parapet of the flat roof.

One of the ropes was stuck and a guy was tugging on it. He got that fixed and they gave up some slack to lower the massive keyboard. Then with a loud crack! one of the pulleys broke loose and the piano swung down vertically, jerked, held, and rocked twisting and creaking. The crowd below backed up emitting gasps. The moving men were yelling at each other. One pulley was holding. The rope for the broken pulley was drawn back and tied off taut again. Slowly the piano was lowered to the sidewalk, a few of us helping it to land.

Our collective sigh of relief could probably be heard across town. Gupta gave the instrument an affectionate pat, and as he did, a BMW turning the corner much too speedily lost control, went into a spin on the wet surface, jumped the curb, and plowed right into the piano smashing it against the brick building, ripping it's covering off, snapping it's lid, and spilling some of its contents out. Gupta tumbled back and landed on the pavement. People screamed and jumped away, glass broke. We all stood in silence, agape as the dust settled. A piano string hanging from the side of the squashed grand was swinging in the air. The owners sprinted down the stairs and stood astonished looking at the results of the melee. The driver leaned, uninjured but in minor shock, on the steering wheel of his smashed vehicle which had bounced back a few feet. Our party stood stunned in the aftermath of the disaster, feeling new intense emotions that had switched from parting to coming apart.

Vargas put his hand on my shoulder. "Where is Ross Bolleter now that we need him," he said, looking with sadness at the ruined piano.

"A brilliant idea," I said to him. "I know exactly what you are thinking. Except this is not Ross's moment. This is yours."

Vargas looked at me intensely. He turned with a sense of resolve, walked up to the piano, took a deep breath, and struck a key, then another. He reached into the crunched Steinway and plucked a string. When the drummer started whacking on the wrinkled fender of the car, the driver sporadically honked his horn and played with the radio—turning it on and off, changing stations—with a deft touch. Gradually this demolition symphony built and the band members joined in with found objects as they meted out the *just this* of the moment, the dirge of a great instrument cut short in its prime. Vargas smashed his fist on the broken key cover, stepped on a bent pedal, ran a hand down the traumatized strings, hammered the piano hammers. The owners of the broken Steinway seemed comforted—one clapped, one sang out. I looked at Gupta's watch. Time to go.

Gelar gunned the engine. Mindy hopped in. Gecko told Frannie to go on with her friends. I stepped on the running board and called out, "Good to meet you Gecko," and he smiled. Mai winked, the woman I'd flirted with blew a kiss. Bye Slim! Vroom, vroom grumbled the hearse. Gupta hopped up with me. Wild strings were sounded in dramatic dissonance, fender drummed. Two figures stood on the curb. "Samo!" We bow. "Techo!" Raised fists. "Love to all WA!" Gupta waved and I called, "Take care dear mates! Bye! Bye!" As the dissonance and random harmonies climbed to a crescendo, the hearse took off with us waving and blowing kisses, Gelar's ooga horn blaring in the finale.

CHAPTER 34
G'BYE

The weight of parting was falling heavily through us. We hovered around the doors to customs, Gupta and me sipping distilled spirits from a flask to squelch the sad and sweet pained emotions. Gelar pushed his hands deeper into his pockets. Mindy and Frannie smiled at us and talked to each other. Running out of things to say, waiting for the moment of departure like condemned prisoners, wishing the axe would fall so our heads could roll into the native baskets to be shipped off.

Speaking of decapitation, a well-dressed man walked up to me as I came out of the men's room. My gosh. It's Stan. He brought, get this, greetings from Fenster, and a gift. It was something special he preferred not to bring into the airport. I would find it waiting for me when I returned to Texas five months hence—naturally they knew my schedule. He handed me an envelope that contained a photo of a sword, a rather familiar looking sword I'd seen Fenster swinging threateningly at me not a great many days prior. With the photo were official looking papers from an auction house certifying the pictured sword was an authentic Yanashi Wakazashi from the late 1700s. Stan said Fenster was handing it over with respect and in recognition of his defeat at our hands. He said Fenster would never have used it as he instantly faints at the sight of blood.

Oh—that explains a lot, I thought, as a handful of scenes flashed through my mind.

I asked Stan who had retrieved the sword out of Crocashit territory. He said he did, but only after the zoo authorities had taken the reptile away. They herded him out the gate for a ways to a large maintenance access in the sewer system. Now he was with new friends and has many admirers—Crocashit not Stan. Stan got the crowbar too. That was thorough of him—I hated to think of a perfectly good tool like that just lying there in the sewer water until it rusted away.

Stan said Fenster was under psychiatric observation ordered by the court. At the time of handing over the sword he had committed himself to a rigorous schedule of meditation in the lotus posture. However since then, possibly due to the pain he suffered in his legs and back from the long hours of sitting, and the strain of all that he's gone through, he's deviated from that practice and now was following the way of Equus convinced that he is Phar Lap.

"Phar Lap?" I asked. "But Phar Lap is, was, a horse. I can see Waxo getting into being Genghis Khan or even the women, Robina and Joan Sutherland, but isn't becoming a race horse a long stretch?"

Stan acknowledged that was so but said Fenster had made that leap. It seems he and his fellow New Zealander, the chestnut colored Phar Lap, were both born in the town of Timaru on October 4th, 1926 (Same as my son Kelly—the month and day that is, not the year and town). Phar Lap and Fenster had identical astrological charts. Fenster insisted they were born at the same instant and had gotten it in his head they shared a soul of which they were, for a time, two simultaneous manifestations, one which passed away prematurely. He had been a rugby star in his youth as well but had injured his left knee. It turns out he was not named Bobby by his parents, but Reginald. Bobby was what Phar Lap's devoted trainer had called him, and Fenster had taken that name on when he was a young man and had first become enamored with the heroic story of that spirited steed. Now he was refusing to stand up or eat anything but oatmeal, as close as he could get to horse posture and fare. Also he was insisting without success he be castrated by the guards as Phar Lap was a gelding.

I thanked Stan for going to all the trouble of coming to see me at the airport, and asked him to tell Fenster a few things. One, that I very much appreciate his gift and will hang it proudly on the wall of the barn when I return. See—I too live in a home for horses. Two, I had gathered from a reliable Internet source that recent research has shown Phar Lap did not die from nefarious causes but from a rare intestinal ailment, which was not even discovered and named until 1980—so he can stop hating San Francisco. And three, even though Buddhism does not use the concept of soul, in the permanent entity that keeps on going forever sense, I am nevertheless confident Fenster and Phar Lap always were and always will be indivisible.

"Oh yes," I said to Stan in closing, "Tell him and... do you see Sid?"

"Every day."

"Give him this message for me as well would you? And to you too and to all involved."

"Most certainly."

"Impressive treasure hunt," I said tilting my head down in a bow.

My shoulder bag was stuffed. I had Simon's sketches and a bunch of light souvies I hadn't gotten around to mailing back home yet—the senior ticket stub for the ferry to Rottnest and another for Ross's concert, brochures for places I'd been like the Swan Bells, the Freo prison, and the Perth Mint. There were a few new ones from the day before when Mindy had gotten that SUV and, with Gelly and Frannie as assistant tour guides, had taken Gupta and me on the countryside tour we'd missed when she'd been kidnapped. I got to see the Vipassana Center though I didn't get to go into any building. Lovely place—spacious. Everyone must have been meditating.

A padded envelope Ross gave me at lunch was in there. There were six CDs in it—three copies of his new tango CD, *Paradise Café*—for Gupta, Frannie, and me. There were copies of another CD in there as well, one he'd made of six songs Gupta and I played with him with Frannie as the engineer operating the on off switch of his recorder. Generous of him. I made a mental note to try to drum him up some business. Let's see, how would I go about doing that? I could suggest that people Google Ross Bolleter and order his CDs online—or they could place an order at their local record store and suggest the store stock his wonderful creations.

Also in my shoulder bag were copies of two newspaper front pages I'd handed out to my mates at our private early get-together back at the nightclub. One featured the photo of Gupta in shock being wheeled into the ambulance. The other had an article on Fenster and the bust at Amenity including a great shot of him as Genghis Khan being escorted into the police station. Amazing—there was no mention of any of us—just the arresting officer, the guy who was tight with Samo. He and the cops got a lot of kudos and the Treasure Hunt Gang stayed out of the whole mess and testifying in court and being whacked and all. Are they really going to be able to keep all this from Rudy? Or maybe he knew—even at dinner. Oh well, all's well that ends without death and destruction—from my human centered point of view anyway. In the big picture I think it could just be said all's well regardless—every day's a good day. Back to the paper. It did mention Johnno—not by name but it was clearly him. An employee had turned on Fenster, would testify, and was getting a new identity. "Waxing on Waxo," read the headline. This informer had been arrested at The Maze where he'd refused to leave at closing time. The police had to go into the loggy thick of it and get him. He protested he was looking for his true love who was in there somewhere and it was very difficult for him to be convinced otherwise.

"That's my fault," said Mindy. "I still feel bad about that. He was sweet."

Gupta and Gelar looked at each other.

The paper quoted a local politician as saying Fenster was an evil man possessed of the devil. I'd agree with that if we define evil as harmful behavior born of greed, hate, and delusion, and the devil as the seeming self thus poisoned.

Mindy said when she was a little girl and Rudy and Fenster were not enemies, she always found Waxo offensive. She said he used to lecture her about morality one minute and tell jokes deriding Aborigines the other. Also, he made her listen to interminable boring opera records while he paced about proclaiming to her how superior the singer's voice was.

"Hmm. Wonder who that singer could be?" Gupta commented.

To me Fenster had that problem, the delusion I'd wondered about when first I met him—misunderstanding emptiness to mean that nothing mattered rather than that all phenomena, all behavior, though non substantial, is quantumly more real thus more significant than we perceive it to be—just not at all what we think it is—nor is it other. Emptiness might be beyond all dualistic ideas including those of good and bad, but I think our intentional actions matter more than we can imagine. There's a name for that—karma. Emptiness doesn't mean you can throw things out, things like morality. As Nagarjuna, the godfather of emptiness said, it's better never to have heard of emptiness than to overemphasize it—or something to that effect. But anyway, it seems Fenster's dealing with other delusions now.

Frannie looked over my shoulder at the newspaper. "There's an

Australian newspaper and in it is an Australian gangster," she said, pointing to the photo of Fenster. "Oh," she continued, "and there's an Australian police station."

"And my gosh," I said looking around, "Australian windows and an Australian floor."

"And an Australian ceiling."

"And Australian mates," I said looking at our comrades.

"And thank you Davo for coming to visit and introducing me to such wonderful and interesting people," she said wrapping an arm around Mindy.

"Thank you for being such a fine hostess and putting up with the little inconveniences."

"All in a month's play."

"I leave you with your new Apollo and Dionysus as well," I said. "He seems to be worthy of you. I may now depart with peace of mind."

"And here's a little something for your trip to Asia," she said as she handed me a small box wrapped in a piece of thick, uneven purple and green material painted with orange swirls. Inside were vials of local oils—Eucalyptus and Emu, herbal potions, hand labeled with an explanatory sheet. Also there was a little delicately painted metal sewing box—too thin to contain spools—just some wound loops of thread, needles, tiny scissors, a few buttons.

I told her to give my love to her family, especially, my voice briefly cracked, to her mother. I gave her a little surprise gift to hang on her wall. It was a familiar quote—in a miniature frame and calligraphed in beautiful tiny script by Techo. It read:

Whatever you would do or dream to do, begin it. Boldness has genius, power, and magic in it.

Frannie didn't know it yet, but she was about to get some good news. She'd won the lottery—sort of. Not an official Australian lottery but the Treasure Hunt Gang Lottery. Earlier that night, when she'd gone off to pick up Gecko, and Gupta had said there was something he'd wanted to talk to us all about, what he had to say was he wanted to split the money he'd received from the Mint, the 300,000 Australian, split it with all of us, since we all were in on the whole thing together and each was as deserving as the next. To make a short story shorter, following his lead we ended up deciding to give the bulk of the bundle to Frannie to do the improvements at the home for her somewhat challenged Mandurah friends. The loot minus a humble share for each of us was tucked away in Vargas's bank. It was all ready for her to use with Vargas as a trustee and advisor to help her spend it wisely and to make sure she didn't get screwed by some shysters. I smiled and told her I knew something she didn't, that she'd learn soon, and she couldn't get out of me.

A long haired young backpacker walked by carrying a guitar case. Gupta went up to him and, thanks to a delayed flight and the natural generosity of this friendly Perthite stranger, Gupta sang one more song for the road in the sky—not only for us but for a large assembly of mutually waiting folk.

Oh my doll, I dream of you
And the garden wall reveals you too
In the wind that winds the blue
I remember who was there
Who took the time the time to care
To one so fair, to one so few
I declare hon
I love you
Yes I do
In the clear, in our brew
And as your wings lift up into
I let you go to fly off where
There is no need to have to wear
The garment or the shoe
And dear indeed as memory bleeds
I'll long remember you
Oh yes I will
Into the veil, beyond the hill
Until I fail here is my heart
It will disappear but there you are
There's no accounting for the stars
That stare at us until
We are the blinking, slowly sinking
To the ocean then
To meet again
As the family, flower, as the friend
As the lion devours the prey
Indra's dancing net within
The changing partners, women men
From children born anew

Such lands will lead us to
Of all places
Always home
Always touching, always lone
Freed by breath and held by bone
You lift me and you blow out then
A daffodil into the wind
I'm floating out into the light and love
Throughout
Our new faces
Always home
Always touching, always lone
Always perfect, Always shown
And going on and on and on and on
And on and on and on

Gupta handed the guitar back with a bow of the head. Mindy gave him a kiss and said, "G'bye good man."

"It's been more interesting than the average vacation," Gupta said. "You were a heavenly hostess." Then turning his glance. "Frannie. Gelar."

"Gupta," said Gelar.

Last hugs all around. "Bye Gelar," I said. "Bye Mindy. Bye Frannie. I lost my quokka stubby but," I lifted up my pants cuff, "the hemp cord is still around my ankle."

"Me too," said Gupta.

"You didn't lose a quokka stubby," I corrected him.

"G'bye Davo," said Frannie. "Be in touch. Come back to George What."

"What? Oh—yes, you remember. Bye Frannie again." I bowed with my palms together—I can't help but do that.

"May I?" I said to the local hippie, put his guitar strap over my shoulder and strummed and sang:

We'll all be back together when she's bloomin'
When she's bloomin', when she blooms
We'll all be back together when she's bloomin'
When she's bloomin', when she blooms

I was a little teary-eyed and waving walking backwards with Gupta who then grabbed me and cried out, "Thank you!"

"Thank you!" I echoed.

"Thank you!" he said rather loudly in my face and then he called out "Thank you!" to our friends who called back, "Thank you!" and then he threw back his arms and yelled "Thank you!" to the whole airport and then "thank you!" to the ceiling and "thank you" to the right and to the left and to the floor. Strangers were calling "thank you" back to him. I had to get him out of there. I was afraid we were going to get arrested for being too gratefully weird in a post 9/11 security situation. And as I dragged him out of sight, one last quick wave and glance—with Frannie.

On the plane and in the air Gupta and I relaxed in our luxurious first class seats, shoes off, stretching, sighing, wiping the corners of our eyes.

"That's sort of the way your thank-you book is toward the end," he said.

"What do you mean?"

"All that thank-you-ing."

"Huh. Yeah. I guess. Sort of. Not quite. I forget. Uh—how do you know?"

"I read it at Frannie's just a few days ago."

"Really?" I said all excited and proud, "I didn't notice that. Well, it seems like an appropriately significant theme to repeat. I repeat it all the time."

"Yes, I know. And I fell under the influence."

"Wow. You read it. That's great."

"Well, the last chapters."

"What do you mean, the last chapters."

"I just read the last chapters."

"You what?"

"I think you heard."

"That's awful. How many?"

"Six, seven. Read them from the back in. Sorry to let you down."

"How could you do that?"

"I just wanted to get a feel for it."

"Why not the first chapter?"

"I like to read the last chapters of books."

"Well gosh..."

"Don't whine. It's unbecoming."

"I give up—okay," I groaned.

"Say thank you," he admonished me.

"Thank you."

"You know, Gupta," I said after a bit of silence, "on the flight in I had this dream, this vision of all the dangerous animals of land and sea attacking me in Australia—spiders, snakes, sharks. Oz is just like everywhere else—it's the two-legged animals that are the most dangerous."

"Like kangaroos?"

"You know what I mean."

"Emus?"

"Okay—it's the occasional two-legged humanoid that is most dangerous."

"Like Mindy?"

"Hmm. Right."

"Well, that's enough love for a while."

"I sympathize," I said.

"How easily we become victims of insatiable desire and romance propaganda. And look at what the in-flight movie is—*Sleepless in Seattle*," he said.

"Better they had that Australian TV show, *Love is a Four Letter Word*," I replied.

"Yeah, that's a Dylan song," he went on, "But no, they've got to fill our minds with the endless lie. It's a sickness. Happily ever fiction."

"Yeah. Mad Magazine did a spoof on 'happily ever after' with examples from fairy tales—I can't remember—you know—long time ago—like Prince Charming getting soft and fat, drinking beer and burping and Snow White in hair curlers bitching or whatever."

"Like how many of the loving couples we were with tonight do you think will be together a year from now?"

"Hey, usually I'm the cynical one about love," I said.

"Just trying to build up my resistance. Never again. It makes me cringe to think of some of the stupid, embarrassing things I said to Mindy in my idiot love dream. I'm gonna miss her for a little while longer though I'm sure. And I'll certainly never forget her."

"I'll miss Francine too. But the chemistry is not painful grieving like yours. It's a little sad and sweet—like missing my boys."

A stewardess glided up to us, oh—that same luscious stewardess who had distracted Gupta so thoroughly on the flight over. His head jerked so fast to face her I was worried he'd twist it off. She was thoughtfully concerned about his wounds, which he milked for all the attention he could get. So much for dispassion.

Soon she was off doing other duties so it was possible to talk with him again. But he didn't want to hear what I had to say. I'd found an article on the Coriolis Effect in the airlines magazine. It had sad news for Gupta. There is indeed such a phenomenon, but it only applies to large weather systems like cyclones, hurricanes. He was right though that they went clockwise in the Southern Hemisphere and counter-clockwise in the Northern. But alas, the Coriolis Effect didn't apply on a small scale. How one got out of a bath or how the inside was designed was what determined which way the water swirled when draining from a tub. It even mentioned the demonstrations at the equator and said they were a trick, determined by how the guide turned when holding the jug.

"So," I said, changing the subject to something less disappointing, "do you think I could write about what happened to us and plug Singapore Airlines and other commercial things like um Emu Beer now? Get a book deal? Make a little something on the side for product placement?"

"Maybe so. If your favorite products won't go for it, just sell out to the highest bidder. Dow Chemical. Wal-Mart."

"Or just for the joy of writing it—if I can't sell out."

I pulled out my notebook and turned back to the first pages. "Here—look," I said. There was a long list I'd been adding to the whole trip—starting with Singapore Airlines.

"What a head case. Ah—give it a try. It was a slightly more eventful trip than I'd anticipated. You'd better say it's fiction though. Don't want to get anyone in trouble."

"Nobody would believe it anyway."

"That's true," he said with a laugh. "That all couldn't have happened. It was a Fig Newton of our imagination."

"And there's another good product placed," I said, writing it down.

"You'd probably have to self-publish."

"POD."

"Die urinating?"

"No silly—print on demand. It's what's happening with vanity publishing these days. It's great. Don't have to invest in stock—it's printed on demand. And—I could fill it with darlings and not let anyone kill them. Cause POD books don't sell much anyway and what the heck. And add a lot of drawings and a CD of songs. And do podcasts and put it on the web for free. Anything I wanted. Whoopee."

"Use Simon's art."

"Good idea."

He took his wallet out and counted his Australian dollars. "Let's not forget to exchange money at the airport," he said.

"Wait, wait, wait," I said as he started to put his wallet away. "Bring that back out."

"My wallet?"

"Yeah."

"Why? No! You want to count my money and do all sorts of unnecessary and neurotic calculating."

"No. Not the money. I want to look in the wallet again. Come on."

"Okay. Here."

"Just open it up—that photo."

"Oh—that's Belfast mom and Calcutta dad."

"Your father's a cardiologist."

"You're not psychic," he said. "I told you that the first day I met you."

"I recognize him!"

"You do? Mmm—all Indians look alike."

"No they don't. Where does he live?"

"California."

"Where in California?"

"Well, he was in LA and then he moved to uh—Petaluma. Where's that?"

"That's like twenty minutes from the barn where I live."

"Oh."

"Gupta, your father did my angioplasty."

Just then our lovely stewardess came over to see how we were doing.

"Oh hello there," Gupta said.

"Gupta! Can you believe this! Your father saved my life."

He didn't hear. She inquired if we would like something to drink.

"Uh—sure," I said, "Jamison's—no ice."

"Me too but ice," said Gupta staring at her. "Thought you didn't drink on planes."

"I don't—usually. But Gupta," I continued, "can you believe that it was your father?"

"That's great," he said gazing at the stewardess who was getting a bottle out of a cabinet not far from us.

"I mean, what are the odds?"

"Well, someone had to do it. He lives in California—so do you. He does them all the time." He smiled at her and she smiled back.

"Well, I think it's the most amazing coincidence."

"Huh? Uh—take your medicine and get plenty of rest," he said continuing his fixation on the lovely stewardess as she handed us our drinks.

I gave up on words, and sat immersed in a feeling of unshakable lonely affection for all my friends, for everyone. I gazed below at the distant bright fishing boat lights, which slowly vanished into the thick blackness out the window of this fabulous silver bird streaming in the big empty sky toward Asia.

IN ADDITION TO THIS BOOK

Color Dreams for
To Find The Girl from Perth

Featuring Illustrations by Andrew Atkeison

AND TO BE RELEASED IN 2022

Audiobook For To Find The Girl from Perth
with 28 homemade songs
Redux of 2009 Edition

Songs for To Find The Girl from Perth Redux
an album by DC with Baliyuga

GIRLFROMPERTH.COM

ALSO BY DAVID CHADWICK

CROOKED CUCUMBER: THE LIFE AND
ZEN TEACHING OF SHUNRYU SUZUKI

THANK YOU AND OK!: AN AMERICAN
ZEN FAILURE IN JAPAN

ZEN IS RIGHT HERE:
TEACHING STORIES AND ANECDOTES OF
SHUNRYU SUZUKI
(FORMERLY TO SHINE
ONE CORNER OF THE WORLD)

ZEN IS RIGHT NOW:
MORE TEACHING STORIES AND ANECDOTES OF SHUNRYU
SUZUKI

*THE ABOVE FOUR BOOKS ALSO AUDIBLE AUDIOBOOKS
(THANK YOU AND OK LATE IN 2022)*

AND FROM CUKE PRESS

THE, THE BOOK

A BRIEF HISTORY OF TASSAJARA: FROM NATIVE AMERICAN
SWEAT LODGES TO PIONEERING ZEN MONASTERY (EDITOR)

David Chadwick's main website is cuke.com.
Links from the home page lead to much more -
podcasts, blogs, Instagram, Facebook.

Chadwick's music site is defusermusic.com.

David Chadwick (born 1945) grew up in Fort Worth Texas, dropped out of college the first year, did some civil rights and SDS work, hitchhiked around, went to Mexico and South America for a year plus, moved to California and began to study Zen as a student of Shunryu Suzuki in 1966. He was ordained as a Buddhist priest in 1971, shortly before Suzuki's death. He continued his Zen study with Richard Baker and assisted in the operation of the San Francisco Zen Center for a number of years, and continues these relationships as a spiritual friend, alum, and independent historian. Through the years he has been involved with sporadic environmental and peace work. In 1988 he went to Japan for four years and continued his Zen study there with Shodo Harada at Sogenji in Okayama. He has two sons born 1973 and 1991. Chadwick has had four marriages, the latter of which with Katrinka McKay continues blissfully. He has written over 1200 songs, too many proposals, and continues to dabble in Buddhism and other matters, mainly working on the Cuke Archives to preserve the legacy of Shunryu Suzuki and those whose paths crossed his. The photo of him by Raymond Rimmer is from around 2000.